The Rhysu Alternative

THE RHYSU ALTERNATIVE

THE ERSTALLIUS CHRONICLES

VOLUME TWO

BY P.D. BLACKWELL

The Rhysu Alternative: The Erstallius Chronicles, Volume Two

ISBN: 978-1-7366096-1-3

Cover design and all interior artwork by: P. D. Blackwell

DEDICATION

For Loren "Lolo" Wolford

An angel on earth, a princess in heaven.

CONTENTS

TERMINOLOGY OF THE ALLIANCE

ACCESS TUBE: Typical deck-to-deck transfer system for crew and passengers on board large space vessels. Various types: pneumatic or magnetic driven capsule systems; hollow micro gravity tubes with either internal rails or conveyor ramps.

AKU: An independent human clan from the Ja'bar river region on Kainogae. They settled GSW-183 (Ni'apinu) after a brief battle for freedom from Clan Tuma in 3360.

ALLIANCE: The Merchant Alliance of Great Clans (Established in 3365). The universal development syndicate created to **1.** control settlement and resource use of surveyed worlds, and **2.** ensure proper control and regulation of support structures.

ALSTEEL: Moldable steel (pliable above 323°C) used only for planet-bound construction. Made by melding carbon crystals with magnesium hydraduranide via the Herz-Gamble fusion process. Resistant to oxidation and common acids.

ATMOCON: Colloquial term for Atmosphere Conditioner. A device used in terraforming operations to alter existing atmospheres for human occupation.

CENOTAPH: A monument built to honor people whose remains are interred elsewhere or whose remains cannot be recovered.

CHAOS YEARS: The interval of time when the merchant clans were not unified by a central governing organization. From 3358 to 3365. Many clans took advantage of the economic and political turmoil and seized holdings belonging to the weaker houses. Fifteen merchant clans were dissolved during this time. Six clans rose to an overpowering prominence: Clan Cormed, Clan Dejoria, Clan Emlito, Clan Sabballi, Clan Sorrell, and Clan Vestlok. They spearheaded the movement that led to the formation of the Merchant Alliance of Great Clans.

CLANMAN: Idiomatic for a member of a clan's security forces.

COMM: 1. A communication device. **2.** Intercom, an internal communication system.

COMCHANNEL: A communication frequency.

COMDRONE: A communication drone, used to relay messages through Hyperspace.

COMNET: 1. The network of communication pathways used by comdrones and/or direct link TAC emitters. **2.** The network created to access data from planet-bound colonies, often with access to off-world data storage centers via comdrones or TAC.

COMPAD: A portable communication device able to access the comnet.

COMPRESSION DRIVE: Main engine system used to propel space vessels through hyperspace. First developed in 2832 by Goddard Simkins during experiments with the less efficient Spatial Warp Generator technology.

COMM TRAFFIC: All messages relayed over communication frequencies and/or via comdrones.

DATA PAD: Portable computation and electronic storage device.

DISPLAY PAD: Portable imaging device used for creating and viewing two-dimensional data.

DESTROYER: Medium size military spacecraft. Average length is two hundred meters. Typical crew capacity: 120. Usually equipped with separate shuttle and/or cargo craft. Standard weapons, including, but not limited to: Plasma Burst Emitters (PBE); Phase Induction Torpedoes (PIT); Tactical Nuclear Mines (TNM); and Particle Disrupters (PD).

DPS: Department of Planetary Settlement. A branch of the Alliance's Commerce Department that has oversight of all settlement operations, which includes Terra-forming operations on holdings owned by Great Clans and/or under contract for development.

DREADNOUGHT: Large military spacecraft. The average length is four hundred meters. Typical crew capacity: 400. Usually equipped with separate shuttle, cargo, and attack craft. Standard weapons, including, but not limited to: Plasma Burst Emitters (PBE); Phase Induction Torpedoes (PIT); Tactical Nuclear Mines (TNM).

DURAPLEX: Glass made from duranide crystals (a product of durillium processing) infused at high temperature within the lattice structure of supaline quartz. Its finished form is usually tinted gray because of the duranide bonding and is an excellent barrier to ultra-violet and other high frequency radiation. High tensile strength (11,000 to 14,000 kilos per square centimeter at one centimeter thickness).

DURILLIUM: Metallic composite (symbol Dr) discovered (2807) by Seth Lorin. The chief source is from certain ores of nickel, sometimes associated with platinum. It does not react with oxygen at normal temperatures nor with common acids. Under certain conditions, most notably in its unprocessed state, it can severely alter surrounding EM emissions, often increasing levels beyond the normal dynamic range by amplifying all frequencies reflected. A primary metal used in Compression Drive coils and other power systems.

EM: Electromagnetic. Refers to radiated emissions of any frequency.

EMP: Electromagnetic Pulse. A brief, powerful wave of electromagnetic radiation.

EVAC LIFT: The main elevator used in underground mining for swift evacuation of large groups of miners. Various types: Hydraulic, pneumatic, or magnetic.

FRIGATE: Small military space vessel usually no longer than one hundred meters. Typical crew capacity: eighty-five. Usually equipped with the standard complement of weapons, including, but not limited to: Plasma Burst Emitters (PBE); Phase Induction Torpedoes (PIT); Tactical Nuclear Mines (TNM); and Particle Disrupters (PD).

FIRST REBELLION: Revolt against the Alliance (3498 - 3501) by independent clans led by Wolfram Sy. Caused by trade restrictions imposed by the Merchant Houses. After three years of feuding the rebels withdrew from Alliance controlled space.

GRAND CRUSADE: The revolt against Trans-humanist technologies from 3226 to 3315. GRAND is an acronym for Genetic, Robotic, and Nano-technology Development.

GLOWBALL: A small globe (usually 50 to 100 centimeters in diameter) filled with lumicrystals. Used for lighting small areas. Activation can be canceled by changing the direction of electronic flow within the sphere.

GPG: Graviton Polarity Generator. A gravity field emitter, sometimes (although incorrectly) referred to as an anti-gravity device when used to counter local gravity fields. Most common use for positive gravity emission is in vessels designed for interstellar transport.

GUILDMAN: Idiomatic for a member of the Guild of Free Traders.

GUILD OF FREE TRADERS: The organization was established after the First Rebellion to help keep the rebels united against further Alliance expansion into new territory.

HELIOSPHERE: 1. The spherical area around a star produced by the outflow of solar radiation that is used to define the boundary of the star's influence. **2.** The area inside the heliopause, where the stellar wind meets the radiation produced by other stars.

HOLDING: 1. A landed estate, usually encompassing the entire surface of a planet. **2.** The portion of land claimed by a Merchant House and secured by contract or deed. 3. Any property by which a Clan may receive benefit.

HOLOMITTER: The source of holographic projections used for large presentations where the ability to zoom in and out of the displayed data is necessary.

HOLOPAD: A portable holoscreen.

HOLOSCREEN: Holographic displays projected from a control console to present a variety of digital information, some of which can be live, interactive media.

HOMEWORLD: 1. Origin point; The planet from which any Clan originates. **2.** The planet on which a Clan has established its central base of operations; the capital settlement of a Clan.

HYPERSPACE: 1. Alternate space, compressed space. **2.** The dimensional warping of normal space. By manipulating hyperspace great distances may be traversed across normal space with minimal dilation effects. The Time Lapse Ratio (TLR), or difference between space-normal time (T) and hyperspace time (τ), depends on energy use and distance traveled but will not exceed the ratio of 1T to .33τ if warp energy is constant above 15.5ζ. Thus, the traveler in hyperspace will, on average, experience the passage of 7.92τ hours for every 24T hours experienced by planet-bound individuals. Average distance traveled in 24τ hours: 5 parsecs.

JAPS: Judge Advocate for Planetary Settlement. **1.** An investigator assigned by the Alliance of Great Clans, Office of Planetary Settlement, to oversee compliance with the Rules of Acquisition. **2.** The legal department under the Office of Planetary Settlement overseen by the Alliance of Great Clans.

KENTAO: A form of martial art. The term is derived from the ancient kuntao, or kuntau, which means, Way of the Fist. Kentao traces back to the oldest organized system of fighting among the Old Worlds, predating the colonial expansion from Terra Prime. Many techniques and weapons of kentao are also associated with ancient silat, and is believed to have been disseminated by the Sino-Iban clans and adopted by the Iban people. Though traditionally passed within the family, aspects of kentao have been identified as the underlying style of martial training for clanmen among the oldest clans.

KOTTREL SPHERE: 1. Composite, multi-element sphere used as a self-regulating, high-energy container at the heart of power generation systems first developed by Marcus Kottrel in 2896 during experimentation with gravity generators. **2.** The heart of ignition systems for Compression Drive engines built between 2997 and 3429 by the Mayfair-Courkos Transport Company, and other spacecraft manufacturers originating among the Old Worlds.

LSC: Life Support Control. The system that regulates the interior temperature and atmospheric composition inside any compartment used for human occupation. Especially pertaining to compartments on board space vessels and living quarters within eco-domes that are used on planets with environments hostile to humans.

MAGAR: Acronym for Magnetically Accelerated Rail used as the propulsion system for a variety of weapons issued by clan security forces. **1.** Magar-pistol: A miniature rail gun developed as a survival weapon for Alliance clanmen. A difficult weapon to detect with standard security scans due to its polymer frame and lack of metallic components. Able to accelerate standard issue projectiles within the 9-millimeter size limit to 400 mps in a vacuum. Actual speed of projectile is dependent upon density of atmosphere and type of ammunition used. Accuracy depends on the type of projectile. Effective planet-bound range about 40 meters. **2.** Magar-rifle: Standard issue for all infantry and special operations clanmen. Rail-length varies from 40 centimeters to 80 centimeters. The maximum projectile diameter is 20 millimeters. Effective planet-bound range is 350 meters. Projectile velocity ranges between 900 mps to 1500 mps in a vacuum.

MAG-JET: Magneto-turbine propulsion system used in a variety of planet-bound aircraft. Often incorporated as a back-up propulsion system in non-planet-bound shuttles for use within atmospheres. Developed in 2653 by H. Lawrence Heldra, the first working model was called SCOMIT (Super-Conducting Magnetic Induction Turbine).

MAG-FAN: Magneto-driven fan propulsion system used for light weight aircraft. Maximum load usually one thousand kilograms. Used for short range transfer of personnel and/or cargo.

MAD: Acronym for Mobile Articulated Drill. A device commonly used for ore extraction.

MERCHANT HOUSE: Any family or defined group (Clan) having reached the status of interstellar entrepreneur, with controlling interest in more than one holding.

MILITARY RANKS:

DIWA: Lowest ranking clanman among the Great Clans. Two levels: **1.** Diwa: Enlisted recruit, general beginning rank.

2. Diwa-Major: A trained specialist, which can include engineering and other technical services, or combat specialties.

NARED: Non-commissioned officer among the Great Clans. Three levels: **1.** Nared: has oversight of a platoon of six clanmen. **2.** Nared-of-the-Corp: Has oversight of a company (30 clanmen). **3.** Nared-Major: Has oversight of specialist disciplines among the clanmen, which includes engineering and other technical services, as well as special combat operations groups up to 30 clanmen.

SEGEN: A commissioned officer among the Great Clans. Three levels: **1.** Segen: Commands a company (30 clanmen). **2.** Segen-of-the-Corp: Commands 1 Unit (60 clanmen). **3.** Segen-Major: Commands specialist Units which includes engineering and other technical services, as well as special combat operations groups up to 60 clanmen.

DEGEN: A commissioned officer among the Great Clans. Three levels: **1.** Degen: Has oversight of a regiment (150 clanmen). **2.** Degen-of-the-Corp: Has oversight of a brigade (300 clanmen). **3.** Degen-Major: Commands specialist Regiments which includes engineering and other technical services, as well as special combat operations groups up to 120 clanmen.

JEGEN: A commissioned officer among the Great Clans. Three levels: **1.** Jegen: Commands a regiment (150 clanmen). **2.** Jegen-of-the-Corp: Commands a brigade (300 clanmen). **3.** Jegen-Major: Commands a division (1500 clanmen).

MERCHANT ALLIANCE OF GREAT CLANS: See Alliance.

OFF-WORLDER: Any person on a foreign world.

OLD WORLDS: The first planets settled by humans. All colonized worlds at the heart of the Alliance. The "heart" encompasses an imaginary sphere 6 parsecs in diameter, centered between Centauri Base and Terra Prime.

PARSEC: A standard astronomical unit of distance equal to 3.262 light-years. The standard parsec is a measurement from the Old Worlds era. It is based on how much Terra Prime's distance from its sun would subtend one second of arc. (< parallax + second2)

PLANET-BOUND: Anyone or anything on the surface of a planet.

PLANET-FALL: Descent to a planet's surface.

RELAY NET: See COMNET.

RULES OF ACQUISITION: The directives of propriety agreed upon by the founders of the Merchant Alliance pertaining to the settlement and oversight of newly acquired holdings.

SALIX: A tree with long flexible branches, narrow leaves, and catkins containing small flowers without petals. Several species are common among the Old Worlds and on several Alliance colonies. Salix - from the ancient Englo'ni designation for this type of flora and often transliterated in other languages.

SAPI: **1.** A derogatory term for a contract laborer who does manual work (informal). **2.** The lowest class level based on the Drupal caste system that originated on Centauri Base in 3152 and continues among some of the clans who trace their origins back to that Old World colony (Clan Vestlok, Clan Sabballi, and Clan Polinda).

SINCOS: Acronym for Supreme Interstellar Commerce Syndicate. (3156 to 3358) The first organization established to control interstellar trade.

STANDARD TIME: The system of time measurement developed in 2880 by The Council for the Unification of Time. Long before humans began colonizing space, they understood that time is relative to location. Every planet orbiting a star has unique properties that determine the duration of a day and the number of days that occur during one orbit of the parent star. Standard Time breaks down the elements of time measurement and unifies them for any planetary system so there exists agreement between colonies regarding the progression of time. This time matrix overlays local time to create consistency regarding date measurement and tracking.

STRAD: unit of measure first introduced on Kainogae c.3120. One strad equals two thousand meters.

TAC EMITTER: A transmitter designed to relay signals via Tachyon Assisted Communication. Frequency band width ranges between 4.5Ghz to 11.7Ghz. The higher the frequency the faster the transmission rate across distance.

TECH: Anyone assigned to perform periodic maintenance on various types of mechanical and/or electronic equipment.

TRANSCEIVER: Portable communication device.

TRANSPORT: The largest space vessel capable of planet-fall. Hauling capacity: 250 metric tons, including crew and passengers.

WORK POD: A mobile, inverse-gravity assisted device (usually basket shaped) used to lift workers and material to great heights. Used during all types of large-scale planet-bound construction.

COLLAPSE

PART ONE

The past always matters. The past creates the future. Some people say if we ignore the past we are doomed to repeat it. Sometimes the past needs repeating, if only to reinforce the need to stick to the correct path.

— From *Conversations at Kuliq'Quad*
By Petra Sitlyn

BEV COLLI: TRANSFORMATION

Bev floated high above the airless surface of the small planet named Simbic Ur, trapped inside a cluster of twitching cyan tendrils of energy—a plasmatic cage that stabbed at her pressure-suit as her cargo shuttle disintegrated.

The Rhysu are the enemy!

That allegation screamed into Bev's mind moments before the plasma encasing her slammed into a white wall of light. She shut her eyes to block the blinding glare and curled into a fetal position as pressure waves ripped through the tendrils of cyan energy and pounded her body.

The Rhysu are the enemy!

Bev recognized the mind searing scream denouncing the Rhysu as a rebuke from the Shoku.

White light pushed away the last undulating filaments of cyan energy and wrapped Bev in a pressing heat that began to erode the outer layers of her pressure-suit.

She dared a peek at the glaring light and saw nothing beyond the white brilliance.

The events that had brought her to this point in time whirled in her mind.

I helped reveal this enemy, and this is what I get!

Her mission to this place had been prompted by her connection to the Rhysu, the aliens from another dimension who had flooded her mind with visions. They sought to retrieve rebels from their universe—the aliens Bev had named Shoku, who had destroyed the mine on Alpha Cephei Four and a dozen Alliance ships. Luring the Shoku to Simbic Ur had been uneventful up to this point. She had expected a quick return to the Erstallius flagship until the Shoku ripped into her shuttle and encased her in their plasmatic cage.

The pressing heat forced Bev to focus on the present. Her quiet fear swelled into whimpering panic as she watched her suit gloves disintegrate. Pain ripped through her arms, and she fell unconscious.

The Rhysu are the enemy!

Bev jerked awake. She floated in white. Pressure eddies rippled against her body, but she could not see her body. She saw only churning wisps of cyan-colored plasma like the Shoku cage, but without the pain.

"Where am I?"

Her query was audible. She heard it plain enough and knew it was from her, but she had no sense she had vocalized it. She searched the white nothingness. There were no shapes to give her a frame of reference.

She shouted: "Where are you?"

"We are here, do not be afraid," a soft tenor voice responded. It wrapped around Bev like a warm blanket. The sound was not a language like Englo'ni, or Akün. It was a thought that came from outside herself, in a language understood but never learned.

"I can't see you!"

"We are here."

"Are you the Rhysu?"

There was a subtle shift in the pressure eddies, and Bev surmised that reaction to be laughter.

"We are the ones you call Rhysu. We are not your enemy."

"Why didn't you speak? Why all the visions and dreams?"

"We communicate, we learn, we adapt."

"That's why you connected with me?"

"Yes. We learn."

Bev recalled the eruption on Alpha Cephei Four and her escape from the mine. She laid on that airless surface and watched churning streams of luminous cyan plasma drift upward into the star-filled sky. One stream broke away from the flow and settled about thirty-meters above Bev, and the miners scattered around her—a churning cloud of charged particles and twitching electric bolts.

The Rhysu weren't in that cloud, she thought. *The Rhysu were the cloud, and they bonded with me.*

That thought pulled up memories of Cynth Halva and the trip to Arrilen Po, where the Rhysu had first contact with humans, and where Cynth had lost both legs and her left arm.

"Do you damage everything you touch?"

"We wish to stop the damage," the Rhysu said.

A spark of realization pushed to the forefront of Bev's mind: After the Rhysu released her on Arrilen Po, she believed the Shoku motivation for entering the human universe had been the euphoric rush of being in three spatial dimensions. The exhilaration the Shoku experienced had been real. She had felt it herself as they transferred their emotional state to her consciousness. Now, after reflecting upon the more recent connection, she understood that elated feeling had clouded the truth. Her first assessment had been correct. The Shoku rebelled and broke into the human universe to free themselves from Rhysu oversight.

"I was right to give you and the Shoku names," Bev said. "I understand you better than you think."

"That is why we chose you," the Rhysu said.

"Where am I?"

"With us."

Bev scanned the white space around her. "Where?"

"Do not be afraid."

"I'm not afraid."

"Good."

In her mind, the cargo shuttle broke apart. She saw herself encased by the Shoku, and then the impact of the white wall. Her mind retreated from her original position until she saw the white wall become a gigantic ball of light orbiting Simbic Ur. She rushed back toward the light and it enveloped Simbic Ur's gray surface.

"Am I in your universe?"

"Yes."

The realization she was inside a higher dimension forced Bev to confront the fact she had been physically altered. Her change had begun on the Halva cruiser while en route to Arrilen Po, when the Rhysu had forced her into a coma to analyze her physical form. The change was completed when the Rhysu pulled her from the grip of the Shoku. *I'm here, but what am I?*

Bev twirled in the white. "What did you do to me?"

"Your essence—everything that is Bev Colli—was transferred into your new form. This allows you to exist here."

"Why am I here?"

"So we can learn."

"How dare you! What gives you the right to interfere with someone's life!?"

"We needed to find the Shoku. We needed you to make that possible."

"What am I?"

"You are Bev Colli."

Bev shrieked and the eddies of pressure holding her grew stronger with every outburst. The restraint held her in place and forced her to quiet. She calmed herself and shifted her focus on the lack of detail in the white nothingness surrounding her. "Where are you?"

"We are here," the Rhysu said.

"Where is here?"

The pressing white retreated from Bev's position and revealed a circular, gray surface a few meters below her.

"What's that?"

Bev moved involuntarily, pulled by the Rhysu toward the rough ground until she hovered a few centimeters above it.

"Dirt?"

"A familiar reference to help you adapt," the Rhysu said.

"Adapt?"

"You are with us. You have no reference for what awaits you. The hard place below you is from the human universe. You can relate to its three-dimensional construction. It will help you adapt."

Bev examined the granular surface and recognized the gray regolith.

"Is this Simbic Ur?"

"The hard place helped us return the ones you call Shoku."

Simbic Ur's gravity well had been used to stabilize the rift between dimensions. Bev never imagined such a rift could transfer an entire planet.

"How am I still here?"

"You are with us."

"Yes, but why am I not dead?"

"You are with us."

"What am I?"

"You are Bev Colli. Do not be afraid."

The white nothingness retreated farther and overlapping bubbles of cyan-colored energy pressed toward Bev like a giant carpet of foam dropping out of the sky. Tendrils of energy encased her. She sensed the warmth of the embrace but could still not see her own body.

"What am I?"

"Do not be afraid. You will adapt. Your body has changed. Your shape is no longer defined by a container of flesh."

Bev focused on the gray soil below her as the energy bubbles pressed around her. She appreciated the familiar, solid reference, and wondered how long she would need to adapt to her new environment and her new body. She looked where her right hand should be and saw only undulating strands of cyan-colored energy.

"I've lost everything!"

"No. Your mind is intact—every memory, everything you learned while human."

"You stole my life!"

"We transferred your life to save you," the Rhysu insisted. "You will need time to adapt. All newborns need time to learn about themselves and their environment. Our environment is much more complex than the human one. Your perception and your ability to move will improve as you become more familiar with our universe and your perception expands. The hard place and the white will help ease you into your new existence. Thrust too fast into this universe and your mind would fracture."

"I'm already fractured. I've lost everything!"

"We understand your loss."

"Do you?"

"Yes."

"I doubt that."

"Why?"

"You've never been human."

"Correct."

"You've robbed me of my life!"

"You are still alive."

Bev forced back a surge of anger. The Rhysu did not understand. Their perspective was alien, not human.

"You are wrong," the Rhysu said.

"What?"

"There are no secrets here. We hear your thoughts."

"Oh, that's just great!"

"We communicate, we learn, we adapt."

"Then adapt me back to my universe!"

"We cannot restore your human body."

"I've lost everything."

"You have not," the Rhysu said, and they backed away to allow Bev time to grieve the loss of her human existence.

Once Bev's mind had moved to a more settled state, the Rhysu approached her again.

"Humans are perplexing," the Rhysu admitted. "They fight each other and yet place great value upon social interaction."

"Yeah."

"You have lost connection. We had not considered that."

"No kidding."

The pressure eddies around Bev weakened.

"Arlud used me," she said. "He persuaded me to help him find the answers he needed. You used me to find the Shoku. In some ways, we're not that different."

"We use each other," the Rhysu said. "That is the nature of existence, the social connection that is broken."

Bev forced her mind into a blank state.

After a lengthy silence the Rhysu said: "We will take you back. You may tell your social group you are still living, but you cannot stay there."

Bev knew her previous life was over, but being able to say goodbye would satisfy a deep need that even the Rhysu understood would help subdue her pain.

"Whoa!"

The rush through the dimensional rift was over before Bev had time to adjust. She recognized the planet Ni'apinu floating below her.

I'm in space!

Bev's mind whirled with the realization she was high above Ni'apinu with nothing to protect her from the vacuum.

How is this possible?

"The links to your social group will pull you back to them, no matter where they are," the Rhysu explained. "Those links can be stronger than the connection that pulled the Shoku to your location above the hard place."

Bev sensed Arlud's presence on the surface, and she found herself in the lower atmosphere, above the ancient, snow-covered stone dwellings in Kuliq'Quad Basin. She could feel her presence push back the cold and watched the snow melt as she dropped closer to the ground.

The Rhysu warned her: "Your new body can endanger the humans. You must reduce your activity, stay calm, and keep your interaction brief."

Bev recognized Arlud and rushed toward him. The pressure wave that preceded her pushed Arlud to the wet ground, and as he lay beneath her, she reached out to touch him.

Remember me?

Arlud heard Bev's voice in his head and gazed up in confusion at the glowing ball of cyan-colored plasma. "Bev?"

Filaments from Bev's energy sphere leaped upon Arlud and wrapped him in their warmth.

I'm here, Bev said. She coiled her energy tendrils around Arlud, lifted him off the ground, and transferred to him a vivid memory of their discussion in the High Regent's house on U'galem. In that memory, she stressed Arlud's infatuation with her to prove her identity. Only she knew the feelings he displayed to her that day.

She set Arlud on the ground and backed away. She focused on her former self and an image of her human body formed out of the swirls of cyan-colored plasma within her energy sphere.

Arlud squinted at the vision. "Bev?"

I'm OK. I'll be fine.

"What happened?"

Don't worry, everything will be OK.

Bev let the apparition of her former self fade. She rose into the overlying fog, then rushed out of the atmosphere to the waiting Rhysu.

Bev hovered above her childhood home on the planet Pigrell. She sensed her parents beneath the corrugated metal roof but stifled the urge to reveal herself to them.

What would they think? Would they even believe it was me?

They hadn't seen her since she left for the mine six years ago. She would not have time to explain everything, which would only give her parents more grief.

She focused on her mental connection with her mother and did the best she could to assure her she was safe. She did not confirm if her attempt to plant that thought had been successful because the Rhysu pulled her away before she could finish.

CLAN ERSTALLIUS: NEW DIRECTIONS

The ceremony to honor the Erstallius engineers had been postponed twice and moved to this cold, snow-covered day in Kuliq'Quad Basin once the Regent, Arlud Reynaldo Erstallius, returned victorious from the Battle at Wan'tei.

Before the ceremony, Arlud agreed to accompany the Aku pilot, Salus, to the memorial tomb of the ancient Aku patriarch who led his people to Ni'apinu. The trip to Seelay's memorial was long overdue and was the perfect opportunity for Salus to help ease Arlud's remorse over losing Bev. The marble colonnade was on the west edge of the basin, above the abandoned stone dwellings of the First People. They had enough time for a brief visit, but Arlud had not expected Bev to drop out of the sky.

Bev Colli was supposed to be dead. Fifteen standard days had passed since the battle at Wan'tei, and only a few fragments of her transport were found along a course that led away from the empty orbital track of Simbic Ur, the planet that had vanished.

The shock of seeing Bev's human form in a ball of cyan-colored plasma pushed Arlud's focus inward. The snow crunched beneath him as he dropped to his knees and watched the cyan light rise and disappear into the gray clouds. *She's still alive,* he thought. *But what is she?*

Salus shook Arlud's shoulder to break his inward focus. "You OK?"

"Yeah."

Arlud stood. His body still tingled from Bev's embrace, and he noticed scorch marks on his thick overcoat where her tendrils had grabbed him. He wiped a tear from his cheek and looked up.

Snowflakes began falling again.

Salus looked skyward. "Was that the Rhysu?"

"That was Bev."

"Bev!?"

"Yeah."

Salus searched the overlying clouds. "Where did she go?"

"She's with the Rhysu," Arlud said. That understanding had come from her. She connected with him the same way the Rhysu had connected with her. He looked at Salus. "You didn't see her?"

"All I saw was a ball of blue fire."

Arlud frowned and looked back up at the gray sky. "She's one of them now. They pulled her into their dimension."

"How?"

"I don't know."

By the time Arlud and Salus crossed to the eastern end of the basin, the award ceremony was in progress. All the inhabitants of the small village in Kuliq'Quad Basin, two hundred twenty-seven men, their wives, and children, were gathered on the tarmac at the Mânu, the landing field where the Aku had stored four of the spherical transports that had brought their ancestors to Ni'apinu. Around each of the empty landing pads, at the four cardinal compass points, polished wooden posts rose thirty meters in a gentle outward arc. Hooks protruding from the tips of each pole no longer held the blue tarps that had covered each transport. Long shadows from the poles fell over the crowd as the late afternoon sun appeared from behind thick clouds.

Winstone Bittle, in his formal blue uniform with the medals and gold sash that represented his twenty-three years of service, accepted his award on the small dais that had been erected in front of the maintenance buildings. Behind Bittle, five other Erstallius engineers, also dressed in their formal blue uniforms, sat in line, holding their awards in their laps—curved silver spikes protruding from hexagon-shaped rings fastened to circular wooden bases.

Salus drove his two-seat ground car along the northern edge of the tarmac, past the assembled throng, and stopped parallel to the dais, near a small group of Erstallius clanmen huddled on the snow-covered tarmac.

Arlud stepped out of the car and was greeted by Gustav Eahuda, whose displeasure was evident on his dark, weathered face.

"About time you got here," Eahuda whispered. "What happened to your coat?"

Arlud smirked at Eahuda's concern. He met the old degen's stern gaze. "Bev's alive."

"What?"

"She's with the Rhysu," Arlud said, and he walked toward the dais.

Salus greeted the stunned Eahuda as Arlud stepped onto the dais and took his place at the podium to a rousing applause from the crowd.

Arlud's speech was brief. He extolled the efforts of his engineers, and ended by saying, "Ni'apinu belongs to the Aku. Our combined effort saved your homeworld from Farquar Polinda's madness. Our continued partnership will ensure that Alliance intrusion will never again threaten your world."

Arlud turned from the podium amid a cheerful applause and greeted the old Aku men who had oversight of the Mânu. He congratulated each engineer then headed for the shuttle parked about fifty meters north of the maintenance buildings. He nodded to the shuttle pilot at the foot of the boarding ramp and clambered up into the squat aircraft. The seats faced inward, five along each side of the hull. He sat in the first seat on the port side.

Eahuda slid into the seat next to Arlud. "What do you mean Bev's still alive?"

"I saw her."

"Where?"

"In a ball of cyan-colored plasma."

"What?"

Arlud leaned back in his seat and watched his five award-winning engineers sit across from him and Eahuda. Petra Sitlyn, the young blond construction engineer who had never worked on aircraft before Clan Polinda attacked, held her silver award in her lap. The other engineers stowed their awards under their seats.

Arlud swelled with pride as he pondered the honor his engineers had received. The repaired Aku transports helped protect Ni'apinu from Clan Polinda's second assault. *Protecting Ni'apinu will be a joint effort moving forward.*

Winstone Bittle entered the shuttle and sat next to Eahuda.

Arlud shifted his focus back to Bev and faced Eahuda. "Bev dropped out of the sky when Salus and I were at Seelay's memorial."

Sitlyn overheard Arlud's remark and leaned forward. "Bev's alive?"

"Yes."

The pilot pulled the hatch shut with a solid thud and entered the cockpit.

Eahuda nudged Arlud's shoulder. "You need to see the Doc when we get back to the outpost."

"Why?"

"You saw Bev in a ball of plasma! What scorched your coat had to have an impact on your body."

Arlud looked at his hands and felt his face—warmer than normal. "Her appearance changes everything," he said, and he noticed all the engineers were now focused on him. "All our speculation about the Rhysu has been wrong. We may never understand what happened to Bev, but she is still alive."

Winstone Bittle leaned forward in his seat. "You're certain it was her?"

"I have no doubt."

The shuttle's engines rumbled to life.

Eahuda focused on Arlud. "Where is she?"

"She left."

"What?"

"She came to tell me she's OK, and then she left."

"How is that possible?" Sitlyn asked.

Arlud looked at Sitlyn and shrugged. Bev had entered Ni'apinu airspace without alerting the orbiting sentries or the planet-bound Aku security patrols.

The shuttle rose into the clouded sky and flew over the basin's northern rim toward the Erstallius outpost in the Yoslyn Mountains.

After seeing the outpost physician, Arlud returned to his office at the landing field and found a message from his father waiting for him.

> **Comdrone E364**
> **Priority - 1**
> **To:** Arlud Reynaldo Erstallius, Regent, GSW-183
> **From:** Armand Reynaldo Erstallius, High Regent, Clan Erstallius
> **Message begin-**
> Come to Pigrell. Your presence is needed during the transition.
> **-Message End.**

Arlud leaned back in his desk chair. His father's request was unexpected. It inferred he would be given oversight of the Polinda homeworld. His clan had defeated Clan Polinda, and Alliance protocol demanded all Polinda holdings would be theirs if they could provide sufficient evidence to the Supreme Council that their oversight would ensure continued prosperity for all the holdings transferred. But Inter-clan conflicts had collapsed Alliance authority, so the only way to keep possession of Polinda's wealth was their own military strength. The struggle to retain control would be a problem for years if the conflict among the Old Worlds continued. *We'll have enough difficulty maintaining oversight of our own holdings,* he mused. And yet he also knew keeping the Polinda homeworld under their control would solidify their victory and improve their strategic positioning.

There are too many paths before us. Which one is right?

He focused his attention on his data pad and sent a reply to his father. The message would be loaded from the local comnet and launched with the next comdrone. Armand would receive the reply about six hours before Arlud arrived at Pigrell.

Gustav Eahuda knocked at the threshold of Arlud's office.

Arlud looked up. "Come in, Gus."

Eahuda stood a few paces away from Arlud's desk. "Have you looked at yourself in a mirror?"

"No."

"You're starting to turn red. Did you see the doctor?"

"I did. Just a mild burn. He treated it and said the redness will fade by tomorrow and I'll have no ill effects."

"What about the Bev situation?"

Arlud slumped back in his chair. "We can't get her back. That's beyond our ability."

Eahuda gestured toward the landing field. "There's a cenotaph out there for Bev. If she's still alive—"

"Her cenotaph honors her deeds," Arlud said, "not her death. She may be alive with the Rhysu but she's just a memory to us. We will continue to honor her memory."

Eahuda bowed his head in a gesture of respect for Bev's loss. "She will always be remembered, but the ability to breach our space undetected is a genuine threat."

Arlud leaned forward and sat up straight. "What do you suggest we do about it?"

Eahuda had no answer.

"What she did earlier today," Arlud said, "and what she has become, are beyond anything we've experienced. We can't prevent a thing we know nothing about."

"And that's what scares me, lad."

Arlud scrutinized his old Guard Captain. Eahuda always used the reference, "lad," when he wanted to appeal to Arlud, not as an officer in the Corp, but as a friend.

"It scares me too, Gus," Arlud admitted, "but I don't think we need to worry about the Rhysu. If they wanted to harm us, they would've done it months ago. My primary concern is the eroding stability among the Old Worlds. Polinda's allies still have strength."

"Yes, they do," Eahuda said. He understood that reality as well as anyone. There were many roads that led to peace, but none of them avoided more battles.

"I've been called to Pigrell," Arlud said.

"Why?"

"My father needs me there. I'll be leaving within the hour."

Eahuda knew that change of duty would also include him because of his position as the head of Arlud's personal guard. He pulled a compad out of his coat pocket. "Petra Sitlyn applied for discharge." He handed the pad to Arlud.

Arlud reviewed Sitlyn's request—an event he never imagined. The clan had just won a decisive battle against one of their greatest enemies, and there was no visible end to the hostilities among the other clans. A clanman was expected to serve under such circumstances until injury or old age forced them to retire.

"Where is she?"

"Waiting outside."

"Send her in."

Eahuda nodded and retreated through the doorway.

Segen Petra Sitlyn entered Arlud's office and stood at attention in front of his desk.

Arlud glanced up from the data pad. The young engineer still wore her formal uniform. "Relax, Petra. Have a seat."

Sitlyn sat on the edge of the chair, knees together, hands folded on her lap.

Arlud leaned forward and crossed his arms on his desk. He could sense Sitlyn's nervousness by her unnatural stillness. "I never expected this."

"Yes, sir. It was not an easy decision."

Arlud leaned back and gripped the arms of his chair. Petra helped save his life. After the shuttle crash, she and Gus had pulled him out of the wreckage and cared for his injuries. "Well, this isn't about being tired, or a lack of initiative on your part. What's the reason?"

"I'm a construction engineer. The build-out is done here. I expect to be transferred back to the homeworld, or another holding that needs my expertise."

Arlud nodded that he understood. The official reports indicated Baleiou, the clan homeworld, suffered major damage from Polinda's attack. Thrum Dau would also need rebuilding for years to come.

"We need you."

"I'm just one person. There are others who can fill that need."

"You're too modest," Arlud said, and his mouth formed a brief frown. "We will have difficulty finding someone to replace you."

"I appreciate that, sir, but I wish to stay on Ni'apinu."

That statement spoke volumes to Arlud. Someone else may have missed it, but to him, Sitlyn's use of the Akün term, *Ni'apinu*, revealed the reason for her request.

"Ni'apinu," Arlud said, "not GSW-183?"

"Sir?"

"You've acclimated to the culture, to the environment. Ni'apinu is a paradise compared to most other holdings. Understandable you want to stay here. I may retire here myself."

"That's not it, sir."

Arlud leaned forward and cupped his hands on his desk. Sitlyn's rejection of his opinion forced a bitter reaction that did not pass unnoticed. Her dismissal was a reproof of one more failed assumption. He seemed to have lost the ability for accurate deduction. He'd been wrong about the Rhysu motive, wrong about Bev's ability, and wrong about her safety. He forced a thin smile and asked, "Then what?"

Sitlyn lowered her eyes. "Salus and I want to marry."

Arlud's intuition had failed him again, but at least this time, no lives would be lost. "Since when?"

"We spent a lot of time together working on the ships. Things just evolved."

Arlud recalled his recent interactions with Salus. The young ciâfey pilot never mentioned an attachment to Sitlyn. "How many clanmen know?"

"Danik and Bril."

"Has Salus discussed this with his elders?"

"Yes."

"And they approve?"

"Not exactly."

"Not exactly?"

"Salus told me Paaq, their Bi'au, insisted I be trained in the way of their people before any joining could take place."

The Bi'au was the mediator who resolved all conflicts. If his requirement was met, the other elders would approve of the off-world bride. That was a wise move on his part. Not only would the coupling help fuse the Aku relationship with Clan Erstallius, Sitlyn would expand the gene pool, which was always a good thing.

The mention of marriage led Arlud to memories of Bev. He was grateful she was still alive, but they lost forever the possibility of a committed romance. *The future is made by the things we choose, and the things we refuse,* he thought. The decisions he had made regarding Bev would haunt him forever. He flicked a comm switch. "Get in here, Gus."

Eahuda appeared in the doorway.

"Petra is discharged," Arlud said. "Please make sure all the correct forms are filled out and filed."

Eahuda blinked. "Yes, sir."

Arlud stood. "Thank you for your service, Segen." He extended his hand.

Sitlyn unfolded from the chair and accepted Arlud's handshake. "Thank you, sir."

"Where will you stay?"

"Salus has a house in Ji'dess."

"We'll be here if you need anything."

"Thank you, sir," Sitlyn replied, then she turned for the doorway, her heart much lighter than when she entered the office. This discharge had gone smoother than she expected.

Eahuda stepped aside to let Sitlyn pass, then nodded to Arlud and left the room.

CLAN HALVA: CARNAGE

Cestratha, the homeworld of Clan Halva, was under attack.

The shock waves from each explosion shook the walls of Cynth Halva's sitting room. The distant bangs and rumbles rattled both the building and her nerves for two hours.

Then silence.

Not since the disaster on Arrilen Po had she felt so close to death. That incident forty-seven years ago had left her with three artificial limbs, and although the metal legs and arm had endowed her with superhuman abilities, she could not survive a direct hit by a plasma burst—she was as frail as any ordinary human. She was seventy-seven years old, and she had expected to die this day.

"Is it over?"

The young, flaxen-haired servant, Tara Quin, moved to the closed duraplex doorway that led to the balcony. She slid the door open just enough to place her hand against the closed metal shutter. "The shaking has stopped."

"Open it," Cynth said.

"But Madame, the security—"

"Open it, girl!"

Quin nodded and slid the transparent door open. She moved to her right and flipped the switch on the wall panel to open the shutters.

Cynth turned on her couch and watched the shutters roll up. She saw shattered buildings along the horizon beneath a smoke-filled, red sky. She rose off her couch and closed her robe against the chill breeze coming through the open doorway and was hit by the stench of burnt wood and melted alsteel from the fires that raged through the distant city.

"See if the comnet is back up," Cynth ordered.

"Yes, Madame," Quin said, and she hurried toward the other side of the room.

Once on the balcony, Cynth could see the demolished buildings on the property north of her estate. Fires still burned there, but the gray smoke told her the local fire brigade had the situation under control.

Why am I not dead?

Quin appeared in the balcony doorway. "The comnet is up, Madame."

Cynth turned to face the holoscreen above the square emitter at the center of her sitting room. The display was a multi-camera view of the carnage on-planet, with a view from orbit at the bottom left that focused on an armada of destroyers identified as Clan Rastee vessels. She left the balcony and sat on her settee to read the reports streaming across the bottom of each view.

"He did it."

"Madame?"

"He did it," Cynth repeated. "Arlud did it."

"Did what?"

Cynth faced her confused handmaiden. "Clan Erstallius acquired allies to defeat Polinda. Based on this report, some of those allies came to help us." She turned back to the holoscreen and enlarged the view of the Rastee ships, which changed to display ships from Clan Sorrell, and then a smaller group of destroyers. "The Guild!"

Quin drew closer to Cynth for a better view of the display. "The Guild?"

Cynth smiled. "I knew he could do it." She had encouraged Arlud to seek help from Wolfram Sy. She was glad he had seen the advantage and ignored the skeptics.

That path changes everything.

The distant roar of mag-jets wafted through the open doorway.

Cynth returned to the balcony. A squadron of Halva attack shuttles, flying in formation around a large, armored passenger carrier, were approaching her residence from the ruined city.

Quin stepped onto the balcony. "Who's that?"

"That would be my brother."

The old High Regent, Gustus Halva, walked down his carrier's boarding ramp and greeted his sister on the southern portico of the ancient family residence. "You survived, Sister. We have much to be thankful for this day."

"Yes, Brother," Cynth said, "and much to mourn. We are fortunate help arrived."

Gustus nodded. "We would have fallen for sure. Our new allies forced Clan Emlito and Clan Vestlok to flee, with just a handful of their forces left. They will not be back."

Cynth turned with a sweep of her hand—an invitation for her brother to enter the residence.

"I cannot," Gustus said. "I had to see you survived, but I cannot stay. We are to meet with our saviors to plan our future."

Cynth recoiled, a subtle movement that revealed her surprise.

"We need the help, Sister," Gustus said. "We cannot continue down our isolated path. The decrees of the Alliance be damned. Our future belongs with our new allies."

Cynth agreed with her brother's decision. She never imagined she would witness a change in the way her family related to the other clans. The embarrassment and loss they suffered because of the Arrilen Po disaster had forced her clan into isolation. As years passed that solitary path became the clan's expected route. They adapted to the restrictions and learned to prosper without off-world contracts.

"A change for the better," Cynth said. "Make wise decisions, Brother."

She left the High Regent and returned to her sitting room. The reports of havoc continued to stream across her holoscreen. She settled onto her settee as the hollow roar of her brother's carrier drifted away, and she hoped he would find common ground with their new allies. *There is much to be done*, she thought, and she knew without help the future of Clan Halva would be in jeopardy.

PETRA SITLYN: STUDENT

Petra Sitlyn crossed the covered porch with her backpack slung over her shoulder and stepped through the doorway into the entry hall of the house that would be her new home. The dark oméu-wood paneling gave the small room a dusky appearance and filled the air with a smell like cedar.

I expected better, she thought. That was not a slight against Salus. She was just surprised his family's home was so gloomy. There was an open doorway to her left and an archway that led to the kitchen on her right. Both adjoining rooms were shuttered and held the same dreary atmosphere. "When was the last time anyone was here?"

An old Aku woman stepped through the doorway behind Petra. "No one has lived here for years," she said. Her voice wheezed and twanged with her Akün accent. "Salus was born here. His grandfather built this house."

Petra turned and faced the old woman. Her name was Lyda. Her title was Na'alief, *Teacher of Children*. From the old woman's perspective, Petra was just another child. "Where can I put my things?"

Lyda gestured toward the kitchen. "Through there. You may not take personal items. Leave everything but the clothes you are wearing."

Petra had shed her clan uniform for the first time since arriving on Ni'apinu. Her light-weight gray trousers were tucked neatly into her thick-soled walking boots. Beneath her light-weight tan jacket she wore a green V-neck pullover, the only casual top she had in her limited wardrobe. She had rejected wearing the floor-length dress Salus had given her. With no clue what her training would include, a dress was the last thing she wanted to wear, even if a dress was the standard attire for Aku women.

She walked through the dark kitchen and entered the sleeping room. It contained a small, single bed and a wooden chest beneath a shuttered window. She dropped her backpack on the bare mattress, withdrew her silver award, and placed it on the dresser.

Looks out of place here.

Lyda stood in the doorway holding a thick, leather-bound codex in front of her waist. "This is for you."

Petra took the book and examined the worn brown cover.

"Your textbook," Lyda said. "Read as much as you can. Your training will begin two days after you arrive at Squa Paln."

Petra flipped through the yellowed pages. It was an Akün language primer. "Two days?"

The old woman huffed. "You have much to learn."

Yes, I do, Petra thought. The first stage of her training would take three months. If she was successful, she would return to this house to finish her education. After one year of study, the Bi′au would decide if her marriage to Salus could proceed. "When can I see Salus?"

"When your training is done."

Petra surmised the mandatory separation was meant to test her devotion, not just to Salus, but to the entire Aku culture. *This may be more brutal than the clan academy,* she thought. She tucked the language primer under her arm and followed Lyda out of the room.

Two hours later, Petra arrived at the landing field outside the tiny village called Squa Paln at the northeastern edge of the *Wassûa Caphâga*, the Valley of Streams. The flight from Ji′dess was via *ciâfey*, the open-air, two-person flyers that were the common form of transportation over the rugged, forest-covered landscape.

Wassûa Caphâga. Ciâfey.

Petra had learned those names months ago after Salus and his band of twenty Aku men had found her with Arlud and Gustav Eahuda along the bank of the Yoslyn River. With only two days to study, she wondered how many more Akün terms she would remember. *Languages take time,* she thought, and she felt the rush to learn was unfair.

She withdrew the language primer from the storage bin behind the pilot's seat and followed him toward a cluster of small wooden bungalows next to the ciâfey landing area. She noticed a few shingled roof peaks beyond the bungalows that jutted above the surrounding trees in various locations north of the landing field.

Squa Paln.

The pilot veered toward a bungalow and opened the narrow door to reveal a cramped room a meter wider than the sleeping pad, with two crates stacked beneath a louvered window.

Petra entered the room to examine the crates—they contained food packets, a ten-liter container of water, and two small lamps. She heard the rush of thrusters and peered out the dirty window to see the pilot had mounted his ciâfey. With a quick downbeat of the wings, he leaped upward, and flew toward the coastal plain to the west.

Now what do I do?

She looked at the leather book in her hand and sat on the sleeping pad. The book was written in Akün, and she knew nothing about the strange characters that filled each page. She surmised from the few illustrations what the topics were in each chapter, but without a translation in Englo'ni she was stifled before she could begin.

This is ridiculous!

As she continued to flip through the pages, she came upon a glossary near the back of the book—page after page of Akün words in columns, with their Englo'ni counterparts next to them in standard Englo'ni characters.

That's better. I can work with this.

She still needed to understand how to pronounce each word, so she searched further and found the Akün alphabet with phonetic equivalents written in Englo'ni.

Odd, she thought, *that the Aku would have a primer for their language with Englo'ni script to explain the pronunciation.*

She searched the front pages for information about who produced the book.

Nothing.

That was also odd, but no matter, she had enough information to learn a few more words, even if she could not string them together in a proper grammatical sequence.

Maybe that will be enough?

For the next two days, she reviewed the words. The bungalow kept her warm during the chilly nights and kept her dry during the light rain that fell early on the third morning.

She heard a ground car once the rain stopped. She stepped out of the bungalow and watched the small, roofless vehicle rumble across the muddy ground toward her position.

"L'dyém," the male driver called out. He stopped the car a few paces from Petra and gestured for her to sit next to him.

Petra grabbed the primer and shut the bungalow door. "Where are you taking me?"

"L'dyém," the driver said.

Focus, Petra told herself. She searched her memory for the correct words. "Mys'bi pak sib gisu?"

The driver chuckled and gestured again for Petra to sit next to him. "Kam."

They drove for an hour over a rutted dirt road that meandered across rolling hills, up into the dense oméu forest in the Umelk Mountains northwest of Squa Paln. This was a wilderness without Aku settlements. The dirt road narrowed, but the driver pressed on through the undergrowth over what was now a foot trail. Low oméu branches snapped against the car, and Petra had to protect her head through a thick outcropping of bristle-bush.

Then the rumbling car stopped. No birds chirped. No wind rustled the trees. The forest was silent.

The stillness caused Petra to gasp. "Now what?"

The driver gestured to a small clearing ten meters from the car. "Sibqu'ta."

Petra translated to herself, *Go there.* "What's—Oui quta?"

The driver ignored her query and said again, "Sibqu'ta, Sibqu'ta." He nudged her shoulder to encourage her to leave the car.

"Okay, Okay, I get it," she said.

"Sibqu'ta," the driver repeated.

Petra stepped out of the car, grabbed the heavy gray shoulder sack from the storage area behind her seat, tucked the language primer under her arm, and trudged through the surrounding brush toward the clearing.

Before she reached the small meadow, the driver had the car moving in reverse along the path they had plowed through the undergrowth. She refused to turn around to watch him leave. *Damn impolite,* she thought, and she assumed this was just the Aku way to test an off-worlder who would dare consider marrying into their clan. She was determined to go through this test, no matter what she had to face.

Three hours later, she was still alone in the meadow, laying on her back in the tall grass, using the sack for a pillow.

Small insects buzzed and wind whispered through the surrounding trees.

When the sun passed the midday mark in the sky, her survival training kicked in. She focused her mind on creating a shelter and sat upright. To her right, along the edge of the meadow, she caught sight of dead wood and a carpet of fallen oméu needles.

Perfect.

By late afternoon she had erected a small lean-to using dead branches. The shelter was beneath a healthy, three-meter wide oméu tree with green needles. The largest needles were half a meter, and they could pierce anyone positioned beneath them when they turned brown and fell from the branches. She used larger dead needles to build an outward-leaning palisade around the open side of the lean-to and picked out two for weapons to discourage any curious klâwpa—the small scavengers were vicious when provoked, and she hoped her make-shift fence would be enough to keep them away. If the fence didn't work, a fire would. She stacked stones along the inside of the oméu needle barrier to radiate heat from the fire-pit she dug in front of the lean-to. The sack had a small heat torch, so making fire would be a simple process.

The sack also contained cooking utensils—a large metal pot with a lid, two small metal cups, one spoon, one knife, a ceramic stirring rod, and another rolled-up gray sack. Unfortunately, there was no food. She was fine for tonight, but tomorrow would be spent gathering nuts and berries.

Damn impolite!

When daylight faded to dusk, Petra reclined beneath her lean-to and prepared kindling to start a fire.

A voice called out: "Ahiah esyah ouik." The words were in the treble range with the timbre of a young female.

Petra stopped arranging kindling in the fire pit. She twisted to a sitting position, grabbed one of the large oméu needles, and searched the tree line for the source of the voice.

"Ilyun ahil'ju edifu."

With that second statement, Petra spied a young girl sitting in the tree to her right. She had black hair gathered in a ring behind her neck, and her light-brown face expressed the humor that had flavored her words.

"Ilyun ahil'ju edifu," the girl said again.

Petra pulled meaning from the girl's statement: *Get up here*. She scooted out from under the lean-to and stood by the fire-pit. "Oul?"

"Because," the girl said in perfect Englo'ni, "it will not work."

"What won't work?"

"Your fence."

Petra examined her oméu needle palisade for flaws.

"Klâwpa will rip it apart," the girl explained. "They eat oméu needles."

"They eat them?"

The girl nodded. "They'd eat you too. You need to get up here."

Petra considered the girl's sincerity and grabbed the heavy sack. She stuffed the language primer into the sack and lugged it over to the girl's tree and examined the lower branches. The large needles presented an impassable obstacle. "How do I get up there?"

The girl pointed to the other side of the tree. "Over there."

Petra walked around the six-meter trunk and saw the opening. She slipped the heavy sack over her shoulder and climbed onto the lowest branch. She rested her body against the tree's rough bark and noticed the girl had moved higher. She followed the girl up—five meters higher to a thick branch free of the larger needles. By the time Petra reached that position, the girl had moved again. "I am not climbing all the way up."

"Almost there," the girl said. She gestured for Petra to keep climbing.

Five meters higher, Petra stopped at an intersection of six branches that formed a wide scaffold with enough room for her to sit comfortably against the main trunk. "Why so high?"

The girl sat near the outer edge of the scaffold, atop a mat of green needles. "They can't smell us up here."

Petra looked down. The view of her lean-to was obscured by the branches and needles below her, but she could see the outer bend of the angled palisade she had built. "Can they climb trees?"

"Not high. They mostly stick to the ground."

"So, we'll sleep up here?"

The girl nodded.

Petra relaxed and examined the girl. Her brown skin looked clean, and her black hair was well groomed. She wore a linen pullover top and calf-length pants. Her feet were bare. "What's your name?"

"Naña."

"Where are your parents?"

"Squa Paln."

"Why are you here?"

"I'm depüfah."

Petra didn't know that word, and her expression revealed her confusion.

"The age of change," Naña explained. "From child to adult."

Petra considered what that implied for the girl and was astonished her parents would send her to the wilderness. "Do all depüfah come here?"

"Yes."

"Boys and girls?"

"Not the boys. They go to another place."

"And you are left alone?"

Naña giggled. "No, you're here. What's your name?"

"Petra."

"Is that a good name?"

"I think it is."

Naña giggled again.

"If I was not here," Petra said, "would you still be here?"

Naña shrugged. "A friend of mine came a few months ago and said there were four other girls here. I never heard of girls coming here alone." She scooted closer to Petra. "Can I touch your hair?"

Petra flinched. "My hair?"

"Yeah," Naña said with a hint of embarrassment. "I never saw yellow hair before."

Petra smiled. "OK," she said, and she leaned forward.

Naña stroked Petra's short-cropped, straw-colored hair. "It's soft. Why is it so short?"

"I was a clan engineer, assigned to the Eighth Corps. The dress code demands short hair."

"Why?"

"Partly tradition, but mostly for safety reasons."

"Safety?"

Petra nodded. "Long hair can be a safety hazard because of the work we do. The same regulation applies to the men."

Naña hugged her knees and pondered Petra's answer. "So, you are from the stars?"

Petra nodded.

"Like the Nela'ogu? They came here from Kainogae."

"Yes, like the First People, but I came from Baleiou."

"Where's that?"

Petra looked up through the branches. Dusk had shifted the sky to violet and the first stars twinkled in the east. She pointed northwest. "That way, about nineteen parsecs."

"Nineteen what?"

Petra considered a measurement the girl would understand and did a quick mental calculation. "About two-hundred and ninety *trillion* strads."

"Wow, that's far."

"Yes, it is."

"Why did you come here?"

"Because my clan came here."

"Oh." Naña turned away, slid along the branch, and stepped to another limb that formed the scaffold. "I'll sleep over here. You can have that place."

Petra felt secure sitting against the main trunk, but she could not sleep sitting up. "I don't think this is the best place for me."

"Sure it is," Naña said. "There's a hollow area in the limb where I was sitting."

The branch was wide enough, and as Petra scooted away from the trunk, she felt the hollow beneath the mat of omèu needles. She slipped the sack off her shoulder, settled into the depression, and reclined with her head resting on the sack. *This might do,* she thought. She moved her arms out sideways to measure the branch. *More than twice my width. Must not roll in my sleep. Must remember to turn in place.*

"Tomorrow," Naña said, "I'll show you how to make a sleep pocket."

"Where did you learn Englo'ni?"

"My parents taught me. I learned it along with Akün."

"Do all your people know Englo'ni?"

Naña shrugged. "I was told we learned the off-world tongue after the Gásah Kaháfa."

"What's that?"

Naña searched her memory for the translation—she had never referred to the Gásah Kaháfa in Englo'ni. "Fast Stars."

"Fast Stars?"

"Yeah," Naña said, "that's what it means."

Petra looked up at the darkening sky. Meteorites could be viewed as fast stars, but there were periodic meteor storms every year, so the Fast Stars had to be something more unique. "How long ago did the Gásah Kaháfa appear?"

"Before I was born, maybe twenty years ago."

That time period coincided with the first survey drones sent here by Clan Erstallius. *The natives must have understood the source of the orbiting satellites and prepared themselves for the inevitable arrival of Alliance Clans.* "Well," Petra said, "I am very glad we can communicate."

Naña smiled. "Me too."

Twilight faded to darkness and chirping sounds came from the surrounding forest.

Petra looked over to where Naña had settled—she was on her side, facing away from her. *If what she said about the klâwpa is true, she saved my life.* "Naña?"

Naña replied without turning: "What?"

"Why do depüfah come here?"

"Kéf'we."

That was another word Petra had not learned. "Kéf'we?"

"Yeah, Kéf'we. We survive."

Petra knelt alongside the destroyed palisade and examined one of the chewed oméu needles. The low-angled sunlight of early morning highlighted the klâwpa tracks that covered the ground around her lean-to. "Looks like there were at least five."

"Ten," Naña said. She stood a few paces away in the soft, dew-covered grass. "They came from that way."

Petra looked across the meadow to where Naña pointed. "There was nothing here to attract them. Why did they attack these dead needles?"

"Your smell. They investigate everything they haven't smelled before. You would have had to fight them."

"Will they be back?"

Naña rested her hands on her hips. "Probably. They travel around their territory. Usually takes them a few days to come back to the same place."

"What's the best way to fight them?"

"Best way is with a gun."

"Then if we can make a loud noise—"

"It's not the noise," Naña insisted. "You have to shoot them."

Petra stood and dusted off her pants. "Then it's good they only come out at night."

"Yep."

Petra placed her hands on her hips, matching the young girl's posture. "Ouahni ouni yi'ou?" The words flowed from her with the phonetic sounds she had read in the primer, but she could see a slight smirk in Naña's reaction.

"That's good," Naña said, "but you still need to work on the accent." She turned around and faced the deep woods to the east. "We'll start over there. There are large pristal bushes there. Kam!" She waved for Petra to follow and jogged across the meadow toward the wood.

This entire endeavor is to test our ability to live off the land, Petra thought. *And avoid dangers like klâwpa.*

She followed Naña across the meadow and focused on gathering food to store in the tree where they slept.

Kéf'we. We survive.

BEV COLLI: QUESTIONS

Bev was pulled away from her childhood home. The Rhysu lifted her from the atmosphere of Pigrell, through space, to a rocky world where she entered a vortex of blue plasma and was thrown back into the Rhysu universe. The entire trip seemed to take only seconds and left Bev disoriented amid blue energy spheres that pressed around her.

"Why did you take me away?"

"Danger," the Rhysu said.

"Danger?"

"War."

Bev recalled the events around her as she floated above her parent's home. She had sensed no danger. "War?"

"Yes."

"I didn't—"

"There was danger."

Confused and worried for her parents, she focused again on her memory of what transpired before the Rhysu pulled her away. She recalled nothing that warned of trouble.

There was danger.

That revelation caused Bev to delve deep into her awareness, to focus on her current surroundings, to sense the limit of her perception. The Rhysu had a broader limit to their sensory input because they had always been Rhysu. *I'm limited because this existence is new to me.* And she wondered: *If the Rhysu could sense danger, why didn't they try to stop it? Could they stop it?*

She focused on her outward self and could sense the limit of her new body—twitching ripples of energy that interacted with, and drew more energy from, the surrounding press of plasma spheres, which she recognized as individual Rhysu. She had no separation, no privacy. She was part of the collective group.

While at Ni'apinu and Pigrell she had been separated from the Rhysu, so she knew isolation was possible, and she assumed the motive of the

Shoku—to be separate, alone, without the constant flux of other voices—was a privacy they could never have here, in their normal state.

Or is it normal?

She recalled her connection with the Shoku. Beyond the overlying presence of the Rhysu she caught a glimpse, a faint impression of the phantoms that had ripped the cargo ship apart. She saw them from a distance, and then she was next to them. She heard sadness, anger, and fear in their voices. Then she was back in the secure embrace of the Rhysu.

"Do not consider the Shoku," the Rhysu said.

"Why?"

"They have disobeyed."

"Disobeyed what?"

"They wish to depart," the Rhysu said. "We cannot allow that."

"Why?"

"Danger."

Bev was flooded with images of the mine disaster on Alpha Cephei Four.

"They ignore the effects their presence has in your universe. We must restrain them."

"Oh."

Bev collapsed her energy sphere into a tight ball to separate herself from the Rhysu embrace as much as possible. She knew no way to remove herself from this place, but based on what the Shoku had done, she knew it was possible. She needed to discover how.

CLAN ERSTALLIUS: GREAT HALL

The journey to the PDN103 star system took two-point-nine hyper-days, or eight-point-seven standard-days. Arlud's transport wound through battle-damaged frigates and destroyers near the orbit of the system's seventh planet. The fighting had been heavy here, and he expected to see damaged vessels all the way to the Polinda homeworld, Pigrell, the fourth planet from the sun called *Surphra* in the ancient catalogs.

The Erstallius Battle Command sent warships to intercept Arlud's transport one million kilometers from Pigrell.

From the forward observation deck, Arlud spotted the four Erstallius destroyers as they emerged from a debris field a few thousand kilometers from his transport.

A holoscreen ignited inside the observation deck window. Jegen-Major Lon Pavan's somber, gray-haired visage peered out of the screen. "Greetings, sir. You will need to halt your approach to Pigrell until we're sure all threats have been eliminated. Once the *All Clear* is announced, we will escort you."

Arlud clutched the railing beneath the window. "What happened? I thought the battle was won?"

"Polinda loyalists mounted an attack yesterday to retake the planet. The capital city was hit hard and most of our positions in orbit were hit. We won the day, but there were many casualties, both civilian and clanman. The Great Hall collapsed. I fear the High Regent may be a casualty. There has been no word of his status since yesterday."

Arlud tightened his grip on the railing as he contemplated the possibility that his father was dead. Armand had kept his clan on a narrow path. Arlud knew his ability would never match his father's, and he worried the cadre would split apart once news of Armand's death reached them. *If my father is dead, the path forward will get mired in useless arguments about my position among the cadre.* He hoped for a better outcome. "No word means nothing," he said. "He could still be alive."

"As we all hope," Pavan replied.

"Damn the threats! Get me there—now!"

Pavan nodded and turned to relay a new command to his bridge crew.

Arlud scrambled over crumbled stone slabs and through a twisted alsteel framework that blocked the road to the charred ruins of the Polinda Great Hall. The three-story structure had collapsed on all sides and only the western portico walls still supported a sliver of the second floor.

Erstallius rescue teams scurried among the destroyed buildings surrounding the Great Hall, using work pods to remove rubble and dead bodies as they searched for survivors.

Arlud met Team Leader Omba Khan at the bottom of the rubble-strewn steps of the Great Hall. The Degen's ebony face was a sullen visage of failure that told Arlud his father was dead.

"I'm sorry, sir," Khan said.

"Take me to him," Arlud commanded.

Khan led Arlud up the stone steps, through the remnants of the portico pillars, then down onto the cracked marble floor of the lobby that had been cleared of debris. Two rows of bagged bodies, eight in each row, filled half of the cleared area. Armand's bagged body lay at the left end of the second row, beneath the sky-blue Erstallius flag with the eagle crest emblazoned at its center.

"Clear the area!" Khan ordered.

The clanmen searching the surrounding rubble stopped their work and clambered off the rubble piles.

Khan turned to Arlud. "We identified the Patriarch with a genetic sample. There were no survivors in the hall. They took a direct hit."

Arlud dropped to his knees beside the flag-covered bag and placed a hand on the clan crest—it was cold. He could tell from the drape of the flag that his father had been crushed.

He hung his head and wept.

Arlud entered the meeting room where the Erstallius officers had gathered to discuss their future, and he paused a few steps inside the doorway. It was a large oval room with a panoramic window on the east side that overlooked the battered city that had been the capital of the Polinda homeworld.

The assembled officers rose from their seats around the black onyx table that dominated the room.

Arlud walked to his seat and stood behind it. He motioned for the officers to sit down and waited for them to retake their seats.

A line of holoscreens ignited along the west wall, revealing two commanders from Clan Rastee, two commanders from Clan Sorrell, and Erlis Pardee, Captain of the Guild armada—coalition allies who would watch this meeting from their ships in orbit.

Arlud gripped the back of his chair and said: "My father once said Clan Erstallius would never be party to unwarranted retaliation. He always preferred diplomacy over battle. Some may say that was his undoing."

A quiet grumble erupted among the assembled officers.

Arlud moved to the panoramic window and gestured to the ruins in the city. "See what our efforts have brought? My father never wanted this, but there was no way to avoid it." He faced the officers. "Who among us could foresee Polinda forces attacking their own people? This is evidence of how little they care for their sapi, and why we must be vigilant. My father's death should strengthen our resolve to end this conflict for good. The Drupal Caste system must be eliminated. The people enslaved by Clan Polinda, and the other clans who practice the Drupal system, must be liberated from that tyranny." He moved back to the table and stood behind his chair. "Our retaliation against our enemies must be complete — we must annihilate every remaining Polinda clanman who insists on perpetuating that despicable tradition."

The officers fell silent, intent on Arlud's words.

Arlud sensed surprise among the assembled officers, but also agreement. He knew his proposed path was fueled by his anger, but he also knew the only path to true peace was to end all possibility of retaliation by their enemies. "Many have died," he said. "We have all lost loved ones. Let's make sure those losses end here!"

The officers stood as one and applauded Arlud's resolve.

THE GUILD: ALLY

Shanna Sy sat on the wooden bench at the end of the stone path that wound through the eastern garden to the hilltop that overlooked the fenced area where groundskeepers were laying sod. This new residence was not as comfortable as she had hoped, but once the landscaping was completed, perhaps she would feel more at home. The four days she had spent in detention for accepting classified information added to her discomfort, and although she knew punishment had been necessary, it pushed her mind into a negative hole, which had no obvious exit. Appreciation of this new homeworld had become as difficult as the journey to get here.

We should have stayed on Al-phaq.

She pulled the wide brim of her sun hat to shade her eyes and turned toward the sound of footfalls coming up the path.

"Here you are, Daughter," Wolfram said. He stopped a few paces from the bench.

Shanna turned back to view the groundskeepers.

"You weren't at breakfast," Wolfram said. "I wondered where you had gone."

"I ate in my room."

Wolfram noticed the sullen tone in Shanna's voice. A persistent attitude he had grown weary of during the past few weeks but knew only Shanna could find the remedy. "Your mother will be released today," he said. "You will be expected to attend the event. The media coverage will be broadcast throughout the Guild."

Shanna bristled at the thought of attending her mother's release from detention, although she was glad her time in jail was finally finished. Her mother's crimes had been unauthorized access to classified data and giving that data to unauthorized personnel. Her mother's penalty was four weeks of detention, with a fine and a public apology. A punishment understood and accepted, but an embarrassing beginning to their new life here on Wald-415.

Wolfram moved off the stone path to stand next to the wooden bench. "We received news this morning from Captain Pardee. He says the Erstallius coalition was victorious against Clan Polinda at Wan'tei."

Shanna twisted on the bench to face her father. "Oh, that's wonderful!"

Wolfram nodded. "Yes, excellent news. Word is the Erstallius also defeated Polinda at Pigrell."

"Oh, my!" Shanna exclaimed. "The fighting has spread to more worlds than I expected."

"And I'm afraid it will spread to more," Wolfram admitted. "The Alliance is collapsing like dominoes."

"Are we in danger?"

"No need to fear. We're far enough from the Old Worlds."

Shanna flashed a brief smile and lowered her head.

Wolfram saw worry creep back into her expression. "Pardee said the entire Polinda fleet at Wan'tei was destroyed. With the capture of Pigrell, Clan Erstallius has won, and our future is more secure."

"Our partnership will endure?"

Wolfram nodded.

Shanna held the brim of her hat to stop it flapping in a sudden breeze. "With Polinda gone, I thought the violence would end."

"There are many clans, and they all have their own motives."

"Then the Alliance was a lie."

Wolfram chuckled. "It wasn't always a lie. Once, many years ago, honor and justice ruled the clans. The birth of the Guild was the beginning of the end for the Alliance."

"How?"

"Our rebellion revealed corruption in the system. Clans began to retreat from General Assembly authority in subtle ways that began to erode central oversight, and long-standing relationships began to unravel."

Shanna sighed. She dropped her hands onto her lap as the breeze subsided. "The carnage will be great among the old worlds."

"Yes, but we will prosper. Based on Pardee's communique, we may return to Al-phaq."

"Really?"

"The district there will see less conflict now that Polinda is gone. I don't intend to move our homeworld back there, but it was a Guild stronghold. The Guild should be there."

"Yes, Father," Shanna said, "the Guild should be there. We have Arlud to thank for that."

Shanna's tone at the mention of the Erstallius heir told Wolfram she still pined for him. "We have the coalition strength to thank for that," he corrected, "which includes Clan Rastee, Clan Sorrell, and the ships we sent to help them."

"Yes," Shanna admitted. Her father's disapproval of Arlud was obvious when he shifted focus to the other clans in the coalition, and that fueled her suspicion he had prevented her from communicating with Arlud when he had arrived to seek help. She tossed aside a surge of resentment and said, "But if Arlud had not come here, the victory at Wan'tei may never have happened."

Wolfram acknowledged that truth with a nod. "Our partnership will bring stability to the region, but true peace may take many years."

Shanna focused again on the groundskeepers. "It's fine with me if the Alliance crumbles, but what of the aliens?"

Wolfram folded his hands behind his back and surveyed the workers laying sod in the field. "They revealed themselves at Simbic Ur."

"Where's that?"

"It orbits the same star as Wan'tei. Pardee said the planet disappeared."

"Oh, my!"

"No one expected that."

"What did the Clans do?"

"Most of them stopped fighting, but Polinda persisted—to his destruction."

Shanna leaned back on the bench as that news whirled around in her thoughts. The aliens were a complete mystery. "Did we learn anything more about the aliens?"

"Pardee said little about them. He said the person who was in contact with the aliens vanished with the planet. She called them Rhysu."

"She?"

"Yes, a survivor from the mine on Alpha Cephei Four."

"How could a miner be in contact with aliens?"

Wolfram shrugged.

"Arlud probably knows," Shanna said.

"Maybe he does," Wolfram agreed. "But for now, we need to get ready for your mother's release."

Shanna frowned.

"I'll meet you in an hour by the shuttle port," Wolfram said. He turned and retreated down the stone path.

❖ ❖ ❖

Wellen Tallilia Sy strolled out of the detention center entrance with Wolfram at her side. Her gait was steady and balanced, showing no sign of the injury to her left knee.

A white canvas canopy covered the stone patio, where a small crowd of media personnel waited for an interview.

Shanna noticed her mother's strong gait as she followed a few steps behind her, and thought: *Well, that's one positive thing about her detention. It gave her time to heal without distractions.* And the memory of the terrible event that caused the injury, when the Cormeds had tried to commandeer Captain Pardee's ship, sent Shanna's mind whirling with thoughts of future reprisal. *That was an infraction more worthy of Guild justice.*

Wellen stopped when pressed by the media. "Good day," she said. "I have finished my detention as mandated by law. I apologize to the Guild for my lack of respect for our security protocols."

A thin reporter with a gray mustache asked, "How will this impact your actions moving forward?"

"We are all under law," Wellen said with a somber expression. "Sometimes our human imperfections need a nudge to keep us on the correct path. I have learned my lesson."

A female reporter asked, "What imperfections caused you to ignore the law?"

Wellen turned toward the plump, middle-aged woman. "I think it's safe to say everyone here has made mistakes. What matters is that we do our best to not repeat them."

The reporter persisted: "But what caused you to ignore the law?"

Wolfram placed a hand on Wellen's lower back as a gesture of support.

Wellen flicked a glance at her husband, then focused on the reporter. "When I was five years old, I went to visit a neighbor. He was an older man who lived on my family's property. We would play stratagem or sit and tell each other stories.

"One day he was busy in the kitchen, and I crept into his bedroom. Inside the closet I found a chest—a very heavy chest, so heavy I could barely move it. I was overwhelmed with curiosity. When he found me, I had half the contents placed around me in a semi-circle on the wooden floor. He squatted next to me and told me it was not polite to poke through other people's belongings. I was stunned by his remark—I had never been told that. I understood I had done something wrong, but I ignored that and said, 'Wow, you're rich!'

"'No, not really,' he said.

"I examined the tiny gold and silver bars I had removed from the chest and said, 'Yes you are,' then dove my hands deep into the chest and pulled up two handfuls of silver coins.

"'Make sure you put everything back where you found it,' he said, then he left me there.

"Later, when I joined him in the kitchen, he asked me to keep my knowledge of his treasure a secret. After he explained why it should be kept secret, I agreed. I never poked around other people's things after that. Unfortunately, the lessons we learn as a child can get lost in the complexities of adulthood."

"Did you take any of the treasure?"

Wellen faced a short, older woman who asked that question. "I placed everything back in the chest and pushed the chest back into his closet. My intent was fueled by curiosity, not thievery."

The short woman asked, "Did he tell your parents?"

"The next day," Wellen said, "he asked me if he should call me *Nosy Nellie*. That hurt a little. No one had ever criticized my actions like that. I quipped that I should call him *Silly Dilly*, and he laughed. The subject never came up again."

Wellen pressed forward through the reporters and slid into the waiting ground car, followed by Wolfram.

Shanna ignored the reporters, took her seat next to Wolfram, and the driver shut the car door. As the car pulled away, she asked, "Why did you tell that story?"

Wellen leaned forward to face her perplexed daughter. "You have a problem with that?"

"Yes!"

"My dear, you must—"

"Oh, that's great," Shanna blurted. "Look!" She held her compad so Wellen could see the screen. The headline read, "Nosy Nellie Released from Detention."

Wellen smirked and leaned back in her seat.

"Ladies," Wolfram said, and he reached out left and right to hold their hands. "Let's not fight all the way home."

"But father, the ridicule—"

"Is deserved," Wolfram said. "You both disobeyed the law. All your mother was doing was stressing the need that we should all learn from our mistakes because we all make them."

"Besides," Wellen said, "my childhood story will help divert the focus of the criticism to something everyone can relate to in their own lives. It makes my actions understandable, and my repentance more acceptable."

"It makes us fools," Shanna said.

Wolfram tightened his grip on Shanna's hand. "No, Daughter. It makes us more real. The people must know we do not sit above them, we sit with them. We have flaws like everyone else." He released Shanna's hand and leaned into Wellen's shoulder. "You did well, my dear. I'm proud of you."

Shanna rolled her eyes and stayed quiet during the remainder of the drive to the shuttle port.

CLAN HALVA: RUINS

Cynth Halva began her day reviewing drone transmissions of the damage caused by the attack against her homeworld. The assault had been well planned and hit the two continents with the four largest cities. The current estimate was eight million dead.

One third of our population is gone.

That number only counted planet-bound dead. The number of Halva clanmen lost in space was estimated to be close to 10,000—7,000 ship-bound crewmen, 1,000 clanmen on the orbital stations, and 2,000 in the fortresses on Cestratha's three moons.

As the data streamed across her holoscreen, with images of the orbiting rubble belt from the destroyed ships and stations, she hung her head and closed her eyes.

We have been decimated!

She thought of her brother's meeting with the allied clans. They would stay and police Cestratha's local stellar neighborhood until the Halva fleet could rebuild. Rebuilding the lost ships would take years, but their new friends promised to lend them ships from their reserve inventory.

"Three months," her brother had said. "With their help, we'll be up to a proper strength in three months."

Clan Vestlok and Clan Emlito had suffered ninety percent casualties, which would forestall any further belligerence from them, but the immediate result of the victory was more danger to Cestratha—falling debris from the rubble streams in orbit would threaten the planet for years.

Two years, Cynth surmised, *before the salvage ships remove all the bits of debris.* Sadness overwhelmed her, and she felt tears pool behind her eyelids.

Tara Quin rushed into the sitting room. "Madame!"

Cynth jerked her head up and wiped her wet eyes. Her hand-maiden's face showed the same fear she had seen during the bombardment.

"Switch to channel five," Quin said. "The report just came in."

Cynth fingered the holoscreen controls and channel five displayed the latest comm-drone report with the headline: "Erstallius High Regent Killed."

"Oh, no!" Cynth exclaimed in an undertone. She leaned forward as she scanned through the report menu and brought up an aerial view of the destroyed Great Hall on Pigrell. The body bag containing Armand Erstallius lay beneath his clan's banner in a rubble-free area of the main lobby. "This is awful!"

As she read the report that streamed across the bottom of the screen, Cynth knew this latest event would propel Arlud into a rage that would send his forces hurling toward their enemies. *Blood will seek blood,* she thought. *He must focus his anger.*

"Call the shuttle hanger," Cynth said. "I need to leave."

"Yes, Madame," Quin replied, and she rushed out of the room.

Cynth peered out the window next to her seat as her shuttle sped over shattered buildings along the river that snaked through the eastern side of the city. She saw the rescue teams removing dead bodies from the rubble, and in the distance, engineering teams clearing debris from the roads. This was her home, her beloved Lichtstad. Now it looked too much like the images she had seen of Capital City on Pigrell. She turned away from the window and closed her eyes.

Thirty minutes later, her shuttle landed on tarmac amid buildings nestled in the pine forest outside the small village named Holte, nine hundred kilometers east of Lichtstad. This was the temporary home for the clan administration where the High Regent would manage the future of Clan Halva.

Cynth discarded her usual robes for this journey. Those coverings were to hide her artificial limbs as much as possible from anyone in her company, to help remove her physical appearance from consideration. This trip demanded more attention, so she emerged from the shuttle wearing her hooded green jumpsuit. She called it her "jumpsuit" because the outfit covered her torso but left her metal legs below mid-thigh exposed and free to move without restriction. The robust blue metal shimmered in the sunlight as she left the shuttle and walked to the steps that led up to the front courtyard, where she met a two-man security team.

The men recognized her but still demanded an ident scan.

Cynth raised her human arm.

The guards stepped aside once the scan confirmed her identity.

"Take the path to the left at the top of the stairs," the guard who scanned her wrist said. "You can wait there."

"Wait?"

"The High Regent is in a meeting," the other guard said.

"Good," Cynth replied. She took one step forward and leaped.

The guards watched as the three-point stabilizers on Cynth's metal feet helped her nail a solid landing at the top of the steps.

She bounded along the stone path that led to the side entrance, ignored two more guards waiting outside, rushed through the doorway, and headed toward the meeting room.

Envoys from Clan Rastee, Clan Sorrell, and Clan Erstallius, along with an aging, silver-haired representative from the Guild, were seated around a holomitter that projected a map of Clan Halva's planetary system. The locations of their forces were identified with blue icons. The routes taken by Clan Vestlok and Clan Emlito were highlighted red and showed how they had retreated from battle in five divergent paths that took them away from Cestratha and out of the system.

Gustus Halva stood beside his chair, directing the discussion on ship movements and defense strategy, when Cynth leaped through the doorway.

The envoys stood as Cynth landed a few paces from her brother. The guildman was the last to stand—he took a step sideways from his chair to give himself more room to maneuver and rested a hand on the holstered pistol concealed beneath his coat.

Gustus glared at Cynth. "How dare you, Sister!"

"Get over it! I've avoided these meetings long enough."

Cynth scanned the holomap, then surveyed the assembled men as two security guards appeared in the doorway.

Gustus waved at the guards so they would leave. "We're fine."

"Gentlemen," Cynth said. "Do you know what we face?"

"We know," Gustus said, his tone indignant. "That's why we're here."

Cynth turned to face her brother and gestured toward the holomap. "You're here to discuss the future of Cestratha. We're faced with much more than that."

"Madame," Lester Isard, the ruddy Erstallius envoy, said, "if you've been following—"

"Silence!" Cynth blurted. "We appreciate your help. We would not have survived without it, but our focus now must be on the future of the allied clans." She spun toward the Guild representative. "Minister Len, withdraw that weapon and you'll regret it."

The guildman moved his hand beneath his coat.

Cynth leaped and was upon the minister in an eye-blink. In one smooth motion, she pushed his arm away with her cybernetic forearm and pulled his pistol from the holster with her human hand. "Idiot!" She shoved the guildman away with her metal hand and stuffed the pistol into her belt.

"How dare you," Len protested. "This is an outrage!"

Gustus moved to console the guildman. "Damn you sister! You want to destroy this alliance before it gets started?"

Cynth huffed. "This alliance? Political favors come with consequences. They will want something in return, and the only thing we have to give is the little we have left. We will not be allies. We will be servants."

Gustus understood Cynth's concern—that was the way the clans had operated for centuries. "Times have changed," he said. "There is no concern for profit here. We are all under threat of anarchy. Our motive is survival."

"The Erstallius patriarch is dead," Cynth said. "Farquar Polinda is dead. How many more High Regents will die before this chaos has ended?"

Lester Isard took a step toward Cynth. "Arlud is our High Regent now."

Cynth flicked a disdainful glance toward the envoy. "Really? And what ensures he will be accepted by your cadre?"

The Erstallius envoy remained silent.

"Arlud is a good man," Cynth said in a softer tone. "But his ascension must be approved by a majority. That won't happen for months, if at all."

"It will happen," Isard said.

"Arlud's rage at the death of his father will fling him into a war he is not prepared to win, and his opposition will grow among the cadre. That could mean our downfall."

Gustus chuckled. "Arlud is not a fool."

"You're right, he's not," Cynth agreed, "but he is an angry man seeking vengeance, and that will cloud his judgment. When his victory turns to defeat, our ability to put down the rebellion will fade—rapidly."

The Guild envoy, still angered at losing his weapon, asked: "What do you see here?"

Cynth blinked at Len's question and surveyed the room. "Four desperate men."

"No," the guildman said. "You see four men concerned with the survival of their people. Each of us has need of the others. We will all live or die because of our next moves."

"And yet, you bring a weapon into this meeting."

"Old habits," Len admitted. "Can you blame me for being cautious?"

Cynth relaxed. "No."

The guildman flashed a thin smile. "Arlud is a brave and thoughtful man, but he is not the point of our spear. Our success will depend on our combined insight and strength."

"Then we are in agreement," Gustus said—a response that caused Cynth to let out a sigh.

"You should listen before you judge, Sister. We are all focused on our mutual survival."

"We need to ally with as many clans as we can," Cynth said. "Arlud's anger can be tempered when more voices join the effort to snuff out our nightmare."

Ronon Venau, the Clan Sorrell envoy, said, "Time is our limitation, Madame. We are separated by days, and sometimes weeks."

Cynth faced the frail-looking man—based on his reputation, she expected a larger man. "Yes," Cynth agreed. "Which is why we need to send out comm-drones to all the clans who are not allied with Vestlok, Emlito, or Sabballi. We need to create a new Alliance Council and purge those who would stand against it."

"We will always have enemies," Jera Pellion, the Clan Rastee envoy, said. "We must move slow and steady, or our efforts may alienate more clans."

"Caution stifles action," Cynth said. She scrutinized Pellion—the lumisilk material that accented his clothing was a sign of great wealth and revealed his ties to the Guild black market. "We must act—as quickly as possible."

Gustus cleared his throat. "What do you propose?"

"Encourage our friends to join us in council at Jai'raan." Cynth said. "That's centrally located on this side of the Old Worlds. If we act now, in two weeks we could have at least twenty clans there, in council, to plan how we move forward."

The guildman fingered the holomitter controls and changed the view to focus on a global map of Jai'raan.

Jai'raan was prized for its exotic mineral deposits. Diverse flora and fauna thrived within a rich atmosphere that protected the surface from the intense radiation coming from Wald-181, a class four gas giant planet and Jai'raan's primary orbital partner within the PDN150 system. Jai'raan had attracted Clan Halva, who profited from her natural resources and benefited from the appeal of the moon's tropical climate. Two settlements had been established, along with a fifty-acre spa that encompassed natural hot springs and serviced thousands of guests each year. But that was before Arrilen Po, and the sanctions imposed upon Clan Halva by the Alliance Council. Since that time, Jai'raan had devolved into a pirate paradise. The Guild moved in to overtake the trade routes, and Jai'raan became the beneficiary of the largest black market among holdings within Alliance controlled space.

Cynth's choice of Jai'raan humored the Guild envoy. "You scold us," he said, "insisting we are profit mongers, and yet here you are, wanting to reestablish your clan on Jai'raan."

"I said nothing about reestablishing our colony," Cynth insisted. She focused on the holomap. "Jai'raan is a minor holding, separated from other Alliance settlements by its reliance on your black market—the perfect location for a clandestine meeting."

Gustus agreed. "Vestlock, Emlito, and Sabballi will never suspect Jai'raan as our meeting place. It's too vulnerable."

"Yes," Isard said, "vulnerable, but not threatened. Our enemies are more concerned with their own immediate problems—Polinda was the driving force behind their plans. With Farquar gone, those who remain will lick their wounds for weeks, if not months."

"Who knows," Pellion said, "they may end their hostilities."

"Wishful thinking," Venau quipped. "We must proceed as if the threat remains the same."

"Agreed," Cynth said.

Gustus ran his fingers over the holomitter controls and changed the view back to the area around Cestratha. "We almost lost our homeworld," he said. "How many more clans will be confronted with the same possibility if we do not act? I vote to approve my sister's proposal."

"I approve," Pellion said.

"I approve," Venau said.

"Agreed," Minister Len said. "We can have comm-drones ready to send within the hour."

"Yes," Isard said. "We'll meet in two weeks at Jai'raan."

"Good," Cynth said. She was glad everyone agreed but knew the issues they would face in two weeks might split this coalition apart if another major holding was sacked.

Courage needs constant energy, she thought, *or the impetus to win will fade, and we'll be forced to cower under the weight of a dissenting argument. If that happens, we lose.*

BEV COLLI: MEMORY

Bev floated amid cyan energy bubbles as she sped a few meters above the gray regolith that was Simbic Ur's surface. The three-dimensional terrain was a substantial frame of reference, but she recognized the landscape blocked full comprehension of her new environment.

Maybe that's the intent, she thought. *The Rhysu want to stifle my growth.* She expected immediate denial from them because they heard her thoughts, but they were silent.

"You do, don't you?" Bev asked.

The energy bubbles pressed against Bev with no change in pressure—a sign the Rhysu were not disturbed by her thoughts.

Of course, you're not disturbed, she realized. *You expect me to have these feelings.*

Bev stopped her motion, collapsed her energy bubble as tight as she could, and dropped through the surrounding Rhysu to settle upon the warm, rocky ground. Her energy filaments stabbed at the hard surface. She focused her effort and penetrated her energy strands a meter into the rock to anchor herself to the planet.

The surrounding Rhysu kept away from the surface, and their pressure against Bev was reduced.

Bev saw that as an opportunity to gain a moment of privacy. She still felt the Rhysu presence, but her physical contact with Simbic Ur changed the flow and transfer of energy and weakened her connection to the Rhysu. And she realized if she bored deep enough, her connection would be severed. *That's how the Shoku escaped! Once they had penetrated into Alpha Cephei Four, their connection with the Rhysu was lost.*

Bev reflected on her connection to Arlud. The Rhysu connected with her when she was human, so she could connect with Arlud, because she was now like the Rhysu—she was in their dimension, she had a body like them, she communicated like them, so she was able to connect like them.

Her memory of Arlud had pulled her to his location once she had passed through the dimensional portal. She wondered if a mental connection could be achieved across dimensions without a portal. She focused on Arlud by recalling her memories of him, from the first day they met in the warehouse where she shot the Polinda retriever, to that last hug in the shuttle bay, before she stole the transport from Jens Orr and flew to Simbic Ur.

Scenes from her past whirled in her mind, and then she burst into a new experience. She recognized Capital City on Pigrell, but it was different now. Row upon row of shattered buildings lined the Great Highway that led to the ruins of the Great Hall. The gray landscape was dotted by fire and smoke, and she saw dead bodies strewn amid the rubble.

A fiery sting shot through Bev's body, and her vision of Capital City vanished. She shook off the pain and realized her anchoring grip on the surface of Simbic Ur was gone.

The Rhysu had pulled her away from the planet and were pressing upon her from every direction.

Bev screamed. "Stop it!"

"We cannot allow your connection," the Rhysu said.

"Why!"

"Your place is here now."

"My connection will always be with my friends."

"Yes," the Rhysu acknowledged. "But contact is not permitted."

"Why?"

"To avoid suffering."

"Whose suffering?"

"Yours."

Bev flowed into a thoughtless calm that did what she intended—the Rhysu released her. She bounced around the environment of energy spheres, careening from one Rhysu to another, getting glimpses of each entity's thoughts as they touched her. She understood their motivation was for her benefit, but she would not abandon her goal. Somehow, she would connect with Arlud again. She had to, otherwise she knew she would go insane.

PETRA SITLYN: DÁGUL JÁSAH

Petra had survived for nine days in the wilderness northwest of Squa Paln. She learned about edible plants, and the plants that would kill. She now knew which Pristal-berries were ripe to pick, and how to cook them so the seeds would soften and break away from the pulp. She discovered how to filter water using tarma leaves, and how to weave a secure sleeping pocket high in the branches of the oméu using the larger, green oméu needles. She learned how to reduce her smell so the klâwpa would ignore her fire pit. She learned the *Ogâhu Esnüphica*, the *Way of the Wilderness*, as taught to her by Naña, daughter of Sêra and Gernatis of Squa Paln. That's how the history would be written, because that's how she would record the facts in her journal once she returned to Ji'dess.

And she perfected her pronunciation of Akün, so Naña no longer responded with a smirk.

She woke on the tenth day to the faint spatter of rain. The oméu shelter protected her and Naña from the wet and the wind, but the drop in temperature caused her to forgo her usual breakfast of raw bump-berries. She slipped out of her sleep pocket and descended to the ground to start a fire.

By the time Naña joined her under the lean-to, the radiant heat from the fire pit had pushed the chill away and a thick pristal-berry stew bubbled in the metal pot over the fire.

"We should pick more berries today," Naña said.

"OK."

The rain stopped an hour later, and Naña presented her *ayulk'salu* to her off-world companion.

Petra examined the three hand-length leather strands that each had five oval stones attached. The strands were tied together and above the large knot, two shorter strands of leather extended in the opposite direction. "What's this?"

"My ayulk'salu," Naña said. "You can wear it today."

Petra translated to herself: *Ayulk'salu, noise maker.* She had been with Naña for nine days and had never seen this. "What's it for?"

"You wear it behind you," Naña said. She turned and held the leather strands against her lower back. "You tie it here, behind you, to a belt loop."

"Why?"

"It clacks as we walk, so we don't surprise a sipá."

"Sipá?" Petra had seen the large gray bears at Kuliq'Quad. She did not expect to see them here.

"Yeah," Naña said. "We've been lucky the last few days. I saw sign yesterday. There's one in the area, maybe more."

"Wild sipá?"

"Oh, no. No sipá is wild. They are raised and trained in special compounds with people. My father told me that sometimes they get difficult when they get older, so they are let loose to roam the ranges without constant supervision. My father calls it, 'Put out to pasture.'"

"Why the ayulk'salu? Are they dangerous?"

"They never like to be surprised. Safer that way for everyone, including the sipá."

Twenty minutes later Petra and Naña made their way down hill to the narrow creek that flowed south of their camp. They crossed the shallow waterway amid the squawk and chatter of birds, climbed the opposite bank, and hiked to where bump-berries grew amid the shade of stunted oméu and broad-leaf evergreens. They spent the next hour collecting the thumbnail-sized, purple fruit.

"My satchel is full," Petra said. She cinched her shoulder sack shut and faced Naña.

Naña paused her berry picking and turned to see Petra's bulging sack. "OK. Give me a few more minutes and we'll head back."

Petra flashed a brief smile at her young friend. Naña taught her many things about her people and how they survive here. This test had become a pleasant experience. Her survival training at the Erstallius academy helped her adapt, but what Naña showed her was invaluable, and deepened her appreciation for the Aku and the mindset that helped them survive here on Ni'apinu.

"OK, let's go," Naña said.

Petra adjusted her berry sack, so it rested behind her left hip. She led the way along the row of bump-berry bushes to the large boulder that marked where they turned north toward the creek. The forest thickened with larger oméu and forced them onto a well-worn path that zigzagged to avoid the clusters of sharp brown needles on the lower branches.

Petra froze at the top of the southern bank overlooking the creek. Five meters below her, a large gray sipá sat on the other side of the shallow waterway. She noticed the shoulder hump and the darker gray neck fur. *A male.*

The sipá looked up at Petra and sniffed the air.

"What should I do?" Petra asked in a panicked whisper. She turned to glance at Naña, but the young girl was gone.

The sipá huffed.

Petra focused on the sipá. *He smells the berries,* she thought. She pulled the bulging sack around so it hung in front of her and lifted the strap off her shoulder. *If he starts for me, I'll toss the sack at him and run.* She took a step backward.

The sipá rocked forward to stand, and his front paws splashed in the creek.

From his stance, Petra estimated his size was at least four meters, so running was not an option.

The sipá kept his gaze on Petra and roared.

The Academy Wilderness Survival Instructions said to play dead when confronted by Ursus Arctos, the common brown bear. Sipás were related to those Old-World animals, but were more intelligent and, by all accounts, more tame.

"You smell the berries?" Petra asked. She saw no reaction in the sipá and realized he never heard Englo'ni. She shifted her mind to the Akün she had learned. "Ileju'es ahipu'pheuk?"

The sipá huffed and bounded across the creek to stand on the southern bank a few meters below Petra. He raised his head and let out a long roar that displayed his large fangs.

Petra lowered the berry sack to the ground and walked backward. "Pheuk il'epha." *The berries are yours.*

The sipá lumbered the rest of the way up the bank and sniffed the sack.

Petra could now smell the sipá's odor—wet grass with a hint of urine. That was typical of the sipá's wild ancestors and caused her to wonder how long this old male had been on his own. She passed the large oméu tree to her right and watched the sipá rip open the sack with his front paws. His focus was now on the berries, so she moved sideways to put the tree between her and the animal. She untied the ayulk'salu from her belt loop, placed it over a low-hanging brown oméu needle, then ran eastward into the dense forest.

Petra fumed: "Where were you!?"

Naña stopped in the grassy meadow a few meters from the lean-to, where Petra stood with her hands on her hips. "I left to distract the sipá," she said. "When I saw you give up your harvest, I knew you could get away. I kept going to save mine." She patted her sack of berries. "At least we'll have these."

"You left me by myself!"

"If I stayed, I may have lost my harvest. Those beasts can eat a lot."

"Your ayulk'salu did little good. I think it attracted him. I might have been killed!"

Naña shook her head. "No. He heard us coming. He wasn't surprised. Sipá can get forceful when they're surprised, but he heard us coming. He wouldn't have killed you."

"You're sure about that?"

Naña nodded and pointed to the tree line behind Petra. "Look."

The old sipá lumbered out of the trees. His mouth was stained with bump-berry juice. He panted and dropped to his haunches.

Petra stepped back from the animal's putrid odor. She surmised from the sipá's demeanor they were not in danger. "What do we do now?"

Naña lowered her berry sack into the tall grass. She advanced toward the sipá with her arms outstretched, and spoke in a soft, comforting tone: "Ieis'pi afil'elk?"

The old sipá moaned and hung his head.

"I hope you know what you're doing," Petra said. "He can rip you in half with one swipe."

"He won't," Naña said. "He's tired and filled with your berries. I think he just wants some company."

"Company? Are you crazy!?"

"No, I'm not," Naña insisted. "Sipas are social. They live in packs during training. They have never killed a trainer."

Petra watched as Naña approached the sitting sipá. Even sitting, he was a meter taller than the young girl. She stopped a few paces in front of the animal and lowered her arms.

The sipá huffed and leaned forward from his sitting position. He planted his front paws in the soft grass and brought his nose to within a few centimeters of Naña's face. He sniffed her and turned away to focus his attention on Petra.

"Told you he wouldn't hurt me," Naña said.

The sipá moaned at Petra. She saw sorrow in the animal's dark eyes, but reminded herself that humans often project their own feelings into the eyes of other mammals. *People have been killed because of the wrong assessment of an omnivore's true intentions,* she thought. She took another step back to increase the distance between them. He was still close enough to lunge upon her in an eye blink, but she forced back the urge to flee. "Afil'elk," she said in a subdued tone.

The sipá moaned and sat back on his haunches.

Petra noticed Naña was gone again. *Where does she go?*

"I'm up here," Naña called from up in their sleeping tree. "Didn't want him to get the rest of our berries."

"What do I do now?"

Naña shrugged and disappeared behind the branches.

The sipá rubbed his nose, then leaned forward and reclined on his side with a grunt.

With her way to the tree blocked, Petra considered another route, but stopped when the old male continued to moan. She knelt a few paces from the sipá's head and examined his tired eyes. "You really are worn out."

Naña appeared at the base of the tree. "What are you doing?"

Petra looked up. "I think he's sick."

Naña giggled. "Probably ate too many berries."

They sat with the sipá until the sun dropped below the tree line west of the meadow. Petra was correct. He was sick. They washed the vomit from his gums and teeth with water and buried what he spewed onto the grass with dirt.

"He needs to fart," Naña said.

"What?"

"He's full of berry gas. That's why he's in pain. He needs to fart."

"How do we get him to do that? I didn't bring a med kit."

Naña chuckled. "He needs to do that himself."

Petra stood and examined the reclining sipá. He was on his side, his breathing even but heavy. "Will he be OK out here by himself tonight?"

"Yeah," Naña said. "The klâwpa aren't due back yet, but if they show up early, they'll smell him, and stay away."

"You're sure?"

Naña nodded. "Klâwpa are afraid of sipá."

"I've heard the opposite opinion. I heard klâwpa are afraid of nothing."

"They won't attack a sipá," Naña insisted, "unless the sipá is dead."

"Then let's hope he doesn't die."

⟡ ⟡ ⟡

An hour after sunset, Petra huddled under the shelter of her lean-to and watched the sleeping sipá. She chose to spend the night on the ground to stay near the sick animal. "If he vomits in his sleep, he could choke to death."

Naña never heard of such a thing, but she also knew that bump-berries made people sick if they ate too many at one time. "OK," she agreed. "Are you going to stay awake all night watching him?"

"Not if you help me."

Naña agreed to take the second shift from midnight to dawn.

Petra listened to the sipá's breathing—a heavy rhythmic rush of air, and she wondered: *Allergic reaction?* Difficulty breathing placed the animal in a danger zone more precarious than a sick stomach and gas-filled intestines. She reached over and tossed more kindling into her small fire pit. The fire's warmth pushed back the chill and illuminated the sipá's head with its flickering light. He was too far from the fire to feel the warmth, but he didn't need it, not with his thick mat of gray fur to protect him from the cold. She focused on the sipá's chest and continued to listen for breaks in his rhythmic breathing.

An hour later, major progress was made when the sipá let loose an audible fart that lasted almost thirty seconds.

The rancid smell drifted across the meadow and wafted into the sensitive nostrils of the ranging pack of klâwpa, who had come back into the area in search of food. The smell they detected was familiar—like an odor produced by a decaying corpse—so they needed to investigate.

Faint yelps caught Petra's attention, and then she heard klâwpa trotting through the meadow.

They're coming this way.

She pushed up into a squat, grabbed one of her dead oméu needle weapons, and focused on the sleeping sipá. *They'll smell him and leave,* she thought—that was more hope than a known certainty.

The klâwpa yelping stopped, but she heard the swish of their movement through the tall grass. They split into two groups to approach the source of the stench from opposite directions.

Petra reached over and grabbed the metal pot. In her other hand she held the needle. She surveyed the meadow and saw two glowing eyes appear out of the tall grass—large circles reflecting the firelight from her pit.

Another set of eyes appeared.

Petra heard a rustling in the undergrowth between the trees behind her, and she calculated at least five klâwpa arrived to inspect the sick sipá.

Although klâwpa were small, less than a meter from tail to nose, they were ferocious when provoked. She glanced over at the sipá—his breathing was heavy but even.

Hopefully the klâwpa will see he's not dead and leave.

More rustling in the meadow grass and six more sets of eyes joined the other two.

Petra heard more unseen klâwpa trotting behind the lean-to, and the glowing eyes in the meadow advanced toward the sipá. She could wait no longer. She yelled: "Get out of here!"

All movement stopped.

Petra stood and banged the pot with the dry omèu needle. "Get out! Get out!"

The glowing eyes shifted toward her and approached with guttural growls.

She expected the klâwpa to flee from the noise, not move toward it. She banged the pot again. "Get out!"

The lead klâwpa stepped into the firelight, growling with teeth bared. Behind him, the pack converged toward Petra. Their sleek, dark bodies glistened in the firelight.

Petra spun at a growl from behind her and caught a leaping klâwpa in mid-air with her omèu needle. She plunged the weapon through the scavenger's torso, then flicked the dead animal aside to free her needle for another attack. Before the dead klâwpa hit the ground, Petra swung the metal pot to the head of another leaping attacker and knocked him to the ground in front of her. She bent a knee and drove her needle through his neck.

Three klâwpa advancing from the meadow leaped toward Petra with screeching growls. She turned to see the lead klâwpa hit by a projectile and fall to the ground. She crouched to face the other two, but one swipe from the sipá hit both of the animals in mid-leap and ripped their torsos open. They dropped to the ground, spilling their guts on the matted grass.

The old sipá stood on his hind legs and roared.

The remaining klâwpa in the meadow rushed back into the grass and retreated for the tree line.

Behind Petra, the swish of grass and snap of branches told her the other group of scavengers fled through the underbrush.

"They won't be back," Naña said. She dropped to the ground from the sleeping tree holding her sling, made from strands of woven omèu needle fiber. She walked up to the klâwpa she shot and kicked the lifeless torso. The stone left a blood-stained hole in the black chest.

"You should show me how to make one of those weapons," Petra said.

Naña smiled. "You did OK with that pot."

The sipá lumbered over to Petra and sniffed her, then turned and sniffed the two klâwpa he killed. He batted the ripped corpses across the ground until they were concealed in the tall grass.

Naña dragged the other bodies to the fire pit and set them ablaze.

"Watch the flames don't get too high," Petra said.

"We're fine," Naña said. The dry omèu needles on the trees nearby were far enough from the fire to not ignite, and the green needles on the tree behind the lean-to would never catch fire. "I'd cook these to eat, but klâwpa taste bad. We should also burn the other ones."

"Hey, boy," Petra said. "Easy there!"

Naña turned to see the sipá nuzzle Petra's back. "He likes you."

Petra turned to face the sipá and caressed his furry head in her hands. His sad eyes seemed to express worry. "Easy now. U'aliou."

The sipá sat back on his haunches, huffed, then leaned to his right and lumbered back to where he'd been sleeping.

"He saved me," Petra said.

"Yes, he did," Naña agreed. "Looks like you've made a friend."

"We've made a friend."

"No. Not me. Just you."

"Why do you say that?"

"He nuzzled you, not me."

Petra watched the large beast recline on the matted grass. "Well, I'm just glad he'll be OK."

"He'll be fine," Naña assured.

"I'll get the other corpses."

"Wait on that," Naña said. "They're all mushy from being ripped open. I'll get a sack." She headed toward the sleeping tree, then stopped and faced Petra. "You're Dágul Jásah now."

"What?"

"Dágul Jásah. One who lives with beasts."

COALITION: JAI'RAAN

Two standard weeks after the death of Armand Erstallius, seventeen envoys from holdings in the outer districts west of Terra Prime arrived at Jai'raan to contemplate their future.

Cynth Halva despised committees, but she knew the only way to resolve the chaos spreading through the Old Worlds was to forge a consensus among the remaining allied clans. She stood at the edge of the round wooden table and scanned the seated envoys—she had just delivered a ten-minute speech and her words had failed to erase their blank expressions. "Clan Vestlok, Clan Sabballi, and Clan Emlito," she concluded, "have proven to have the same heart as Polinda. War rages before them as they seek to enrich themselves and rule what remains."

Still no reaction from the envoys.

Cynth clenched her metal fist and struck the table. "Are you deaf? Wake up!"

Milos Fore, the fat little envoy from the Cormed colony on Roth-513, rose out of his chair across from Cynth. "Madame," he blurted, "control yourself! Rage won't solve anything."

"Sit down, little man," Cynth retorted. "You're like the others—stone-faced with nothing of consequence to bring to this table. Have you nothing to say about all we have lost?"

The Guild envoy was five seats away from Cynth but felt adrift in a sea of corpses. "Madame, Gentlemen, I appreciate you allowing me into this discussion. I had believed you all appreciated the seriousness of our predicament. Apparently, that is not the case." He pushed his seat away from the table and stood. "Madame Halva is correct in everything she has said. If you prefer to wallow in your indecision, then I see no benefit for the Guild to be present." He turned toward the doorway and crossed the room under the silent gaze of the envoys.

Cynth watched Minister Len leave the room, then turned her attention back to the impotent envoys. "You are idiots, all of you. Your inaction will destroy us all."

Milos Fore, still standing, asked: "Did you expect us to arrive at a solution the first day?"

Cynth glared at the Cormed envoy. "Yes," she said. "The path we need to take may be difficult, but it's in plain sight and waiting. Your delays threaten to block access to it."

"We must be cautious," Milos said.

"We must act!" Cynth demanded. She turned and stormed out of the room.

Arlud Erstallius walked down the shuttle's boarding ramp behind Gustav Eahuda, flanked on both sides by six guards. They wore civilian attire, and the guards carried their weapons concealed. Jai'raan's dusky sky was thick with moisture and filtered the multi-colored cloud bands on Wald-181, the massive gas giant planet that filled the southwestern sky. Under the ruby haze, heat radiating from the tarmac rippled above the path that led to the debarkation center. Arlud's guards could protect him from aggression, but not from the pressing humidity. He removed his overcoat and slung it over his arm as they crossed the tarmac. "U'galem was hot, but this drippy sauna is unbearable."

Eahuda kept his gaze forward. "I'm with you, lad. I'll never understand how people can flock to such a stifling climate and enjoy it."

Once through the debarkation center and into the cooler atmosphere, Arlud and his entourage were taken via monorail to the Suralpai Resort in the jungle two kilometers west of the landing field, where the envoys had gathered to discuss their future.

Arlud had balked when he received the invitation. "We need a fast response," he had told his advisers. "The conference will delay everything."

"Delay is necessary," Eahuda had insisted. "We need to develop a unified strategy. That takes council and time. Our enemies are not going anywhere, and they won't attack while they lick their wounds. Besides, I once heard you say: 'A cool heart can see reason that a man enraged can't.' We need to cool our hearts before we strike back and find ourselves unprepared."

Arlud remembered the words Eahuda had quoted. The situation then was different, but the logic was the same—pause to formulate a detailed plan of action to improve chances for success. He buried his rage under a tenuous calm and agreed to pause hostilities.

Eahuda inquired at the front desk regarding the whereabouts of the Merchant Symposium and was directed to the conference room where the clan envoys had gathered. He showed Arlud the location on the large wood map displayed in the lobby, then headed down an adjoining hallway with two of the guards.

Arlud met Cynth as she bolted from the conference room. Anger was evident on her face. “Madame?”

Cynth halted as the doors swung shut behind her. “About time you arrived. What kept you?”

“I’m here now. That’s all that matters.”

Cynth glanced at the guards flanking Arlud. “Where’s Eahuda?”

“Busy,” Arlud said in a curt tone.

Cynth caught the none-of-your-business attitude in Arlud’s voice and took a step backward. *He’s dismissed me,* she thought. She understood the pressure Arlud was under, but never thought he would respond to her with such disrespect. Her initial reaction to retaliate against that rudeness was held in check by the greater need to confront the mob in the conference room. “Well,” she said, “we don’t need him here. We need you.”

“Not going well?”

“No. Not well at all. They’re idiots!”

Arlud nodded that he understood. The clans had a history of long, drawn-out negotiations. “Our culture must change, and that’s a difficult thing for most people. Almost impossible for politicians.”

“You can change it.”

Arlud flinched at that statement. “Everyone must change it.”

“Yes, but you can lead the way. They won’t listen to me.”

“Is Gustus here?”

Cynth smirked. “He’s just as stubborn as the rest. He stayed on Cestratha and sent me to represent our clan.”

“How many clans are here?”

“Twelve, plus the Guild, but the guildman left the conference. He has no patience for their inaction.”

Arlud turned to one of his guards. “Go find the guildman.”

The guard nodded and hurried away.

“I need to announce myself,” Arlud said.

Cynth stepped aside and gestured toward the conference room doors. “Good luck.”

Arlud pushed through the doors and the conversation among the envoys stopped as they turned their heads to face him. His guards followed him into the room and flanked his position as he stopped behind the empty chair across from Milos Fore. "Greetings, Gentlemen."

Milos stood. "Arlud Erstallius, my condolences to you and your family. Armand was an effective leader, held in high esteem by everyone who knew him. His loss will be felt throughout the Alliance."

The other envoys stood and voiced their mutual sympathy.

"Thank you all," Arlud said. "Please sit."

Milos hesitated. "I never thought I would see you again, especially after Polinda hit GSW-183."

"That problem has been resolved," Arlud said. He draped his overcoat over the back of the chair, pulled a flat metal cylinder out of the side pocket, and slid it to the center of the table. "Observe, gentlemen."

Milos sat and focused on the cylinder.

The edge of the metallic device emitted a ring of blue light. A holo-projection of the crumbled buildings surrounding the rubble-strewn foundation of the Great Hall on Cestratha burst upward out of the center and floated above the table.

"You have all read the reports about this," Arlud said. "I need to know you've seen it. Watch closely."

The holo-projection displayed aerial views of the battle damage on Cestratha's surface, then showed rubble fields in orbit—shattered frigates, destroyers, and the twisted framework of bombarded orbital stations.

"Without the aid of Clan Rastee, Clan Sorrell, and the Guild," Arlud said, "Clan Halva would not have survived."

The holo-projection ended, and the emitter's blue light faded.

"More clans are threatened. The Alliance is done. There must be changes—drastic changes—before peace and order can be restored."

"That's obvious," the young envoy from Clan Tuma said.

Arlud faced the red-haired representative. "The changes begin now," Arlud said. He flicked a hand signal and two of his guards flanked the Tuma envoy. "Fiorello Darmanti, you are under arrest for sedition against the assembled clans and for promoting the rebellion among the Old Worlds."

The guards grabbed the envoy and pulled him out of his chair.

"What!?" Darmanti blurted. "How dare you accuse—"

A guard injected a sedative and Darmanti went limp.

The envoys stood as one around the table and protested Arlud's actions.

Eahuda entered the room followed by ten more guards and the envoys went silent.

"Levion Cellius, from Clan Brandi," Arlud said. "You are under arrest for sedition against the assembled clans."

The white-haired envoy backed away from the approaching guards and withdrew a compact pistol from beneath his coat.

One of the advancing guards fired a capture net that wrapped around the envoy's weapon and sent a surge of electricity into his body that dropped him to the floor.

"Jacob Vindel, envoy for Clan Tuma," Arlud said. "Sedition."

Vindel did not protest the allegation. He walked toward the guards and submitted without a fight.

Once the arrested envoys were out of the room, Arlud said: "Please, everyone, return to your seats."

Cynth bounded back into the room and stood next to Arlud. "So, Gentlemen, now we know who was dragging this assembly toward inaction. Their smooth words should be forgotten."

"The rebellion is not just happening at distant locations," Arlud said. "It has occurred within our districts, among clanmen we once embraced as allies."

The Guild representative was escorted into the room by two guards.

"Minister Len," Arlud said. "Welcome back."

The old trader nodded and returned to his chair.

"This holding is now under Marshall Law," Arlud said. "Security of all our holdings is more important now than it has ever been. The Guild will leave ten warships in this system to monitor all vessels. Debarkation centers will have increased security, and all markets will be under greater scrutiny. The Guild has agreed to be a partner in these changes with Clan Halva."

"Outrageous," Milos said. "The Guild has no authority—"

"The Guild has partnered with Clan Erstallius," Cynth said. "Guildmen died defending Wan'tei and Cestratha. They are partners in our Coalition and will be shown the same respect you expect us to show you."

Minister Len cupped his hands on the table. "And this was sanctioned by Wolfram Sy? I have not been informed."

"That's correct," Arlud said. "The decision to have the Guild share the defense of Jai'raan was made before we left Pigrell and was sanctioned by Sy's representative."

"Who?"

"Erlis Pardee."

"I will have that confirmed," Len said.

"Of course you will," Arlud said. He spoke again to the entire assembly: "Security adjustments will be implemented for all holdings. They will be enforced by local clanmen and will not be optional."

"Under whose authority?" Milos asked.

"Coalition authority."

Milos huffed. "And if the clans refuse?"

"They will be considered in league with the rebels."

Arlud watched the reaction to his words and saw concern in the envoys. "You may feel your authority has been usurped. It has. We are at war, Gentlemen. The time for gentle conversation is past. We must plan our campaign to stop the violence, and to do that we must remove those who would try to stop us. Our Coalition strength is our military, and we will enforce security where necessary, and pluck sedition from our midst when necessary."

"You once accused me of moving too swiftly," Milos said. "Now you may be guilty of the same. Or worse."

"The attempted blockade of Al-phaq was just the beginning of a greater plan," Arlud said, speaking to Milos. "That plan was instigated by Farquar Polinda with the aid of Sabballi and Emlito. Clan Cormed supported the blockade of Al-phaq, but your part in the rebellion was blind allegiance to Alliance decree, not sedition—otherwise, you would have been arrested with the others. The rebellion you unknowingly helped instigate will not be easy to stop, and along the way you may not be comfortable with what must be done, but it will be done because the blood flow must stop."

Milos was offended by Arlud's assertion that his clan had been deceived into supporting Polinda's rebellion, but as he reviewed in his mind everything that had transpired, he accepted where his clan had failed. "We were fooled," he admitted. "We moved too fast, and that's the warning I give to you."

"We must get hold of this mess before it's allowed to fester and afflict more holdings."

"Authoritarians never win," Milos said.

"The Alliance is done," Cynth said. "The security measures are necessary and have been developed by consensus. If your homeworld was devastated, you would have a different view."

Milos frowned. "I think we all understand the seriousness of our situation."

"Changes are needed," Arlud said, "but Marshall Law will not last forever. We are at war. The Commanders must have free rein to take the battle to wherever it needs to be."

The envoy from Clan Bree cleared his throat. He was seated six chairs away to Arlud's right. "We understand the reasons," he said. "The clans should have more input in how these changes are implemented."

"They will," Arlud assured. "All new security restrictions will be enforced by local clans. It's your job as representatives to educate your regents and help them comply with what must be done. We must unite to protect our districts. We must help those who are at the front lines against Vestlok, Sabballi, and Emlito, and any other clans who join their rebellion."

"Like Clan Tuma and Clan Brandi," Cynth said.

The Guild envoy spoke from the other side of the table: "And what of these aliens I keep hearing about?"

"They left," Arlud said. "They are no longer a concern."

Len was shocked by Arlud's dismissal. "What? They destroyed Polinda's mine, crippled many ships, devoured an entire planet—and they just left!?"

"It's complicated," Arlud said. "They caused much of the confusion in the days after the mine disaster, and that led to false accusations and the death of hundreds of clanmen. We can't change the past, but we should have no fear of them—they have left."

Milos leaned forward. "And that's been confirmed?"

"Yes," Arlud said, "it's implied in their exit."

Milos slumped backward. "Implied?"

"You don't know," Len implied. "No one knows. We could wake up tomorrow to an invasion."

"That won't happen," Arlud insisted. "We had a mediator who communicated with them. All they wanted was to retrieve their people and leave."

"What mediator?"

"Bev Colli," Arlud said. "She was caught in their exit and pulled into their universe. We know this because she appeared on GSW-183 and told us."

The assembled envoys were stunned silent.

"You'll get all the info about that," Arlud said. "For now, we need to discuss our immediate future." He flicked a hand signal to Eahuda.

The remaining guards left the room and ten coalition commanders entered and formed a silent wall behind Arlud.

"Jegen-Major Lon Paven," Arlud said, "will begin with a briefing about our force status around Pigrell."

Cynth moved away and stood against the wall near the doorway. She listened without reaction as the commanders presented their reports. *Now it begins,* she thought. *Now Arlud becomes High Regent in name and in deed. His future is set.*

THE GUILD: RETREAT

Erlis Pardee settled into his seat in his ship's Command Intelligence Center. The entire Guild armada had regrouped at Jai'raan from the two battles where they had helped the Erstallius Coalition defeat the Polinda insurrection—Wan'tei and Cestratha. Ten of his ships orbited Jai'raan with his dreadnought, while the remaining forty-five Guild ships were in a holding pattern beyond the system's outer belt. His remote conference with Minister Len had left him disturbed. The Erstallius intention to push their war deeper into Alliance territory was against his better judgment—it would spread out the Guild armada again and put their local interests at risk. He exhaled and flicked the switch on his command panel that sent a hail to Arlud's flagship, also orbiting Jai'raan.

"Set course, Helmsman," Pardee said. "Notify the fleet, we will rejoin them at the outer belt in two hours."

"Aye, Sir."

Pardee knew Arlud would be furious about his decision to leave. This would be the first major split between the Guild and the Erstallius Coalition. *He'll learn diverse priorities are often at odds, and every agreement has its limitations.*

The communication panel buzzed.

Pardee flicked another switch, and a holoscreen appeared in front of him, displaying the Erstallius eagle crest. He shifted his weight and sat tall on his seat.

Arlud's face replaced the eagle crest. "Captain," he said. "How are you?"

"Disturbed," Pardee replied. "Len tells me your command has planned a campaign that pushes toward Anders Prime."

"Yes. News out of district two tells of Sabballi and Emlito planning attacks against Clan Bree. We need to hit them hard there."

"You may weaken your position in this district."

"We will proceed cautiously, but if we delay Anders Prime may be lost. Clan Bree cannot defend the holding by themselves."

"Your force is not large enough."

Arlud caught the subtle implication in Pardee's statement—*Your force?* "Have you broken our partnership?"

"No, but we will limit our participation. The aliens have left, and Polinda has been defeated. Your need for our help has ended. Internal Alliance struggles are beyond our original agreement."

Arlud kept his surprise hidden behind a calm expression. He lowered his eyes and considered Pardee's candor. He could sympathize with the Free Trader's viewpoint—the Guild had lent their support to defeat Polinda and confront the aliens. The new campaign would force them to deploy their armada at too many locations, across too great a distance. "I understand," he said, and he looked into the holoscreen. "I appreciate what you have done for us. Thank Wolfram Sy for me. I consider us partners—that's a bond that will never fade."

Pardee nodded. "I will tell Wolfram of your appreciation."

"Thank you."

"We will leave the ten ships at Jai'raan as agreed. I wish you success."

Pardee cut the transmission and leaned back on his couch. That was more difficult than he had imagined, and yet easier than expected because of Arlud's lack of protest. *He took that well,* he thought, and he wondered if his decision would impact their partnership in the future. He turned toward his first officer. "Mister Egin, alert Alpha Group. We will depart in five minutes."

"Aye, sir."

Pardee leaned forward and peered into the holomap floating above the navigation pedestal. The Beta Group ships that will remain at Jai'raan had settled into a lower orbit where they would deploy into their assigned defensive positions. *This pact with Clan Halva reaffirms our place in this district,* he thought. *This should motivate Wolfram to send us back to Al-phaq.*

CLAN ERSTALLIUS: RETURN

Arlud peered out his cabin window at the bright limb of Ni'apinu. Remorse for his father's death morphed into anger, and the anger fueled thoughts of revenge. The plan put in motion at Jai'raan was just the beginning. If his path forward was successful, all the clans who supported Polinda's rebellion would be defeated.

He had secluded himself in his cabin during the thirty-six hyper-hour trip from Jai'raan, focused on status reports and news from the Old Worlds about the continued Alliance collapse. Amid all the transcripts, there was one report from Wan'tei about the disappearance of Simbic Ur, but nothing about the aliens who took the planet, and no sign they, or Bev, had returned.

His pining for Bev lurked behind every thought. He had suppressed his feelings for her, but now, isolated in his cabin, he wiped a few tears, and heaved a sigh at the knowledge he would never see her again. One regret rolled into another, and he wondered if happier times would ever return.

Bev and my father. Who else will I lose before this mess is over?

The door buzzer sounded.

Arlud looked toward the hatchway and saw Gustav Eahuda's face on the small, square holoscreen next to the door. He flicked a switch on the wall panel below the screen, and the door slid open.

"We'll be in orbit in twenty minutes," Eahuda said. "The base commander has requested a meeting as soon as we reach the outpost."

Arlud gestured for Eahuda to enter the cabin. "Trouble?"

"Could be," the old Degen said as he stepped into the cabin. "Some command staff are wondering why we're not headed to Baleiou."

Arlud gazed out the window. Ni'apinu was now a thick blue crescent covered by wisps of white cloud and filled half the view as his flagship descended into a lower orbit. To his right, he saw a white glint near the inner moon—an Aku ship deployed to secure that area. "All twenty Aku ships are in service now?"

"Yes."

With the Aku ships in orbit, Ni'apinu was secured by the native forces. Erstallius forces would continue to patrol the outer reaches of the system, and salvage ships would continue to clean the debris fields in Ni'apinu's orbit and around the gas giant that dominated the middle of the system.

"We can't abandon this outpost," Arlud said. He faced Eahuda. "Baleiou survived. Thrum Dau survived. We still have enough forces to defend each holding, and I doubt they will see another attack now that Polinda is gone. Our focus should be at Anders Prime, and other holdings under direct threat."

"Understood," Eahuda said, "but Baleiou is our homeworld. The commanders—"

"The commanders must focus on what's needed, not on their own desires."

Eahuda jerked into a more formal stance. "You are the presumptive High Regent now. Your place should be on Baleiou."

Arlud returned Eahuda's stern gaze. "My place should be where I can do the best for my clan."

Eahuda let his shoulders slump, disappointed by Arlud's answer. "Should I inform the commanders you will reschedule?"

"No," Arlud said in a flat tone. "I'll meet them after we planet-fall."

Eahuda nodded, spun for the doorway, and left the room.

Arlud turned back toward the window as the cabin door slid shut. The Jai'raan trip had been successful, and a small armada had been dispatched to Anders Prime, but the delicate partnership between the clans in the coalition could crumble if Clan Erstallius imploded because of Armand's death. The split among the outpost command officers wasn't expected, but it was a legitimate protest that needed careful handling.

Three steps forward and two steps back.

He closed his eyes against tears that returned without warning.

Arlud bounded down the shuttle exit ramp and headed across the tarmac toward the tower complex along the north side of the landing field. Once inside, he paused at the entrance to his office lobby. Ten commanders mingled around the vacant reception desk, chatting in low tones—three senior Jegens, and seven Degen-Majors.

Arlud cleared his throat. "Gentlemen."

The officers fell silent and turned in unison toward their Regent.

The meeting lasted less than fifteen minutes. The officers filed out of the office, leaving Arlud psychologically numbed. He slumped into the reception chair, more worried than ever about his clan's future.

Gustav Eahuda appeared in the lobby doorway. "You Okay?"

"They rejected my ascension. They have that right, and I cannot argue against it. This schism will weaken our effort against the rebellion, and we may lose more than we gain."

"You are still regent here," Eahuda said. "The local—"

"Without a majority vote from the cadre, my position in the clan will always be in question."

"There *are* protocols."

"They will leave with their clanmen—half of our force here—and there's nothing I can do to stop it without arresting them."

"That would not be wise."

Gus is always direct when he needs to be, Arlud thought. He appreciated that honesty. The commanders had chosen to return to their families on Baleiou and Thrum Dau. He could not slight them for that—his own worries about his mother and cousins gnawed at him daily, but he buried that anxiety as soon as it appeared beneath the need to retaliate for the death of his father. "I may be many things," he said, "but I don't expect everyone to handle this crisis the same way I do. We don't need to start our own civil war—one war is enough."

Eahuda nodded and sat in one of the available chairs. "Politics is not my specialty, but there are many possibilities ahead of us, and we can't disregard tradition. Clan law must survive."

"I have been made impotent. The Guild has left, half our local forces will leave, and the other clans can't seem to agree on the simplest things. We were lucky to put together that small armada to send to Anders Prime. Without unity, we are doomed."

"We're not doomed yet, lad. This is just a minor setback."

"What do we do, Gus?"

"Stick to the plan."

"I fear this mutiny may spread. We must unite the clan. Maybe I should go to Baleiou."

"That's one possibility."

Arlud folded his arms and shook his head. "Yeah, but it's not sticking to the plan. I'm being pulled in two different directions."

"Then you need to decide which one is the best route."

Arlud pursed his lips. *So much has happened,* he thought. *So much has been lost.* "Get me a list of everyone who will leave, and the adjustments we must make once they're gone. We will adapt, and we will stick to the plan."

PETRA SITLYN: BONDED

Petra Sitlyn reclined in the meadow, eyes closed, with her back resting against the sipá's back. The grey sipá lay on his side and didn't mind the human using his body as a pillow. The tall grass formed a green wall around Petra's legs and above her the sun was a glaring disk shining through a line of puffy clouds that drifted from north to the south.

She had been in the wilderness for almost four weeks. The sipá bonded with her and refused to leave—he followed her everywhere and slept at the base of the tree where she and Naña slept. At first the sipá annoyed her, but as the days progressed, she became more accepting of his presence, and she was never afraid. Naña had been correct—he wanted company.

I'm Dágul Jásah now.

A shadow moved across Petra's closed eyelids from left to right, then again from right to left. She opened her eyes and saw two ciâfey, the two-seat low altitude flyers used by the Aku, circle silently about fifty meters above her. She sat up, shaded her eyes from the sun with her hand, and watched the ciâfey circle toward the far end of the meadow.

A rustling behind her in the meadow caused Petra to stand. She looked over the reclined body of the sipá and spied Naña jogging toward her through the tall grass.

Naña stopped a few paces away from the sipá. "They're here to pick us up," she said, excited her time in the wilderness was over.

"Are you sure?"

"Yeah, look!"

Petra turned to watch both ciâfey flutter downward in controlled spirals to land at the far end of the meadow. "I thought they'd pick us up in ground cars, the same way they brought us here."

Naña shrugged. "Why else would they be here?" She walked around the sipá and stood next to Petra.

One of the ciâfey carried a passenger, which told Petra if they came to retrieve, they would not be taking both of them, unless the passenger stayed here. "There's only one empty seat."

"Then what do they want?"

The three Aku men removed their helmets and trudged through the tall grass. They stopped a few paces away from Petra. "L'dyém," the lead pilot said. "You have a sipá with you."

Petra glanced back at the grey sipá. "Yep, that's what he is."

"Is he sick?"

"Not anymore," Naña said.

The lead pilot pinched the ring around his neck and spoke Akün in an undertone.

"They came to get me," Naña said. "They're leaving you here."

The passenger walked up to Petra. He was middle-aged, with a shoulder-length scalp lock gathered by two wooden rings. "I am Mérol from Squa Paln. I am the overseer of the Depüfah'ahuah. Naña has completed her test. She will leave with us. You will wait for ground transportation."

"For how long?"

"Before sunset."

"Why ground transport?"

"You are Dágul Jásah," Mérol said, and he nodded to the reclining sipá.

Two hours later Petra sat under her lean-to and stuffed the utensils the Aku had given her into the shoulder sack for the trip back to Squa Paln. She pushed the Akün primer between the large pot and the thick canvas so it would rest against her and prevent the metal utensils from poking her side. She finished stuffing the sack and sat still by the empty fire pit. The afternoon sun was still high above the tree line, and she wondered if the car would arrive before dusk.

A light wind whispered through the trees and a few birds squawked in the distance.

The sipá was walking the border of his territory in the surrounding wood, refreshing his scent markings. Petra had not seen or heard him for close to an hour and dreaded leaving without seeing him again. And then she heard a mechanical rumble. It was much louder than the car that brought her here, and as the noise drew closer, she could discern more than one vehicle. She stood and watched a tan-colored transport bust through the tree line at the opposite end of the meadow. It was a large, six-wheeled, open-air ground car like the ones used at Kuliq'Quad. The driver sat in an open turret at the front left. The two seat wells held five Aku soldiers. A second car followed—a cargo truck with a covered storage bed behind a two-seat open-air cab for the driver and one passenger.

A sipá transport, Petra surmised.

Both vehicles stopped about ten meters into the meadow, side-by-side.

Petra picked up her sack and walked toward the Aku along a path the sipá had trampled through the tall grass. When she came within thirty meters of the vehicles, one of the soldiers stepped out of the six-wheeled car.

Petra focused on all the soldiers. They all wore the wide-brimmed hats used by the road patrols, so their faces were shaded and difficult to see in the high sun. The mystery behind this encounter forced caution, because she did not know how well she had performed during her first test. The legends about Aku ferocity she heard as a child still lingered in her mind and fed doubt that gnawed at her confidence. She stopped walking when the sipá roared behind her.

An undulating mass of grey fur behind white fangs ran toward Petra through the tall grass. The sipá covered fifty meters and was beside her in less than four heartbeats. He stood on his hind legs, stretching to his full four-meter height, and roared at the soldiers.

The soldier in front of the car stood immobile, but not from fear. He called to Petra in Akün, "I'dalahieh ouah. Esie yaju?"

Petra translated to herself: *He protects you. What is his name?* "He has no name," she replied in Englo'ni, curious if the man understood.

"All sipá have a name," the soldier said. His pronunciation of the common language was perfect.

The sipá dropped to all fours and bumped into Petra's side, forcing her to take a step sideways to avoid falling to the ground. *He's telling me he's here to protect me,* she thought. She reached up and brushed the thick grey fur along the sipá's shoulder. "Ikyu ahpsu," she said. *No trouble.*

The sipá huffed and glanced at Petra, then returned his gaze back to the soldiers.

"You are Dágul Jásah," the soldier said. He pulled a small metallic cylinder from a pouch on his belt and pointed it at the sipá. "His name is Aluk. He is thirty-four years old. He is from the Quel Pass Hybrids. He was released from the cavalry four years ago."

Petra was put off by the mater-of-fact tone in the soldier's voice. "So, you breed them, use them, and then abandon them."

"He was not abandoned," the soldier said. "He is monitored constantly. His implant not only carries all his data, it transmits all current information."

"Oh."

"Your bond is strong with this one."

Petra leaned sideways into the thick fur—she had become used to the smell. "Is that a problem?"

"No."

"Where do I go from here?"

"You are Dágul Jásah. We will take you to the Quel Pass Hybrid Farm."

The open-air ground car rumbled over the dirt path that snaked between the forested peaks of the Umelk Mountains, followed by the covered cargo truck.

Petra relaxed in the passenger seat of the cargo truck. She was impressed by the concern shown to Aluk by the Aku soldiers. She surmised their consideration was born out of their respect for the bond that had formed between herself and the old sipá. *They could have left him in the meadow,* she thought. She turned and peered through the small window behind the passenger seat. Aluk was sleeping—his large body filled the cargo space. She slid the window open a few centimeters and heard his rhythmic breathing over the van's rumble.

I'm Dágul Jásah now.

They arrived at Quel Pass two hours after sunrise, on the second day after leaving the meadow. The narrow road cut a steep descent into the eastern wall of the pass and presented Petra with her first view of the waterfall that roared down the western cliffs about fifty meters away. The water dropped one-hundred meters into a churning pool and was funneled out of the pass toward the main artery that sliced through the Wassûa Caphâga toward the eastern sea. The surging water masked the rumble of the two ground cars and Petra understood why the Aku had named the waterfall, *Jegáh ahi'Nudah, Mist that Thunders.*

Two days on the road had been enough for Aluk. The sound of the falls roused him from boredom. He raised his head and roared.

Petra turned in her seat to face the old sipá. "He remembers this place."

The driver glanced at Aluk. "Sipá remember everything." He turned back to watch the road. "He may not enter the compound. Old ones shy away from the fences."

Petra faced forward as the car descended closer to the river and the wooden bridge that led to the hybrid ranch along the western bank. Her first glimpse of the compound defied her expectations—It was nestled amid the grass-covered hills south of the pass. The entire thirty-acre ranch was surrounded by a one-meter-high picket fence made of omèu wood. On the western side of the property, five rectangular wooden buildings with gable roofs housed the medical facilities, living quarters, food storage, vehicle storage, and waste reclamation facilities. The breeding stalls were along the southern perimeter and surrounded by a five-meter-high picket fence. Eight training paddocks adjacent to the stalls—grass-lined, forty-meter pens—were separated by two-meter-high fences. She expected metal fencing and armed guard towers, but that was her off-world mindset failing again to deduce the Aku reality. The Aku viewed the sipá like any other livestock, not as a military weapon. The hybrid ranch was built after a passing remark by Seelay about the cargo of sipá cubs discovered on one of the transports they commandeered in their war against Clan Tuma. Using the animals as military cavalry had begun after the third generation produced more social offspring.

Petra noticed sipá in three of the training pens. She leaned forward and asked the driver: "How long does their training take?"

The soldier spoke without turning his head but raised his voice above the din from the falls: "They are handled from birth, but the most intense training begins after they are weened."

"Do they all adapt?"

"Yes, but there are different levels of success."

Trained, but not domesticated, Petra thought. She remembered Salus telling her that and she wondered, "If the training stops, do they revert to their natural tendencies?"

The driver shot a quizzical look at Petra. "They are sipá, not bears."

Petra took that to mean their social interaction with humans had been hard wired in them via the breeding process, like the difference between dogs and wolves. "Then from birth, they don't have the same wildness in them as their ancestors."

"Correct," the soldier said. "Their mothers pass along behaviors that reinforces the bond with humans. They do not consider us a threat."

"But you train them like attack dogs. Doesn't that contradict the human bond?"

"No more than it does for dogs. Each species has an inbred need to bond with humans that produces loyalty tuned to protect their bond mates. They will not attack another human without first sensing a threat or instructed that a threat exists. That's why Aluk stood up to us in the meadow and why he placed himself against you—his first reaction was to protect you against unknown people."

"Then he would have attacked you if I had voiced the correct command?"

The driver nodded.

Petra had not realized how much potential control she had over Aluk. *I must consider my words carefully,* she thought. She turned again to watch the old sipá. *Sipá cavalry are used like horses, but with six-inch front claws and the strength to crush a man's head with one blow.* She chuckled to herself as she considered an introduction for her next letter to her parents: *Hi, Mom and Dad. I retired from the Corp and will be getting married to an Aku savage next year, and by the way, I've bonded with a four-meter bear I know you'll just love to meet.*

The two vehicles stopped outside the farm's main gate.

Inside the cargo truck, Aluk sniffed the air and huffed. He twirled his body to face the rear, pushed against the closed ramp that blocked his exit, and caused the truck to rock backward.

"Stay here," the driver said to Petra. He jumped from the front cab and ran to the rear of the vehicle.

Through the narrow window, Petra watched Aluk push the closed ramp again, and the truck rocked backward.

The driver yelled, "Ka'hid!"

Aluk sat on his haunches and huffed.

The rear ramp dropped with a thud, opening the way for Aluk to exit.

The old sipá bounded out of the truck and into the grass field next to the road.

The driver closed the ramp, returned to his seat, and the truck moved forward through the open gate.

Petra leaned over the passenger door to see Aluk standing in the field. "Ka'hid," she told the driver.

The truck stopped with a jolt a few meters into the compound as the other car continued toward the main buildings.

Petra jumped to the dirt road and walked back to the open gate. "U'aliou, Aluk."

Aluk swayed side to side and huffed.

"U'aliou," Petra repeated in a soft tone. She approached the anxious sipá and could see his eyes squint as he continued to sway. "These fences won't hold you in. You're free now. You've nothing to fear. Yáhir guáfi." Naña had shown her how to calm the beast with words and how to stroke him to assure him. She stepped closer to hug his head, but he lumbered forward and pressed his face against her chest, forcing her to grab his neck fur and take a step backward to avoid falling to the ground. "U'aloiu," she whispered. She regained her balance and stroked his neck.

After a few minutes of embrace, Petra realized Aluk would not budge a centimeter closer to the gate. She turned to face the ground car and was surprised to see eight soldiers standing in a line next to the car, watching her and Aluk. The driver was in that line. She had never seen the other seven Aku men. They all smiled when she turned to face them.

"He won't come in," the driver said. "He smells the other males." He gestured to the training pens.

Petra glanced at the enclosures and could see adult males in three of the paddocks. "I thought sipá had shed the traits of their ancestors?"

"He'll be fine out there," the driver said. "He'll stay in the area as long as you are here."

Petra turned and looked into Aluk's brown eyes. She held his face in her hands and whispered, "So you're not that tame, eh? You still fight for dominance and you're too old to face them, is that it?"

Aluk lowered his head onto Petra's chest and huffed.

Petra rubbed Aluk's cheeks. "Stay out here, old boy, I won't be gone long." She stepped away from the sullen old sipá, walked into the compound, and the wooden gate was pulled shut by a soldier.

Tryol's gray scalp lock revealed his age, but his sinewy frame still had the strength of younger men. He was the camp overseer. He showed Petra the breeding stalls where two sipá females nursed their cubs, then guided her to the training paddocks.

Petra leaned on the fence to watch a trainer introduce saddle and bridle to a young male who resisted the attempt to place the saddle blanket by stepping sideways. When the trainer persisted, the sipá twisted his torso, pierced the blanket with his six-inch claws and flung it across the pen.

Petra stepped back from the fence. "Do they always resist?"

"Usually takes a few days for them to get used to riding tack," Tryol said.

Petra noticed two other sipá were training with saddle and bridle, but no riders. "How long does it take to break them for riding?"

Tryol chuckled. "Sipá are not broken, they are trained to accept the rider. Once they're comfortable with the tack, they usually have a rider within a week."

"And they all accept a rider?"

"No. Those who can't be ridden are assigned to the road patrols. Some will accept a cargo pack."

"Like Aluk?"

Tryol flinched. "How did you know he was not ridden?"

"By the way he carries himself."

"What do you mean?"

"I have seen sipá cavalry bow to accept riders. Aluk doesn't bow. He's friendly enough but has never prompted me to mount him."

"You're a woman. Females don't ride. He knows that."

"Then why did you bring me here?"

"You are Dágul Jásah."

After a quick tour through the different buildings, Petra was taken behind the breeding stalls to the trainee stable. Two large skylights in the roof bathed the pathway between the stalls with warm light. Each side of the walkway had twenty stalls, three were being cleaned for weened cubs.

As she walked between the stalls, Petra asked: "You house both the males and females here?"

"Yes," Tryol said.

"Even during mating season?"

"They're separated as needed. We remove competition among the trainees as much as possible."

Petra stopped and faced the guide. "Why am I here?"

"You are Dágul Jásah."

"Yes, I live with beasts. What's important about that?"

"You are an off-worlder who wishes to join our community. The Depüfah'ahuah helps determine the path for our young. No Aku female has ever been Dágul Jásah."

"Why?"

"To be Dágul Jásah, you must bond with a sipá. The bond does not originate with you, it is the sipá's choice."

"I'm the first woman?"

Tryol nodded. "The elders see importance in that. You are one of the engineers who helped repair our transports. The honor you received for that is deserved. Bonding with a sipá increases your value and improves your chance of being approved for Salus."

Petra folded her arms across her chest and turned away from the guide. *My future on Ni'apinu is still on trial. This is my first test.* She looked at the old man. "What do you want from me?"

"You will be shown how we train sipá, and perhaps if you learn the skill, you will also be a rider."

Petra continued to advance down the stall way. *I just left one army and they want me to join another!* "And if I fail?"

"We will discuss that if it happens," Tryol said.

"And if I do not want to be an Aku soldier?"

"We are not asking you to be a soldier. Aku women are not soldiers. We are offering you a chance to train sipá."

Like all members of the Erstallius landing team, Petra had been schooled in Aku culture before coming here. What she had learned since her arrival had proven many of the sources about Aku culture to be inaccurate—not surprising since the most recent histories were over two hundred years old. Their fight for freedom and their isolation had altered some of their customs, but their view of each person's place in the clan had not changed. Aku women were not soldiers. No woman had bonded with a sipá because sipá breeding and training was done by the military.

I'm an odd one from their perspective, Petra thought. *I was in the military, and I bonded with a sipá. Perhaps that makes this assignment more agreeable to them? Or perhaps they see an advantage in having an Erstallius clanman train their cavalry?*

"I'll do it," she said. "When do I start?"

CLAN ERSTALLIUS: FORTIFIED

Salus guided his ciâfey toward the Erstallius outpost just as the sun was breaking over the eastern tree line. The morning mist had cleared, and clouds formed a white canopy above the landing field. He circled the east end of the field until cleared to land by the control tower, then spiraled downward with cupped main wings, and touched down in the area reserved for planet-bound aircraft. After he folded the wings into their stowed position, he dismounted and was surprised to see the tarmac empty of the usual ground personnel.

Something has changed, he thought. He paused for a few heartbeats to scan the field but saw nothing that urged caution. A lone field manager strolled toward him from the central tower. A maintenance crew was busy in the main hangar, preparing a new Kottrel Sphere for transport to Kuliq'Quad.

The last sphere.

Every Aku transport had reached orbit and was stationed to defend Ni'apinu. Only one still had an old power core. Once the last Kottrel Sphere was installed, any potential reliability issues would vanish. Arlud's promise to repair all the ships would be fulfilled.

That's odd. There is no shuttle here to accept the load.

Salus stowed his helmet behind the ciâfey pilot station, greeted the field manager, then strode toward the tower complex, which brought him near the white marble memorial for fallen Erstallius clanmen and the red granite cenotaph for Bev Colli. He paused in front of each monument and gave a somber salute. Before he reached the walkway to the main tower, Arlud stepped out of the doorway, followed by two guards. He met Salus at the edge of the tarmac and they shook hands.

"It's quiet here," Salus said. "Where is everyone?"

"We had some reassignments," Arlud said. He had kept news from the Aku about his father's death and losing half the clanmen assigned to this outpost, believing that knowledge would cause unnecessary concern regarding clan stability. "The build-out is finished here, and we have obligations elsewhere."

Salus nodded that he understood. News of the Erstallius victory over Clan Polinda had been received among his people with cheers and heartfelt praise—a powerful Erstallius clan meant the Aku would keep their autonomy. They were united with these off-worlders now, and that could lead to more benefits than just the repairing of their disabled transports. "Your ships are still in the system?"

"Yes. Everything here is stable."

"Good."

"Where have you been?"

"I was across the western sea, in Dol'anar, at our primary manufacturing facilities. Your shuttle made the trip from Kuliq'Quad in only two hours. We could use a few of those."

"Yes, you could," Arlud agreed. The Aku transports were the only aircraft that could leave the atmosphere. All the other native flyers had the limitations of the ciâfey. *We will both benefit,* Arlud thought. *A subtle way of expanding our forces here. The Aku will never be true Erstallius clanmen, but they will be friends in arms—an effective way to expand the defense of this holding by getting more Aku off-planet, where most of the fighting will happen.* "I'll review our needs with my commanders. We may lend you a few. Pilots will need to be trained. I'll ask the Commander of Flight Operations to make arrangements."

"Thank you," Salus said. "Would it be possible to create new manufacturing facilities so we can build our own?"

That would push Aku technology well beyond current standards, Arlud thought. Constructing an entire spacecraft was far beyond what the Aku had achieved. "Shuttles are a thousand times more complicated than ciâfey."

"Yes."

"You must make many changes to accommodate that complexity."

"Yes," Salus said. "The elders understand. To survive, we need to change. They sent me to confer with you about building two facilities. One in Kuliq'Quad, and the other in Dol'anar."

They've had a taste of Alliance tech, and they want more, Arlud thought. *Their vulnerability is more apparent to them now, and they see the need to advance.* "To build shuttles like ours, you must mine and process the raw materials here, on Ni'apinu."

Salus nodded. "We can do that."

"And you'll need to barter for off-world material you can't create here, like durillium."

"Yes."

"I'll have my people create a report listing everything needed to make that happen."

"Thank you."

Arlud nodded, and his curiosity forced him to change the subject. "How's Petra?"

"I won't see her until she returns to Ji'dess."

"Why?"

"The Bi'au agreed to our joining, provided she completes the Ogâhu Esnüphica. It's tradition."

"How long will that take?"

"One year."

Arlud found that interesting when compared to the Aku request for new manufacturing facilities. "You realize with change comes the loss of tradition?"

Salus flinched. "The old men won't allow that. Tech changes won't change everything."

Arlud smirked and said with a hint of sadness: "No one is prepared for the changes that come. Cultures that change because of technology often lose traditions within three generations. People move on when the old ways get in the way."

"The transports Seelay commandeered didn't change us."

"They were a means to move you from one location to another—a location untouched by the tech that brought you here. Once here, you set that tech aside, made it off-limits to the general population, kept it secure, almost sacred. It changed you but had no impact on the average Aku life. Your people continued the agrarian ways you have known for centuries. Your victories against Clan Tuma, and the isolation, helped your traditional culture survive."

Salus pondered everything Arlud said. "Maybe that was wrong," he admitted. "Perhaps my people should have changed."

"No," Arlud said. "Your ancestors made the right choice—the better choice for their time—but circumstances always change. Your people are on the cusp of many changes."

"And so are yours. Your Alliance has ended. Clans battle clans for dominance. Your culture is threatened as much as my own."

"Yes, it is," Arlud admitted. He gestured toward the maintenance hangar. "Walk with me."

Salus strode alongside Arlud as he led him into the hanger where the Kottrel Sphere was being packed for shipment to Kuliq'Quad.

Arlud stopped next to the exposed side of the five-meter metal sphere secured within a six-meter yellow shipping stand.

Four clanmen were wrapping the sphere in a thick blanket of duralax, a layered gray composite material, to protect the conduit plugs and the connection points for the gravitic compression boxes.

Arlud gestured for the clanmen to pause their work to silence the crinkling of the duralax and told Salus: "These engineers have spent the last two days making sure it's ready to install. Now they're packing it to ship. Do you know what this is?"

"A Kottrel Sphere," Salus said. "We brought two of these back from U'galem."

"Yes, I remember. But do you know what this is?"

Salus was dumbfounded.

"This is the modern result of over six-hundred years of engineering. The first Kottrel Sphere was thirty meters in diameter and was only active for about five minutes. This five-meter version, if maintained, will burn for two-hundred years. Do you know why?"

"No."

"Technology," Arlud said. "Or rather, improvements in technology. The components in this version did not exist in your transport's original spheres, but they lasted ninety years. Technology never stands still, it always evolves. You want to build shuttles. You must realize you will also build a platform for technology that will continue to change, and it will change your people. It's inevitable."

Salus took a deep breath and contemplated the potential impact.

"Don't worry," Arlud said. "Your people are strong and wise. If the changes are managed as you've managed everything else, you won't face your own GRAND Crusade."

Salus knew about the GRAND Crusade. That revolt against technology lasted almost ninety years. By the time it was over, the majority of holdings under the protection of SINCOS rejected the robotic and trans-humanist abominations that failed to bring utopia. The Aku people rediscovered their agrarian roots because of that rejection of automation. "It seems," he said, "no one can hold back technology forever, no matter how much we may regret the changes."

"It's like the sea," Arlud said. "We can't stop the waves that pound against the shore, but with good planning, we can control the damage they cause."

"There are no alternatives?"

"No. There are no alternatives for anyone."

Arlud gestured for the clanmen to continue packing the sphere and led Salus out of the hangar. "A cargo shuttle will be here in about thirty minutes to pick up that sphere."

Salus matched Arlud's pace. "What about the aliens? Have you discovered anything new?"

Arlud stopped. "When Bev dropped out of the sky, what did you see?"

Salus halted a step ahead of Arlud and faced him with a quizzical look. "I told you—a ball of blue fire."

"I saw her in that fire—a perfect rendition in flickering plasma. She must have formed that image in my mind if you didn't see it, which means she connected with me like the Rhysu connected with her. After our trip to Arrilen Po, Bev's connection with the Rhysu got stronger day by day. If she's like them now, why isn't our connection getting stronger?"

"Only she can answer that question."

"I can't sense her anymore."

Salus stepped forward and put a firm grip on Arlud's shoulder. "I feel your pain, my friend, but she's gone. She will always be gone."

"I know her, Salus. I understand how determined she can be. She would be here if she could. I've a feeling the Rhysu are keeping her away. That suspicion has been gnawing at me since the day I saw her, like she implanted that idea inside of me."

Salus patted Arlud's shoulder and stepped back. "What do you want me to do?"

"Ponder this," Arlud said. "When the Alliance armada was attacked on their way to Al-phaq, two Sabballi frigates disappeared and have never been found. The Rhysu took Bev. Maybe they also took the Sabballi frigates."

"Why would they do that?"

"Why did they do any of the things they have done? All we've been able to do is speculate."

"They're aliens from another dimension. We may never know."

"They took Bev," Arlud said. "That means they either need her or had no other option. She came here to tell me she's still alive, which is a good sign they mean her no harm, but there are too many unanswered questions to accept the assumptions we've made in the past."

"Then what do we do?"

"Keep looking for answers."

Arlud continued walking toward the tower complex.

Salus kept pace and wondered about the stability of Arlud's clan. "Do you have enough resources to fight the clans and also search for answers about the aliens?"

"We'll be fine," Arlud assured. "Our enemies have fled and most of the local clans support our coalition. I plan on sending out teams to gather more data about the Rhysu."

"Where will they go?"

"To the mine on Alpha Cephei Four and to Arrilen Po."

Salus considered all he had been told of the destroyed mine and the ruined colony on Arrilen Po. "There could be danger in that."

Arlud had no fear of the Rhysu, but there was a possibility that penetrating the caverns on Arrilen Po might unleash another vortex. No one knew if the eruption was triggered or if the Rhysu had been there monitoring the site, waiting for Bev to arrive. Clan Halva had not heard from the survey team, and he hoped that failure was just because of the lack of comm-drone access. "Anything of value is worth a little risk," he said. "The knowledge we'll gain overshadows the danger."

"That's true," Salus said, "but I hope your first focus will be on the clan wars."

Arlud reached over and patted the ciâfey pilot's shoulder. "Don't worry, my friend. That has always been my priority. The Anders Prime campaign should be underway as we speak."

COALITION: ANDERS PRIME

The Coalition armada—one dreadnought, three frigates, four destroyers, and two fighter carriers from Clan Erstallius; one dreadnought, two frigates, and one destroyer from Clan Sorrell; three frigates, and two fighter carriers from Clan Rastee—arrived at the boundary of the PDN2204 star system six-point-eight standard days after leaving Pigrell. Six sensor drones were launched into the cometary debris cloud surrounding the system and ten hours later, after they passed the inner planets, the data returned from each drone revealed no rebel ships.

Jegen-Major Lon Pavan examined the data streaming across the holoscreen hovering in front of him. "PDN2204 is status normal," he said in an undertone. He let his body relax in his seat, and asked himself, "Where are the rebels?"

The clanmen seated around Pavan were busy at their stations in the C.I.C., preparing for the eventual push to Anders Prime, the homeworld of Clan Bree, where they expected to engage Clan Sabballi and Clan Emlito.

Pavan turned in his seat and leaned toward his Reconnaissance Officer. "What do you think, Mister Dal?"

"They could be hiding inside the outer asteroid belt. There are two lobes that are dense enough, but that would also limit their data collection. They'd be sitting partially blind. Not a good option unless they're waiting for more ships to arrive."

"What do you recommend?"

"Remote sensing is easy to deflect, especially inside a rubble field. If we pinpoint a location to search and surround it, we could find them if they are there. We can send out more drones."

Pavan sat up straight. *We don't have time to hunt ships that might not exist.* "Show me the status at Anders Prime."

The holoscreen in front of Pavan changed to display Anders Prime: The mottled-blue class 2 terrestrial holding that supported eight-hundred million humans was joined in its orbit around PDN2204 by two spherical moons.

Red icons appeared in the holoscreen that identified where Clan Bree had positioned defenses nine-hundred thousand kilometers from the planet's surface at sixty locations—fortresses that encircled the planet and her moons.

Pavan zoomed out the holoscreen view to see more area around the fortresses. "Status normal?"

"Yes," the reconnaissance officer said.

Pavan faced his communication officer. "Send to all attack groups: Proceed to Stage One and hold until further orders. Heads up, condition yellow." *That'll place the armada in a good defensive position,* Pavan thought. "Contact Bree security. Tell them this flagship will arrive at Anders Prime in two hours."

A faint rumble sounded in the C.I.C. as the dreadnought surged through the heliosphere into the outer cometary debris cloud.

Thirty minutes from Anders Prime's outer moon, Pavan's dreadnought was met by five Bree frigates that escorted the ship into a high orbit around the planet, about five-thousand kilometers inside the orbit of the inner moon.

A young Bree liaison officer appeared in Pavan's holoscreen. Her sand-colored hair was gathered in a bun on top of her head, which made her large ears a prominent feature and caused Pavan to force back a chuckle at the sight of her.

"Greetings, Jegen-Major. What brings you to Anders Prime?"

"We came to save you."

"Save us?"

"We have reports Clans Sabballi and Clan Emlito are heading here to claim your homeworld for themselves."

"Oh."

The surprise on the liaison's face told Pavan there was a major flaw in the data.

"We detected a few passing ships seventeen days ago," the liaison said. "The telemetry indicated Clan Emlito. Their flight path never crossed the orbit of Aegir. They did not pause or change course."

Pavan examined the system holomap above his course-plotting pedestal. Aegir was the fourth planet in the system, a Class Three gas giant that helped define the limit of the inner asteroid belt. "I recommend you place all your forces on high alert," he said, "and help us scan the system for intruders."

"I will notify command. Please hold."

The liaison's face was replaced by the House Crest of Clan Bree.

Five hours later, after a deeper scan of the outer asteroid belt by twenty sensor drones, and a closer examination of the four outer planets and 24 largest moons, no Sabballi or Emlito ships were found.

Pavan pondered the implications of the data and decided to stay in the system a few more days, just in case their enemy arrived later than expected. His decision was appreciated by the Bree High Regent, and the Bree security force developed a coordinated plan that kept the Coalition forces in position to defend the system periphery.

Once his dreadnought was positioned in the security grid, Pavan continued to review the data that had brought him here. He huddled with his First Officer and Mister Dal, the Reconnaissance Officer, around the plotting pedestal in the C.I.C. "Looks like the comm-drone that brought us news of the threat to Anders Prime originated from GSW-34."

"That makes sense," Dal said. "It's only 1.67 parsecs away."

"Yes, that's a logical point of origin," the First Officer agreed. "If the rebels are rallying near GSW-34, that would be worthy info for the loyal clans. But what if their target isn't Anders Prime? What if the target is GSW-34?"

"Clan Brandi owns GSW-34," Pavan said. "Unlikely the rebels would hit their own mates."

"Clan Dejoria had partnerships with Clan Vestlok," the First Officer said, "but they attacked Dejoria at Wan'tei. Partnerships can no longer be trusted."

Pavan fingered the holomitter controls and pulled up a map of GSW-34. "What do you think, Mister Dal?"

"Sir, based on the intel, I expected to be engaged in battle by now."

The First Officer added the most recent list of security forces at GSW-34 to the holomap. The list was extensive. "We may have been misled, sir. Clan Brandi's homeworld would have been the perfect source of false info about the rebel intention to strike Anders Prime."

Pavan wondered: "Did they lure us here to keep us from focusing on the actual target?"

"That would explain why the Emlito ships passed through this system," Dal said. "Their presence would seem to support the reports, but perhaps they were headed toward a different battlefield."

"What do we do, sir?" the First Officer asked.

Pavan knew Clan Brandi had been found loyal to the rebels and had planted seeds of doubt among the allied clans. "If Anders Prime isn't the actual target, finding the real one will be impossible until it's attacked. If we leave this system, Clan Bree will be more open to attack. We will stay here and help protect Anders Prime."

"Aye, sir," the First Officer said.

"Send two drones to GSW-34," Pavan said. "We need to see what's happening there."

BREACH

PART TWO

Our goal is to win. Sometimes losing is better than winning when it impels us forward with renewed commitment, with the knowledge of how to clear our path of the things that stalled our advance.

—From Conversations at Kuliq'Quad
By Petra Sitlyn

BEV COLLI: PRISON

Every time Bev dug her energy tendrils into the regolith of Simbic Ur, the Rhysu pulled her away. After the one-hundredth time she kept clear of the surface and the Rhysu said, "Thank You." They were tired of preventing her isolation—Bev could feel the exasperation in their response.

"Why did you bring me here?"

"We learn."

"Well, how does it feel to learn I'm a stubborn bitch?"

The Rhysu did not respond.

Bev focused her thoughts inward and spent what seemed like days examining her new body. During that time, the Rhysu were quiet as she floated among them above Simbic Ur's surface. And she realized she had entered a mental state void of their voices—the first time since her arrival she seemed to be alone. She focused on the Rhysu around her and noticed they were dimmer, as if the influx of energy had dropped. She examined herself and could sense no change in her energy output—she was still feeding off the energy of the Rhysu touching her, but they did not appear to be as energetic. She wondered if there was a cycle to their existence, like the human sleep cycle. She had been conscious since her arrival so had assumed that was the normal state for the Rhysu. She pressed close to a Rhysu next to her and as her energy tendrils encompassed the alien, a sudden influx of energy sent a burning sting through her body.

"Eetah!"

The voices came back and the Rhysu surrounding her returned to their normal brightness.

"You should not impose yourself," the Rhysu said.

"What?"

"You should not intrude into the Rhysu."

Bev understood that to mean she should not wrap herself around another Rhysu. "Sorry," she said. "I didn't realize what would happen."

"You have much to learn."

Bev focused her thoughts inward again, examining up close the small rivulets of energy that protruded from the larger fire that was the center of her new body. The boundary of her plasma tendrils formed the energy sphere that encased her and was the limit of her physical form. Punching through the sphere of another Rhysu had caused the burning that broke her solitude. Now aware of that limitation, she let herself float as she dove deeper into her mental space and found herself once again surrounded by silent, dimmer Rhysu.

I can finally think in private!

This new state was a welcome change, and a possible key to returning to her own universe if she could search for answers without being forced to connect with the Rhysu. She concentrated on moving in a specific direction, along a mountain ridge in the gray landscape below her.

The Rhysu spheres around her brightened, and the voices came back.

Damn!

Any conscious movement reignited her connection with the Rhysu. She focused her thoughts and her privacy returned. She reviewed the few facts she had learned about her new environment—limited, secluded, a prison. Simbic Ur was the key to her isolation. The planet may have allowed the Rhysu to capture the Shoku, but it was also a barricade that kept her from experiencing the real Rhysu universe.

That's how they're controlling me. I must break free from this place.

She knew she could do it if she took slow steps.

I must break free from the community.

That understanding seemed to initiate itself, as if planted in her mind by the Rhysu.

They may view themselves as communal, but there is nothing open or unrestricted here for me. I am not part of any community. I'm an outsider, an alien, a prisoner.

A surge of frustration broke Bev's inner focus and restored her connection with the Rhysu.

"Everyone learns," she said, as if responding to the last Rhysu statement.

Hearing anger in Bev's voice, the Rhysu retreated to reduce their pressure against her body, and they did not respond.

Bev flew over Simbic Ur, keeping her average distance above the surface to three meters as her course mirrored the terrain and kept her body in contact with the Rhysu spheres above her. The small airless planet had three prominent mountain ranges that covered forty percent of the surface, and thousands of craters pock-marked every feature—there were no smooth plains. The ice fields around the southern pole had vaporized during the transfer through the dimensional portal and exposed fissures where gases spewed up from deep below the surface.

The Rhysu did not interfere with Bev's survey.

"This planet is my anchor," she told them. "I want to visualize all of it because one day I hope to leave it."

The truth in her statement was recognized by the Rhysu. Telling the truth was her best ally—there was no deceit in that, and the Rhysu had no reason to wonder about her motives.

As she sped over the rugged southern landscape on her third circuit around the planet, she searched for a crevice clear of up welling gases, and deep enough to allow her to separate long enough to break her connection with the Rhysu. The terrain was illuminated by the combined brilliance of the Rhysu and the white glare surrounding the planet. The broad illumination reduced shadows, and she found it difficult to judge depth, but she flew over a steep ridge and noticed the terrain drop into black shadow between near-vertical cliffs.

That must be deep for the shadows to be so dark.

She crossed the chasm and made a U-turn to examine it again.

No Gases!

She rushed down into the crevice, her self-illumination pushed away the shadows as she descended between the jagged cliffs. The gap narrowed, so she slowed her advance to avoid protruding folds of rock that forced her path down a meandering slit to an impassable crack. She looked back up the chasm to see Rhysu spheres descending toward her.

My only chance!

Bev focused on the narrow crack below her and jammed her energy tendrils deep into the rock. She felt a harmonic reverberation that caused her to pause—just long enough for the Rhysu to reach her. Their connection returned, and she felt the familiar tingling along edges of her sphere. She ignored the voices to stop, focused her plasma emissions into the rock, and dug downward six meters before the Rhysu pulled her out.

The sting that tore through her body stopped her plasma emissions and her advance through the rock ended. She rose through the crevice in the Rhysu's grip, her energy level almost depleted. She was weak, angry, and silent. The Rhysu questioned her on the way back to the surface, but she refused to answer.

Bev's recovery seemed to take days as her energy was restored to normal levels and ended with a stern warning from the Rhysu that another attempt to bore into the planet could kill her.

"Kill me?"

"If you deplete yourself in isolation, you will not regain consciousness."

"Then how do you bore into the rock?"

"Properly."

Bev waited for more explanation and when nothing else was said she focused inward and entered her private state. As she bobbed between the surrounding Rhysu, a new plan formed in her mind.

If I can't go down, I'll go up.

She was cut off from Simbic Ur by the intervening layers of Rhysu. Above her, more Rhysu pressed against her energy sphere.

There must be an end to this gathering, she thought. *If I can break free, I may have more opportunity to stay free.*

Bev returned to her normal state, and as the surrounding Rhysu spheres grew brighter, the persistent drone of voices bombarded her with questions she did not wish to answer. She pushed upward through the Rhysu and paused for a few moments before pressing through the next layer. She repeated the process—a casual movement that advanced her one layer at a time until she reached the outer layer of spheres, beyond which she could only see the glare of whiteness.

"What's out there?"

"We are out there," the Rhysu said.

"Why can't I see beyond the white?"

"You are not ready. You still have much to learn."

"Why can't I learn out there?"

"You are not ready."

Bev felt the press of the surrounding spheres—the Rhysu were tightening their grip, which told her they expected her to flee.

"I will not disappoint," Bev said. She compressed herself and let loose an energy blast that freed her from the surrounding Rhysu. She rushed upward into the white, leaving the stunned Rhysu in her wake.

"Come back," the Rhysu yelled, and they surged after her.

Bev pressed onward through the white, free, but with no idea where she was headed. She looked back—the Rhysu were far behind her.

You won't catch me this time—there's nothing to slow me now!

The white glare began to fade.

Bev pressed onward until the white shifted to a blazing, cyan-colored glow filled with rippling tendrils of streaming plasma. She looked behind her—the white glare was a glowing ball amid the plasma sea that churned and flowed around her. The twisting streams mesmerized her as they folded and twisted in a higher-dimensional fashion she found difficult to follow.

They didn't want me to see this.

And she realized she was no longer moving.

The Rhysu pressed upon her. "You are a stubborn bitch."

"I told you I was."

Held by six Rhysu, Bev was pulled back toward the white glare. Before she entered the white, she glimpsed something familiar, something she did not expect to see. Far outside the white glare, two ships that looked like Alliance frigates were trapped within undulating ripples of the cyan-colored energy. They were distant, perhaps five kilometers away, based on their relative size. She kept that sighting to herself as the Rhysu pulled her from the sea of energy back into her white prison.

THE GUILD: HOME

Wolfram Sy strolled along the stone path that followed the northern curve of his residence. The landscaping crew had installed velvet grass in the adjoining field. Bunches of roseweed filled the narrow area between the path and the gray building. The nearest trees were along the perimeter fence—young salix trees that would shade the ornamental ponds Wellen had designed for their collection of terra-carp.

This is beginning to feel like a home.

His decision to leave Al-phaq was more successful than he'd imagined. He always knew the change would benefit his family and the Guild, but never to the extent realized.

And now Pardee has arrived with plans to retake Al-phaq.

Wolfram's decision to abandon the original Guild stronghold was based on the need to survive - the Alliance had advanced beyond Al-phaq's position, and that forced isolation would have led to a blockade and inevitable defeat. Leaving Al-phaq strengthened the Guild by avoiding direct confrontation. Going back would have been a slap in the face to the Merchant Houses who ruled the Alliance, but now the Alliance was crumbling, and the Guild could return to the old stronghold without a fight.

Our presence there will strengthen that portion of the district, he thought. *The Erstallius will welcome our presence, and we may even get a slice of Polinda's mine on Alpha Cephei Four.*

He glanced up at the hilltop where Shanna sat on the wooden bench. That had become her place to meditate. He had seen her there every morning during the past week. He thought of waving, but her side was facing him, and her head was bowed in contemplation, so he halted the gesture before his hand rose above his waist. *She's isolating herself,* he thought, and he wondered how long he'd have to put up with her sullen mood. *She needs to snap out of it.*

"Wolfram?"

Wolfram turned to see Wellen approach from the house. Her thick black hair glistened in the early morning light, and her silver lumisilk dress hugged her slim figure.

"Pardee is here," Wellen said, and she stopped on the stone path about five paces from Wolfram with a gesture to follow her back inside.

Wolfram returned a smile and followed Wellen into the house.

Captain Erlis Pardee stood by the entry to the sun-room and watched his patriarch follow Wellen through the open glass doorway. He tipped his head as Wellen passed and retreated down the adjoining hall but kept his eyes on Wolfram. "Good morning, sir."

Wolfram gestured for Pardee to sit in one of the cushioned chairs. "How was the trip back?"

"Uneventful," Pardee said as he eased into the plush chair. It made him feel trapped because his knees were higher than his hips. "None of the clans have come out this far."

Wolfram sat on the edge of the chair across the low table from Pardee. "I have a feeling they won't be coming this way for many years."

"You never know. Some may want to leave the conflict behind."

"And lose all the wealth they've acquired?"

"Wealth has no value if you're dead."

Wolfram sat back. His chair was harder than Pardee's and allowed him to stretch out his legs. "Any additional deaths?"

Pardee sighed. Two-hundred and eighty-seven guildmen assigned to his armada did not return. "No. Everyone else survived the trip back."

"Good. I expected more from the injuries you reported. We fared well considering the clans we fought. The Erstallius are good tacticians, and the Coalition fighters stood up well." He noticed a slight frown in Pardee's expression. "You disagree?"

"No, sir. It's this chair." He pushed up with his arms and stood. "Too soft for me."

Wolfram gestured to the low settee to Pardee's left.

Pardee sat on the edge of the quilted cushion—it was a firmer support. "We were fortunate to have stealth on our side," he said. "At Wan'tei, we took Polinda by surprise, blocked him on three sides—there was no way for him to win. At Cestratha, the Coalition forces came in behind the Vestlock and Emlito ships—a complete surprise. Our effort at Pigrell was minimal—the main battle was done when we arrived. We were part of Arlud's small armada, more for show than for fighting. He wanted his father to see his new allies."

"I see it differently," Wolfram said. "We took advantage of the circumstances. That's how any battle is won."

Pardee nodded. "Yeah, we took advantage. We won't always have an advantage."

"Then we must take as many as we can get."

"Armand Erstallius is dead."

"What!?"

"Sorry, sir, I wanted to tell you in person."

"When? How?"

"Armand won at Pigrell about the same time we demolished Polinda's siege at Wan'tei. Arlud sent a convoy with Farquar Polinda's remains to Pigrell to fulfill the Alliance tradition of returning a defeated patriarch to his homeworld. Apparently, the commanding Jegen paraded through the capitol city and dumped Farquar's remains on the steps of the Great Hall. That angered the surviving loyalists, and the day before we arrived with Arlud, they hit the capital with a counter-strike and everyone in the Great Hall was killed."

Wolfram grunted. "Fools!"

Pardee shrugged. "I understand the symbolism in what the Jegen did—they've been feuding with Polinda for decades."

"Still foolish."

Pardee leaned forward. "Armand's death has sent Arlud on a revenge-driven campaign, and he is weakening his forces. The Coalition sent an armada to Anders Prime to defend Clan Bree."

Wolfram closed his eyes and tilted his head back. He knew Arlud's reaction to his father's death was normal regret-driven anger, but his position wasn't normal. *He needs to stop and think before jumping too fast into a conflict he cannot win.* "Where is Arlud now?"

"I left him at Jai'raan," Pardee said. "But he will most likely return to GSW-183."

"Why?"

"He's respected there. His clanmen helped restore the Aku's small fleet. He never had much respect on Baleiou—he was candid about that. The cadre refused to support his promotion to Regent."

"They should support him now—he deserves it."

"With the death of Armand, his future path is not clear. I believe he fears the clan will split apart."

"Politics—the clans revel in that," Wolfram said, thinking of his own ouster and eventual rebellion. "Should we send a dreadnought task force to strengthen his backside?"

"That would delay the convoy we had planned to send to Al-phaq. Supply and maintenance systems would need to be redirected to accommodate the new directive."

"Yes, but you didn't answer my question."

Pardee weighed the ramifications of his answer, then: "No."

"And why not?"

"If we delay our return to Al-phaq, we might lose her for good. The clans in that district are scrambling for every scrap of wealth available. And our hope at gaining a foothold on Alpha Cephei Four might also be lost."

"Then you propose we take the selfish route and ignore a friend's need?"

"No, sir. I propose we strengthen our house while our ally is not under direct threat. His enemies have fled. His house is secure."

"Good," Wolfram said. He unfolded from his chair and walked to the threshold of the open doorway. The air outside was warm, and the sky was a cloudless, pale blue. He turned back to face Pardee. "Send the convoy to Al-phaq. We can address the Coalition's needs once our strength in the district is firmly fixed."

Shanna stormed down the vaulted hallway toward her father's study. The news about the death of Armand Erstallius had been broadcast over the comnet and she was furious that Pardee had returned and left Arlud's coalition weaker.

The rebellion is spreading, and we abandoned him!

She stopped a few paces from the closed double-doors. The stained wooden barrier was enough to force her to rethink her actions. The last time she intruded into her father's study, she spent four days in jail. She knew that wouldn't happen this time, but that memory reinforced the reality that there was no way to predict how her father would react, and she knew if she entered angry the situation could escalate and she would be the one to suffer for it.

And perhaps Arlud would suffer too.

Her father liked the Erstallius Regent, but when she mentioned him, it was obvious he preferred she focus on other things. She reassessed her plan and reformulated what she would say. She gulped a breath, stepped toward the doors, and rapped against the hard wood.

A deep voice sounded from inside the room: "Come!"

Shanna could tell by the tone that her father was in a bad mood, but she shrugged that aside and turned the door handle.

Wolfram sat in one of the wing-backed chairs that bracketed the low wooden table where a holoscreen displayed comnet reports. He glanced up at Shanna as she entered the room. "Daughter," he said, "what a privilege to see you."

Shanna halted. Wolfram was being sarcastic, and that was not a good place to start. "Hello, Father," she said with a hint of apology. "I just found out we will return to Al-phaq."

Wolfram stood and his face softened. "Yes, Pardee recommends we reclaim our old home. With the Erstallius victories, our options have expanded."

"That's wonderful," Shanna said. A slight smile separated her lips for an instant. "I'd love to return to our old home. I had to leave so much there."

Wolfram nodded agreement with his daughter's loss. "I apologize for that. We brought as much as we could. The need to leave was great, and I didn't want—"

Shanna rushed forward, threw her arms around Wolfram's shoulders, and pressed the side of her face against his chest. "You don't need to apologize. You saved us from the Alliance."

"I almost lost you," Wolfram said, and he returned his daughter's embrace.

"That wasn't your fault," Shanna said. She leaned away and added, "the Cormeds paid for their crime. That was the past. I'm more concerned about our future."

Wolfram released his hug and took a step backward. "I'm glad you're over that mess. I was worried it would scar you. Are you sure you're over it?"

Shanna flashed another brief smile. "Yes."

"Then tell me, what are your concerns?"

Shanna heard the shift in her father's tone—his anger had subsided. *I must choose my words well,* she thought, *lest his anger return.* "There is growing chaos among the clans. The old worlds are plagued by war. Millions have died. I do not want to see the Guild pulled into that conflict."

"Nor do I."

"I want to help."

Wolfram blinked. Shanna's request was a welcome expression, but as the daughter of the Guild patriarch, her obligations ended with obeying the rule of law and preparing the house for official events. "You serve here," he said.

"That's not enough," Shanna insisted. "You told me, 'The people must know we do not sit above them, we sit with them.' How can I sit here in comfort when guildmen have died and our old home is in danger of being overrun by Alliance clans?"

"We abandoned Al-phaq for good reason, never expecting to go back."

"But now we have an opportunity to reclaim it. I want to be part of that."

Wolfram saw the sincerity in his daughter's eyes. He moved away and leaned against the back of his leather chair. "What would you do?"

"Lead the expedition to reclaim our old Keep."

Wolfram suppressed a chuckle. *Lead?* he wondered. He loved his daughter but considering her to lead anything had never entered his mind. "That's new," he said. "What makes you think you're qualified?"

"Who knows the layout of our old home better than me? Who knows the secret chambers? Who knows what items to retrieve first?"

"I can think of a dozen guildmen who would do just fine leading that expedition."

Shanna balked at that reply—her argument was lost. Then: "Prestige."

"What?"

"Prestige. The prestige of House Sy."

Wolfram considered Shanna's new argument: *In her mind, the ridicule she suffered because of her incarceration lowered her value to the Guild. She seeks to regain her standing.*

"Clan Sy is doing just fine," Wolfram said. "We could confront Alliance scavengers at Al-phaq—we did abandon the place. The situation could get dangerous."

"The clans know we've aligned with Clan Erstallius. There has been no confirmation Alliance ships have entered the system, which means they're respecting our claim to that holding even though we abandoned it."

That was true, and Wolfram acknowledged it with a nod. He knew allowing Shanna to lead the expedition would raise her reputation and send the message throughout the Guild that House Sy serves the Guild as all guildmen serve. "I will need a detailed Operation Plan from you by tomorrow."

"Then you agree?"

"No," Wolfram said in a flat tone. "Bring me your plan and we can discuss this further."

"Thank you, Father," Shanna said, and she stepped forward to embrace him.

Wolfram gestured for Shanna to stop by showing her the palm of his hand. "Get me your plan, and we'll talk."

Shanna nodded and spun toward the doorway. She left the room with the slow gait of confidence. Her father had agreed to review her plan, and that was encouraging. *One step closer,* she thought, and she smiled.

CLAN ERSTALLIUS: RESOURCES

The Aku transport had been under maintenance review at the Mânu in Kuliq'Quad for eight days.

Arlud stood bundled in his thick coat on the tarmac with Winstone Bittle, near one of the spherical transport's landing pads. A group of ten Aku engineers huddled nearby—they had paused their search for a solution to allow Bittle time to discuss the problem with his regent.

Arlud glanced up at the ship—one quarter of the hull panels had been removed to reveal the inner support girders and the pathway to the new Kottrel Sphere that had been installed. He faced Bittle and noticed the old engineer's forlorn expression. "What's the problem?"

"All twenty ships are the same make and model, but there have been customizations to each ship's power system. Those alterations produced unique changes in this ship. I think Seelay may have been experimenting with different ways to power his weapons. We restored the original gravity furnace without removing it during our first upgrades, which preserved the altered connections and settings. Replacing it with the new one created problems we didn't expect."

"Is this like what happened to Transport Two?"

"It's related, yes."

"You can fix it?"

"Yes, sir."

"How much longer?"

Bittle shrugged. "Can't give you a definite time. We've tested every connection at the sphere six times. That's two-thousand one-hundred and sixty tests. Seems to be a back-pressure issue somewhere down stream. We could be at this for a few more weeks before she's flight-ready again."

"So, the problem is not in the furnace?

"Correct. The furnace appears to be working as it should. Once the power rises above ten percent, a cascade failure occurs in the surrounding systems."

Arlud turned and walked toward the center of the exposed interior to get a better view of the Kottrel Sphere. It was the heart of the ship, obscured behind a network of conduits and cables. He called to Bittle: "You're sure the problem is because of Seelay's weapon modifications?"

Bittle nodded and began walking toward Arlud.

Arlud asked: "Are the other transports in danger of this same failure?"

Bittle stood next to Arlud. "Not likely, but other failures are bound to occur—they're old, and old ships always need repairs."

"OK," Arlud said. "One grounded ship isn't a disaster. Just make sure this doesn't grow into a bigger problem."

"There's no fear of that, sir," Bittle said with confidence. "We're on top of it."

Arlud sat in the small conference room across the table from Grénu, the gray-haired overseer of the Mânu. Narèndu, the overseer of the Aku Defense Force, sat at Grénu's side. Four lower ranking Aku military overseers filled the chairs next to Narèndu. Gustav Eahuda sat to Arlud's right, along with Jegen-Major Kurt Sari, the Erstallius officer who replaced Lon Pavan as fleet commander at GSW-183 before the battle at Wan'tei.

"Our position is strong," Narèndu said. "One ship down will not limit our ability."

Arlud heard the conviction in Narèndu's voice—the same calm commitment he had heard during the escape to U'galem, when the Aku officer helped devise the strategy that lured Farquar Polinda away from Ni'apinu. Yet Narèndu's conviction could be interpreted as arrogance.

"Your strategy is sound," Arlud said. "My concern has more to do with the age of your transports."

"Have you doubts regarding your own engineers?"

"Beyond a certain point, all technology will fail. Our engineers resurrected your dead ships. You should not suppose their second life will last as long as their first. That transport stuck on the tarmac should impress upon you the need to modernize."

Narèndu leaned forward and rested his hands on the table. "What do you propose?"

"I have already agreed to support your request for modern shuttles, and the construction of facilities here at Kuliq'Quad and at Dol'anar to build and support them. Larger vessels will need much larger facilities, and thousands more engineers to build them. The best option for you, considering the time needed to build the facilities and the ships, is to purchase what you need from the clans."

Grénu and Narèndu exchanged a quick glance. They had foreseen the need to partner with off-worlders and they were both opposed to that solution. "That will not happen," Narèndu said.

Arlud understood their reluctance to increase contact with off-world clans. "We are bound by our commitments. Clan Erstallius can be your conduit to the other clans and all the things they can offer."

"We will not allow more clans on Ni'apinu," Narèndu said.

"I understand," Arlud said. "This issue with your transports must be resolved soon. To keep your ships in top condition, I asked Jegen-Major Sari to assess the situation, and he has a proposal."

Arlud leaned back and flicked a hand signal to the Jegen-Major.

"Based upon past issues," Sari said, "and the current complications with Transport Fourteen, we recommend the following:

"First: only ten ships in orbit. This will allow proper maintenance and ensure that no ship is rushed back into service before maximum competence.

"Second: Once we have established credible up-times, a rotation schedule will be put in place for regular transfer between maintenance and service.

"Third, this rotation should continue until all ships are replaced by modern spacecraft."

Narèndu leaned forward and cupped his hands on the table. "That will impact how Ni'apinu is defended."

"Yes, it will," Sari said. "We will readjust the deployment of our fleet to compensate."

"Your fleet is half the strength it was two months ago," Narèndu said. "Grounding our ships will put us at a disadvantage."

Arlud sat up straight. "If your ships fail while in orbit, the disadvantage will be greater. Keeping ten on planet ensures sustainability and a ready reserve should the need arise to use them against an attacker."

"There is no real downside to this," Sari said. "Ni'apinu will still be protected."

Grénu and Narèndu engaged in a quiet Akün discussion that lasted a few minutes, then Narèndu turned to Arlud and said: "We understand the purpose behind your proposal, and we accept it. However, what is your timetable to acquire the modern vessels?"

"I have sent a drone to U'galem," Arlud said, "with a request to the High Regent to prepare and deliver four class five destroyers as soon as possible. Clan Dejoria has the largest system-bound fleet in the district, and their ship-building yards are in constant operation. I expect delivery to happen within weeks. Before the standard year is over, I am hoping your entire fleet can be replaced."

Narèndu translated Arlud's words to Grénu.

The old man smiled and nodded his approval.

"Your crews will need to be retrained," Sari said. "We should begin that process immediately."

Narèndu nodded his approval. "We can begin with the crew of Transport Fourteen."

THE GUILD: AL-PHAQ

Shanna Sy looked out her cabin window at the bright orange star whose ancient name was Eta Cephei. The Guild armada had reached the edge of the system and was probing for Alliance ships before advancing toward their abandoned homeworld.

Al-phaq is almost ours again.

Her father had agreed to send her on this campaign, giving her oversight of the resettlement. Erlis Pardee was in charge of the armada—two dreadnoughts, six frigates, six destroyers, and ten cargo transports—so Shanna's influence was restricted to the planet-bound scenarios. That limitation was fine with her. Once resettled on Al-phaq, the armada's focus would change, and she would have more leeway regarding her underlying motive. Her return to Al-phaq had always been the first step in her plan to reunite with Arlud Erstallius.

A bell dinged, and a holoscreen ignited inside the window. Erlis Pardee's face filled the screen.

Shanna pressed the comm-channel button on the wall panel to accept the call. "Yes, Captain?"

"My lady, our drones detected no Alliance presence in the system. We are beginning our entry as I speak."

Shanna noticed a shift in the star pattern outside the window.

"We will reach orbit of Al-phaq in sixty-eight minutes," Pardee said. "Planet-fall should begin as soon as we've secured orbit. Please come to the debarkation center to review preparations."

"Yes, Captain. Thank you for notifying me."

Shanna ended the conversation by pressing the holoscreen-off button. Normal protocol stated the caller should always end the connection. Pardee may have thought it rude of her to end the call, but she did not care. She respected Pardee, and she knew he respected her, but his attitude expressed misgivings regarding her oversight of the resettlement—the indicators were subtle, but all too obvious to one skilled in reading body language and the tone behind words.

His attitude will change once we're back on the ground and secure in our old keep.

◈◈◈

Planet-fall happened as Pardee had promised—as soon as the armada achieved a secure orbit. Ensuring the integrity of the pressure domes and restoring the atmosphere throughout the capitol complex took five hours. The engineering teams reported everything was found as it had been left, which meant the Alliance Clans had stayed away. The twenty other settlements on planet had also not been disturbed. That discovery reassured everyone the things left behind could be retrieved.

Shanna peered out the small window next to her shuttle seat and watched the landing bay dome split open like a flower into eight leaves that bent outward to accept the shuttle. *The Clans see no value in this planet with a poison atmosphere,* she thought. *I suppose that's a positive thing. Not having to chase away the clans will make this reclamation easier.*

The Guild shuttle dropped through the open roof of the hanger and touched down on the circular landing pad. The domed ceiling closed, then the cold carbon-dioxide atmosphere was evacuated and replaced by a breathable mixture of oxygen and nitrogen heated to the standard twenty-two degrees Celsius.

Shanna stepped out onto the shuttle's boarding ramp into the dim bluish light of the shuttle bay. Her ankle-length white dress fluttered as the thin air circulated in a clockwise motion. She took in a deep breath.

We're home.

Her life began in this manufactured atmosphere. The taste of it brought back feelings of security—the familiar comfort she'd known until her ill-fated journey to Wald-415 by way of Ni'apinu.

She walked down the boarding ramp, followed by two female attendants who wore white linen pants tucked into calf-length leather boots, and long-sleeve tan blouses secured at the waist by thin belts. The attendants each pulled small GPG-assisted carts that floated behind them, stacked with flattened shipping containers. They crossed to the doorway that opened to the staging room and met the gray-haired leader of the engineering team, who restored the life support and internal power systems.

"Good work, Mister Han," Shanna said.

"Thank you, lady," Han replied with a curt bow. His crooked smile emphasized the deep scar along his right jaw.

"All rooms are open?"

"Yes. You'll have unrestricted access to all areas."

Shanna nodded with a smile and led her cart-pulling attendants from the staging room through the access tunnel that led to the debarkation center, then up the wide ramp to the vaulted corridor that led to the central residence.

Guildmen scurried through the passageway, nodding to Shanna as they hurried past, focused on their assigned duties to secure the complex and retrieve items for transport back to Wald-415. Two guildmen rushed in front of her, discussing machinery displayed on a compad. Wolfram had made a list of equipment and supplies for retrieval that would keep the guildmen busy for days. She understood the goals for this trip, she helped define them, but was amazed at the rush each guildman displayed in their effort to complete their tasks.

Once inside the family residence, away from all the bustle and hurry, Shanna paused under the subdued lighting in the circular foyer—the ornate columns around the perimeter gave the room a grandeur uncommon in pressurized dwellings. She turned to the young attendant on her left. "These columns were brought all the way from Makenzie, our ancestral home."

The attendant had never seen this keep. She had been raised on Sisus Nine, a Guild settlement in district four. "Very impressive," she said in her quiet contralto. "I am honored to be here, my lady."

Shanna turned to the older attendant, reached down, and took one of the flattened shipping containers off her cart. "Gretel, take Cala to my study and start packing. I'll meet you there after I've collected a few things from my private quarters."

Gretel nodded and led Cala across the foyer. As they entered the dark vaulted corridor, Gretel touched a wall switch that brightened the hallway.

Life returns to Clan Sy's Keep, Shanna thought. She held the flattened container in front of her and advanced down the hall to her right.

Shanna placed a folded lumisilk dress into the expanded storage container that rested on the bare mattress of her old bed. The dress was the last garment she would retrieve from her private quarters—what remained could be replaced. She scanned the room for anything she might have missed. Satisfied she had packed everything she wanted, she sealed the container's top and lifted the box off the bed. It was lighter than expected.

I spent twenty-three years in this keep and this is all I value?

Leaving Al-phaq had been a persistent regret that shaded every thought Shanna had after her capture by the Cormeds. Now that she was back in her room, the comfort she felt upon exiting the shuttle had morphed into overwhelming emptiness, and from deep within her awareness, a thought formed: *There is nothing here for me any longer.*

Her compad buzzed for attention.

She dropped the box on the bed and raised her compad to her lips. "Yes?"

"Pardee here, Lady Sy."

"Yes, Captain?"

"Everything going well down there?"

"Yes, Captain, what can I do for you?"

Pardee could hear the impatience in Shanna's voice. "I would like your team to return to my ship as soon as possible."

That request implied trouble. Shanna froze for a heartbeat as she contemplated possibilities. "Are we in danger?"

"No, but it's best to be cautious. We received a drone transmission that may imply a coming threat."

"May imply?"

"Yes," Pardee said in a matter-of-fact tone. "It may be nothing, but I would like you up here if things unravel."

Shanna knew Pardee would not cut short her stay on Al-phaq unless there was a legitimate reason, which meant his concern was justified.

A coming threat.

"Lady?" Pardee pressed.

Shanna focused again on her compad. "Yes, Captain. I'll have my team return to the shuttle."

Shanna read the message displayed on the small holopad Pardee handed her:

Comdrone E987

Priority - 1

To: GSW-183

From: Jegen-Major Lon Paven, Commander-in-Charge, Coalition Task Force Alpha

Message Begin- Anders Prime is stable. No threat imminent. The large flotilla detected near GSW-34 has

moved. Compression plot stream points to the outer district near PDN198.
-Message End.

“We’re in the PDN198 system,” Pardee said. He stood next to Shanna in his ship’s C.I.C. at the plotting pedestal that emitted a holographic map of the region one light-year in diameter around PDN198. “We’ve detected nothing unusual in the area, but I set mission status to level three.”

Shanna peered into the holomap. The drone’s course was plotted with a solid green line that arched upward from the direction of Anders Prime toward Al-phaq, then continued on toward GSW-183. “Is that course accurate?”

“It’s an estimate, based on the transmission’s blue-shift as we tracked it, combined with the origin code embedded by the sender. It’s an Erstallius transmission. They sent a small armada to Anders Prime to help Clan Bree defend their homeworld. If the message is still accurate, that effort was a waste of time.”

Shanna faced Pardee. “Why?”

“The large flotilla that’s mentioned is heading this way—Anders Prime was never a target.”

“Their coming to Al-phaq?”

“Possibly, but most likely to GSW-183.”

“We must warn them!”

Pardee leaned away from Shanna’s intensity. “I’m sure the Erstallius have gotten the message by now.”

“But you don’t know that for certain.”

“Correct,” Pardee said with a hint of regret. “Warning them by drone or frigate would do no good. Based on the timing of the Erstallius transmission, if the target is GSW-183, our drone message would arrive after the large flotilla reaches the system. If we leave Al-phaq to support the Erstallius, and the large flotilla is headed here, they will overtake our holding without a fight. We cannot leave Al-phaq unprotected.”

Shanna turned back to the map and examined the positions of the different holdings.

GSW-183—Ni’apinu—Erstallius colony.

“The distance between Anders Prime and Ni’apinu is sixteen-point-zero-seven parsecs on a direct route, the travel time would take nine-point-six standard days at standard cruise speed.”

Al-phaq—Guild stronghold.

"The distance between Anders Prime and Al-phaq is fifteen-point-forty-four parsecs. On a direct route, the travel time would take nine-point-three standard days at standard cruise speed."

"Yes," Pardee said. "We're a tad closer."

"That's about ten hours closer to the origin point of that drone, and that's based on a direct route. Based on your estimated course for the drone, we might be an entire day closer."

"Closer to the drone, not the flotilla. We do not know their course. I assume the flotilla left before the drone. They could have already reached GSW-183."

Shanna peered into the holomap again. She gripped the railing that surrounded the plotting pedestal and let her hips rest against the cold metal. "We would still be a deterrent."

"To what?" Pardee quipped. "At optimum speed, travel time to GSW-183 from Al-phaq is over three standard days. If they have been attacked, the battle will be finished before we get there."

"So we abandon them?"

"We will guard Al-phaq. That is our primary mission, by Wolfram's decree. If the Erstallius have fallen, that would also mean the Aku have fallen, and I doubt that scenario is possible. The myth of Aku prowess may be overblown, but they defeated clan Tuma with their ancient ships, and they scuttled the ships Polinda left in orbit. Clan Erstallius is not alone."

"The odds will be better for the Erstallius, even if we arrive late. Our arrival will be a surprise to their enemies."

"I understand," Pardee admitted, "but the mandate—"

"What if we're the target? What if the Erstallius recognize the threat and refuse to come to our aid? Where is the honor in our partnership?"

Pardee looked at the holomap. The calculated path for the drone told him the coalition forces at Anders Prime hoped contact with the Guild was possible. That hope was based on previous communication he had authored to prepare Clan Erstallius for the Guild's return. But Wolfram's mandate was still in force. "I can't leave Al-phaq unprotected."

"You're a hypocrite," Shanna stated with disgust. "Arlud helped remove those ungrateful Cormeds off your freighter. He gave me shelter, repaired our shuttle, and gave you the three Cormed officers who took part in the uprising to commandeer your ship."

Pardee flinched at that last revelation. "You knew about the three prisoners?"

"I did. How could I not? Do you think me an idiot?"

"Never."

"Arlud went out of his way—ignored Alliance protocol—to help us. And now you stand here and refuse to help him based on a mandate given by my father ten days ago, sixteen parsecs from here."

Pardee paused for a few heartbeats to consider Shanna's logic. "Wolfram's mandate was voiced under different circumstances," he agreed, "but still took into account hostilities at Al-phaq. That's why we came armed with two dreadnoughts leading the way." He leaned toward Shanna to add weight to his words. "Clan Erstallius is honorable. They have earned our friendship. But our first loyalty is to the Guild. I cannot abandon Al-phaq."

Shanna slapped Pardee's left cheek.

The captain turned his head with the strike—the sting burned for a few seconds, but the inner pain from Shanna's disrespect lingered. He straightened his posture and glared back at the raven-haired beauty. Her action was mutiny, by all Guild standards. He had the right to have her flogged and vented, but she was Wolfram's daughter and that kept him from striking back. "Would you feel the same if Clan Bree was under siege?"

"What?"

"It's known how you pine for that Arlud fellow—everyone at the landing field saw you kiss him the day we left."

"How dare you!"

Pardee caught Shanna's wrist as she tried to strike him again. "Calm yourself, lady. It's no secret, and no one thinks less of you for it."

Shanna yanked her arm free.

"You're letting your feelings override your logic," Pardee said.

"So it's logical to ignore a friend in need? I did not realize that was the Guild way."

"We must always choose the better course. Protecting Al-phaq is the better course."

"My father will hear about this."

"Yes, he will," Pardee intoned. "Mister Cordova, escort Miss Sy to her quarters."

Ross Cordova unfolded from his security station and gestured for Shanna to leave the C.I.C.

Shanna flicked a disdainful glance at the old marine and stood defiant. "You may aid an Erstallius defeat!"

"If you won't go peacefully, I'll have Cordova drag you to your cabin by your hair."

Shanna sensed the sincerity in Pardee's statement. By striking Pardee, she had rejected his authority in front of his crew. She was now in a place where there was no safe exit if she continued to oppose him. She forced back her anger and strode from the C.I.C. with Cordova pressing close behind her.

Pardee returned his attention to the holomap. He zoomed out the view to include Anders Prime and GSW-183, then fingered the control panel and GSW-34 was highlighted next to Anders Prime. He selected the map's measuring tools and saw GSW-34 was only a tenth of a parsec more distant to GSW-183 than Anders Prime. *Not enough to make a difference,* he thought. Since the flotilla had not appeared near Al-phaq, it was most likely headed to GSW-183, and he imagined a battle that would press Clan Erstallius to their limit. He turned to his navigator. "Plot a course to GSW-183."

"Aye, sir."

Pardee flipped the talk switch on the plotting pedestal's communication panel. "Attention all ships, this is Pardee. Battle Group One, prepare to leave orbit. I am sending your course via a secure link. Battle Group Two, defensive scenario Alpha One. Engage."

Shanna reached her cabin as Pardee's voice sounded from the ship's intercom: "Battle Stations, Battle Stations. All personnel report to Battle Stations."

Klaxons blared the emergency siren.

"Are we being attacked?" Shanna wondered. She turned and faced Cordova. "What should I do?"

"Stay in your cabin."

"But I want to help."

Cordova checked his compad. "Sometimes a slap in the face is enough to turn a man's opinion. Half the armada is leaving for GSW-183. The other half is moving to defensive positions around Al-phaq."

"I knew he would come to his senses."

"You're lucky he's a sensible man, but don't press him again. You may be Wolfram's daughter, but this is Pardee's ship, and he's in charge of the armada. Stay in your cabin and don't come out until you're called, or you may find yourself left on Al-phaq. We are heading for battle. Pardee will not tolerate any more insubordination."

Shanna accepted Cordova's advice with a nod and retreated to her cabin.

BEV COLLI: CONNECTION

Bev floated in the white, surrounded by Rhysu. Her mind was in her private space, and she bounced among the energy spheres of her captors.

Yes, that's it, she thought. *My captors.*

She had asked multiple times—too many to remember—but the Rhysu had never explained why she was still imprisoned in the white.

Kidnappers are not obligated to explain.

She had resisted asking about the Alliance frigates. She assumed they were the Sabballi ships Arlud had told her about. Their existence here with the Rhysu was a mystery that needed an answer, and she wondered if knowing that truth might threaten her existence here.

"The Sabballi frigates just disappeared," Arlud had said. "That happened while the Alliance forces were on their way to confront the Guild stronghold on Al-phaq."

When she learned about the missing frigates, her mind was centered on her own problems. She now wished she had asked Arlud more questions. *I might have learned something to help me understand why the frigates are here. The crews must be prisoners like me. If they're still alive.*

Since her two attempts to escape the white prison, she had kept her thoughts private even while focusing on things that had previously pulled her back to full connection with the Rhysu. She wondered why this was now possible and surmised two potential reasons: She had either become adept enough to evade Rhysu awareness, or the Rhysu had become bored with her mental meanderings and ignored her.

A perfect opportunity.

She had seen the Alliance frigates from a substantial distance—two vessels entangled within the rippling tendrils of the cyan energy sea outside her white prison. If the crew were still alive, she might detect them long enough to determine their condition. She focused her mind on the ships and found herself floating next to an energy-scarred hull but could not penetrate the metal plating to peer inside.

She pulled her mind away from the ships and focused on her own energy sphere. She was still in her private space. She had not disturbed the Rhysu.

With renewed confidence, she tried to penetrate the hull again.

The black metal was a solid barrier she could not breach.

Her mind snapped back to her energy sphere, and she relaxed.

They must be empty.

The thing that had pulled her to Arlud, and to her parents, had been their consciousness.

An active mind allows connection. Where there's a mind, there are thoughts, where there are thoughts, there is energy, where there is energy, there can be a connection. There is no energy in those ships, just solid matter.

The gravity furnace in each ship was dead. The crews in the ships were also dead or taken somewhere else.

That must be the reason I can't latch on and peer inside.

And maybe that was why the Rhysu ignored her effort. They knew she would find nothing.

She forced back the urge to scream her anger and focused instead on the Shoku. The Rhysu forbid her to connect with the hated rebels, but now was as good a time as any to make another attempt. She relaxed and focused on the memory of her approach to Simbic Ur and the disintegration of the cargo shuttle, then the electric sting of the Shoku's grip as they held her in their plasmatic cage.

The Rhysu are the enemy.

Bev's memory of the verbal warning was submerged by an influx of images—mental scenes of blazing cyan fire flowed into glaring white heat that revealed the charred hull of a frigate. The close-up view of the destroyed human spacecraft was joined by images of burnt bodies adrift in space. This recollection was not coming from her own memories. These scenes were new, and deep within her she sensed the pain that came with each scene of destruction, and the anger that lingered once the scenes ended.

That memory is from the Shoku.

She sensed their presence behind the emotion. The same feeling she had when they connected with her before the cargo transport was ripped apart.

Bev turned around and expected to see a glowing sphere pressing behind her, but only the dimmed spheres of the Rhysu bumped against her.

The Rhysu are the enemy.

Bev twirled in her energy sphere—the lusterless Rhysu were clustered around her. Somehow the Shoku bypassed the Rhysu blockade and connected with her. And she wondered: *If the Rhysu are blocking me from reaching out, how can the Shoku contact me?*

The Shoku presence—a tingle on the edge of her awareness—gave Bev hope that one day she could break through the Rhysu blockade. *I must learn how they did it,* she thought. *I must press them for answers.* She focused again on her connection with the Shoku and dove into a mental query to impress upon them her need for more precise communication.

The Rhysu spheres flared brilliant cyan, and the Shoku were gone.

Bev screamed as a searing jolt pierced her body and caused her energy sphere to flicker and dim.

The violent shock forced Bev's mind to dive inward, and everything around her faded into a gray fog.

The Shoku are the enemy.

That thought burst into Bev's mind as she regained awareness of the Rhysu spheres pressing against her. Their brilliant blue tendrils of energy stabbed at her dim sphere and sent electric daggers into her body.

"Stop it!"

The stabbing tendrils stopped.

"You must not contact the Shoku," the Rhysu said.

"They contacted me."

"You contacted them."

Bev stifled a belligerent response—although the Shoku started the contact, she had reached out to them. "They contacted me first."

The Rhysu spheres retreated enough to give Bev space to move without restriction. "When will you heed our warning?"

"When you convince me I should."

"You have much to learn."

"How can I learn when you won't tell me what I need to know?"

"You have not been listening!"

That hard statement was like a slap in the face. It forced Bev to analyze her attitude toward the Rhysu. Fueled by anger, she had rejected every attempt the Rhysu had made to help her adapt. Even her gratitude for being allowed to return to Arlud and her parents had been buried beneath resentment. "I know I haven't been cooperative. Can you blame me?"

"Yes, we blame you."

That mater-of-fact Rhysu admission stung Bev deeper than the Rhysu tendrils. "I'm sorry. I know it's my fault. There's just so much to take in."

"You have much to learn."

"As you keep telling me," Bev protested. The brilliant cyan spheres of the Rhysu floated around her—a gentle motion that calmed her. She transferred her visual memory of the dead frigates to the Rhysu and framed the scene with the question, "Why are the Alliance ships here?"

"They are relics of a mistake."

"What mistake?"

"They were taken during the escape."

"The Shoku escape?"

"Yes, when the Shoku fled from the hard place."

Bev recalled the moment on Alpha Cephei Four when she lay on the hilltop and two Polinda frigates flew overhead and disappeared in a blinding flash of light. *They're Polinda, not Sabballi!* "Why did you attack them?"

"We did not attack them, we retrieved them."

"Why?"

"We were drawn to their energy and assumed they were the Shoku."

"How could you make a mistake like that?"

"We were unfamiliar, we did not recognize. We only saw the energy, not the objects. We were distracted, and the Shoku escaped."

"What happened to the crew?"

"We did not understand. We did not prepare them like we prepared you. Flesh and blood cannot exist here."

Bev let that revelation roll around in her mind, and the truth became clearer. The rush to retrieve the Shoku thrust the Rhysu into her universe so quickly they had no time to prepare for what awaited them. They reacted from instinct alone, and hundreds of people died.

"I wondered why there was no debris cloud left in orbit," Bev said. "Do you know why the other ships heading to Al-phaq disappeared?"

"Energy. We followed the Shoku until the cold and darkness made us turn back. We could sense their presence but could not navigate your space without a greater loss of energy. Their journey would have depleted them if they had not found a way to recharge themselves."

"The Shoku attacked the other ships for energy—just as Arlud thought."

"Yes."

"Why did one ship survive?"

The Rhysu contemplated what they could discern from the Shoku and replied: "They transferred everything into energy. In their starving frenzy, they did not consider what they were doing, or to whom. Only later, when their hunger was under control, did they leave the source of their feeding intact."

"People still died."

"Yes," the Rhysu admitted. "Shoku also died."

Bev had never considered Shoku deaths. "If the human universe is so deadly to you, why did you open the portal on Arrilen Po?"

"Knowledge."

"Knowledge of what?"

"Our place is parallel to yours," the Rhysu said, "within what you call a different spatial dimension. We detected disruptions in our energy streams that could not be explained from local changes. The anomalies create harmful fluctuations that damage many Rhysu. We opened the portal to investigate the cause."

"What's the cause?"

"Your mode of travel."

"Mode of travel?"

"How you move from one hard place to another hard place. We did not suspect intelligence behind the anomalies until we found the dying woman."

"You almost killed her. You killed the man with her. You killed twenty-three other people on that planet."

"Your mode of travel creates harmful fluctuations," the Rhysu said. "Our presence created harmful fluctuations on the hard place where we found the dying woman."

"So Rhysu and humans can't exist together," Bev said. "You changed me so I wouldn't die, and you could continue to learn."

"Yes. We must learn."

"What's the purpose?"

"To stop the harmful fluctuations."

"Without Compression Drive, the colonies will be isolated. Communication between most holdings will stop. Trade routes will cease to exist. Human civilization will fracture."

"No. Humans will continue on the hard places."

"Yes, but people will be confined to whatever planet they're on when the harmful fluctuations stop. That will cause major disruption, especially for people on colonies that depend on trade with other holdings. More people will die."

"We have learned that your people began on one hard place, separate, alone. You breached confinement and survived in the dark outside that should have killed you. Your need to explore took you to harmful places, and you still survived. You will survive much easier if you stay on your hard places."

"Some will survive. Some will not. Not all hard places are the same."

"The fluctuations must stop."

"How do you plan on stopping them?"

"We must learn. You will help us learn."

Bev retreated into her private space and pondered what the Rhysu wanted to do. Humans had two-thousand years of history in the void, and the hyperspace routes were the arteries that kept civilization moving. The Rhysu wanted to bleed those arteries dry. *No way*, she thought. She twirled around and glared at the Rhysu spheres as she emerged from her private space. "You're the enemy," she said. "You won't need to defeat the clans in battle. All you'll need to do is block their Compression Drive. If you do that, human civilization will be planet-bound again. Planet-bound forever. I will never help you do that."

"We must stop the harmful fluctuations."

Behind the Rhysu determination, Bev sensed something else—something the Rhysu were unwilling to admit. She sensed it in the tone, heard it in the cadence of their words, saw it in the flicker of their mental images. Pressing them about it would lead nowhere—their power was too great to force them to reveal what they hid—but sensing their lack of complete truthfulness strengthened her resolve to resist them. "You tell a wonderful story, but there's more you're not telling me. If a story is truthful, every piece fits together with no gaps. There are too many gaps in your story."

"Gaps?"

"You're keeping something from me. Is it the Shoku?"

"We cannot permit the harmful fluctuations to continue."

"If you stop humans from traveling between their holdings, you might strand thousands of people in the void, condemning them to death."

"We will do our best to avoid that."

"How?"

"We will find a way."

"The humans will not permit the loss of Compression Drive. They will find a way to continue interstellar travel."

"Then we will find another way to stop them. The harmful fluctuations must stop."

"By causing harmful fluctuations for the humans?"

The Rhysu fell silent and backed away from Bev, creating a gap between them that was double her sphere's diameter. The result was an immediate break in her connection with the Rhysu. She revolved in her sphere and sensed nothing from her captors. *They are definitely keeping something from me.*

For the first time since Bev woke in the white, fear stifled her thoughts.

And the Rhysu spheres flared brilliant cyan.

CLAN ERSTALLIUS: RUPTURE

Arlud followed Jegen-Major Kurt Sari out of the elevator into the windowed command center on the tenth floor of the central tower. The operations personnel were busy at their stations monitoring shuttles and orbiting spacecraft, including the Erstallius salvage vessels that continued to clean the debris clouds from the battle with Clan Polinda. "How recent is the info?"

"Normal TAC delay from that distance is four minutes," Sari said. He led Arlud to the holomap that displayed five diamond-shaped icons. "They crossed the system boundary thirty minutes ago."

Arlud examined the holomap—the markers where fifty-million kilometers from the Erstallius command station orbiting the blue gas giant, which put them close to one-billion eighty million kilometers from Ni'apinu, on the opposite side of the system from the primary sun's companion star. "You've confirmed their identity?"

Sari flicked a switch on the holomap console and replayed the first incoming transmission:

TAC Comm 2
Sender: Dejoria Defense Force, D-737
Target: Erstallius Command, GSW183
Priority: Alert 1
Message begin:
"This is destroyer seven-three-seven from the D.D.F. Alpha-nine-four-zero-Delta. Requesting to rendezvous with your command station for transfer to the Erstallius Fleet, by permission of Jhared Dejoria, High Regent."
—Message end

"They are not D.D.F. ships," Sari said. "The command code is wrong, and the ship ident markers are not current."

"Who are they?"

"We'll discover that after we disable them. We've got twelve cruisers bearing down on them now. We'll have them under fire before they get within forty-million kilometers of the command station."

"They're all destroyers?"

"Yes. Class 5."

Arlud relaxed and activated the course plots that identified the Erstallius cruisers sent to confront the intruders. The cruisers were stealth ships and would not be detected until they fired upon the intruders. "We'll have them surrounded," he noticed. "Good. Interrogate all survivors."

"All?"

"Yes," Arlud said in a flat tone. "Even the cooks."

Sari nodded. "Yes, sir."

One of the operations personnel called out: "Jegen-Major, more ships in sector three!"

Arlud turned toward the voice and saw eight concentric circles pulsing on a holoscreen across the room.

Sari changed the view on his holoscreen to display the other incoming ships and noticed five Aku ships were heading toward the eight intruders. "They dropped out of hyperspace inside the orbit of our third moon. Risky move."

"Got them past our outer defenses," Arlud said. "This is a—"

The building shook from the concussion of a plasma burst that hit the tarmac and filled the east-facing windows with the rebounding fire.

Sari hit the emergency switch on his console that opened evac tubes to either side of the main elevator and triggered the warning sirens. "Everyone into the bunker. Now!" He pushed Arlud back into the elevator, held the door open from inside for three other clanmen, then pulled the emergency decent lever that closed the doors and dropped the lift.

Arlud's feet left the floor as the lift fell and he floated with the clanmen in the grip of activated GPG's that kept them in the air and protected them as the elevator landed in the basement with a hard jolt.

Sari flipped the emergency switch to the off position. The GPG's died and the elevator doors opened.

Arlud's feet hit the floor, and he rushed into the dark bunker. He could hear rumbling above as plasma bursts continued to pound the field.

Holoscreens came to life as the clanmen who had used the evac tubes activated their stations.

Gustav Eahuda stepped through a hatchway from another room in the basement complex and approached Arlud. "You OK?"

"Fine," Arlud said. "Everyone make it to the bunker?"

"No. We lost the field crew, the maintenance personnel in the main hangar, and eleven specialists in the tower."

Arlud turned to face the console where Jegen-Major Sari stood. The holoscreen displayed the only active data feed and showed eighteen enemy ships in orbit above them. "Are we not responding?"

"The Aku are moving into position now," Sari said.

The rumbling above them stopped.

Arlud faced Eahuda. "Send out a recon drone."

Eahuda nodded and left through the hatchway.

"A drone attack, propelled by compression drive," Sari muttered.

Arlud overheard Sari's comment. "Compression drive plasma bursts?"

"Yes. Precision deployment and return to normal space about a meter above the field."

Arlud pulled a chair away from an empty console and sat. He pondered the new tactics and realized he and his clanmen had underestimated their enemy. "They split our forces by inventing the threat against Anders Prime. That opened holes in our defenses."

"Yes, it did," Sari admitted, "but even with our original strength intact, we wouldn't have been able to stop the drone assault."

Another holoscreen came to life and displayed images from the recon drone on the surface. The main hangar and service buildings were piles of charred rubble. The central tower was a blackened, jagged remnant, only three stories tall.

Arlud turned back to the console next to Sari and watched the plot schematic of six Aku ships engaging the eighteen enemy ships. "Who are they?"

Sari faced Arlud. "Vestlock and Emlito."

"What's happening with the five destroyers?"

"Our link to the outer system has been lost. We can only access data from close orbit."

Arlud slumped in the chair. Once again, he was cut off from his clanmen in orbit. *We can't stay here,* he thought.

Another holoscreen displayed four ground survey transmissions that covered the terrain around the landing field. The clanman at the console focused the south-facing camera to a ridge in the Umelk mountains. "We have drop ships landing," he said.

Arlud moved to the ground survey console and watched three small troop ships drop out of sight behind the ridge. "That's at least thirty troops."

Sari stood next to Arlud. "If they have hover-pods, they'll be here in about twenty minutes."

"We need to leave the bunker," Arlud said.

Sari faced Arlud. "This is the safest place right now."

"If they place a siege on us—"

"That won't happen," Sari insisted. "They'd only do that if they meant to capture us. Based on the first assault, they have no intention of doing that. We need to see if more troops will be deployed. Once we know their intentions, we'll have a clearer picture of how to retreat. I don't want us going above ground too soon and running into another troop drop or drone strike. From their perspective, we're all dead. Let's keep them believing that as long as we can."

Arlud pondered his commander's logic. This bunker was built to hide the occupants from detection. The enemy would come to examine the results of their assault, which meant the troop count would be limited to a recon unit. If they detected survivors above ground, they'd either fire another drone assault or send in more troops, and that choice would depend on what was happening in orbit.

"OK," Arlud said. "I trust your judgment, Jegen-Major. Let's hope the fight in orbit is to our advantage."

PETRA SITLYN: BRIGADE

The sipá cub bounded across the grassy paddock a few paces behind Petra. He was two years old and stood one meter at his shoulders. This was his second training period with his novice instructor, and he enjoyed loping behind her as she jogged around the paddock.

Petra looked back at the energetic cub. "Come on Serra, keep up!" She started each training session with a quick two-lap jog around the training pen—it was good exercise and used enough energy to help calm him so he would focus on his training tasks without too much resistance. He was the first cub to be trained by an off-worlder using Englo'ni instead of Akün. He would be Petra's sole project for one year.

Outside the paddock, beyond the exterior fence, Aluk sat on his haunches and watched Petra and Serra jog. He had come to this same place every morning and waited for Petra to exit the fence and bring him a basket of fruit.

At the first turn during their second lap, Petra stopped and looked upward as a high-pitched whine cut through the clouds from the southwest with spiral turbulence that dissipated as the whine shifted to a low-pitched roar north of the camp. "What was that?"

Serra hugged Petra's leg and gnawed playfully at her boot.

Petra tapped the cub's head. "Stop!"

Serra released his grip and bounded away along the fence line.

Aluk stood on his hind legs and roared.

Petra glanced over at Aluk—he was looking northward. She turned to follow his gaze and noticed a patch of clouds glowing red. *The same glow I saw when Polinda attacked,* she thought, *and it's above the landing field!* She jogged toward the paddock gate. "Serra, come!"

The cub ran to Petra and rubbed against her leg as she stopped at the gate.

A bright flash forced Petra's attention to the sky.

Above the clouds, the expanding shock front from an explosion in high orbit formed a fiery sphere that filled the southwest sky.

"Oh my!"

Another explosion flashed to the southeast over the Dekeg foothills.

Then another burst erupted farther to the east, above the Wassûa Caphâga.

Petra flipped the gate latch and ran for the breeding stalls.

Serra bounded through the open gateway and rushed after Petra.

Aluk sat in the soft grass with his eyes focused on the glowing debris blooms expanding in the sky.

Petra asked, "What are we supposed to do!?"

Tryol turned from the trainers who had gathered in the main office to face Petra standing in the doorway with a sipá cub nuzzling her legs. "You should know that more than any of us." He flicked a hand signal, and a trainer led the cub away from the doorway.

Petra stepped into the room. "Why should I know that?"

"It is your enemies who are attacking."

Three sonic booms rattled the building.

Petra rushed out the doorway into the clearing between the buildings and looked up.

Three troop transports dropped deeper into the atmosphere as they sped north across the valley and disappeared into the clouds above the Umelk range. The red glow was gone in the north and the debris blooms Petra had seen from the paddock had faded, but a new explosion was expanding overhead.

Tryol stepped off the porch and dropped his gaze to Petra. "A ciâfey squadron will be here soon. They can take you to Gráal in the Highlands, where you can join the Fifth Brigade. The Fifth Brigade can take you to your outpost."

Petra was surprised by the offer and shifted her gaze back to the northern sky where the red glow had been. *He knows my loyalty to Clan Erstallius will force me into the battle,* she thought. "Thank you, but why can't the ciâfey take me to the outpost?"

"They will lead a counter-strike against the troops in the ships we saw descend—having you as a passenger will get in the way of that."

That's true, Petra thought. The outpost had been hit from orbit, so the aerial fight would focus on the troop transports.

"The brigade will advance to the field from Khemyak Gorge," Tryol said. "An easier climb and a more tactful approach. You will be in less danger with the brigade."

Petra was impressed with how fast the Aku had devised a counterstrike, then realized they had planned their campaigns when Clan Erstallius began building the landing field. And the obvious truth about these Aku men burst into the forefront of her mind—they were all soldiers, trained and willing to protect their land even if not part of the regular militia. "I'm not afraid of a fight."

"I believe you," Tryol said. "It is not my wish to put you in harm's way. I hope to keep you safe. But I will not stop you from defending your regent. The Fifth Brigade will take you to your outpost."

"Aysillé," Petra responded, using the formal Akün expression of gratitude.

"Thank me when you return. You may not thank me once you are there."

Petra crouched behind a large-trunk evergreen near the edge of the tree line surrounding the Erstallius outpost. She wore a light armor vest over her civilian clothes and the wide-brimmed hat of the Aku militia. The long-barreled rifle she held was heavy and unfamiliar. She had been given the clothing and weapon because of her military training—Aku women could not touch a rifle—no Aku women were here prepared for battle. That understanding came to the forefront of her mind and she thought: *Despite the differences between us, the Aku have allowed me, a woman, to attend this assault, but only because my Clan is under attack, and I was trained to be a soldier.*

That reality also told her she would never be accepted into Aku society. She would always be viewed as an off-worlder, no matter how long she stayed here, no matter if her marriage to Salus was approved, no matter that she was Dágul Jásah.

The Aku Fifth Brigade was spread out to her right and left, waiting for the signal to advance. Sixty meters away, beyond the ground cleared of trees, the crumbled buildings and crater-strewn landing field displayed no sign of activity. The perimeter fence was still standing but had buckled outward along the northern strip next to the ruins of the central tower complex.

From the concussion, Petra thought, and she wondered if anyone could have survived the assault. She looked up at the sky. Explosion blooms were still erupting in orbit from horizon to horizon. *A massive battle up there!*

In the forest-covered hills of the Umelk range south of the outpost, three separate columns of black smoke billowed upward, marking the site where the ciâfey squadron engaged the troop transports. The sky was clear of flyers, which meant the battle there was finished.

A man's voice sounded from the receiver in Petra's left ear: "Dhon, anwâlu!"

To her right, a line of thirty Aku soldiers crept out of the forest and rushed across the cleared ground toward the outpost. She had been ordered to stay with the second platoon and would advance once the first platoon called the all-clear. She watched the soldiers advance one by one through the open main gate, scramble over the rubble from the shattered service buildings, and disappear behind the ruins of the command tower.

A few minutes later, another voice sounded in Petra's left ear: "Suli, fu'ani!"

She stood with the other soldiers assigned to the second platoon and adjusted her grip on the magar rifle.

Another command in Petra's left ear: "Badé!"

She jogged across the cleared ground with the second platoon, then slowed her pace to watch a large explosion bloom expand above her. The pink and orange debris wave covered one quarter of the sky in an eye-blink.

"Jiwu!"

Petra jerked at that command from a nearby Aku soldier. *I am moving*, she thought, and shifted her gaze toward the crumbled Erstallius outpost.

A fireball flashed about five meters above the landing field, and the shock front from the plasma burst pushed Petra backward through the air. She hit the low-hanging branches of an evergreen and dropped unconscious into the thick underbrush.

Searing pain shot through Petra's rib cage—the first sensation she felt after being hit by the shock wave. Her head was spinning, and her vision was blurry.

"Is she alive?"

The voice was male—a quiet tenor—and pulled Petra's attention toward her feet, where she saw a gray figure standing above her. She squinted her eyes to improve focus and saw the gray was military armor with the chest insignia of Clan Emlito.

"Yeah, she's alive," another voice said. "She opened her eyes. I'll close them."

A second figure moved into Petra's blurred vision and aimed the weapon in his hand toward her head.

Petra rolled to her right to reach through the grass for her rifle, but the pain in her ribs halted the action.

"Stay still," the man said, "you'll just—"

The impact of a projectile pushed the Emlito clanman back a step with a thud as it tore a six-centimeter-wide hole in his chest armor. He fell into the tall grass and disappeared from Petra's vision.

The other clanman pivoted toward his fallen comrade as the sweeping claws of a sipá came from behind him, ripped into his armor, and flung him away from Petra.

The din of small arms fire erupted around Petra, and she heard multiple roars from the sipá cavalry. She looked up—a squadron of ciâfey soared toward the outpost with magar cannons booming. She raised her head to peer beyond the surrounding grass and saw the flattened rubble at the outpost, swarming Aku soldiers and sipá cavalry press back a retreating line of Emlito ground troops, and ciâfey blasting the forest south of the outpost with their cannons.

Then two Aku soldiers were on their knees next to her.

"Luán nouy!" one of the men commanded.

Petra dropped her head, and the other man secured her neck in a brace that expanded into a back brace with handholds so they could lift her. "What's happening?"

One soldier bent close to Petra's face. "Oufu ruáher ilé igifu."

We are getting you out of here.

The two men lifted Petra off the ground and retreated deeper into the forest.

By the time Petra was placed on the ground in the boulder field near the sloping ground that led back to Khemyak Gorge, the clamor from the counter-strike against the Emlito clanmen had become louder.

One of the Aku soldiers who had carried her said, "Ilés pucágu iufu," then he rushed back into the trees after his comrade.

You'll be safe here.

Petra blinked, and her vision cleared. She released the neck brace and glanced around—wounded Aku men reclined around her, some with bandaged heads, others with bandaged legs, some with no apparent injury, and a few covered by blood-stained blankets. *This is our triage,* she thought, and she noticed two physicians moving from one body to another, assessing the injuries. *Most battles between the clans have no wounded,* she recalled. *The weapons are too deadly. If you're hit, you're dead.* She assessed her own situation—her ribs ached, but she felt no swelling or bleeding. She pushed up through the pain to a sitting position.

Someone called: "Iue! Sai'palk!"

Petra glanced toward the voice—a doctor. She translated to herself: *Hey! Lie back!* "Eája gêyu," she replied. *I'm fine.*

"Ous jêyu ahiah!" *I will determine that!*

Petra smirked. *No,* she thought, *I'll determine that!* She leaned sideways, used a hand for support, and prepared to stand.

Three booms shook the trees surrounding the outpost and black smoke billowed into the sky while an expanding wall of flame inside the forest ignited the underbrush.

Aku men fled from the forest and ran across the boulder field toward Khemyak Gorge.

Petra stood as two Emlito assault fighters screeched through the sky above her and banked northward. *They're turning to hit the outpost again.*

The triage physicians ordered two withdrawing soldiers to help evacuate the wounded.

A retreating Aku soldier glanced at Petra. "Fey!"

Petra nodded to the soldier's command to flee as he ran past her, and she looked around the triage site for a weapon.

Two explosions boomed and the two Emlito fighters cartwheeled out of control to the northeast, spewing flames and smoke. They fell into the forest and the smoke from their wreckage rose in black billows as the sound waves from the impacts hit Petra's ears. *About two kilometers away,* she thought. *Who hit them?*

Her query was answered as three triangular assault ships with black hull plating dropped below the clouds above her and flew toward the outpost. She spun to watch the black triangles as they moved over the burning trees and saw five more ships emerge from the clouds.

The fleeing Aku men paused their retreat, and a doctor approached Petra. "Oula afuahi?"

Petra searched the hull of the nearest ship. "Yâlah léfa," she said. *They're not ours.* "They have no markings."

"Oula les'ahupu?"

"Who could they be? Pirates."

NI'APINU: REINFORCED

Petra walked on ash-covered ground between charred trees, with a long-barreled rifle slung over her shoulder. She followed a line of Aku soldiers advancing toward the cleared ground around the Erstallius outpost. Fire suppression drones had dowsed the flames to create a path to the outpost and continued to attack the fire flickering among the trees on either side of the path. *The pirates saved us,* she thought. *Clan Emlito would have killed everyone.*

As the soldiers advanced closer to the clearing, Petra could see burned bodies of Aku men and sipá scattered between the forest and the outpost. To her left, a large Guild shuttle rested on the cleared ground next to the outpost's main entrance. To her right, a smaller executive shuttle sat in the clearing just beyond the burned ground. Guildmen scrambled over the rubble inside the fence line.

They're searching for survivors.

The stench from the dead caused Petra to cover her nose and mouth with her hand as she trudged across the clearing behind the soldiers. A few paces into the burned ground, she noticed the executive shuttle drop her rear exit ramp. Three guildmen walked down the ramp. Two wore helmets with breathing filters, heavy armor, and carried magar rifles. The third person wore light armor and the helmet with a breathing filter but carried no weapon.

That's a woman, Petra thought, recognizing the more graceful gait beneath the lighter armor.

The Aku soldiers stopped on the ash-covered ground next to the buckled fence.

Petra watched the Aku commander greet the leading guildman with a handshake. The language barrier would hinder further communication, so she stepped out of the line. "I'm Petra Sitlyn," she said, "Segen with the Erstallius Eighth Corps."

The armored woman turned her head. "Petra!" she exclaimed, then rushed forward and wrapped the Erstallius engineer in a tight embrace. "I'm so glad you're alive!"

Petra did not recognize the voice behind the breathing filter. She gripped the woman's armor shoulder pads and pushed away from the hug. "Who—?"

The woman pulled her breathing filter away from her face. "It's me, Shanna!"

"Oh, my!" Petra returned Shanna's embrace. "I didn't expect to see you!"

Shanna whispered: "We came as soon as we could."

Petra stepped back to look at Shanna face-to-face. "What are you doing here? Why aren't you with your family?"

"My father sent a convoy to resettle Al-phaq. We received a comm-drone message that warned of this attack. Where's Arlud? Is he safe?"

"I'm not sure," Petra admitted. She faced the shattered buildings. "The last report said he was here."

One of the armored guildmen stepped toward Petra and pulled aside his breathing filter. "So, it's Segen now. Congratulations!"

"Ross Cordova," Petra replied. "Good to see you." She reached out and shook the guildman's gloved hand.

The other guildman extended his hand to Petra. "Donté Cegla," he said. "I'm glad you're well, Segen Sitlyn."

Petra smiled at Cegla and shook his hand. "I never expected to see any of you again." The memory of her first meeting with these guildmen whirled in Petra's mind—they stood huddled against the rain on the tarmac outside their crippled shuttle, their clothing stained with blood. "You saved us."

Shanna flashed a brief smile. "Just returning the favor."

Once the land around the outpost was declared free of enemy combatants, a drone designed for ground-penetrating surveys searched the rubble for survivors. Thirty Aku soldiers joined the ten guildmen under Shanna Sy's command. They sifted through the rubble by hand while two GPG-powered work pods used their articulated claws to move the larger chunks of debris.

Petra stood near the edge of the five-meter-thick layer of debris on the west side of the tower complex. "There are two basement exits," she said. "One ten meters east of the service buildings, and one here beneath this pile of rubble."

Shanna stood with her armored guards a few paces from Petra. She examined the data from the survey drone on her holopad. "Then we'll focus on clearing those two areas. We can sift for the dead after we've freed the living."

As the two work pods cleared the rubble, Petra watched the data graphic on Shanna's holopad. "The drone sensors won't penetrate the basement. It was designed to prevent detection, but you can see the squared shape of the foundation."

Shanna examined the live display. "How many people are down there?"

"That depends on how quickly they could evacuate. The shock front and heat bloom from an average-size plasma burst will vaporize anyone within twenty-meters of the ignition point—without proper fortification. As you can see," she gestured to the collapsed tower complex and hangers, "proper fortification is impossible when you use alsteel."

Shanna felt her eyes swell with tears. "We should have come here first."

"First?"

Shanna wiped her eyes. "We went straight to Al-phaq. We should have come here first."

"Then you'd have been caught in the attack."

"Yes," Shanna admitted, "but we may have been able to prevent this."

"Maybe," Petra said, and she remembered the earlier attack by Clan Polinda. "We abandoned this place once to prevent this. The outpost survived, but we still lost hundreds of clanmen. Revenge survived Polinda's defeat. This will continue until all his allies are neutered."

"I would assume Polinda's allies feel the same about our coalition," Shanna mused. "Is there no other way to end this?"

"No. And I fear the Aku may withdraw their support. We promised to protect them. We promised to prevent this."

"Pardee told me no one can avoid this conflict. The Aku would be worse off without you—without us."

"If we hadn't come here, Ni'apinu wouldn't have been attacked."

"It would. Knowledge of the weakened Aku defenses would have leaked to the clans eventually—that's data even the Erstallius could not keep a secret for long. Without you here, this holding would have been inundated by survey teams—even the Guild would have sent reconnaissance patrols—and the Aku would have been forced to fight once again for their freedom, but without allies."

"That's true."

"We can't let ourselves whine over what might have been. We need to focus on what to do moving forward."

Petra nodded at Shanna's advice. *She was a scared, escaped hostage when we first met,* she remembered. *A naïve young woman, removed from her insulated life on Al-phaq, who only wanted to return to the safety of her home. Now she stands here confident, in command of a Guild survey team—an armored, weaponized survey team!* "You're right," Petra said, "we need to focus."

A work pod pulled the last chunk of melted alsteel off the sealed west entrance to the basement. The rectangular duranide cover was intact—a smooth gray plate flush with the ferroconcrete used for the tarmac.

Shanna examined the entrance via the remote data feed from the survey drone. "Can you open it?"

"Not without the security key," Petra said, and she walked toward the entrance.

Shanna followed Petra. "Then how do we open it?"

Petra reached the entrance, knelt, and brushed away a layer of dust from a circular access plate. "A security key may not be necessary." She opened the round cover and pulled up a small metal handle, turned it clockwise one-half turn, then pushed it down to its seated position. "That should signal anyone inside we're at the west entrance."

"What if it doesn't work?"

"Then we'll dig."

Arlud squinted at the shaft of light that poured into the stairwell when the reconnaissance team opened the hatch to the surface. The bright glare brought with it the odor of burnt trees and the faint stench of charred bodies. Whoever had activated the all-clear alarm at the western exit was familiar with the safety protocols, so he was confidant Clan Erstallius still held the outpost. He turned to Jegen-Major Kurt Sari. "Let's get everyone to the surface ASAP."

Sari nodded and returned to the control room to begin the evacuation.

"We have the field," Gustav Eahuda said, as he stopped behind Arlud. "The recon unit reports all buildings collapsed, but the Guild and Aku forces defeated the Emlito assault."

Arlud turned to face the old Degen. "The Guild?"

"Yeah. They joined the off-world fight with a dreadnought, three frigates, and three destroyers."

Arlud glanced up the stairwell to the bright rectangular opening at the surface.

"They sent down eight heavy assault ships," Eahuda said. "That was enough to end the ground assault."

"Then we owe them another debt."

More Erstallius clanmen entered the stairwell. Arlud and Eahuda stood aside as the survivors passed them single file and ascended the long staircase. Ten minutes later, only Arlud, Eahuda, and Jegen-Major Sari remained in the basement.

Arlud made the climb last. He followed Eahuda into the sunlight and found himself surrounded by his clanmen and the Aku soldiers. He surveyed the destroyed buildings.

"Excuse me, my Regent."

Arlud whirled to face the voice. "Petra! You're an Aku soldier now?"

"They allowed me to join them. I could not stay away."

Arlud grinned and thought: *She'll always be an Erstallius.* "How—"

"Sir," Petra insisted, "the Guild representative." She turned and gestured to the three armored Guildmen who pressed through the crowd.

Shanna Sy stepped forward and removed her helmet.

Arlud gasped. "Shanna?"

Shanna's hug was brief, but firm enough to give Arlud the impression that her joy was sincere. She released her embrace and took two steps back. "I am so glad you survived!"

As Arlud stood dumbfounded by Shanna's presence, Jegen-Major Sari issued verbal orders to repair the Erstallius TAC link to their off-world assets, which sent six Erstallius clanmen back into the basement to retrieve equipment. The remaining clanmen dispersed to join the Aku and Guild search teams.

Eahuda moved next to Arlud and asked Shanna, "What's the status of our off-world forces?"

Shanna turned and took a holopad from Cordova. She fingered the pad and handed it to Eahuda.

Eahuda scanned the info and passed it to Arlud.

Arlud focused his gaze on the data stream. *This is terrible,* he thought, *but at least we prevailed with a third of our force intact.* He glanced up at Shanna. "How did our enemies fare?"

"We annihilated all who came against us."

"Because of your surprise attack," Eahuda said. "When your enemy has their back to you, the odds are always in your favor."

Shanna smiled at the old Degen. "Captain Pardee is a fine tactician."

Arlud fingered the holopad. "Are we sure Clan Emlito has been purged from the system?"

Shanna stepped forward and touched the holopad to redirect Arlud's query. "Look here."

The data stream showed the latest stats from the Guild command ship. A Clan Emlito dreadnought orbited the second planet of the system's distant second sun.

"That's their Command Center," Shanna said. "Our forces should have them surrounded in about five minutes. They will not leave the system."

"How many clans attacked us?"

"Those who attacked here were Emlito and Vestlok. The five destroyers that attacked your command center in orbit of the gas giant were from Clan Tuma."

Arlud didn't expect Tuma to be involved, but the more he considered it, the more it made sense. *They returned to reclaim their Aku slaves.* "Did any Tuma survive?"

"All destroyed."

Arlud handed the holopad back to Shanna, then turned and walked alongside the piles of rubble that had once been the central tower complex. He watched the searchers sift through the debris. Four bodies had been found and now lay in body bags along an intact stretch of tarmac near the main entrance. *This outpost is done,* he thought. He stopped and looked up at the blue sky. *Beyond this atmosphere lies the greater graveyard—the debris clouds that will define this system as a place of death for years to come. We promised the Aku peace. We brought them nothing but death.* He dropped to one knee and rested a hand on a large chunk of chard alsteel. Touching the remains of the central tower reinforced the reality of its destruction. He hung his head and closed his eyes. A tempest erupted in his mind—visions of the tumultuous events of the past few months whirled from his memory: *Farquar Polinda's siege of Wan'tei was defeated, but Bev was lost; The Polinda homeworld was captured, but my father died; Lon Pavan's strike group escorted me to Pigrell, then moved on to Anders Prime, further reducing defenses here. And the Guild ships left, further weakening the Coalition. Then our forces at Ni'apinu were divided by loyalty, and that sent half of what remained back to Baleiou.*

The path that lay before him was no longer obscured by anger and the need for revenge. *Every step we've taken has pushed us farther from where we need to be,* he thought. *I've been rushing headlong toward oblivion while believing the Coalition had the upper hand. Our enemies weakened our forces by manipulating our every move via fake reports and political subterfuge. Polinda was obvious in everything he did. His cohorts are more subtle—devious warriors whose power is not only in their military strength, but in their ability to distribute propaganda.* He raised his head to see Petra Sitlyn standing a few paces away. He saw uncertainty in her deep blue eyes as she looked down at him. "We've lost a lot, Petra, but we'll overcome this."

"Yes, sir," Petra replied, but her eyes betrayed her doubt.

Arlud stood. "I failed the Clan because the path I chose was short-sighted and twisted by revenge."

"You did not fail—we did not fail."

Arlud heard the pride in Petra's response — she helped design this outpost and had overseen the construction. He closed the space between them and held the young engineer's shoulders. "You did everything you were supposed to do. This is all on me."

"You didn't—"

Arlud stifled Petra's response with a wave of his hand. "It's on me," he insisted. "I see the correct path now—I know why I failed." He backed away from Petra and faced Jegen-Major Sari, who stood ten paces away, next to Shanna Sy and her armored guards. With the flick of a hand signal, Arlud told Sari to approach him, then he turned back toward Petra. "How's Salus?"

"Salus? I haven't seen him."

"You're still in training?"

"I am."

"Do you know if Salus fought here?"

"He's in Dol'anar."

Sari stopped a few paces away. "Yes, sir?"

"Jegen-Major," Arlud said, "once the dead are collected and buried, transfer all clanmen off-planet. We will leave the system once we've set a security plan with the Aku for the ships that will stay."

"We're evacuating?"

Arlud nodded. "Part of our fleet that survived will stay to help secure the system and train the Aku how to pilot and support the new ships coming from U'galem. The remaining clanmen will return to Baleiou."

"Yes, sir," Sari said. "We should have everyone off-planet by tomorrow afternoon."

"Good."

Sari bowed his head to Arlud, then turned and strode toward Gustav Eahuda, who stood near the basement entrance.

Arlud looked at Petra. "You can come with us."

"Thank you, sir, but I'm staying here."

"You really are committed."

"I am."

"Then I will look forward to the day I return here to attend your wedding."

Petra's smiled. "That would be wonderful, sir."

And Arlud saw a glimmer of hope overtake the doubt in Petra's eyes.

BEV COLLI: PROTECTION

The fluctuations must stop!

That thought burst into Bev's mind as she revolved in her energy sphere.

The Rhysu pressed around her, glowing brilliant and hot. Along with their intense plasma streams, the Rhysu inundated Bev with visions—a return to their earlier method of communication. As the visions of attacks on human spacecraft whirled in her mind, Bev's awareness was flooded with the harsh reality—the Shoku intent was to destroy every ship using Compression Drive. *These are the ships Arlud plotted in the Stellar Cartography room on board his flagship*, she thought, and she remembered seeing the positions of the destroyed vessels inside that dark void filled with miniature stars.

"The harmful fluctuations must stop," the Rhysu said, "but we cannot allow the Shoku to destroy an entire species."

"Wow!" Bev exclaimed. "I never sensed the Shoku wanting to do that!"

The Rhysu released their pressure against Bev, and the heat from their energy tendrils cooled to create a warm cocoon around her. "They tried to kill you."

Bev tumbled into the memory of the Shoku assault on the cargo ship speeding toward Simbic Ur.

"They have one goal," the Rhysu said. "They would kill every human to stop the fluctuations."

"The Shoku *are* the enemy."

"Yes. Your enemy."

"Why do they say the Rhysu are the enemy?"

"Because we stopped them."

"They'd kill all humans?"

"Yes."

Bev went limp, allowing herself to carom off the surrounding Rhysu as she digested this new information. "How do the harmful fluctuations injure you?"

The Rhysu pondered how to respond to Bev's question and showed her a memory of one event: a cluster of Rhysu spheres in the cyan energy sea outside her white prison. A rippling in the energy streams began nearby, rushed over the Rhysu, ripped their spheres apart, and left them splayed together—contorted energy tendrils that twitched and dimmed.

"Did they die?"

"No," the Rhysu said. "They were repaired."

"Have many Rhysu been hurt?"

"Yes. Thousands and thousands more expected."

Bev pondered that and thought of the chaos among the Clans. "That's probably because of the clan war. More ships moving through hyperspace. More ships moving in large armadas."

"The harmful fluctuations must stop."

"Why haven't I been affected by the fluctuations?"

"You are protected by the white. It dims the effect. You may feel the ripples like a light caress."

Bev recalled soft undulations. "If you can block the effect here, why not do it everywhere?"

"Can humans gather all their settlements under one shield to protect them from another dimension?"

"No."

"Neither can we. The harmful fluctuations must stop, but we must find a way without harming humans."

Bev sensed the fear and pain from the Rhysu, and she remembered the regret they expressed when they discovered the damage they had caused on Arrilen Po. "You saved Cynth Halva's life. That's the reason I believed you. I believe you now because you protected me. You changed me—which I hate—but that kept me alive."

"Yes. We changed you."

"I'd be a floating corpse or a ring of particles drifting in your energy sea."

"Yes, your human body was ripped apart."

"Is that what happened to the crew in the frigates?"

"Yes."

Bev sensed truth behind the Rhysu wish to avoid harming more humans. "What can I do to help you?"

The Rhysu spheres pressed against Bev's energy sphere. The pressure had a softer touch than their earlier encounters. She relaxed and allowed the Rhysu to pierce into her deepest thoughts. The melding minds drew her into multiple Rhysu personalities that bypassed her defenses and flooded her awareness with thousands of questions about her previous life. She let the queries flow through her and the answers sprang unfettered from her mind, free of her inhibitions, a torrent of truth that the Rhysu accepted without protest.

In return, Bev received more knowledge about the Rhysu—knowledge that once analyzed might reveal how to breach the barrier between dimensions. She would need to collate the data while in her private state and she wondered: *Do the Rhysu know my plans? Do they realize what I'm learning?*

The Rhysu disappeared.

The sudden release of pressure left Bev stupefied. She twirled in her energy sphere and saw only her white prison. "Did you learn what you needed to know?"

The Rhysu did not answer.

"Are you there?"

Fear crept into Bev's mind. Without a connection to the Rhysu, she would lose energy. *Did they get what they wanted and now toss me away like trash?*

"Where are you?"

The Rhysu did not answer.

Bev focused her mind and calmed her panic. *They saved me, they won't abandon me.*

Now alone, she tried to connect with Arlud again. The damaged buildings she had seen in Capital City caused doubt that Arlud was safe. *Our connection pulled me to that place, which meant he was there.* She knew he had survived the battle at Wan'tei, but that did not mean he was safe. *Why is he on Pigrell?*

She focused on Arlud and was thrust into a vision of Ni'apinu. She saw the planet, a blue globe covered with swirls of white cloud, surrounded by rings of battle debris and two separate armadas—one Erstallius and the other Guild.

They're not fighting. The battle is finished.

Her vision descended through the debris into the warm atmosphere and brought her to the damaged Erstallius landing field. She hovered above the cratered tarmac and saw Arlud outside the buckled fence with a group of Guildmen near a shuttle.

He's alive!

Relief pushed away her doubt. She moved above Arlud. She could not hear the conversation he was having with the Guildman and then realized—*Guild woman!* By the look of things, it appeared the Guild was still an Erstallius ally.

That's good. He needs friends.

Bev dropped to ground level next to Arlud. He never flinched from his conversation with the woman, which told her he could not sense her presence.

I can see him, but we can't communicate. How did the Rhysu connect with me?

Bev relaxed and watched Arlud's interaction with the Guild woman. *She likes him,* she thought. The hints of attraction in the woman's manner were obvious. A tinge of jealousy flared in Bev's consciousness and spiraled into a regret that she rebuffed and shed like a winter coat in summer.

Let's see if this makes a difference!

She pushed her consciousness into Arlud's body.

The sensation was immediate—an electric sting that flooded her with Arlud's thoughts. "Eetah! I'm so glad you're OK. Can you hear me?"

Bev backed away and watched Arlud wince, tilt his head back, and roll his shoulders. *I'll hurt him if I continue to touch his mind,* she thought, recalling the muscle aches, nausea, and mental confusion she suffered when the Rhysu first connected with her.

She rose upward and floated above the assembled clanmen.

How can I communicate without hurting him?

Then without warning, she was back in her white prison.

Snapping back to her own reality left Bev expecting a Rhysu reprimand, and yet there were no Rhysu waiting to confront her.

What happened?

Bev moved forward into the white and hit a transparent barrier. "So now I'm in a cage!?"

The Rhysu did not reply.

NI'APINU: OUTCOME

Shanna Sy stood behind the Aku and Erstallius clanmen who had gathered to observe the burial ceremony for their fallen comrades. Her soft, ankle-length dress, light gray with a flat collar, was the best choice from her wardrobe for this somber occasion. She watched the ceremony with genuine sadness, but beneath that emotion she was relieved Captain Pardee had come to his senses.

I must remember to thank him for saving the Erstallius from total defeat.

The grave for the fallen was dug between the memorial for the Erstallius clanmen who died when Polinda attacked four months ago, and Bev Colli's red-granite cenotaph that was damaged during the Emlito attack—the central pillar was a jagged stump.

Shanna had heard the stories of Bev Colli's mission to expose the alien intruders during the Battle at Wan'tei, but a cenotaph for Bev was something she did not expect.

Bev was just a sapi from Clan Polinda. I must ask Arlud why she deserves such a prominent monument.

The ceremony ended, and the gathered soldiers dispersed. The surviving Erstallius clanmen filed out the outpost's main gate to board shuttles for their transfer off-planet. The Aku soldiers separated into three groups on the cleared ground along the outpost's damaged fence line. Petra Sitlyn said farewell to Arlud and Shanna, then joined Aku Group One and retreated through the burned forest via the trail to Khemyak Gorge, followed by Aku Group Two. They would wait in the gorge for ground cars and ciâfey to take them back to the Gráal Highlands. The remaining Aku marched down the road that wound eastward through the evergreen forest to the coastal plain and the city of Ji'dess.

Arlud walked with Shanna outside the buckled fence toward her small executive shuttle. Ross Cordova and Donté Cegla trailed ten paces behind them with Gustav Eahuda.

"We won't rebuild," Arlud said, "unless the Aku elders agree."

Shanna flinched at that revelation. "You'd abandon this place?"

"It's not ours to keep."

"If you leave, others will replace you."

"No," Arlud said. "The Aku won't allow that. Eight of their ships survived the battle and their strength will increase once they receive the additions to their fleet. Some of our ships will stay to help make sure no one else can take advantage."

Shanna was impressed by Arlud's resolve to protect the Aku. She stopped at the foot of her shuttle's rear boarding ramp. "If the other Clans had your integrity, this war wouldn't have begun."

Arlud flashed a thin smile but shrugged aside the flattery. "Clan Erstallius has always honored our commitments. Those who populate our holdings are our partners—most clans work to benefit themselves at the expense of their populace."

"Yes, they do. But at least the killing might end now that Polinda's allies have been defeated. We have reports—the Alliance continues to fracture as the clans fortify their homeworlds. That should reduce the amount of belligerence—they'll be focused on defense, not attack."

"The battle we fought here was planned by at least four Clans—Emlito, Vestlok, Tuma, and Brandi. Clan Sabballi may also have been involved. They have their own coalition—an axis of rebellion—they are not fracturing."

"True. But Pardee feels the fighting will slowly fade as more clans, prompted by defeat, regroup, and look inward. Is that not a good thing? Will that not make our campaign against them simpler?"

"If Pardee's assessment is correct, there will be no reason to continue our campaign."

"You would allow them to rebuild?"

Shanna's sparkling green eyes reminded Arlud of Bev, and that unspoken attraction was not what he wanted to focus on, so he shifted his gaze toward one of the Erstallius shuttles that lifted off the ground and sped over the eastern tree line on its way to orbit. "Killing each other won't solve our problems. As much as I'd like to annihilate all our enemies, that's not possible. There will always be survivors and survivors breed revenge—the same revenge I felt when my father died. We must stop the killing."

"There will be no revenge. There will be no killing once our enemies are gone."

"Our coalition has been successful," Arlud admitted, once again avoiding Shanna's eyes. "Our people fought together and turned back our enemies. But we've allowed our enemies to dictate our actions, and that led to this disaster. We can no longer move at the prompting of our enemies if we hope to survive. We must find another way forward. Our path must not be cluttered with war."

Shanna was dumbfounded by Arlud's words. "Are you cowering because of this?" She gestured to the destruction that surrounded them. "We won the day. We destroyed our enemies. All of them! Beauty can rise again from these ashes."

Arlud flicked a glance back at Shanna. He had not expected such criticism from her. *That mindset must stem from her father*, he thought. "There's more at stake than this meager outpost. Our civilization is on the brink of collapse. War will continue unless we stop it. I have decided to stop it."

"We can't control what our enemies do."

"There is another way. We can force our enemies to react to *our* prompting."

"Without more fighting?"

"Your father avoided war with the Alliance for years by making peace more advantageous for the Clans. We can do the same."

"How?"

"By making peace the best option for their survival."

Shanna frowned. "That may have been possible in the past, but it won't be possible now."

"Why?"

"Because of what Pardee said. Keeping our coalition together has been difficult. As more clans retreat to defend their homeworlds, our combined power will be reduced. We'll be island fortresses too remote from each other to maintain our combined strength."

"Yes," Arlud agreed. "The Guild retreat after the Jai'raan conference is a perfect example of strength reduced."

"That was a mistake," Shanna admitted.

"Does your father know that?"

"Pardee knows it," Shanna assured. "That was a terrible decision."

"Our path must change," Arlud insisted. "I am leaving for home—for Baleiou. Once our realignment is complete, I will know how to proceed—with the clan behind me or on my own."

"You will not follow your father as High Regent?"

"That's up to the cadre."

"Oh—" The realization that Arlud's position, or rather his lack of position, might take him away for good, left Shanna speechless.

"They will make the best choice for the clan," Arlud said. "I will accept whatever they decide."

"Well, whatever happens, you will always be welcome on Al-phaq. You should visit. It's quite unique—unlike any other holding."

Arlud could see the regret in Shanna's eyes, and wondered if she feared his potential demotion, or the possibility he might be stuck on Baleiou and unable to return to this district. *Is she enamored with me or my position? She wants to be more than a casual acquaintance—that's obvious from our last encounter—but will her enthusiasm decline if the cadre rejects me?* "I'll consider your offer," he said, "once I know where I stand."

"Even if you are not chosen to be High Regent?"

"Who I am and what I do is not dependent on a title," Arlud said. He rolled his shoulders and tilted his head back in reaction to a sudden twinge in his back muscles below his neck. An image of Bev jumped to the forefront of his thoughts, and he heard her say, "I'm so glad you're OK! Can you hear me?"

Shanna saw fatigue in Arlud's pained expression. "Well," she said with a resurgent hope in her voice, "whatever position you hold, may your path lead to success."

"Thank you," Arlud said as Bev's voice faded like a whispering wind in his head.

"Now tell me," Shanna queried, "why does a sapi from Clan Polinda deserve a memorial at an Erstallius outpost?"

Arlud frowned. The vision of Bev faded, and he focused on the destroyed buildings. The derogatory tone Shanna used to emphasize the word *sapi* sparked his anger, which he subdued, knowing Shanna's attitude toward sapi was most likely a concept learned during her childhood. "Just as I am not dependent on a title," he said, "neither is Bev Colli. She was a sapi because she was born into the Drupal Caste System on Pigrell, but that does not define who she is."

"I apologize," Shanna said. She sensed Arlud's resentment and the rift her words had created—the one thing she hoped to avoid. "I did not mean to be disrespectful."

"Of course not," Arlud said. He turned to gaze upon Shanna's cream-colored face and her sparkling green eyes. "I will send you all the details about Bev's mission."

"I would like that," Shanna said, and she smiled. "So, the memorial commemorates her deeds, not her death?"

"Yes."

"Where is she?"

Arlud shifted his gaze skyward. "With the aliens."

"Oh, my!"

"She returned here to tell me she's still alive and left before I could question her. I assume we will never see her again. She was one of the bravest people I have ever known. I will never forget her."

Shanna heard the pain in Arlud's words. "The aliens took her?"

Arlud nodded. "She's no longer human."

"What?"

"They changed her so she could survive. I hope to contact them."

"To find Bev?"

"That's part of it," Arlud admitted. "They unknowingly sparked the war between the clans when they erupted out of Alpha Cephei Four. Maybe they could help end it. I thought revealing them would stop clan hostilities, but the shock was too brief. If we can start a lasting connection, that might trigger genuine change among the clans."

"That would change everything."

Arlud nodded.

Shanna stepped toward Arlud. "My stay on Al-phaq was to be brief, just long enough to retrieve items left behind and oversee the repopulation of our abandoned settlements. Send me all the details about the aliens. I will extend my stay and use the resources we have on Al-phaq to help you. We can create a dedicated comm-drone cycle between Al-phaq and Baleiou to exchange data."

Arlud heard the sincerity in Shanna's voice, but a caution flag raised in his mind as her father's words echoed in his memory: *"I prefer she not contact you."* That restriction was set because of Shanna's infatuation, as demonstrated months ago by her farewell kiss before leaving Ni'apinu with her stranded guildmen. "I appreciate the offer," he said. "I assume you'll get your father's approval. I do not wish to cause discontent."

"Discontent?"

"Your father insisted on limits to our partnership. He requested I not contact you."

So, Father did prevent Arlud from contacting me, Shanna mused. She refused to let her rage surface again. "My father has always done what he believes is best for me. Sometimes he goes too far."

"That's between you and him."

"Yes."

"We should also setup a cycle between Al-phaq and Ni'apinu," Arlud suggested. "Wolfram will understand the benefit in that, but I would feel better with his direct permission."

"We'll have it," Shanna assured, "even if it comes after the comm-drones are in motion."

That's understandable, Arlud thought. The average communication delay between Al-phaq and Wald-415 was twenty standard days.

Shanna turned to walk up the boarding ramp. "Have a safe trip to Baleiou." She flicked a hand signal that prompted Cordova and Cegla to proceed her into her shuttle — they gave Arlud a casual salute as they passed him.

Arlud returned the salute, and the Guildmen trudged up the ramp. He faced Shanna. "Have a safe trip back to Al-phaq. Give my thanks to Pardee. We wouldn't have survived without him."

Shanna bowed her head in a gesture of respect. "May peace fill your days, Arlud Erstallius. I look forward to meeting again."

CLAN HALVA: ANOTHER MISSION

Cynth Halva, wrapped in her sleeveless crimson robe, sat on a marble bench in the atrium connected to the ground floor library of her new residence in the city of Holte, on Cestratha. She had moved here after returning from Jai'raan to be closer to the clan administration while the rebuilding campaign was underway.

Three curved holoscreens floated around her and displayed data from the rebuilding effort.

She had spent the last hour reviewing the off-planet clean-up of battle debris, which was progressing faster than she expected. The new on-planet data also revealed positive results. She touched the holo-emitter on her mechanical wrist and tuned off two of the holoscreens.

The crest for the Judge Advocate for Planetary Settlement appeared on the remaining holoscreen, then faded to show the official Arrilen Po disaster report, authored by the Sabballi Degen, John Avrim Parker, on 113.11.8.

We should have fought his allegations and revealed the truth!

Cynth closed the advocate's forty-seven-year-old report and opened the latest data from the survey team at Arrilen Po. The com-drone cycle between Cestratha and Arrilen Po was thirty-nine-point-six standard days.

The team's data is ten days overdue. Something has broken the com-drone cycle!

And Cynth wondered if the Rhysu were to blame, although she knew there were more mundane things that could cause a drone failure.

She did a quick review of the old data. The survey team had cataloged the status of one third of the ruins. They listed items that could be retrieved, structures that could be repaired—only two out of the seventeen examined—and had detected no unusual weather patterns.

But that report had been received forty-nine days ago.

Something has happened!

She turned off the holoscreen and stood. "Quin!"

Cynth's flaxen-haired servant, Tara Quin, rushed into the atrium and stopped five paces from her. "Yes, Madame?"

"Call a car, and layout my purple jumpsuit."

"Yes, Madame," Quin said. She nodded and turned to leave.

"Wait," Cynth cautioned. She took a step forward and examined the girl's flowing pastel dress. "Change into traveling clothes. You're coming with me."

"Madame?"

"It's time you experienced more than the interior of my house."

Quin nodded with a brief smile. "Yes, Madame."

"Now hurry," Cynth demanded. "We need to get to my brother's office before noon."

Gustus Halva, High Regent of Cestratha, leaned back in his office chair and cast a blank stare at Cynth, who sat in a high-backed chair on the other side of his desk. "I agree there must be a problem, but I do not want you to go there. We will send a rescue team."

"I must go!"

Gustus chuckled. "Why, sister? What makes your presence there mandatory?"

Cynth rose from her chair. "I know the place. All the others who survived the colony are now dead."

"Yes, but what benefit is there in your presence?"

"I know how to manage a search under the worst circumstances that planet can deliver. I know what signs to look for, how to read the environment, but most important, I left the survey team there. They're my responsibility."

"Yes, they are your responsibility," Gustus agreed. "Which is why I do not want you to go."

"What?"

"The last time you were there, those aliens reappeared. You're lucky to have escaped, twice. A third time may end your life—don't push the odds!"

"Odds need pushing if we're ever to find—"

"You're old sister, as am I." Gustus pushed his obese body out of his chair and moved to the window behind his desk that overlooked the manicured garden surrounded by the new administration buildings. "Let younger ones handle this."

Cynth fumed. She was old on the outside, but her mind was just as crisp as it was in her thirties. "Being old isn't a handicap."

Gustus turned and looked at his bionic sister. "In your case, I suppose not." He stepped closer to Cynth and held her human hand. "We almost lost you once."

Cynth nodded. "The aliens made sure I came back. I sense no danger from them."

"But something has gone wrong."

"There will be no danger from the aliens. I'm certain of that. There are many things that can cripple a drone."

"Will the survey team not send another?"

"They will not suspect a drone failure for thirty-one more days, when our response to them is not received."

"Oh, right," Gustus mused. He turned back toward the window. He was genuinely concerned for Cynth's safety, but he also knew a trip to Arrilen Po would keep her attentions off the rebuilding effort, which had been a source of strain for some administrators. *She can really be a nag!* He faced Cynth and nodded his approval. "Just don't take any chances. If the command is to leave, then leave!"

Cynth shrugged off the reprimand—that was a reminder of her trip to Station 38 that delayed her evacuation from Arrilen Po and cost her three limbs. "Thank you, brother."

Tara Quin watched the back of Cynth's metal feet clack against the metal deck as she followed her down the narrow corridor outside the guest quarters.

"That's your cabin," Cynth said.

Quin stopped in front of the cabin hatch.

Cynth stopped outside the adjacent cabin hatch three meters farther down the passageway. "I'll be in here."

"Oh," Quin said, "I thought you'd have a suite."

"This is not a luxury cruise," Cynth said. "This a Defense Force cruiser. Only the captain has a *suite*—if you can call it that. Get settled in and I'll show you where we'll eat."

Quin nodded and pushed through the hatchway.

The cabin was small. The single-sized sleep alcove across the entry filled half the room, leaving one meter by three meters of open floor space. The only seat was folded into the wall to her left. A pocket door to a narrow shower room was in the wall to her right. Cabinet space was limited to the area above the bunk.

She tossed her travel bag onto the bunk and frowned. *Not what I expected.* This was her first trip off-planet. She had anticipated more luxurious accommodations because she was traveling with Lady Halva.

Hopefully, the entire trip won't be so lacking.

She transferred her garments from the travel bag to the cabinets—two extra pairs of calf-length cotton pants, chosen because they would tuck inside her walking boots, and five cotton shirts with pockets on both sleeves for the small utility items she would take to the surface of Arrilen Po.

"Are you ready?"

Quin turned to see Lady Halva standing in the hatchway. "Yes."

Cynth stepped into the room. "This was Bev's cabin."

"Bev?"

"You'll learn about her during our voyage. I want you to be an expert by the time we reach Arrilen Po."

"An expert? In ten hyper-days?"

"Bev's story is brief, but very important to this mission. Her full name is Bev Colli. She was a sapi from Pigrell who became familiar with the same aliens I encountered. Like me, she is one of the few who survived the encounter. I expect you to read all the info we have on Bev before we reach our destination. Your insight may be helpful."

"Yes, Madame."

Cynth took in a deep breath through her nose and whispered, "Her smell is still here."

Quin flashed a grimace and sniffed the room.

"Oh, stop worrying," Cynth insisted. "The cabin is clean. Bev had a unique scent about her—a pleasing aroma, not a rancid stench. Can you smell it?"

"No, Madame."

"You would if you had known her. Now come, I'm hungry."

Cynth turned and left the cabin.

Quin scanned the cabin and sniffed again. *Nothing,* she thought. She smirked and followed Lady Halva to the mess hall.

CLAN ERSTALLIUS: NEW PATH

The House Crest of Clan Dejoria appeared on the holoscreen—gold lion on hind legs, rearing up in profile, with forelegs raised. Below the lion a single white star, with two stars above the beast, one to the right, the other to the left, all in a black circle, framed by the circular Alliance belt.

Once that belt symbolized unity, Arlud thought.

The crest faded and the fat hairless head of the High Regent, Jhared Dejoria, filled the screen.

"This message arrived an hour ago," Eahuda said. He stood beside Arlud in the forward lounge of the Erstallius dreadnought, D2430, the flagship of the local fleet.

Arlud focused on the message.

"Greetings, my friend," Jhared said. "Thank you for your help at Wan'tei. My commanders sing your praises. This message is my official announcement that our gifts to you have arrived. The four class-five destroyers are our newest design, the most reliable, and the most powerful yet. Use them wisely. Peace with you and yours."

The Dejoria House Crest replaced Jhared's face, and the holo-image faded to reveal the local star field outside the window.

"I knew we could count on him," Arlud said.

"He sent that before we were attacked," Eahuda remarked. "When he hears about what happened, will he be willing to send more ships?"

Arlud nodded. "Ni'apinu is still an Erstallius holding. We can count on him."

Eahuda fingered the holoscreen controls and the image of Jegen-Major Kurt Sari appeared in the window.

"Greetings, Jegen-Major," Arlud said. "The Aku training should keep you busy while I'm gone."

"Yes, sir," Sari said. "Will be an interesting few months, especially for them."

"They're talented engineers. Segen Bittle has high regard for their abilities. Train them well and we'll have a more powerful ally."

Sari nodded. "I'm sure you will be pleased upon your return."

"I look forward to that day," Arlud said. "Thank you for your sacrifice. Your willingness to stay behind on Ni'apinu does the clan great service."

"Thank you, sir. Semper Paratus."

The motto of the clan, Arlud thought. *Old language, long dead, but preserved for military songs, clan banners, and the hearts of those who serve. The secret words that bind us together.* "Semper Paratus."

A clanman handed Sari a compad. He lowered his eyes to read the message. "The Guild ships have left the system."

"And so must we," Arlud said. "See you in three months, Jegen-Major."

Sari flicked a formal salute. "Safe journey, sir."

Arlud returned the salute.

Eahuda fingered the holoscreen controls, and the image of Sari winked out. He brought up a course plot. They were eighty-thousand kilometers from Ni'apinu and maneuvering into formation with the other Erstallius ships before the transition into hyperspace. "Our course will have us home in twelve standard days."

"She spoke to me, Gus."

Eahuda shot a quizzical glance at Arlud. "Lady Sy spoke to many before she left."

"Not Shanna. Bev."

"When?"

"At the field, during my conversation with Shanna."

"Where was she? I didn't see her."

"I felt her. Her voice was in my head."

"What did she say?"

"She was glad I survived."

"That's all?"

"Yeah." Arlud gripped the hand railing below the window and lowered his head. "Felt like a pinched nerve—a sting below my neck, along my spine. She suffered discomfort often when the Rhysu connected with her. That's how I know it wasn't an illusion."

Eahuda patted Arlud's shoulder. "That's a good sign, lad. She connected with you. This may lead to regular contact with her."

"I'm not so sure it's a good thing."

"Why?"

"She left too soon. As if she was yanked away."

"She could have sensed the discomfort she caused."

"Maybe."

"Well," Eahuda said, "If it happens again, don't just listen. Speak to her."

"If it happens again."

Arlud focused on the stars outside the window. "If we can connect, Bev could be our mediator again." He knew that was an unreachable prospect floating on a wayward wind, but it might still be possible.

Eahuda stepped closer to Arlud. "If she could convince the Rhysu to display regret for what happened at Alpha Cephei Four, and establish a persistent dialog, their presence could end the rebellion. That's a worthy goal to strive for, lad."

The deck rumbled as the dreadnought's compression drive ignited and a wispy green halo formed outside the window.

"Until that happens, we must focus on this reality. Hopefully, what we find on Baleiou won't stall our effort."

PETRA SITLYN: QUEL PASS

Petra stepped off the ciâfey once the pilot folded the wings out of the way. He had landed at the Quel Pass Hybrid Farm, ten meters inside the fence line south of the administration buildings.

Petra looked around—no one was there to greet her.

She still wore the wide-brimmed hat and armor vest of the Aku militia but had left the magar-rifle with the brigade. Her rib cage stung, but she showed no sign of that as she walked toward the trainee stable.

A trainer in the stable greeted her before she reached Serra's stall and told her the cub was in one of the training paddocks.

Serra bounded through the thick grass, wrapped Petra in a tight hug, then bounded away as if expecting her to run after him.

He hasn't a clue, Petra noticed. *To him, this is just another day for training.* That naivete saved the cub from the horrors of battle, but not from the threats still lurking above the sky. *Is Serra's ignorance a better place to be?*

A deep roar turned Petra's attention toward the southern perimeter gate.

Aluk stood on his hind legs in the tall grass as he did every day. He sniffed the air. Petra carried no fruit, so he rocked back and sat on his haunches. He huffed as she approached him.

"L'dyém, Aluk," Petra said.

Aluk reached out and swiped the wide-brimmed hat off Petra's head and brought it to his nose.

"Hey!" Petra reached up to grab the hat.

Aluk let her take the hat but put a paw on her back and pulled her into his chest and held her with his forelegs.

Petra stifled the urge to push against Aluk's grip—she realized he missed her, and this was just a welcome-back hug. She stroked the fur under his chin. "Easy boy, I'm still here."

Aluk eased his grip and huffed.

Petra twisted to step out of the hug, but Aluk pulled her back. She tried three more times to separate from the old sipá, but each time he pulled her back and the last time he lifted her off her feet. "Ok, I'll stay." She relaxed and stroked his chest fur. She had never bonded with another animal like this, and found the attachment heartwarming, but also sad—he had been forced to leave everyone he had known. Unlike his ancestors, this sipá needed companionship. *The Aku reject the old ones, thinking they are doing them a favor by putting them out-to-pasture, but all they are doing is quickening their demise because of loneliness.*

Petra looked into Aluk's sad brown eyes. "You can be the first," she said. "I'll convince them to find a better solution for old sipá like you." She focused on his rhythmic breathing. "If you could talk, what would I learn?"

Three ciâfey soared overhead from the south and caught Petra's attention. They banked toward the farm and dropped in spiral descents behind the administration buildings.

A few minutes later, Tryol led a pilot through the main gate and stopped ten paces away from Aluk and Petra. "Petra," he said, "I'm glad you made it back. Can you join us for a conversation?"

"I'm stuck at the moment."

"Give him a firm tap on the nose."

Petra considered Tryol's solution, reached up, and tapped the old sipá's nose with her palm.

Aluk huffed and released his grip.

Petra's feet fell to the ground, and she twisted away from her furry friend. She walked a few paces toward the men and stopped. "What's happening?

Tryol moved closer to Petra. "This man is here to take you to Kuliq'Quad."

"What?" Petra stood firm and placed her hands on her hips. "Why? I'm Dágul Jásah."

"Yes, you are," Tryol said. "You are also an engineer."

"There are plenty of engineers at Kuliq'Quad."

"Not Erstallius engineers. Most of your clanmen have left."

"So?"

"Jegen-Major Sari has stayed with twenty instructors to teach us about the new warships. Winstone Bittle is one of them. He recommended you design our new facilities. He said you're the best construction engineer he's ever met."

Petra smirked. "That's just him being ironic."

"Ironic?"

"To Bittle, constructing buildings is inferior to making spacecraft. If you listened well, you would have caught his emphasis on the word *construction.* He reduces my value compared to himself while still recommending me."

Tryol pondered Petra's opinion and said, "Well, whatever the reason, this man is here to take you to Kuliq'Quad."

"I'm Dágul Jásah."

"Yes. You will always be Dágul Jásah. We would also like you to be an engineer."

Petra contemplated what that request implied. "One thing I admire about the Aku—you adapt quickly."

"Drastic events demand drastic changes."

"What are the new facilities?"

"Spacecraft maintenance and construction," Tryol said. He could tell from Petra's raised eyebrows she had not been told about the pact made with the Erstallius Regent. "Your clan agreed to help us modernize. Now that only a few of you remain, we need your help."

"I cannot go to Kuliq'Quad."

"Your status as Dágul Jásah —"

"I am still bound by the Ogâhu Esnüphica."

"You are done with the Ogâhu Esnüphica," Tryol said.

"I am?"

"Yes."

"But I'm not done with my training. That's why I was brought here."

Tryol nodded. "You are done here, for now. Drastic events demand drastic changes."

Petra folded her arms across her chest. *That's the second time he said that,* she thought. *That means the decision about me won't change.* "What will happen to Aluk?"

Tryol glanced over at the sitting sipá. "We will care for him."

Petra turned and faced Aluk. "He needs companionship. I'm not comfortable leaving him alone."

Tryol folded his arms. "I knew this one when he was a cub. We will care for him. He will not be alone."

Aluk rocked forward and plodded through the grass to stand next to Petra.

Petra wrapped an arm around Aluk's foreleg. "You'll bring him a basket of fruit every morning?"

"Every morning."

⁂

The ciâfey pilot looked behind him to make sure Petra was in her seat, had secured her feet in the leather straps on the metal deck, and had goggles in place. "Hold on tight," he said.

Petra gulped a breath and gripped the hand railings to either side of her seat. *I hate this part.*

A quiet hum erupted from the nacelles.

The pilot pulled back the main lever. The four wings flexed upward, then dropped in a powerful downbeat and the ciâfey was a meter off the ground. The thrusters engaged, and the aircraft rushed upward at a thirty-degree angle.

As they banked south above the farm, Petra could see Aluk outside the fence in his favorite spot near the main gate. He stood on his hind legs and roared as they flew above him.

They better take care of him, she thought, *or they'll have another war on their hands.*

THE GUILD: REQUEST

Four standard days after leaving Ni'apinu, Shanna Sy was once again resident in the old family keep on Al-phaq. This time, her focus was not on the items she left behind. She spent the morning in her father's old library. She downloaded data from Pardee's dreadnought about the history of the Polinda mines on Alpha Cephei Four. The data Arlud had given her about Bev Colli provided insight about the disaster and its aftermath but presented only assumptions regarding the cause. The two independent reports from Clan Cormed and Clan Sabballi failed to answer why Alpha Cephei Four was the focal point for the Rhysu appearance—they made no reference to the aliens except in addenda written after Simbic Ur vanished.

The facts are accurate, but the reason is lacking.

She spent the next two hours reviewing all the histories a second time, aided by the keep's comnet logic engine. Her eyes narrowed as she read one paragraph in the logic engine's correlation analysis.

"Raw durillium amplifies electromagnetic emissions. In the mine this happens because of electro-static discharge between the drill and the raw metal, creating voltages less than 40kv. Six electro-magnetic pulses greater than 150kv occurred during the twelve days before the alien plasma streams erupted. An E.M.P. greater than 300kv was detected one hour before the emergence of the alien plasma streams. Thus, a correlation between these higher voltages and the alien plasma appears valid."

Shanna pushed her chair away from the desk. *Just more facts. The aliens caused the higher energy pulses. But why did they cross over? Why did they appear in the rock?* She stood and fingered her compad.

A secure hail was sent to Pardee's ship, and the comm-officer replied, "Lady Sy, how may I direct your call?"

"Is Captain Pardee available?"

"One moment."

Five minutes later, Shanna raised her compad to her lips. "If the captain is busy, we can talk later."

"He'll be just a moment longer," the comm-officer replied.

"Never mind," Shanna said. "We'll talk later." She closed the comm-channel and walked out of the library. Pardee had been distant since her insubordinate act in the C.I.C. He had allowed her to planet-fall at Ni'apinu once the fighting subsided, but otherwise, he ignored all of her inquiries. *His attitude needs to change.* She blamed herself for the distance between them and knew she had to prove her repentance, or she could never help Arlud.

She strode down the vaulted corridor that led to the foyer and met Cala by the entrance to the dining room. "What are you doing?"

"I've finished packing the utensils and will meet Gretel in the pantry to sort what we can take back with us."

"Good. Things are progressing as we planned."

"Yes, lady."

"I'm leaving for the flagship and may be gone a few days."

Cala nodded. "Yes, lady."

"You're doing a great job. Don't forget to relax occasionally."

Shanna turned to continue down the corridor but stopped in mid-stride and spun to face the young girl. "The work you do is important. You are not a sapi. You are family now. You are a member of Clan Sy."

Cala tipped her head. "Yes, lady."

Shanna returned a thin smile, then continued down the corridor.

The starboard observation deck was a narrow hall, three meters wide and twenty meters long, with meter-high windows that revealed the star field opposite the direction of the sun. Shanna was glad for that. Eta Cephei's brilliance would cause the duraplex windows to dim to the point of blotting out all the stars.

"Wow," she whispered to herself. "Such a great view."

"Yes, it is."

Shanna twirled to face Pardee. He stood at the other end of the deck. "Captain. I didn't see you."

"I just arrived," Pardee said. He moved toward Shanna and stopped about five paces from her. "What do you wish to discuss?"

Shanna looked at the stars. "My father made a pact with Arlud Erstallius. The partnership created was not between him and Arlud alone. All members of the Guild and Clan Erstallius are responsible for the success of the partnership."

Pardee stood silently as Shanna's gaze shifted to him.

"The pact my father made," Shanna said, "has not been fulfilled."

Pardee folded his hands behind his back. "How has it not been fulfilled?"

"The agreement was to track down the alien intruder."

"The aliens left."

"Really? How do you know?"

"Since Simbic Ur disappeared, there has been no reported alien presence."

"That does not mean they are gone."

Pardee nodded at Shanna's logic. "Yet no more ships have been attacked. No planets have been invaded. No more planets have disappeared."

Shanna returned her gaze to the stars. "Not yet."

"You imply they are hiding from us?"

"They got what they sought, but that does not mean they are done."

Pardee faced the window and grabbed the hand railing. "Perhaps, but there is nothing left to track."

"Do you agree we should learn as much as we can about the Rhysu?"

"Yes."

"How do we do that?"

"We don't, unless they return."

Shanna smirked. *He's being short-sighted.* "Have you ever hunted animals?"

"Human animals," Pardee quipped. "That's what soldiers do."

"When I was a little girl, my father told me about hunting wapiti in the forests on Makenzie. The animal's branched antlers are a deadly weapon, so the hunter stays far enough away to avoid being gored, but close enough to slay the beast with his arrow. How do they do that?"

"Stealth," Pardee said.

"Yes, but how do they find the wapiti?"

Pardee did not answer.

"A hunter must learn everything they can about the animal," Shanna said. "What they eat, migration patterns, how to read hoof prints in the dirt, how to identify a buck from a doe, and much more. My father told me he tracked a large buck once only to find the stag had circled back and followed him for almost an hour. Read the signs wrong and the hunter goes home empty-handed."

Pardee nodded. "No different from hunting enemy clanmen."

Shanna smiled. "And no different from hunting Rhysu." She took a step closer to Pardee. "We must learn more about the aliens. We must examine what they left in their wake."

"I agree."

"Then you'll understand why I wish to investigate Alpha Cephei Four?"

"Alpha Cephei Four? Clan Cormed may have an issue with that."

"Clan Cormed?"

"They're defending the holding. They forced the Sabballi investigators out of the system after the Battle at Wan'tei."

"Clan Erstallius defeated Clan Polinda. So Alpha Cephei Four should be under Erstallius authority."

"Yes, under Alliance Law, but the Alliance is done, and Clan Erstallius has not enforced their right-of-ownership."

"They've had other matters of more concern."

"Yes, as do we."

That's correct, Shanna thought, but she also knew the recent battle made this district less likely to erupt with more violence. "With our victory, our concerns are reduced. We could go to Alpha Cephei Four as representatives of Clan Erstallius. Our partnership allows that."

"Why would we do that?"

"Durillium."

Pardee stepped back from the hand railing and folded his arms across his chest. "The mine was destroyed, and we don't have the equipment to restart operations."

"Your right, but we would keep the Cormeds from claiming rights, and that would ensure favor with the Erstallius."

And Wolfram wants a piece of that prize, Pardee remembered.

"As a partner," Shanna added, "the Guild would benefit. By helping Clan Erstallius, we help ourselves."

Pardee came to his decision before Shanna stopped speaking but was curious how Shanna would proceed. "How would you investigate an inaccessible mine?"

"We can modify work pods to deliver drones into the deeper tunnels."

"And what do you hope to find?"

"Wapiti leave hoof prints. Rhysu must also leave tracks of some sort."

"I would assume Rhysu tracks are much more difficult to find."

"Which is why we need to investigate."

Pardee grasped the hand railing again and gazed at the stars. He thought about the data regarding the Rhysu. He considered what he learned about the condition of the mines and the current status of his fleet. The last report about Clan Cormed's presence at Alpha Cephei Four encouraged a rapid deployment to prevent the clan from increasing their strength around the holding.

Shanna's impatience returned. "Well?"

"I'll discuss this with my commanders," Pardee said. "If they approve the assessment, Battle Group One will leave for Alpha Cephei Four." He moved to the exit. "Sketch your proposal for the investigation and bring it to the C.I.C. in one hour."

CLAN ERSTALLIUS: BALEIOU

Gustav Eahuda sat on his bunk and gazed at the green wisps of hyperspace flowing past his cabin window. After four hyper-days, the Erstallius armada was less than a minute away from the PDN306 system and he wondered what they would find there. Based on the reports he read, the attack by the Polinda Axis had been brutal—Baleiou lost one million people and much of the orbital infrastructure between planets had been devastated beyond repair.

He felt a rumble as the ship's compression drive diminished and the green wisps outside faded away to reveal a normal star field.

We're here.

The comm-panel next to the window buzzed.

Eahuda flicked the talk switch. "Yes?"

"This is Arlud. Are you dressed yet?"

"Yes."

"Come to the C.I.C."

"On my way."

Eahuda was in no hurry to witness the damage, so his pace was slower than normal as he walked through the narrow corridors. What awaited them was not only the physical destruction, but a governmental revolt against Arlud's status. *The lad deserves better than what awaits him. Maybe the opposition won't rescind his position in the cadre.*

The C.I.C. was crowded with clanmen illuminated by the glow of the surrounding sensor stations and the central navigation pedestal. Arlud stood next to the flagship commander at the pedestal's control panel. Above the panel, a holomap displayed the system's five inner planets. Baleiou was the fourth planet orbiting the sun labeled PDN306.

Arlud waved to Eahuda to join him.

Eahuda shouldered through the crowd. "Any contact yet?"

"Had a response to our beacon," Arlud said. "We were told to wait."

Ten minutes later, the holomap was replaced by the thin face of Nared-Major Rena Veillon. Her frosted-brown hair was gathered in a braided tail that hung over her left shoulder. "Greetings," she said. "All your ships have been identified. Please advance along the coordinates we are sending to you now. Your armada has been granted an express route to Baleiou. Please maintain a tight course, otherwise you will be fired upon."

Vellion's image winked out and the system image returned.

Eahuda was puzzled. "Fired upon?"

"Security rules have been amped up since the attack," Arlud explained. "Expect to see damage."

The flagship commander sent instructions for the armada to keep formation as they advanced toward Baleiou.

An express pathway allowed the Erstallius armada to reach the orbital boundary of Baleiou's binary moon in two standard hours, rather than the ten to twelve hours needed for a standard flight from the system's heliosphere.

The returning clanmen were silent as they passed the splintered remnants of outer-system orbital stations and received transmitted imagery of crushed surface installations on the sixth and fifth planets.

Eahuda focused on the small data station next to the navigation pedestal. He replayed the progression of the Polinda attack that revealed a massive invasion had intruded into the system from four positions. The outer defenses were overwhelmed, and the rush toward Baleiou fractured half of the inner-system defenses before the Erstallius counter-strike pushed back the invaders. The binary moon installations survived, but two continents on Baleiou had large swaths of chard landscape where nine of the largest cities once stood, and four of the ten orbital stations were now compact streams of rubble.

Worse than I thought it would be.

Once the fleet was in orbit a few thousand kilometers outside the orbit of the binary moons, Eahuda switched his data analysis to real-time broadcasts from the surface. He leaned toward Arlud. "Look at this."

The small screen displayed transmissions from a faction within the cadre who preferred Avery Barick Erstallius wear the mantle of High Regent.

"My uncle always pined for the Regency," Arlud whispered. "He honored my father, but he will not honor me. The vote in two days will decide our future."

❖ ❖ ❖

Eahuda relaxed in his shuttle seat, pulled down the window shade. The view outside the small oval window revealed the rubble clouds that remained after the battle, and the salvage ships that were scooping up the debris. He closed his eyes. He had seen enough of the damage and this forty-five-minute flight from the flagship to Baleiou's new capitol city was a chance to take a nap.

Arlud heard the window shade close behind his seat, and he frowned. He had noticed Eahuda's stamina decrease during the past few weeks. His physical condition was within clan guidelines for the defense service, but his mental health was borderline and had lowered his energy level. *He's become a tired old man,* he thought. Eahuda had served him as Personal Guard for twenty years. He knew the time would come when Eahuda retired, but he never considered removing his friend from his entourage.

Flashes of light erupted at the periphery of Arlud's vision. He closed his eyes against the sparkling intrusion and heard Bev's voice scream in his head: *Can you hear me?*

Pain stung Arlud's shoulders, as if his muscles had been ripped open. He bent over in his seat as nausea forced him to grab a vomit bag from the back of the seat in front of him.

Can you hear me?

Arlud looked beyond the flashes of light and did not see Bev anywhere. *This isn't like your appearance at Kuliq'Quad. I can hear you, Bev, but I can't see you!*

Bev asked: *Where are you?*

I'm home. Baleiou.

Don't forget me! I'm still here!

I'll never forget you!

Don't forget me!

Bev, where are you?

Don't forget me!

Bev?

Arlud's vision cleared and the pain in his shoulders faded. He clutched the vomit bag and leaned back in his seat. "Gus!"

Eahuda stirred from his nap and sat up. "What's wrong, lad?"

"I heard Bev again."

Eahuda stood and leaned over the back of Arlud's seat. "What did she say?"

"She asked me to not forget her."

"She's still reaching out to you. That's good."

"Yeah."

"You should see a physician once we're on-planet. A neurologist might find a way to make the connection permanent."

"The Rhysu changed Bev. I doubt we can do that to me."

"We have the medical records from the Halva and Guild physicians."

"Yeah."

"As soon as we planet-fall, I'll find the best qualified neurologist and give him the data. Worth a try, lad."

"OK."

Eahuda nodded and dropped into his seat.

Arlud strolled up the sunlit path to the new residence where his mother waited. This new home, surrounded by manicured lawns and hedges east of the small village of Mancipa, had a similar stone-and-wood facade, but not the history, or the size, of the ancient family residence that had been destroyed. A modest entry porch protruded from the two-story, gable-roofed building.

My home was a castle, he remembered. *This is a manor house for servants, not the residence of a High Regent.*

Beneath his disappointment, he understood the cause—millions dead and a once beautiful capitol reduced to piles of rubble.

A House Guard stepped off the porch and raised an Ident reader.

Arlud stopped, raised his right arm, and exposed his wrist.

The guard snapped to attention and saluted.

Arlud returned a quick salute.

The guard turned and escorted Arlud to the door.

Once in the foyer, Mister Tupo, the gray-haired house manager, greeted Arlud and led him through the vaulted corridor to the small sitting room where his mother waited.

Tupo retreated as Arlud stood in the open doorway.

Madame Benita Gale Waldu-Reyes Erstallius sat on a padded bench next to the bay window across from the doorway. She was clothed in her black mourning dress and veil, the attire she would wear for another month until the official grieving period for Armand was over—a custom she embraced. Her attention was on something in the garden outside the window. She did not turn as Arlud stepped into the room.

"Hello, Mother."

Benita flicked a glance at her son, then returned her gaze to the garden. "About time you got here. Where have you been?"

"Protecting our interests."

"That's what your father told me before he left. He returned in a coffin."

Arlud took another step into the room. "Our enemies are powerful. Many clanmen died."

"I was told you almost died, more than once, and that you failed to secure our new outpost."

"We faced many obstacles. Our allies rallied to our side, and we prevailed. Our outpost is secure."

Benita reviewed Arlud's posture and his calm expression, then turned back to the window. "What is it about Erstallius men? Why do you enjoy putting yourselves in jeopardy?"

"I'm not one who enjoys battle," Arlud said in a flat tone. "Father always hoped to avoid it." He meant to be conciliatory but noticed his mother had taken his words as contradicting her statement — the perfect fuel for an argument.

Benita huffed, still looking out the window. "Avoiding the battle made it worse."

"Yes," Arlud admitted in a softer voice. "Much worse."

"You allied us with pirates."

"The Guild of Free Traders is now our partner in the peripheral district."

"Many in the cadre are opposed to that partnership."

"I know."

Benita turned on the bench and faced her son. "The cadre will remove you from your post. Your reckless deeds have lost us the Regency."

"The cadre is ignorant of—"

"Do not speak of ignorance! You have lost your position. You will not be High Regent."

"I never wanted—"

"Silence!" Benita turned back toward the window and lowered her head. "Your father would be appalled."

"Appalled?"

"I've heard the stories from the clanmen who returned from your assignment. You blamed the rebellion on the unwitting actions of aliens. And you relied on a Polinda sapi to stop the battle at Wan'tei!"

Arlud exhaled. His mother was in no mood to listen to the truth. "What you heard is lacking facts. People ignore the important things when they have contrary agendas. We can speak about this after you have reviewed all the data." He turned to exit through the doorway but stopped for a heartbeat, expecting his mother to protest his decision to leave.

"There is a place for you in the west wing if you wish to stay," Benita said. She turned and watched Arlud leave the room.

The day after he arrived at the new Erstallius residence, Arlud met Eahuda in the foyer.

"This is Vero Singh," Eahuda said. "I found him at the Regency Medical Center in Mancipa."

The grizzled neurologist nodded to Arlud.

Arlud shook the old doctor's hand, then gestured to the doorway on the west side of the foyer. "We can talk in the library."

A round, light-wood table dominated the room, surrounded by four high-backed wooden chairs that matched the color of the table. Bright morning sunlight streamed through the large bay window and cast shadows across the table from the evergreen trees that flanked the view.

Eahuda shut the library's double doors while Arlud moved to the table with Singh.

Arlud rested his hands on the back of the chair opposite the window. "What did you learn, Doctor Singh?"

"Very interesting case," Singh said. He pulled a metal disk out of his coat pocket and placed it on the table. "What happened to the patient did not change her personality. I understand that some have interpreted the data that way, but that's not possible—even if aliens were responsible."

"Then what happened?"

"Her mind was expanded."

Eahuda pulled out a chair and sat. "Expanded?"

"Neurons are the cells in the brain which transmit data using chemical and electrical impulses. Neurons communicate with each other through connections called synapses. The brain's plasticity allows it to remap as new data is stored and new skills are learned. In this patient's case, an external force caused new synapses to form, changing her synaptic pathways, which changed the flow of data and enhanced certain areas of her brain to accept an increased flow of external data."

Arlud folded his arms across the top of the chair. "The Rhysu improved their connection so Bev could hear them better, which meant they could also hear her better."

"That would seem to be the reason," Singh admitted. "Think of the network of synapses as an internal antenna. Bev's network was altered to improve reception, but also to improve transmission."

Eahuda leaned forward and cupped his hands on the table. "Why did they do that? They could communicate with her from the moment they met her."

Singh touched the metal disk and a transparent, holographic schematic of a human brain floated above the table. "This is Bev's brain, from a scan taken on the Guild freighter. You can see her brain's electrical signals."

The holo-schematic displayed roaming flashes of light inside Bev's brain.

Singh continued: "All electrical signals radiate into space. The bone and tissue around the brain reduce the signal strength before it leaves the skull, which is why telepathy is difficult to achieve under normal circumstances. An external signal entering the skull is also reduced by the bone and tissue. To strengthen the signal, it must either be amplified, which can adversely affect nerve cells inside and outside the brain by causing them to be over-stimulated, or the incoming signal can be focused at a frequency which allows it to be heard internally but avoids over-stimulating nerve cells. I would guess, based on the data, that the first dreams Bev experienced entered her mind directly without having to pass through her skull on a carrier wave—they popped into her consciousness from another dimension, and she felt only emotional pain. Later, when the Rhysu widened their influence and infused physical discomfort, their mode of contact changed to keep the connection stable under different circumstances, like traveling in hyperspace. And then there's the other issue of opening her mind so the Shoku could also connect with her."

Arlud watched the flashes of light in the holo-schematic. "Is there a way to focus the incoming signals with an external device to allow the communication to be heard but blocks the debilitating effects?"

"Maybe," Singh said. "To be successful, we would need to know the frequency and strength of the specific carrier wave used for the communication."

"How do we find it?"

"Analyze a real-time event. Like they did on the Guild ship."

"The med-tech called it interference," Eahuda said. "They had no clue how to stop it."

"True," Singh said. "But we would not be trying to stop it, just evaluate it. It doesn't matter who is sending it, or where it is being sent from. What matters is isolating the carrier wave so we can control how it's received."

"How would you do that?"

"Monitor the receiver until the signal is identified. Then isolate it from the other radiant electro-magnetic noise. Is Bev available?"

"Bev's not the receiver," Arlud said. "She's the sender."

"Oh." Singh focused on the holographic brain. "How far is she from the receiver?"

"I'm the receiver," Arlud said. "Bev is—where she is depends on your point of view."

"What?"

"The Rhysu took her," Eahuda said. "She's in another dimension, a different universe, so her position is problematic."

"Oh."

"That's not the problem," Arlud said. "It's not something we expected but is no reason for alarm. She's trying to communicate with me, and it's very painful. The Rhysu altered her brain to reduce the pain and improve their connection. I'd like you to do the same thing, without altering my brain."

Eahuda focused on the doctor. "Why is Arlud feeling pain? He's not traveling in hyperspace like Bev was when she began reacting physically."

Singh shrugged. "I would assume Bev is under a lot of stress. If her effort is out of desperation, then perhaps her communication is like a scream—a forceful, unfocused call blasted out in all directions. Even if her voice is popping into his brain from another dimension, avoiding the need to enter through his skull, the force of the interaction could still over-stimulate Arlud's nerves as the energy radiates in his brain."

Eahuda leaned back in his chair. "Then getting her to calm down would reduce the pain?"

Singh nodded. "Perhaps." He faced Arlud. "How often does she connect with you?"

"There's no specific schedule."

Singh pursed his lips. "Well then, to isolate the carrier wave, we would need to keep close and monitor you until a connection is made. Whenever it happens, we would need to stop everything else and focus on analysis."

"Then be prepared to change your schedule for the next few weeks."

Singh pondered Arlud's expectation. "I haven't agreed to that. There are demands on my time—"

"I understand you're busy with other things," Arlud said. "I am not High Regent, so my request cannot be taken as a lawful demand. But what I am is a connection to another dimension that could have an impact on our present situation. The war we've survived was sparked by a misinterpretation of the Rhysu eruption out of Alpha Cephei Four. Creating a dialog with them could change attitudes among the clans, and that could lead to real peace."

Singh looked at Eahuda. "Do you agree with that analysis?"

"We saw the Rhysu on Arrilen Po and have recorded data to back-up that claim. We have the medical evidence that Bev was altered, which you agree happened. Based on what we've experienced, yes, I agree."

Arlud stepped away from the chair and approached Singh. "Bev's mind was expanded. The nature of her connection with the Rhysu has never been analyzed by someone with your medical expertise. Now that I'm experiencing similar events, you have an opportunity—"

"I'll do it," Singh said, "but I must make arrangements with my family. You and I will spend a lot of time together, Mister Erstallius, at least for the next few weeks."

The hidden camera on the south wall of the library relayed Arlud's meeting with Singh and Eahuda to a holoscreen floating above the ornate wooden desk in Benita's sitting room. The black clad matriarch leaned back in her chair with her veil pulled aside so she had an unobstructed view of the meeting. Her reaction upon first learning about Bev Colli's encounter with aliens produced thoughts of schizophrenia. Arlud's meeting with Doctor Singh proved that theory wrong, but she knew her son would find only ridicule from the cadre—a political weapon to keep him from the Regency. *He's never been honored by the cadre,* she thought. *They blame the loss of the clanmen he led to GSW-183, an example of his incompetence, and labeled him a coward for fleeing to U'galem.*

Benita fingered the controls on her desk and turned off the holoscreen. She loved her son and regretted snapping at him when he arrived. Her own misgivings fueled that reaction and had nothing to do with how the cadre viewed her son's accomplishments. She knew he always made thoughtful decisions, and that was the important thing when leading others.

Decisions must never be rushed, but that does not mean thoughtful choices cannot fail. Arlud deserves the benefit of doubt regarding his decisions. If the cadre won't honor him that way, I will.

She reached out and flicked a switch that hailed the house manager.

"Yes, Madame?"

"Mister Tupo," Benita said, "please contact Fleet Command and tell them I wish to have my cruiser prepped for a journey with the required escorts."

"Yes, Madame. When will you be leaving?"

"As soon as possible. Notify me once everything is ready."

"Yes, Madame."

Tupo closed the comm link and Benita leaned forward on her desk. She could not help Arlud achieve the position of High Regent, but she could help him in his quest to contact the woman who had been taken by the aliens.

The assembled cadre was a boisterous crowd—two-hundred and fifty-six representatives gathered in the new Hall of Assembly; a tiered auditorium once used as a theater. They took their seats when the Chairman stepped up to the podium.

"Greetings to all assembled here today," the Chairman said. He waited for the murmuring to stop. When silence filled the hall, the Chairman continued: "Among those assembled here today are sixty-two members of the Erstallius cadre who gathered to debate during the past two weeks to select two candidates for the office of High Regent. These two candidates have gone through an extensive review, and we will cast our votes today to select our High Regent."

Arlud watched the proceedings from an aisle seat in the last row of the eastern balcony. He wore black clothing—bland business attire more typical of government envoys—a break from his preference for blues and grays. His five-day-stubble formed a sparse beard but did not keep his identity hidden from the more senior members. Many acknowledged his presence with a nod and brief condolences regarding Armand's death. Few greeted him by name, which he accepted as a display of their low view of his status. He leaned to his left, elbowed Eahuda, and whispered: "As soon as they make the announcement, we're leaving."

Eahuda nodded.

"The two candidates are both worthy of the position," the Chairman said, "yet only one can lead the cadre. All those in favor of Avery Barick Erstallius, please cast your votes."

The assembled crowd cast their votes by depressing buttons on the arms of their chairs.

"All those in favor of Hugo Rusan Erstallius, please cast your votes."

Arlud cast his vote and waited for the tallies to display in the holoscreen behind the Chairman.

The numbers next to each candidate's name shuffled as the votes were counted.

Arlud expected different results:

Avery Barick Erstallius: 102
Hugo Rusan Erstallius: 154

Eahuda leaned toward Arlud and whispered: "Good, it isn't a tie."

Arlud nodded. A tie would have moved the cadre into another debate. "Let's go," he said, and he stood to leave.

Applause erupted as Hugo Rusan Erstallius stepped up to the podium. He stood only 1.4 meters high so had to step on a riser to reach the controls on the podium.

Arlud halted on the landing behind the seats to watch the new High Regent begin his first speech.

Eahuda stopped next to Arlud. "This has to be a mistake."

Arlud shrugged. Hugo was the least favored candidate based on recent polls. He was Arlud's cousin by his father's older brother, Patrus George Erstallius. He last saw Hugo eight years ago—he was still short, but his voice had become deeper, and his dark curly hair was now sun-bleached at the tips.

"Greetings to all the Clan," Hugo said. "I, Hugo Rusan, am honored to serve the clan and will do my best to uphold the mantle of Erstallius."

Arlud listened as Hugo rambled through his speech. A few comments received polite applause, but the general response was more courteous than enthusiastic.

"We defeated our enemies," Hugo said, "but at what cost? Millions of lives lost on our three main holdings. Tens of thousands of our clanmen are dead. Half our fleet crippled or destroyed. Armand's folly was his refusal to confront Polinda years ago, before our enemies could band together and strengthen their forces. The Alliance is in chaos. Clans continue to battle clans, devastating more holdings. Many clans believe the Alliance has already crumbled beyond repair. So, what do we do?" He surveyed his audience as if searching for an answer. "Our focus," he continued, "will move inward, to restore what we have lost and strengthen our holdings by retreating from unprofitable expansion."

That means my position has been erased, Arlud thought. *GSW-183 will be abandoned.*

"While we honor those we have lost," Hugo added, "we must abandon the past."

Arlud touched Eahuda's elbow. "Let's go. Doctor Singh is waiting."

THE GUILD: SUPPORT

The comm-drone dropped out of hyperspace 550,000 kilometers outside the heliosphere of the PDN1592 system. This was a normal course evaluation stop, one of many along the route from Al-phaq to Wald-415. As it compiled a three-hundred-and-sixty-degree image of the surrounding star field, it detected a spatial anomaly. The spherical bulge in the star field covered an area ten degrees in diameter behind the drone, nine degrees below its course trajectory. The navigation plot system saw the anomaly as an error and compiled another image.

Twenty compiles later, the drone had recorded movement of the anomaly to the starboard side of the drone, across one-hundred and ninety degrees at a constant angle of plus sixteen degrees, then the anomaly vanished.

With the surrounding stars once again stable, the comm-drone adjusted its course heading, jumped back into hyperspace, and entered the PDN1592 system.

Wolfram Sy paced in front of the holoscreen that displayed his daughter's calm, cream-colored face.

Wellen appeared in the doorway to Wolfram's study. "Is she OK?"

Wolfram stopped pacing and looked at his wife. "She's fine."

"Then why do you look so glum?"

"Clan Erstallius was attacked again at GSW-183."

"Oh."

"They survived with the help of Pardee's armada. Our daughter convinced him to help."

Wellen entered the study, stood behind one of the leather-backed chairs that faced the holoscreen, and asked: "How much did we lose?"

"We lost nothing. Pardee caught the attackers off-guard."

Wellen turned to the image of her daughter. "And what about Al-phaq?"

"It's ours again," Wolfram said in a flat tone. "No one claimed it after we left."

"Then what's bothering you?"

"The attack depleted Erstallius strength at GSW-183. They would have lost everything if Pardee had not intervened."

"Even with the Aku?"

"The Aku are not the power they used to be."

"How does that affect us?"

"I'm not sure."

Wellen sat in the chair, rewound the report from her daughter, and watched the entire ten-minute recap of the Guild mission to Al-phaq and the military support of Clan Erstallius. "Is Al-phaq safe with the Erstallius strength reduced?"

"For now," Wolfram said. He moved to the other chair and sat. "The rebel forces had no survivors. Recovering their losses could take years."

"Then—"

"Pardee wants to take Alpha Cephei Four and claim it for the Erstallius."

"Why?"

"Because it's Clan Erstallius' right to claim it, but their forces are so depleted they could never defend it by themselves. They're divided between their twelve holdings, Pigrell, and Anders Prime."

"If they can't defend it, why claim it?"

"To prevent Clan Cormed from taking it."

"Oh."

"Our partnership will increase in value with the Polinda mine under Erstallius control. We will benefit from the profits."

"Profits are never attained without sacrifice."

"Therefore, my dilemma," Wolfram said. "Taking Alpha Cephei Four will weaken our defenses at Al-phaq, and Pardee has already engaged his forces to acquire it."

"Without your permission?"

Wolfram nodded.

"Pardee would not press forward without good reason," Wellen stressed.

"Exactly," Wolfram said. "Delay would allow the Cormeds to strengthen their presence, which would take Alpha Cephei Four out of our reach for good. I understand Pardee's motive, but it strains our own strength almost to the breaking point. Our resources are limited."

"If we had never left Al-phaq—"

"We'd most likely be dead."

Wellen straightened her posture. "Perhaps, but our strength there would be ten times greater if we had done there what we've done here."

"The clans would have stopped us once they realized what we were doing. One way or another, we'd be dead."

Wellen retreated inward from the conversation and turned to focus on the holoscreen. "When is Shanna coming home?"

"I don't know."

Wellen twisted to face Wolfram. "What?"

"There's a second message in the comm-drone's transmission. Shanna has gone with Pardee to Alpha Cephei Four."

"What!? Why?"

"To find evidence left by the aliens."

"Aliens?" Wellen stood. "Stop her!"

"The comm-drone took fifteen standard days to get here. Al-phaq is only seventeen standard hours from Alpha Cephei Four. They're already there."

Wellen held her voice and dropped into the chair.

Wolfram saw the worry in Wellen's brown eyes. "She'll be OK," he said. "Pardee won't let anything happen to her."

Eber Kurnes entered the study clutching a small folio under his arm. "Excuse me, sir."

Wolfram stood. "Yes?"

Kurnes handed Wolfram the folio. "This data was downloaded from the last comm-drone."

Wolfram flipped through the pages of the report and stopped where the data revealed the anomaly that followed the drone.

Wellen moved to Wolfram's side. "What is it?"

Wolfram handed Wellen the folio and said to Kurnes: "Contact central command. Set security to alert level two. Activate Third Fleet for movement to Al-phaq."

Kurnes nodded and left the room.

Wellen looked up from the folio. "What does this mean?"

"The thing that attacked the Cormeds has returned," Wolfram explained.

"Are we sure?"

"Look at the data. It appeared behind the comm-drone, then moved past it before it disappeared."

"And?"

"It was probably tracking the drone, then lost it when the drone dropped out of hyperspace."

"Oh." Wellen flipped through a few more pages. "Why would it do that?"

Wolfram pursed his lips and folded his arms. "Based on what happened to the Cormeds, I would guess nothing good."

"I thought the Erstallius said the aliens only wanted to retrieve their lost comrades?"

"They were wrong."

The sixty ships of the Guild Third Fleet waited in sailing formation two million kilometers from Wald-415. Once Wolfram Sy's order to proceed was broadcast, they would engage compression drive and speed toward Alphaq.

Wellen leaned into Wolfram's shoulder. They stood in the communication room next to Wolfram's study and viewed the remote broadcast of the fleet on the large holoscreen set against the wall opposite the doorway. "Do we need to send the entire fleet?"

"Better to have the whole and not need it," Wolfram said, "than to have only a portion and be short-handed. If I could, I'd send everything we have to get our daughter back."

Wellen smiled and hugged Wolfram's arm. "I know you would. Let's hope they're not needed."

Wolfram pushed a button on the holoscreen control console, and his deployment message was sent.

A few minutes passed, and the fleet surged forward a few thousand kilometers, but the expected hyperspace shimmer did not appear, and they slid into a sub-light advance.

The communication station erupted with incoming messages from the fleet.

Wellen looked up at Wolfram's frown. "What happened?"

"The Erstallius were wrong."

ALTERNATIVE

PART THREE

When our path crumbles, the only way to advance is to change course. Sometimes the change will create more obstacles but will enable us to keep moving toward our goal. Our goal is the only thing that matters. Once our goal is reached, we are not finished. To maintain the results of our accomplishment, we must create new goals. Our quest never ends. It morphs and adapts, but always leads us down a path to another goal, and hopefully to a better future.

—From Conversations at Kuliq'Quad
By Petra Sitlyn

BEV COLLI: LINKS

"Can you hear me?"

Bev's call to Arlud was a hopeful plea from inside the transparent cage. Beyond the unbreakable barrier the white glare now hid the gray regolith that was Simbic Ur, and she had no contact with the Rhysu—a perfect opportunity to contact Arlud again. Her mind focused on her last memory of Arlud, and she saw him—a vision obscured by a gray haze, a faint impression of his body in a shuttle seat.

"Can you hear me?"

Arlud's response was muffled—a distant whisper: *This isn't like your appearance at Kuliq'Quad. I can hear you, Bev, but I can't see you!*

"Where are you?"

I'm home. Baleiou.

"Don't forget me! I'm still here!"

I'll never forget you!

Bev felt the grip of the Rhysu as they flooded her mind with raging voices to block her connection with Arlud.

"Don't forget me!"

Bev, where are you?

"Don't forget me!"

The connection broke.

Bev shrieked at the Rhysu: "Leave me alone!"

The Rhysu went silent.

Bev revolved in her transparent cage. She retreated into herself, gathered her energy tendrils into a tight ball, and blasted the invisible barrier. The shock front rebounded against her, and she slammed into the opposite side of her cage.

"Eetah!"

Time flowed, and Bev's anger receded into frustration. She focused her thoughts on the Rhysu.

They'll keep me here if they believe I can't live in their universe.

She was glad she had made contact with Arlud. Although she could not be with him physically, seeing him and hearing him was encouraging.

He said he would never forget me!

Arlud's words lifted her above the frustration.

I promise to never stop trying to communicate with you, Arlud. Never!

Twitching tendrils inside cyan-colored energy spheres burst through the white beyond Bev's cage.

"What now!?"

The Rhysu advanced toward Bev, wrapped her cage in their tendrils, and it disappeared. "The time has come for you to shed your three-dimensional perspective."

The white glare dissipated and revealed the sea of cyan-colored energy streams that filled the Rhysu universe.

Bev wondered if her place in the sea had changed. "Where's Simbic Ur?"

"We removed the hard place," the Rhysu said. "It is no longer needed."

"Why?"

"You must learn. You must adapt to our universe."

Bev rotated to examine the energy streams. "Where are the frigates?"

"We absorbed them."

"Absorbed?"

"Matter is energy. Their energy is now with us."

Bev let that admission roll around in her thoughts as she peered past the Rhysu spheres at the interlaced streams. *This existence is more complicated than I imagined,* she thought, and a realization burst to the forefront of her thinking: *Objects from my universe are not compatible with this place.*

"Correct," the Rhysu said. "It was easier to absorb the alien objects than to keep them intact."

"Was Simbic Ur absorbed?"

"We removed the hard place."

"Removed to where?"

"To where it belongs."

Bev considered the impact Simbic Ur would have upon returning to its original orbit. "You put it back in the same place?"

"No," the Rhysu said, "that was not possible. It resides with its neighbors in a different position."

"But still at the same distance from its sun?"

"It follows a similar path to the one it once followed."

Bev mentally sighed and shrugged off the fear that Simbic Ur's return would cause disastrous orbital disruptions to the other worlds nearby. The Rhysu decision to return the small rocky planet to its own universe impressed her. "That's good you did that. You should always return what is not yours."

The Rhysu saw Bev's praise as a veiled statement against her continuation in their universe. "You must learn and adapt to our universe. You must shed your three-dimensional perspective."

"You're right. I must learn."

"Once you learn, you can help us."

"How?"

"Help us understand how we can stop the harmful fluctuations without causing harm."

So, there it is, Bev thought. *They finally admit to the folly of their original plan to stop Compression Drive.*

"It is not a folly," the Rhysu said. "We must do it, but not cause harm."

"I told you I would not help you do that."

"Then help us find an alternative."

Bev felt a genuine willingness to compromise in the Rhysu statement—a position she never expected.

Their request is sincere.

Once she acclimated to their universe, she would understand what it means to be Rhysu, and knowing that, she might resolve the harmful fluctuation issue without causing harm. *At the least, that is my hope.*

"That is also our hope," the Rhysu said.

The pathway through the energy sea was not obvious, but the Rhysu guided Bev through the twists and turns of the higher-dimensional universe. Her three-dimensional mindset adapted faster than she expected. The human restrictions she'd known since birth were gone—she could see the enfolded higher-dimensional pathways and learned how to anticipate shortcuts with the aid of her Rhysu guide.

"Once you master this level of movement," the Rhysu said, "then we will introduce you to tunneling."

"Tunneling?"

"Movement without moving."

"Huh?"

"When you returned to the human universe, the links to your social group pulled you back to them at the hard place you call Ni'apinu. You can move like that here."

Bev recalled examining the Polinda frigates, but that was movement of her consciousness, not physical transportation. “Do I need to make links with a Rhysu, or can I just think myself to another place?”

“You’ll need prior knowledge of your destination. We will demonstrate at the proper time.”

“Oh.”

A Rhysu touched Bev with an energy tendril. “Follow me and stay in contact. Do not separate.”

“OK.”

Bev followed the Rhysu through energy streams that grew larger with each plunge into more energetic areas. They stopped at a dark, rippling barrier they could not penetrate.

Bev focused on the undulating shape, surrounded by twitching ribbons of energy. When she shifted her view, the barrier shifted with it and the energy ribbons changed shape with the change of perspective. “What am I seeing?”

“This is the limit of our expanse,” the Rhysu said. “It is not at one particular place, it is at all places, intertwined within our energy sea. It constrains our movement.”

“The limit of your expanse?”

“It is a barrier we cannot penetrate on our own.”

“What’s on the other side?”

“The place you came from, and other places.”

Bev pondered that revelation. The Rhysu were confined to their spatial dimension. Although they could connect with humans, the way she had connected with Arlud, they could not physically cross into the human universe on their own. She had always sensed that limitation, but seeing the thing that restricted their movement gave this higher-dimensional existence a finite limit she could understand. The microscopic waveform was everywhere within the energy sea, but appeared only when an attempt was made to cross it.

The Rhysu tugged at Bev. The barrier shrunk and disappeared as they rushed from the microscopic back into the normal state of the energy sea.

“How did you cross over if you can’t pass through the barrier?”

“We manipulate energy to open a rift. It opens for only a moment, but a moment is all we need.”

“And you use gravity from the other side?”

“Yes,” the Rhysu said. “A large gravity well helps stabilize the rift so we can pass through.

“But you don’t need a rift to communicate across the barrier.”

"Correct. Some frequencies can pass through the barrier."

"Why do the harmful fluctuations pass?"

"The fluctuations do not pass through. They are disruptions in the space between dimensions."

"Between dimensions?"

"What humans call hyperspace."

"The problem does not emanate from the human universe?"

"The root cause is from the humans because humans access hyperspace."

"What if humans could alter Compression Drive to reduce the disruptions?"

"The act of entering hyperspace creates the disruptions. To reduce disruptions, they must not enter hyperspace. Manipulating hyperspace changes the spatial relationships in our streams. The effect does not pass through the barrier. It warps our space from hyperspace."

"Oh."

Bev's awareness was filled with new data as the Rhysu downloaded the schematics of their proposal to stop Compression Drive. "You want to change how Compression Drive interacts with the fabric of space to stop the harmful fluctuations. You know how to do that?"

"We are testing the process."

"I thought you were willing to find an alternative?"

"We are willing, but we will not stop testing the process."

Bev followed the Rhysu through the energy sea and saw enfolded structures made of braided strands of plasma. Inside the structures, she saw Rhysu spheres. "What are those?"

"Nests."

"Your homes?"

"Where we congregate. The energy sea is our home."

The flow of the energy streams around them jerked upward.

Bev was tossed sideways and lost her connection with the Rhysu as rolling waves pushed her and the Rhysu apart. Her energy sphere collapsed, and she screamed from a brief jolt of searing pain. Her body was flayed in three directions as she tumbled along the wake of the fluctuation that progressed through the streams and disappeared in the distance.

"Eetah!"

The Rhysu surrounded Bev and worked to repair her body so her sphere would regenerate.

"Now you understand why the harmful fluctuations must stop," the Rhysu said.

Once her body was repaired and her sphere returned to its full energized condition, Bev retreated into herself to hide her thoughts from the Rhysu. She could not prove it, but she had a feeling they planned her injury.

They wanted me to experience the pain. They think I will be more eager to help if I understand the danger to myself.

She floated in her sphere between the surrounding Rhysu and considered her options.

I need more information, she thought. *They'll sense my sincerity and provide the info I need if I focus my intent properly. Once that happens, I'll know how far I can go. I escaped Clan Polinda once, a thing impossible in the minds of most people. Escaping the Rhysu, a deed improbable but not impossible. If the Shoku could do it, so can I.*

THE GUILD: HYPERWAVES

The Guild investigation of the destroyed Polinda mine had been underway for seven hours, and the lead drones had reached the lower tunnels near the eruption point.

Shanna Sy stood behind the two seated drone pilots and watched new data populate the holoscreens in front of each man. Sensors on each drone relayed electro-gravitic, visible light, and infrared data as they descended through the damaged tunnel system. Two additional sensors focused on a spectral analysis of the rock, and another scanned for hyper-dimensional disruptions.

Leru Canter, the officer-in-charge, had balked at adding the hyper-dimensional wave detector. "It's too heavy and unlikely to relay useful information."

"Yes," Shanna had replied. "I know it's unorthodox, but so are aliens erupting from inside the planet. We need to gather as much data as possible."

Shanna examined the hyper-dimensional wave graph on the holoscreen for Drone Two. The data feed revealed odd hyperspace fluctuations in combination with a faint radiation with unusual harmonics. "That's what we found in orbit."

Canter peered over Shanna's shoulder at the data screen. "Yes, it is."

Shanna turned and faced the officer. "What could cause that down there?"

Canter shrugged.

Shanna smirked and looked at the holoscreens. Drone One was in a different section of tunnel, one level deeper than Drone Two. "Drone One is nearing the eruption point," she said, and she noticed static in the telemetry feed on the holoscreen. "Is that interference caused by the durillium?"

"Most likely," Canter said. "Look at the electrostatic numbers. That tunnel is a sea of electromagnetic waves."

"Is the drone in danger?"

"No, but we may lose telemetry further in if the energy level increases."

Shanna moved away from the drone drivers and looked out the shuttle's port window. They were parked near the western excavation the Cormed and Sabballi teams had dug to reenter the mine—a ten-meter, circular hole that bored through the twisted rubble of the old mine complex. They had been on the surface for seven hours, but Alpha Cephei, the massive blue-white sun, had barely moved above the horizon because of the planet's slow rotation.

Shanna turned toward the officer-in-charge. "How much longer can we stay here?"

Canter looked at the timer on his wrist pad. "Twenty hours. Plenty of time."

Shanna breathed a quiet sigh of relief. *Good,* she thought, *no need to rush.* She returned her gaze to the dark terrain outside the window. The tinted duraplex reduced the brilliant glare from the sun and revealed its smooth limb about two degrees above the horizon. Shanna understood the hazards posed by direct exposure to that giant star. Once it rose more than five degrees above the horizon, transmissions to the surface from the drone relay network would suffer interference from the intense solar radiation. "Why would anyone come here to mine?"

"Profit," Canter said. "Durillium creates a lot of profit."

"We're there," the driver of Drone One said.

Shanna spun to view the holoscreen. The visible-light monitor displayed a gaping hole in the dark rock at the end of a short tunnel, beyond a large lump of melted metal and the scattered remains of charred environment suits. *The first ones who died,* she thought. *Bev Colli was there. Amazing she could escape.* She watched as the drone entered the hole and rotated down to view a corkscrew-shaped tunnel. "How far can the drone go?"

"Until we lose contact," Canter said.

"What happens then?"

"The drones are programmed to stop and reverse course."

"Good."

Canter touched Drone driver Two on the shoulder. "Can you backtrack and reach that hole?"

"Yes, sir, that'll take about five minutes."

"Do it. You'll hover inside the entrance and relay Drone One's transmissions."

"Yes, sir."

Twenty minutes later, Drone One's descent through the twisting tunnel, relayed to the shuttle crew via the twelve-drone network in the mine, stopped.

Shanna flinched at the dark holoscreen. "What happened?"

Canter moved to the data console and replayed the last ten seconds of Drone One's transmission. "All sensor data stopped."

"Aliens?"

Canter examined all the sensor graphs. "No. Looks like we lost contact because of terrain."

"Terrain?"

The holoscreen for Drone One winked to life and displayed a visible-light image of the twisting rock.

Canter looked at Shanna. "It backtracked to reacquire our link. To keep our connection, we need more drones."

"There are no more drones."

"Then we're done."

Shanna stood behind the drone drivers. Drone One's transmission revealed a sharp turn in the jagged rock. "How deep is that?"

"Five point two kilometers," the driver said.

Shanna faced Canter. "Call Pardee to send down more drones. We still have time."

"It's time we returned to the flagship."

"Why?"

"We should analyze all the data before we proceed. Going further may not be necessary. Besides, that tunnel may go to the center of this rock. We don't have enough drones to cover that distance."

"If the data tells us we need to go further, what do we do?"

Canter shrugged.

Shanna stepped into Captain Pardee's ready room and nodded to Canter, who sat on the bench next to the closed window, his feet crossed on the deck and his head resting against the backrest cushion. "Where's Pardee?"

"On his way."

Shanna moved to the guest chair next to Pardee's desk but remained standing. "So, are we done?"

"That's up to the captain."

Pardee entered the room, prompting Canter to stand. "Please, sit," Pardee said, and he sat behind his desk.

Canter sat, but Shanna hesitated. All she wanted was to know if the investigation was done, but under Pardee's impatient stare, she held back her query and sat in the chair.

"You've had two days to review the data," Pardee said. "Tell me your impressions."

"Overall," Shanna said, "our results are like the Sabballi/Cormed analysis, with minor differences. The hyper-dimensional waves and the electro-magnetic flux in the deepest tunnels are new data."

"Those are facts," Pardee said. "What do you think it means?"

Shanna flicked a glance at Canter, who appeared willing to let her continue. "It means we need more information," she said. "We are witnesses of the aftereffects of a cross-dimensional transfer of energy. We need to know if that crossing is closed or if it's still open. Did the aliens leave anything inside Alpha Cephei Four?"

Pardee shifted his attention to Canter. "Is that possible to know?"

"Maybe," Canter said. "If we continue the tunnel survey, we may discover if anything was left here, but the survey could take months and we may still be without an answer."

"I disagree," Shanna said.

Pardee met Shanna's steady gaze. "Why?"

"We have a thousand years of planetology with which to compare our findings, combined with the fact we know the aliens exist, that their origin is from another dimension. The physical evidence of their passage is all over the destroyed mine."

Canter sat up and leaned forward, as if to add weight to his words. "We can never prove the existence of another dimension because we can't physically interact with it. Every determination about the alien dimension and the reason for the alien contact is all theory, no matter what we find."

"Not so," Shanna said. "The hyper-dimensional evidence supports the eyewitness accounts of what happened. The aliens are real. How they affected this environment is real."

"The aftereffects of the eruption are not evidence of an extra-dimensional cause," Canter insisted. "They are three-dimensional results of a massive release of energy. Hyper-dimensional waves are the aftereffects of three-dimensional energy manipulations. That's how Compression Drive can access hyperspace."

"When was Compression Drive ever used in a mine?"

Canter looked at Shanna with a smirk. "It's the energy, not Compression Drive, that caused the hyper-dimensional waves in the mine."

Shanna contemplated Canter's answer and replied: "If three-dimensional energy manipulations create hyper-dimensional waves by warping three-dimensional space, then higher-dimensional energy manipulations should also create hyper-dimensional waves, since hyper-dimensional waves result from warping dimensional space. Hyper-dimensional waves are evidence of a higher-dimensional presence in the mine."

"That's your theory?" Canter asked. "You're implying that hyper-dimensional waves are felt in all spatial dimensions?"

Shanna nodded and faced Pardee. "We have the security camera recordings of the plasma streams. We have Bev Colli's recording of the eruption from inside the mine. We have unusual radiation readings deep in the rock, beyond anything durillium would cause. All this, combined with remnants of hyper-dimensional waves, indicates a higher-dimensional alien intrusion."

"That tells us nothing about why it happened," Canter said.

Shanna shifted her focus. "When Clan Halva went back to Arrilen Po with Arlud Erstallius and Bev Colli, they examined the tunnel where Cynth was found. While not as deep, they found a sharp turn like the one we found. That's a significant similarity."

"I agree," Canter said. "I understand the significance, but beyond that I can see no reason to continue our effort."

Shanna flicked a disdainful glance at Canter. "No reason? Beyond that turn on Arrilen Po was a spherical cavern with two circular tunnels opposite from where their drone entered. We should push beyond the bend to see if a similar cavern is here on Alpha Cephei Four."

Pardee leaned back in his chair. "And if we find no cavern?"

Shanna faced Pardee. "Then you can do as you wish with no argument from me."

The investigation team reset the drone relay network to free five drones for reassignment in case the bent tunnel went deeper than expected. The shuttle with the receiving station sat on a landing pad twenty meters below the surface at the bottom of the Sabballi/Cormed excavation—the underground position blocked interference from the rising sun.

Shanna watched the recording of the lead drone's transmission in the comfort of her cabin on the flagship. Pardee had stopped her from returning to the surface. Knowing what happened the last time someone entered an alien cavern, he would not allow Wolfram Sy's daughter anywhere near it.

On the holoscreen, the lead drone stopped in the tunnel where it bent ninety-degrees. The dark rock face twisted clockwise, and the surface presented a glazed sheen from the intense heat it had suffered.

As the visual recording played on her holoscreen, Shanna monitored the sensor data on a smaller holoscreen that floated next to the main display. All the data was similar to the readings the team had collected earlier that day. The hyper-dimensional waves jumped a few degrees higher as the drone entered the horizontal tunnel.

Shanna advanced the playback to speed-up travel time through the tunnel until the rock passage widened and the glazed walls illuminated by the drone's forward lamp disappeared from view. She paused the playback.

There it is, she thought. She restarted the playback at normal speed and watched as the drone entered a huge cavern. The radar data revealed a hollow sphere thirty meters in diameter.

That's larger than the one on Arrilen Po.

Shanna changed the view to infrared and the black screen turned a dull red.

Residual heat.

The drone rotated three-hundred sixty degrees and the infrared image showed one circular tunnel nineteen degrees below the sphere's equator.

Shanna advanced the replay again and returned to normal playback as the drone came closer to the circular tunnel.

The holo-image went black as the drone left the spherical cavern and entered the circular tunnel.

The radar data mapped the tunnel length at only ten meters with a smooth concave end.

Shanna paused the data replay and focused on the data graphs. The hyper-dimensional wave detector jumped off the scale. She dialed through the spectral analysis settings. At the three-quarter mark, a rotating sphere of diaphanous orange and green hyper-waves appeared at the back of the tunnel.

"Wow!"

PETRA SITLYN: KULIQ'QUAD

The morning sun had not yet risen above the eastern cliffs of Kuliq'Quad basin, bathing Petra in cool shade. She rested against the front fender of her utility cart and scanned her data pad. She compared the digital foundation plan for the shuttle construction building to the surveyor's stakes sticking out of the ground cleared of snow. A new durroconcrete tarmac would extend one hundred meters north from the Mânu, which would merge with the new building's foundation and extend twenty meters beyond the building's northern face.

This is a good start, Petra thought. *We should have the foundation blocks set by mid-day.*

She turned toward the low-pitched whine of a utility cart approaching from the Mânu. Winstone Bittle sat in the driver's seat and guided the cart across snow covered ground outside the survey markers. Behind him, the gray sphere of a grounded Aku transport stood on its four legs on landing pad Two—the aft hull plates removed for access to the main engine compartment.

Bittle stopped the cart a few paces from Petra. "Good morning. Looks like you've made good progress."

"Yes, we have. What do you want?"

"Another transport will planet-fall in about an hour. You will want to cease your activity until the ship is safely grounded. Standard precaution."

"My crew won't be here."

"Oh," Bittle said. "I assumed you'd get an early start."

"I knew about your flight operations, so rescheduled our start time."

"Oh."

Petra noticed a brief disgruntlement in Bittle's expression. *Typical,* she thought. *He always needs to have the upper hand.* "Anything else?"

"The transport will planet-fall with two tons of supplies for your work crew. We'll help you offload it."

"Thank you."

"Once your tarmac is completed, we'll deliver your supplies via cargo shuttle."

"Good."

Bittle nodded. He turned the cart to leave, then paused and looked back at Petra. "You know, if leadership changes at home steer the clan in another direction, our stay here may be ended."

"Really? You believe that?"

"It's possible. If Arlud does not return—"

"We made a pact with the Aku."

"We?"

"Clan Erstallius."

"You left the clan," Bittle stated in a flat tone.

"I was allowed to retire from the Defense Force. I did not leave the clan."

"Some say you rejected your duty."

Petra caught her temper in her throat and stopped remarks Bittle would find offensive. "Our regent approved my request to retire."

"Well, you can't control what some people think."

"What will the Aku think if the clan abandons them?"

"We'll make sure their ability to defend themselves is sufficient if we leave. They'll have at least four class five destroyers, maybe ten if Clan Dejoria is generous."

"Sounds like command already decided to leave."

"No," Bittle assured, "just voicing possibilities. I thought you should know. If we leave, you'll only have one chance to return home with us."

"I'm staying here."

Bittle frowned. "As you wish." He hit the cart's accelerator and headed back to the Mânu.

Petra stopped her cart on the snow-covered ground west of the Mânu, a hundred meters from the spot where Jens Orr had been forced to land the shuttle with the guild survivors. She relaxed in the driver's seat, remembering that day and her first sight of sipá cavalry.

Magnificent beasts.

Those memories led to thoughts of Aluk and the Hybrid Farm. They were close, less than one-hundred kilometers northwest of Kuliq'Quad basin.

I could be there in a few hours with this cart.

Her regret at leaving Aluk was a nagging disruption to her internal focus—she never expected to develop such a close bond—but her promise to Salus was a commitment that overshadowed everything else and stifled the thought of returning to the farm.

I must do whatever the Aku ask of me.

Salus was in Dol'anar where combat ships would be built—ships three times the size of the shuttles built in Kuliq'Quad Basin. *His project dwarfs this one,* she thought, and she hoped it would not delay their marriage beyond the year promised.

A spherical Aku transport plunged through the high clouds over the basin's western rim wall.

Petra watched the ship drop toward the Mânu enveloped in the white atmospheric halo typical of the tri-pole compression engine. Thirty meters above the tarmac, the landing gear deployed, the four plasma thrusters attached at the sphere's equator ignited, and the white halo disappeared. The ship landed on pad four and the plasma emissions stopped.

Perfect.

As the ground crew rushed to the transport, four open-air ground cars filled with passengers rumbled east out of Kuliq'Quad Village along the snow-lined dirt road that led to the Mânu.

My Crew. Right on time.

Petra turned her cart around and followed the tracks the cart had left in the snow to meet her crew at the construction site.

CLAN ERSTALLIUS: VISIONS

Doctor Singh placed a slim, white medpad on Arlud's forehead and pushed the switch to activate it. "This will help me isolate the correct waves. Are you feeling pain?"

"A little," Arlud said. He reclined in a lounge chair in the Erstallius residence library. "She's asking if I can hear her."

"Tell her," Singh encouraged. "Tell her with your mind."

Arlud closed his eyes. *I hear you. Where are you? Are you OK?*

I can barely hear you, Bev said. *I'm OK... I need... to tell you...*

Bev's voice faded, and the pain in Arlud's neck vanished. He sat up and pulled the medpad off his forehead.

Singh looked up from his data pad. "What happened?"

"We lost the connection."

Singh sat at the table and examined the transmitted data. "Well," he said, "the relay worked. This is good. I can make adjustments from this." He faced Arlud. "The analyzer's filter must have blocked her. I'll know more once I've examined all the data."

Two hours later, Singh adjusted the medpad and placed it on Arlud's forehead. "Don't take it off. We need to catch her signals as soon as you get them."

They spent the rest of the day in the library, but Bev's voice never returned.

Arlud was immersed in a dream at the edge of a calm lake surrounded by pine trees. Bev Colli appeared in front of him, standing with her arms crossed, wearing the clothes she had worn on U'galem. He could see a bulge under her pullover shirt from the retriever's pistol stuffed in her pants. "I thought you left that gun on U'galem?"

Bev examined the bulge at her waist. "I did. This is your imagination."

"You're not real."

"Not my appearance, just my mind. You see what you want to see."

"How is this possible?"

"It's a dream."

"I know that. How can you—"

"The Rhysu taught me," Bev said. "We exchanged thoughts. I learned many things."

"This is how they connected with you."

"Yes, but I can speak to you. They could not speak to me when I was me."

"When, what?"

"When I was my old me. My human me."

"Oh."

"I don't have a lot of time, so pay attention."

Arlud moved in front of Bev and held her shoulders—toned muscle beneath thin fabric. "I'm not going anywhere."

"Focus," Bev insisted. "This is important."

"OK."

Talking slowed communication, so Bev shifted to the Rhysu method and transferred her memories of the plan to end Compression Drive directly into Arlud's mind.

Arlud flinched. "Wow!"

"Yeah," Bev said. "They're serious about it. Hurts a lot when those waves rip you apart. Happened to me once."

Arlud let Bev's memories replay in his mind. He let go of her shoulders and took a step backward. "If they succeed, our universe will be changed forever. Our holdings will be isolated, thousands of people will be stranded in space."

"Yeah."

"What do we do to stop them?"

"Find a solution to stop the harmful fluctuations. Nothing will stop the Rhysu. I can try to delay them, but I will never stop them."

Arlud focused on his vision of Bev. "I miss you."

"I miss you too. Be brave. Find a solution."

Bev's image faded.

Arlud jerked awake.

Stop the harmful fluctuations.

Doctor Singh burst into Arlud's bedroom, and the yellow light from the hallway illuminated Arlud on his bed. "Is she gone?"

Arlud flung aside the blue flannel blanket and swung his feet to the floor. "You recorded my dream?"

"She appeared in your dreams?"

Arlud nodded.

"This is more than I expected!"

"I felt no discomfort," Arlud said. "Was that because of the medpad or because she spoke to me in a dream?"

"I need to analyze the data. This is great!"

Singh turned and rushed out of the room.

Arlud leaned forward and plucked off the medpad. Bev's warning about the Rhysu alternative ignited a fresh fear for the future. *The Alliance may crumble,* he thought, *but that's nothing compared to the Rhysu threat*. He reached over to the table next to his bed, grabbed his compad, and sent a message to Eahuda.

> "Alert status: One. Notify your security team to prepare to leave. Meet me in the library ASAP."

The dark hall concealed Benita as she watched the grim-faced conversation through a slit between the library's double doors. Inside the room, back-lit by the yellow light from two glowballs that flanked the bay window, Arlud, Eahuda, and Doctor Singh sat at the table and discussed the warning from Bev. Benita slid open the double-doors. "We usually sleep at this hour on Baleiou. Is your time sense so different?"

The three men stopped their conversation and stood to greet the Erstallius matriarch. She was clothed in a floor-length, black night coat with flared sleeves, her dark hair disheveled and draped over her shoulders.

"I apologize, Mother," Arlud said. "Something happened that needs our immediate attention."

"Bev Colli contacted you, and there's a dire situation you need to fix."

Arlud exchanged glances with Eahuda and Singh, then returned his attention to his mother. "How do you know?"

"You thought you could keep that from me, in my house?"

Eahuda glanced around the room. The surveillance devices were hidden well. He wasn't uncomfortable about being under constant scrutiny, but disappointed Lady Erstallius found it necessary to spy on her own son. "Madame, our aim was not to deceive you, it was—"

"Good Gustav," Benita said. "I know your aim. I'm here to help."

"I did not want to add to your burden," Arlud admitted.

"My burden?"

"You're in mourning, and you seemed to regret my presence."

Benita moved closer to her son. "Now that Hugo Rusan is High Regent, your status is in jeopardy. I expect you to lose your assignment on GSW-183, and all access to our fleet. If you're stuck on-planet, your quest to resolve the alien issue may end before it can begin—the cadre will ignore you. You must gather allies who have the resources to find a solution and the power to influence the clans. You won't find them here."

Arlud knew his mother's assessment was correct. The Erstallius cadre would ignore his warnings, just as they had ignored the warning Jhared Dejoria had broadcast to the Old Worlds. That reality was a stab to the heart. *They continue to reject me, despite what I've done to secure our position in the outer district.* "Jhared will continue to help us," he said, "as will the allies who fought with us at Wan'tei. The Guild also understands the threat. Together, we will create a voice even the cadre cannot ignore."

Doctor Singh rapped his knuckles on the table. "We need a solution in hand before we broadcast the problem."

Benita faced the doctor. "Why?"

"Presenting a problem without a solution breeds skepticism. I recommend we contact the clan's science division."

Arlud faced Singh. "The cadre control access to all clan facilities."

"I never thought our own clan would be our greatest obstacle," Eahuda said in an undertone.

"The clan isn't the obstacle," Arlud said. "The cadre is the problem. The High Regent's path will be focused on restoring our fleet's strength and stabilizing our holdings. Diverting resources to counter the Rhysu will not happen."

Benita stepped toward Arlud and placed a hand on his shoulder. "We need to ignore the naysayers and broadcast your evidence across the comnet for everyone to see. That will increase the odds of finding engineers who understand the physics involved." She clasped her hands at her waist. "How many drones can you send?"

"Ten should be enough," Eahuda said.

"My cruiser has thirty comm-drones," Benita said. "I recommend we board her ASAP and use that arsenal to contact more holdings. If we delay too long, we'll be stuck on-planet."

Singh asked: "Will Hugo really limit access to your transport? Can he do that?"

Benita folded her arms across her chest. "He can and will. My status as Lady of the Clan ended the day Hugo was appointed. I'll keep my current residence and all the benefits guaranteed to a High Regent's widow, but in a few days my access to fleet transport will end."

Arlud faced Singh. "Once I'm officially deposed, I'll lose all access to clan infrastructure—no more free rides on clan dreadnoughts."

"I need more time to analyze the medpad data," Singh said. "If you want the ability to contact Bev, I must have more time and more data."

"Then you'll come with us."

"I can't. My family is here."

"Bring them with you."

A wave of panic flowed across Singh's face. "I have five children still at home."

Eahuda's jaw dropped. "Five?"

"Yes," Singh said. "From eight to sixteen years."

Benita asked: "Five children still at home? How many do you have?"

"Ten. The other five are on Thrum Dau with their mother. I can't leave my children and taking them is not an option. If this Rhysu thing happens, I will not risk them being marooned in space."

"That's understandable," Arlud said. "Stay here and continue to analyze what you have. Thank you, Doctor. You've been a great help."

Singh nodded his appreciation. "Thank you."

"Bev may be the most important part of any solution," Eahuda said to Arlud. "Can you maintain effective contact without the doctor?"

Arlud nodded. "I'll just need to wait on her to make the contact."

"In time," Benita said, "your connection with Bev may improve to the point it becomes constant, much like her connection with the Rhysu."

Arlud pondered his mother's comment and frowned. "That might not be as beneficial as you think."

"Why?"

"A continuous stream of thoughts between us may allow the Rhysu to eavesdrop."

"If they haven't done that already," Eahuda said.

Benita rested her hands on her hips. "Are we certain the Rhysu can accomplish what they intend?"

"Bev was certain," Arlud assured. "She revealed no time frame for when but was adamant that it would happen."

"Then we must do our best to stop it."

The air traffic above the landing field was sparse in the pre-dawn darkness—one arrival per hour, no departures scheduled until after sunrise.

A guard blocked the ground car that rolled up to the VIP gate.

Another guard approached the driver's side. "Your I.D., please."

The driver gave the guard an Erstallius Regency pass.

The interior of the car was dark, so the guard asked, "How many passengers?"

Benita lowered the passenger window. "Three. Our shuttle is waiting, Diwa-Major."

"Yes, Madame," the guard responded. He gave the pass back to the driver. "Hanger four to your right." He pointed to the row of buildings. "Your crew called and told us to expect you, Madame. Have a pleasant trip." He saluted Benita and backed away from the car.

Once they reached the hangar, Benita, Arlud, and Eahuda were rushed into the shuttle. Twenty minutes later, they were speeding past the orbiting debris streams, heading for Benita's cruiser ten-thousand kilometers inside the orbit of the binary moon.

Benita leaned in her padded passenger seat toward the bulkhead to peer out the small oval window. "Looks like we'll make it."

Arlud nodded from the seat, facing his mother. "If a hold order is sent, will the Commander-in-Charge honor your request?"

Benita smiled at Arlud. "No worries. This crew is loyal to our family. The devotion to your father was genuine."

"How did Hugo—"

"Hugo won because your actions were ridiculed by the majority."

Arlud let the sting in that truth pass through him. "We defeated Polinda and secured Pigrell for the clan. Why is that ridiculed?"

Benita returned her gaze out the window. "The cadre viewed your actions at GSW-183 as a weakness. You've done nothing that deserves an apology. It's just politics—propaganda to rally supporters. They ridiculed your father also—they said he died because he was too moderate, that he should have hit Polinda first." She looked at Arlud. "We can't control the actions of others. The clan will go forward as the cadre wishes—even if that path is questionable. The past should not dictate our actions. Our actions should be a response to what needs to be done, not an attempt to repair the past or confiscate the future."

"Confiscate?"

"Hugo."

"Oh." *She implies Hugo stole the election,* Arlud thought. *A reward for his charity to opposition leaders, which fuels suspicion the vote was rigged. A deplorable event if proved true.* Arlud looked out the window next to his seat. "I would like to repair many things."

"As would we all," Benita said in a contemplative tone. "With our thoughts focused on the past, we often miss options to improve the future."

"This mission could improve the future. Hopefully, the clans will agree."

"And if they don't?"

"Then our civilization is doomed."

Benita leaned back on her couch and did a quick mental analysis of her son. "Not doomed," she said. "We'll still exist, just under different circumstances."

"I suppose that's one way to view it."

"The Rhysu don't want to destroy us, just limit us."

"Isn't that the same thing?"

"No," Benita stressed. "We should consider options in case we fail. We might find a solution that circumvents the worst-case scenario."

"It would help to know how much time we have."

"Yes, it would," Benita said.

"That'll be the first thing I ask Bev."

A precarious position, Benita thought. *Our future may depend on the ability of a Polinda sapi. Armand would never have accepted that.* She focused on Arlud. "Your faith in Bev is strong. She must have been a unique woman."

"Yes," Arlud said. "She is."

CLAN HALVA: SURVEY

Cynth stepped out of the shower stall, draped a towel around her shoulders, and stared into the small mirror above the washbasin. The drying elements in the stall had evaporated the moisture off her body and metallic limbs, but her gray shoulder-length hair framed her face like twisted cords of a worn damp mop. She brushed the strands behind her ears and examined her face. The bags under her eyes were larger, the seams to either side of her mouth had grown deeper, and her jowls sagged more with the turn of a new year. Today was her seventy-eighth birthday. There were cosmetics to tighten the skin and revive the appearance of youth, but that solution was a vain one.

I'll not hide behind a false return to my youth.

She raised the towel to dry her hair and the cabin holoscreen buzzed for attention. With a towel on her head, she slid open the shower room door, moved to the holoscreen panel next to the cabin hatch, and hit the response button for audio only. "Yes?"

"This is Commander Russo, Madame. We have passed the heliosphere."

"Good. Any response yet?"

"Not yet. Our drone will reach orbit in about thirty minutes."

"The drone's close enough to relay communication. We should have heard from the survey team by now."

"Yes, Madame."

Russo's brief answer revealed his misgivings about the survey team's status, which mirrored Cynth's worst assumption. "How long till we get there?"

"Two hours."

"Thank you, Commander. Keep me updated."

Cynth ended the call. She rubbed the towel against her wet hair and returned to the shower room.

Tara Quin entered the dark observation bay and joined Cynth by the window.

Cynth focused on Arrilen Po—a small blue disk flanked by its two moons, surrounded by the brilliant star field, with the disk of the Milky Way slicing vertically through the view thirty degrees left of the planet.

"I finished the reports," Quin said.

Cynth glanced at her assistant. "Good. What are your impressions?"

"It's a tragedy."

"Why?"

"They used her and then abducted her."

Cynth returned her gaze out the window. "They didn't take her life."

"Yes, they did."

"She's still alive."

"Our lives are more than physical existence. Our lives include everything we experience. They took her humanity from her."

"They took her human form, not her humanity. Look at me, I'm still human despite these limbs."

"Yes, Madame, but you are still part of this universe. Bev lost everything but her consciousness."

"Consciousness is the core of who we are. No one can take that from her."

Quin focused on Arrilen Po. "I suppose not killing her was an act of kindness, but she's no longer human—that's worse than death. She must feel alone in that strange place."

Cynth agreed. "No doubt."

The comm panel next to the window buzzed for attention.

Cynth flicked the call switch. "Yes?"

"This is Commander Russo, Madame. We are still not receiving from the cruiser in orbit. I have changed our approach path. We will enter orbit one-thousand kilometers outside the orbit of the second moon. We will drop to our intended prime orbit only after we've determined all is safe."

"Thank you, Commander," Cynth replied. She switched off the comm panel and noticed Quin's worried expression. "Nothing to fear, Quin. The Commander-in-Charge won't place us in jeopardy. We'll leave if we must."

The Halva task force, three cruisers and two freighters, settled into cautionary orbits beyond Arrilen Po's second moon and launched an

Explorer Class drone to examine the survey team's unresponsive cruiser. The data was transmitted to a receiving station in the task force flagship's C.I.C. and displayed on a holoscreen above the plotting pedestal.

Cynth watched the drone's visual analysis of the cruiser's hull—no damage. Energy signatures from the engine pods appeared normal, yet the ship was spinning around her Y-axis at a rate of 30 degrees-per-hour, in an elliptical orbit 520 kilometers by 110 kilometers from the planet's surface.

"That ship was pushed out of her prime orbit," Cynth said in an undertone. She turned toward Jegen-Major Russo. "That wouldn't happen if the crew were still on board."

Russo faced the pilot at the drone control station. "Gandri, breech the forward hatch."

"Aye, sir," Gandri said. He guided the drone along the port side of the vessel, then under the forward engine pod to the circular access hatch. The drone's articulated arm extended and turned the hatch release. The door slid open and revealed an empty airlock.

Thirty minutes later, after passing through the forward engine room cluttered with five dead clanmen floating in the micro-gravity; after speeding through empty corridors past the shuttle bay; after negotiating up four stairwells to the med deck, then past the crew cabins and up five more decks, the drone reached the C.I.C. The command crew bobbed in the micro-gravity, restrained by their seat straps.

Cynth read the data feed on the holoscreen. "All dead. How?"

Russo turned to his Operations Officer. "Get a team over there, Degen Magol. Retrieve those bodies and transfer all ship data."

"Aye, sir," Magol said, then he turned and rushed out of the C.I.C.

Cynth stood under the low light in the flagship's forward lounge and examined the graphic overlay in the window that outlined the twisted radiation belts around Arrilen Po.

Quin stood a few paces from Cynth, toward the lounge entrance, her expression a mixture of confusion and silent dread. "What caused that?"

"Aliens," Cynth said, without a hint of emotion.

Jegen-Major Russo entered the lounge, moved to the narrow table, and dropped a thin folio onto the sleek black surface. "Ladies, please sit."

"I prefer to stand," Cynth said without turning.

The Commander-in-Charge looked at Quin and gestured to a seat on the other side of the table. "Please sit."

Once Quin sat, Russo angled his chair so he could face both women while seated. "This is not the final report, but we have enough data. I'm confident our assessment is correct." He flipped open the folio. "There were eruptions from the planet—something emitted hyper-dimensional waves from the poles and the hyper-nodal points. They caused—"

"Hyper-nodal?"

Russo nodded at Quin's interruption. "All spinning planetoids with active cores pull in energy from a higher dimension. The energy radiates to the surface at nodal points based on hyper-dimensional geometry, usually around nineteen point five degrees above and below the planet's equator. The emitted waves warped the magnetic field and caused the poles to change location. That altered the magnetosphere and created the twisted radiation belts you see in those graphs." He gestured to the graphic in the window. "They'll migrate to a stable, more balanced condition if there are no more emissions, but the data indicates that may take a few months."

Quin leaned forward. "How did that kill the clanmen in the cruiser?"

"The waves not only twisted the magnetosphere, they altered the fabric of space around the planet, which disabled the cruiser's Compression Drive. Based on the recorded data, bio-electric systems were disrupted like the magnetosphere. The crew's nervous systems shut down, and they died. The waves continued outward and brushed the surface of the inner moon. The moon's geography was affected, and its orbit was changed."

"They were attacked," Cynth said.

Russo nodded. "Based on the history of this holding, I agree with you, Madame. The aliens are the cause."

"The aliens?" Quin asked. She faced Cynth. "I thought the aliens helped you. You told me we had nothing to fear from them."

"Yes, I did," Cynth admitted. "I was speaking of the ones Bev called Rhysu. There are also ones she called Shoku."

"The ones who attacked the Cormed ships?"

"Yes," Cynth said. She turned her attention back to Russo. "What about Arrilen Po's surface?"

"Massive damage."

"So, the survey team—"

"All dead."

Quin leaned back in her chair. "What do we do now?"

Russo closed his folio. "I've sent more drones to the surface to locate the original eruption point. If we can find it, we may stop it from happening again."

Cynth chuckled. "How?"

"We'll know how once we have more data."

"Absurd," Cynth said in an undertone. "We'll never know. We're limited by our dimension—we can't peer into their universe. We can only detect the effects they leave."

"Not absurd," Russo responded with dry conviction. "We know from Bev Colli's dialogues that the aliens need specific conditions to breach the barrier between dimensions. They failed many times here on Arrilen Po because of physical traits in the rock."

"What traits?"

"Pitchblende. We found hints of that the last time we were here."

Quin's worry faded. "What's Pitchblende?"

"A radioactive mineral," Russo said.

Cynth huffed. "That's a fool's path."

"Their failed crossover sites all show evidence of—"

"How can Pitchblende stop them from creating a rift?"

Russo shrugged. "We need more data to determine that."

"They can fly through space," Cynth said. "Space filled with all sorts of radiation. They can alter magnetospheres, burst through solid rock, endure temperatures that can melt durillium, and Pitchblende will stop them? Rubbish!"

"But it's a factor in their failures," Russo said with calm resolve. "We must investigate it."

"At what cost?"

"Madame?"

"If we stay, will we also be dead?"

Quin gasped. "Oh my! I don't want to die."

"We need more data," Russo answered, focused on Cynth. "I have set an eight-hour time limit to retrieve the dead from the surface—a search team left thirty minutes ago. We'll take that time to gather as much info as possible."

Cynth rested her hands on her hips. "Then we leave?"

"Yes, then we leave," Russo assured, "unless something happens before time is up."

Quin leaned forward and slapped her hands on the table. "What?"

Russo looked at Quin's confused expression. "We'll leave sooner if there's a need."

"Oh," Quin relaxed and leaned back in her seat. "Good. That's good."

BEV COLLI: PASSAGE

The Rhysu surrounded Bev and pressed against her. Their tendrils wrapped around her energy sphere and pinched her plasma flow.

"Ouch! What are you doing?"

"Relax," the Rhysu said. "We will teach you how to enfold."

"What?"

The Rhysu dove into Bev's consciousness and revealed through detailed images how to restrict her dimensional reach.

"You have been unrestricted until now," the Rhysu said. "You must learn to limit your presence in the human universe so they cannot detect you."

"I thought you said I could not return there."

"We must take you there. You must see what the Shoku have done."

"What did they do?"

"You will practice how to enfold once we cross the dimensional barrier."

The lack of an answer to her question told Bev the Rhysu wanted to show her what the Shoku had done rather than tell her.

There was a loud pop, and a cyan-colored, swirling energy vortex erupted in front of Bev. Moments later, she rushed through the rift and tumbled out of the vortex into a smooth spherical cavern. She looked back at the brilliant, churning passageway to see more Rhysu burst through the rift. The vortex vanished, and the dimmer Rhysu energy spheres illuminated the glazed rock surface.

"Practice," the Rhysu said.

Bev could not see the results of her effort. Her senses were beyond the limits humans experience—she saw no change in her appearance. "How will I know I've done this right?"

"You'll feel it, and your reflection will no longer be visible. Focus on our example. Follow each step exactly. Restrict your reach."

Bev repeated the steps the Rhysu showed her, but the glow from her energy sphere still reflected off the rock.

I can't leave this cavern until I can do this, she thought. *I'm a higher dimensional being now, but I'm in a three-dimensional world. Unless I pull back from revealing myself, humans will see the shape of my higher dimensional body as a glowing sphere.*

She tried again, and again. Twelve times her energy streams bent and twisted, folding into her higher dimensional self. And then the glow from her body vanished from the rock wall.

Yes!

The Rhysu pulled Bev upward, through a long, narrow tunnel, and emerged into a clear blue sky above a rock-littered valley bordered on the north and south by rugged granite hills. She felt the heat from her presence push away the thin atmosphere as she rotated to examine the landscape. "Enfolding only hides our visual presence, not the effects we have on this universe?"

"Correct," the Rhysu said. "Proceed with caution and do not relax your body."

Bev surveyed the terrain. Thirty meters below her, eight dead humans lay scattered around the rock walls of a research station. Patches of flesh had decayed to reveal segments of bone. The uniforms, unaffected by the decay, displayed their clan crest on the shoulder of the right sleeve. "This is Arrilen Po! They were part of Clan Halva's survey team. Who killed them!?"

"The Shoku."

"Why!?"

"The Shoku are consumed by their goal. They activated our weapon."

"Weapon?"

"They found an enfolded path that allowed them to flee to the origin point and open the rift. Once here, they activated our weapon. Humans within range did not survive."

"Your weapon is here?"

"Our prototype. We deactivated it to avoid killing more humans."

"Are the Shoku still free?"

"No. We caged the Shoku to keep the humans safe, but it is difficult to cage them forever—alternative paths emerge as the energy sea fluctuates. When they escaped, we caged you to protect you."

"Me?" Bev remembered the transparent sphere.

"They still see you as an enemy."

Bev focused on the word *enemy* and the Rhysu showed her visions of their struggle with the Shoku—twisted strands of energy, entwined in a fight that left many Rhysu maimed.

"The humans will want revenge for these deaths," Bev said.

The Rhysu were pleased at Bev's mental separation from *humans.* "They cannot war with us."

"Are you sure?"

"We are confident."

"Once these deaths are discovered, the humans may use Compression Drive to inflict more harm. You are not immune to retaliation."

"Which is why we oppose the Shoku, and why we seek a solution that will not cause harm."

Bev sensed movement in the atmosphere and turned to face the western horizon. *Two large shuttles.* "Humans are coming!"

The Rhysu grabbed Bev and pulled her toward the tunnel.

Bev twisted free. "I need to know who's coming!" She focused on the approaching aircraft. Too much time had passed for the occupants in the aircraft to be contemporaries of the dead survey team, otherwise the dead would have been retrieved by now. In her mind she saw the shuttles, and thoughts of Cynth Halva jumped to the forefront of her thinking. Her mind's vision leaped out of the atmosphere, and she sped toward cruisers orbiting beyond the second moon. "Cynth has come back!"

The Rhysu grabbed Bev again and forced her into the tunnel. "We must not reveal ourselves!"

Bev's focus jumped back to her immediate reality, and she felt a pressure wave pulse through her body as she tumbled out of the Rhysu grip deeper into the rock tunnel. "What was that?"

"Our solution," the Rhysu said.

A thud echoed once from a distant hollow in the rock, and Bev sensed a change in the environment. *A shift in air pressure? A change in gravity?* "What did you do?"

"We changed the polarity of the flux."

"The what?"

"The material precursor of this universe. We generated this change from within this hard place, and it radiates outward to encompass the space nearby. It is a minute change that affects the formation of the compression fields."

"It alters hyperspace?"

"No. It changes how the compression field interacts with the hyperspatial environment."

Bev moved further into the tunnel, focused on Cynth Halva, and saw her standing at a large window, gazing at Arrilen Po and its two moons.

The grief revealed in the old matriarch's eyes overwhelmed Bev's awareness, and her focus returned to the rock tunnel. "Will it kill them?"

"No," the Rhysu said. "It will not cause harm. We will monitor the process and evaluate."

"How long will that take?"

"As long as needed. We need to know if it's sustainable and the range of effectiveness."

"Why did you bring me here?"

"You needed to see this to affirm the truth in our desire to not cause harm."

Bev sensed the sincerity in the Rhysu motive. They would not proceed without caution. She moved back into the spherical cavern, receded into her private state, and focused on the Halva clanmen. The two shuttles landed on the rough ground next to station 38. The crew from one shuttle retrieved the dead. The crew from the other shuttle placed new equipment inside the rock walls beneath the collapsed drill rig.

The Rhysu solution hasn't affected them.

With that positive observation, Bev focused on the cruisers, and her mental vision jumped to Cynth Halva. The old woman sat with a young girl at a black table. They both looked distraught.

Are they saddened by the dead or something else?

While in her private state, Bev could not communicate nor hear Cynth's conversation. The Rhysu would break any attempt at communication and prevent her from leaving the cavern, so she focused her mind's eye beyond Cynth and roamed through the ship's corridors to find the bridge.

No panic among the crew, but they appear upset.

Once on the bridge, Bev moved to the propulsion console and noticed the failure of the drive system frustrated the helmsman.

It worked!

Bev relaxed her focus and returned to the cavern, uncertain how to proceed—she was glad the Rhysu could reduce the harmful fluctuations without causing harm, but if their solution proved sustainable harm may still impact humans via the aftereffects—stalled ships, and stranded settlements.

There must be a better alternative!

The Rhysu surrounded Bev and carried her to the center of the cavern. A cyan energy vortex blazed around them, and they were pulled through the rift.

Once she could isolate herself in the energy sea, Bev focused on Arlud. Her mind's eye jumped across the dimensional barrier, sped through space, and came to rest next to him in a dark room. *Can you hear me?*

"I've been waiting for you," Arlud replied. He sat on the settee in his cabin and touched the medpad on his forehead, ready to remove it if Bev's voice faded. "How much time do we have?"

The Rhysu were successful, Bev said in a mournful tone, and she downloaded into Arlud's mind what she had seen on Arrilen Po. *They plan to open rifts in every colonized world and emit energy waves that will prevent Compression Drive from working wherever human colonies exist. Not sure how much time you have.*

"Time may not matter."

Why do you say that?

"It's unlikely we can alter how our engines interact with the flux and still achieve an efficient compression into hyperspace. The process needs to be specific to work."

Then don't counter the Rhysu wave. There must be other options beyond Compression Drive.

"If you know of any, now would be a good time to tell me," Arlud said in a sarcastic tone. "What can *you* do?"

Bev flinched. *What do you mean?*

"You're with them now. You're one of them. You must have abilities they have."

I'm like them, but not them. They have knowledge I don't. They have stuff I don't understand how to use. The flux changing is done with some kind of device that gets power from the planet in your universe. They called it genic energy.

"In my universe?"

Yeah, Bev said. Her tone implied she had accepted her new life with the Rhysu. *There are no planets in the Rhysu universe.*

"They can't alter Compression Drive unless they crossover into the human universe?"

Apparently not. Is that important?

"It's a beginning," Arlud said.

Good. Bev's tone was more upbeat. *Please don't give up.*

"What happened to Cynth and her clanmen?"

They were safe when I left Arrilen Po, but they could not use Compression Drive.

"They're stuck there?"

Yeah, but if they can move out of range of the Rhysu device, they'll be able to return to Cestratha—unless more devices are activated and the route they take is affected.

"And the Rhysu still need to test the process."

Yeah.

"I must pass this info to people who know more about the physics end of things—it's beyond me, but it is helpful. Thank You."

Good.

Arlud's thoughts shifted to Doctor Singh's effort to improve his communication with Bev, and Bev uploaded every detail. *Thank the doctor for me,* she said. *I have to go now.* She could feel Arlud's adoration for her, and she flooded his mind with her deep admiration for him.

CLAN ERSTALLIUS: LIMITS

Arlud floated through micro-gravity in the circular access corridor to cruiser 1108's aft engine pod, followed by the Commander-in-Charge, Jamira Melkor, and Science Officer, Newt Vellion. Once they reached the engine pod hatch, Vellion punched in the access code on the lock plate. "Follow me," he said, "the Chief is in the control room."

Engine Chief Maxillian Sands watched through the window in the control room door as the three visitors entered the engine pod and drifted forward beneath bundled conduits, flanked by the man-sized capacitor banks that lined the short passage to the control room. He activated the control room door, and it slid open. "Welcome," he said with a hint of surprise—guests were a rare sight in the engine pods. He closed the door once everyone was inside the cramped space. "Why meet here, sir?"

"Privacy," Melkor said. "This is Arlud Erstallius. He has questions for you."

Sands flinched. "Arlud?" He straightened his body in the micro-gravity, steadied himself by clutching a hand railing, and saluted.

Arlud grabbed a railing and returned the salute. "Thank you for allowing me access to your domain, Engine Chief. Of all the clanmen on this ship, I was told you are the one I should talk to about Compression Drive."

"Me?"

"There are manuals and theories I can read," Arlud said, "but I need more than technical specs. I need your real-world experience."

Sands grinned at the compliment. "Ask away, sir."

"Can a compression wave be attenuated and still function?"

"The normal range is between 13.7 zetas and 16.9 zetas."

"Yes," Arlud agreed. "Can the energy level be reduced below thirteen point seven?"

"Below that level relative speed diminishes, and time of travel is increased—not effective for interstellar travel."

"But it can be done?"

"Yes. Lower levels are used in most shuttles and planet-bound aircraft built during the last twenty years."

"Why?"

"The compression wave at all energy levels creates a slipstream—a spatial well the ship is pulled into—that reduces drag and allows for faster speeds without the negative effects of friction. That's how modern shuttles avoid friction-induced plasma effects during planet-fall."

"Do the compression waves that pull the ship into hyperspace create a bow shock?"

"Bow shock? All waves have leading edges. The size of a bow shock depends on the energy output of the engine and the density of space. That's never been an issue."

"Can the bow shock be reduced to standard operating energies
by changing the frequency of the wave?"

"A reduced bow shock would mean the wave has less energy."

"Yes, under normal conditions. Can we alter the wave generation to maintain normal operating efficiency but reduce the impact on hyperspace? In other words—streamline the wave so the bow shock creates a gentle roll and not a bashing hammer?"

Sands looked confused. "I've never heard that analogy before. Seems overblown, sir. The compression wave pulls the ship into hyperspace. Streamlining the wave would change the effectiveness."

"Has it been tried before?"

"A lot of testing was done to improve the old Spatial Warp Generator technology, so I would assume—"

"I'd like you to try some modifications."

Sands raised his palms as if pushing Arlud's request away. "Whoa. With these engines? Never!"

"Mister Sands," Melkor said, "Mister Erstallius is not asking you to change the operating specifics of our engines."

"That's correct," Arlud assured. "I would just like you to model a few changes to the process so I can analyze the data you generate."

"Why?"

"I understand the mindset—if it isn't broken, don't fix it—but we can always try to improve it."

"What's the reason? Would help if I understood your goal. I don't see a benefit—"

"Can we change the underlying structure of our universe?"

"No."

"What happened at the Battle of Wan'tei?"

"We defeated Polinda and his allies," Sands said, more confused now than before.

"Yes, we did. Simbic Ur also disappeared."

"Oh, yes, sir. I heard about that."

"The aliens who took Simbic Ur can change the underlying structure of our universe. They intend to stop our use of Compression Drive because it produces detrimental effects in their universe. If we can't produce a solution, Compression Drive will no longer work, and thousands of people will become stranded in space. Interstellar travel will stop, and you'll be out of a job, Mister Sands."

"Oh."

"Mister Vellion will assist you," Melkor said.

Vellion moved forward and gave Sands a data chip. "I've created an encrypted link between the Engineering systems and the Science Data systems. This is a Top-Secret project. Only the four of us will have access to the test results."

"Your schedules have been updated," Melkor added. "You will begin testing immediately."

Sands examined the chip in his hand, then looked at Melkor. "Aye, sir."

"What are our chances?"

Arlud flicked a side glance at Melkor as they walked through the corridor toward the guest cabins. "Slim," he said.

Melkor stopped and forced Arlud to stop by grabbing his upper arm. "There is another solution."

"What?"

"Target the alien emitters. We can send a task force to Arrilen Po or Alpha Cephei Four and test the effectiveness of our arsenal against them. If we can disable the emitter before they finish testing, that might upset their plans."

"Clan Halva is already at Arrilen Po, and the Guild is at A.C.4. If they can't disable them, no one can."

"Halva will want to preserve the holding and the Guild covets A.C.4's durillium. We should demolish the planets."

"That's a little extreme, don't you think? What if that doesn't dissuade the aliens? We can't use that option for every holding."

"If it works, we won't need to target every holding."

Eahuda leaned back in his cushioned chair and folded his arms. "That's insane."

Arlud moved to the settee across from Eahuda and sat down. Eahuda's cabin was a mirror image of his, same furniture, same gray walls. "Melkor's thinking is correct," he admitted. "If we disable them before they have a chance—"

"You agree with her?"

"No. I understand her logic."

"We can't expect to disable them based on what Bev said. We need to focus on finding a solution on our end."

"Are the drones ready?"

"We just need to agree on the final message. Madame Erstallius is reviewing the last version."

Some will ignore the warning, Arlud thought. *Some, like Melkor, will encourage a military strike.* "We can't control how the clans will respond," he said, "but it will impress upon them the need to prepare. Hopefully, the engineers will find a solution."

"For five-thousand years mankind has moved from one reality to another," Eahuda said. "Each generation believed they understood the universe and how it worked, and each was proved wrong by those who came after them. We were able to leave our homeworld and colonize our holdings because our ancestors broke the shackles that kept them chained to the ideas of the past. There has always been resistance to facts that contradict mainstream beliefs, but those facts create new discoveries. We are now at a crossroads, Lad. Old ideas must die so a new understanding can change the future."

"Unlike the past, we don't have a choice. We must change, or our civilization dies."

"Some might consider that a good thing—our civilization dying."

Arlud nodded his agreement. "Maybe it would be a good thing. The Alliance has been a sham for years."

A comm-channel buzzed.

Eahuda flicked the talk switch on the wall next to his chair. "Degen Eahuda."

"Hello, Gustav," Benita said. "I will approve the final version."

"Thank you, Madame. Please forward your signed copy to the Commander-in-Charge."

"I will. Is Arlud there?"

"I'm here."

"Can you come to my cabin?"

"On my way."

Arlud pushed the door buzzer. The cabin hatch clicked. He pushed the hatch open and saw his mother seated on the settee by the closed window, dressed in the clan's dark-blue work uniform with the clan crest at right shoulder, but missing rank insignia and section badges. He entered the cabin and stood next to the available chair. "Why the uniform?"

"Robes and skirts are not ideal attire when shipboard," Benita said. "This is more comfortable. Please sit." She watched Arlud drop into the chair, then asked: "Is the Rhysu threat as severe as the message indicates?"

"Yes."

"You're sure about that?"

"Yes. We've already discussed this."

"I know," Benita said. "I'm just having second thoughts. If we warn the clans and nothing happens, they'll see us as fools and never listen to us again."

"If that happens, I can live with the ridicule. Better to warn them and nothing happens than to not warn them and people become isolated in space."

"You said the Rhysu energy waves will be emitted from inside each holding, but there is a limit to how far they will reach."

"Yes."

"Then Compression Drive would still work farther out in space."

"Yes."

"Then that's not a real solution for the Rhysu."

"It's a beginning. The waves will propagate over time and make interstellar travel very difficult by current standards. A journey from the heliosphere into the habitable zone of most systems could take years. A journey between planetary systems will be extended by hundreds of years if the disruption reduces the interstellar efficiency of Compression Drive by only twenty percent."

"And that's spelled out in the data files uploaded to the drones?"

"Yes."

Benita folded her hands on her lap and focused on the thin silver ring on her left index finger. "Lasting relationships are a rare jewel. You and Bev were close, yes?"

"I'd like to think so."

Benita raised her eyes to look at Arlud. "She was transformed into a Rhysu."

"Yes—a Rhysu with a human mind. Only her body was changed."

"The Rhysu have a collective mind, so she knows what they know—yes?"

"Some things are hidden from her, but she told me she has learned many things."

"Can you ask her something for me?"

Arlud nodded.

"The Rhysu live in a higher dimension parallel to our universe," Benita said. "The only way we can affect their universe is by entering hyperspace. They cannot affect our universe unless they crossover by creating a rift. How is it possible for them to identify holdings?"

"Good question," Arlud said. "I'll ask her. I assume they must be able to detect the things in our universe and isolate acceptable gravity wells."

"That assumption should be replaced by facts. The facts may help us block the Rhysu waves. If they can't open a rift, they can't prevent Compression Drive."

"Right," Arlud agreed. He leaned back in the chair and folded his arms. "The Commander-In-Charge wants to destroy Arrilen Po. She said without the planet, they can't open a rift. I would hate to discover that was the only solution."

"Talk to Bev. Find a better path."

"I will." Arlud watched his mother relax her shoulders.

Benita leaned back against the pillows on the settee. "Good." She reached over and ignited a holoscreen.

Arlud watched his mother sign the warning message and considered her argument: *If they can't open a rift, they can't prevent Compression Drive.* The ability to block the Rhysu seemed a viable solution. *But*, he thought, *what happens when the harmful fluctuations continue? Would the Rhysu not turn to a more forceful solution like Melkor's plan to destroy Arrilen Po?*

Benita sent her approved message to the Commander-In-Charge and closed the holoscreen.

The holoscreen above the course-plotting station displayed trajectories for fifteen comm-drones. Eight would broadcast their message among the Old Worlds, and seven would relay their message in the Outer Districts.

Melkor checked the paths for each comm-drone, then turned to Eahuda, who stood a pace away next to the C.I.C. Operations Officer. "If the aliens activate their anti-compression wave, these drones will never reach their targets."

Eahuda frowned. "If they activate. Split odds are better than no odds."

"Just stating for the record," Melkor said. She turned to face the drone control station. "Launch the drones, Mister Ryn."

Mister Ryn flicked a switch for each comm-drone and the message-bearing missiles separated from the cruiser, propelled into hyperspace by their small Compression Drive engines.

CLAN HALVA: WEAPON

Illuminated only by the glowing holoscreen floating above the narrow black table, Cynth watched the transmission from the forward camera on Shuttle One. Two shuttles had followed the coordinates transmitted by the drones and landed on Arrilen Po in a rocky basin twenty meters from the standing monoliths that protected Station 38. She could see at the left edge of the holoscreen a small part of the twenty-meter-wide circular hole the Rhysu had bored in the side of the southern ridge during her last visit. "That's the hole they came out of when they took Bev."

Quin leaned closer to the holoscreen. "Where?"

Cynth pointed to the left edge of the screen. "There."

"Can you rotate the camera so I can see all of it?"

"No. The shuttle crew are in control of that."

Quin slumped and leaned back in her chair. She had expected to planet-fall, but because of the discovery of dead clanmen, that expectation had vanished. She watched four clanmen in teams of two pick up the dead clanmen and carry them on stretchers to Shuttle One. Four clanmen from Shuttle Two lugged two large crates to Station 38 and disappeared behind the granite monoliths. "What's in those crates?"

"Probably sensing equipment," Cynth said. "My old meters are most likely dead."

"Why would they do that?"

"Why not?"

"Well, things went awry here. What purpose is there?"

"To a scientist, more data is always a good thing."

A half-hour later, the shuttles left the station and headed back to their mother ship in orbit. Two hours after leaving the surface, they flew past the derelict cruiser and two more shuttles joined them.

The Commander-In-Charge stepped inside the lounge and paused. He saw Quin seated at the holoscreen watching the shuttles approach, and Cynth standing at the panoramic window contemplating the view of Arrilen Po and her moons. *They should not have come here,* he thought.

"Greetings, ladies," he said, and advanced toward the table. "All teams are off planet."

Quin watched Russo sit in the chair next to her. "The dead and the search teams?"

"Everyone. The last of the dead are on those shuttles."

Cynth glanced over at Russo. "It'll be night soon at the station. It's good we got them off-planet before then."

Quin squirmed in her chair as she watched the four shuttles merge into a standard approach formation. "Why is it taking so long? I read an article that said a shuttle can leave Mackenzie and get to its outer moon in twenty minutes. That's a lot farther than we are from Arrilen Po."

"The Mackenzie shuttles are newer hybrid versions that use Compression Drive," Russo said. "Our shuttles are older Zavos built models that only use fusion engines and mag-jets. Trips take longer, but they won't fail if the aliens activate more anti-compression waves."

"Oh." Quin frowned and rose out of her chair. "I'm going to the mess. Can I get you anything?"

"No," Cynth said.

Russo shook his head and watched Quin leave the lounge. "Why did you bring her?"

"A housemaid's life can be a dreary one," Cynth said. "I thought she could use an adventure, and I wanted to pass on to someone what I experienced here." She moved to the table—her feet clacked on the metal deck. She sat in front of the holoscreen. "She's an intelligent girl."

"I'm sure she is," Russo said. He was silent for a few heartbeats as he watched the shuttles maneuver closer to the cruiser. "The derelict ship is not retrievable. Too much damage from the alien emission—burned fuses, fried relays. The principal components are in working condition, but the drive systems will need a complete overhaul before attempting an interstellar voyage. We've realigned her orbit to keep her out of the atmosphere. We can return with a full maintenance crew to get her moving again, or we can leave her as-is."

"We can debate that after we return home," Cynth said.

Russo nodded to Cynth's recommendation. "The Sabballi ship and the three satellites are gone."

"Gone?"

"They must have been kicked out of orbit. No sign of them within Arrilen Po's gravity boundary. No debris on the moons."

Cynth recalled the most common attribute associated with the aliens. "Maybe they were vaporized?"

Russo preferred to ignore that possibility, but he could not discount the terrible heat of past alien confrontations.

The comm-channel buzzed for attention.

Russo flicked the talk switch on the control panel next to the holoscreen. "Russo here."

"Incoming from Cruiser 47, sir. Shall I transfer to you?"

"Yes."

The holoscreen blinked and the face of Jegen-Major, Sidon Arom, appeared—a swarthy, round-faced man with a short, silver goatee. "Russo," he said, "are you there?"

Russo activated the comm-channel, and his image was transmitted to Arom. "Yes, Sidon, I'm here."

"We began our course correction for departure and my Engine Chief said the C.D. is slipping. I had the science division analyze the situation and we've been swamped by an anti-compression wave, although without the magnetic disruptions. The data has been sent to all ships. We should leave at once."

"I agree," Russo said. "Thanks for the update." He cut off Arom and hailed his C.I.C.

"C.I.C., First Officer Lep."

"Russo here, Mister Lep. Notify the Task Force to begin departure. Anti-Compression waves detected. Engage C.D., full speed. If we stall, switch to full fusion."

"Aye, sir!"

Cynth looked out the window and watched Arrilen Po move out of view as the ship changed position to depart. She felt the deck rumble as the engines ignited to pull them into hyperspace, but the star field did not change. "Are we trapped?"

"No, just slowed down," Russo said. He fingered the holoscreen controls and brought up his ship's engine schematic. The Compression Drive was at 15.5 zetas. "Once we get farther away, our engine problems should disappear."

"If they don't?"

"We have a contingency plan."

"What?"

"The crates you saw unloaded on the surface—Tactical Nuclear Mines."

Cynth pushed away from the desk. "What!?"

"Each crate has two mines. They were lowered into the abandoned drill hole. If we see no engine improvement, I will order them ignited. The blast will do a lot of internal damage, but the radiation is what I'm hoping will shut down whatever is stifling our engines."

"You won't kill them. You'll just piss them off."

Russo rose out of his chair. "I'm not trying to kill them. I'll be in the C.I.C."

Quin walked through the narrow corridor toward the forward lounge and met the Commander-In-Charge as he rushed out the lounge doorway. "Oh, Commander, I—"

"Not now," Russo said. He brushed past Quin and entered the nearby access tube. The doors closed, blocking him from view.

Quin watched the lights on the tube control panel indicate Russo was heading for deck five. "So rude!"

"What are you doing?"

Quin spun to see Cynth standing in the lounge doorway. "Coming back from the mess." She held up a bottle of red juice. "What's wrong? Russo seems upset."

"Get in here," Cynth demanded. She led Quinn into the lounge, past the glowing holoscreen, and stopped by the panoramic window. The two freighters were now visible outside the window, three-hundred meters away—one was two-hundred meters to the port side, the other two-hundred meters to the starboard side. The core of each ship's aft engine pod emitted the blue glow of fusion thrust.

Quin stepped up to the window. "Where are the other cruisers?"

"Behind us."

"When do we enter hyperspace?"

"I don't know," Cynth said. She moved to the holoscreen, fingered the control panel, and accessed an external camera.

A crescent view of Arrilen Po appeared on the screen.

Cynth pulled a chair closer and sat. She entered more commands and numbers appeared by the blue limb of the planet—distance and speed measurements that updated every five seconds. They were moving away from the planet at thirty-thousand kilometers per hour. *That's too slow.*

Quin noticed the worry in Cynth's expression. "What's wrong?"

"We should be in hyperspace by now, but we're not."

"Because of the alien wave thing?"

"Yes."

Quin folded her arms across her chest. "That's why Russo was upset."

"Yes."

"Are we stuck here?"

"We're moving, just not very fast," Cynth said. She entered more commands and a red marker—a circle bisected by a cross—appeared on the holoscreen above the day side of the night/day boundary on Arrilen Po.

Quin stepped closer to the table. "What's that?"

"The position of Station 38."

"Is that where the aliens live?"

Cynth focused on the speed measurement. Relative speed from Arrilen Po had increased to thirty-eight thousand kilometers per hour. She glanced out the panoramic window and noticed the fusion engines still glowed blue. *Full power.* "Damn."

"What?"

Cynth ignored Quin, fingered the comm controls, and hailed the C.I.C.

"C.I.C., First Officer Lep."

"This is Cynth Halva. I need to speak to Jegen-Major Russo."

"The Commander-In-Charge is busy, madame. I can have him call you back."

"Please do," Cynth said. She broke the connection to the C.I.C. and refocused on the holoscreen. Relative speed from Arrilen Po was now forty-two thousand kilometers per hour. "We've lost compression drive."

"What's that mean?"

"With constant thrust our speed will gradually increase, but the trip to the heliosphere will take months."

"Months?"

"Once past the system boundary, Compression Drive may be active again, maybe sooner."

"What if it's not?"

"Then we'll have a very long—"

A bright white spot appeared under the red marker on the holoscreen—a brief flash that turned orange and faded as the shade of night overtook the area.

"Idiot," Cynth said in an undertone.

Quin sat in the chair next to Cynth. "What was that?"

"A mistake."

The cruiser lurched froward and Cynth noticed the speed indicator was in the hyperspace range. Green wisps of hyperspace obscured the stars and freighters visible through the window. "We might make it." She opened the comm-drone control panel and launched her emergency message. The tracking window displayed the drone's course—it left the cruiser propelled by its small fusion engine, then engaged Compression Drive and disappeared on the holoscreen as it headed for the heliosphere.

It's faster than this cruiser, Cynth thought. *It will escape. In twenty standard days, it will reach Cestratha and transmit my message.*

On the holoscreen, the disk of Arrilen Po was now half the previous size as the ship sped away, and from a point under the red marker, strands of cyan colored plasma streamed outward over the surface. Within seconds, the entire planet was covered in undulating strands of the alien energy.

Cynth turned to Quin. "Get to your cabin and put on the environment suit!"

"What?"

"Go, now!" Cynth pulled Quin to her feet and pushed her toward the doorway. "Go!"

Before Quin reached the door, Arrilen Po flared white on the holoscreen. The brilliant ball of light engulfed both moons and continued to grow until the entire holoscreen was blazing white.

Cynth watched Quin rush into the corridor, then turned and looked out the panoramic window. The green hyperspace fog was gone.

The cruiser jerked backward, and Cynth noticed the aft end of both freighters were white hot—their blue fusion glow was gone.

Metallic-gray shutters activated outside the window to protect the ship's interior from increased radiation.

Cynth dropped into her seat and saw a black holoscreen because the exterior cameras had failed. And she felt what she feared the most—her skin prickling from heat—a terrible reminder of her first contact with the Rhysu.

Heat upon heat upon heat. . .

THE GUILD: OBJECT

Captain Pardee looked at the image on the floating holoscreen above his desk and squinted. "What is it?"

He must realize all we can do is speculate, Shanna thought. She glanced at the rotating sphere of diaphanous hyper-waves on the holoscreen—green to orange ripples near the end of a smooth rock tunnel. "We know it's not a doorway," she said. "Based on Cynth Halva's reports, the rift opens inside the large spherical area outside the tunnel where that object rests and generates a vortex of high energy plasma that would melt the drones."

Pardee leaned forward and folded his arms on his desk. "Can we interact with it?"

"The drone passed a laser through it. There was no reaction."

"The laser wasn't refracted?"

"Went straight through."

Pardee watched the hyper-waves ripple outward from the sphere—orange-to-green. "It's not three-dimensional?"

"Not as we usually perceive a three-dimensional object," Shanna explained. "It's in our three-dimensional space, but more like a shadow. It's a shadow of a higher dimensional object we cannot see."

Pardee rubbed the side of his face. "So, the Rhysu left something from their universe in that tunnel that's invisible to human vision."

"Yes," Shanna said. "We can only see its shadow because we can manipulate the spectral frequencies and bring them into our visual range."

"And the real object looks very different from what we see there?"

"We will never see it as the Rhysu see it."

Pardee leaned back in his chair. "Ok. How do we discover what it does?"

"I'm not sure that's possible."

"It must have a purpose."

"Absolutely."

Pardee leaned forward again and zoomed in the view on the holoscreen. He examined the tunnel's smooth rock walls. "The aliens created the tunnel, so I would think the invisible parts fit inside."

"I agree."

"If we collapse the tunnel, would that destroy the object?"

Shanna flinched. "Oh, we shouldn't do that."

"Why?"

Shanna glanced at her hands resting on her lap. *He's reviewed all the reports,* she thought, *but has missed the main argument.* She lifted her eyes to match Pardee's stare. "Captain, I know you see this object as a threat, but we should be cautious—"

"It's an alien intrusion," Pardee insisted. He leaned forward. "We can't allow them—"

"They know they intruded into a universe inhabited by humans," Shanna stressed. "They did everything they could to prevent harm once they understood their presence—"

"They attacked Alliance ships and took a planet!"

"The Shoku attacked, the Rhysu stopped them. The last comm-drone message reported Simbic Ur was returned to its orbit."

Pardee rocked back in his chair. "That doesn't remove the fact every time these aliens show up people die."

"I understand that, but Bev has said—"

"Bev? That Polinda sapi died because of the aliens."

"No."

"Where's the proof she's still alive?"

"She appeared to Arlud. You read his report."

"Yes, I did," Pardee muttered. "Why not collapse the tunnel?"

"That might destroy the object and we should avoid that. We should use it."

"How?"

"Canter and I think it may be a beacon. From the alien perspective, planets are gravity nodes—matter concentrations that allow them to focus their energy streams for crossing from their dimension into ours. Once here, they set-up a beacon to identify the crossing point."

"What evidence points to that conclusion?"

"Those waves you see only radiate inside that small spherical space—there are no emissions beyond that, but the waves might radiate into the alien dimension, like a beacon."

"That implies they intend to return."

"A beacon can also identify where not to return. They understand the damage they caused."

"Planting a beacon also implies they crossover to other places. Why are they crossing over?"

"We may find out by using that object to communicate with them."

"How?"

"They must be able to connect with it from their universe. Arlud said the Rhysu could connect with Bev across the dimensional barrier. We know the frequencies they used to connect with Bev. We could try to signal them via the object."

"Whether it's a beacon or something else, we don't know how it works. How can we send a signal?"

A comm channel buzzed for attention.

Pardee flicked the response switch. "Pardee here."

"Comm Officer Nordal here Captain. We received a comm-drone transmission. Our Third Fleet arrived at Al-phaq twenty-seven hours ago. A three-ship task force will arrive here in seven hours with the mandate to retrieve Lady Sy, per order of the Director."

Shanna slumped in her chair upon hearing the news. *Just like my father,* she thought. *Pull me out when I've just got started!*

"Thank you, Nordal," Pardee said. "Send the data to my ready room."

"Aye, sir."

Pardee switched off the comm link and looked at Shanna. "He's concerned about your safety."

"As he always is."

"Canter can continue the investigation. I'm sure—"

"Without me, we never would have found that object," Shanna said. "Canter wanted to end the investigation."

"His opinion was premature," Pardee admitted. "He'll not make the same mistake twice."

"Give me a week."

"Go against your father's command?"

"A one-week delay is reasonable. He can't expect me to leave without properly delegating my duties."

Pardee pondered that option and nodded his agreement. "One week."

Shanna straightened her posture. "Thank you."

"How can we send a signal through that object?"

"I hope to have that answer by the end of the week."

⯁ ⯁ ⯁

Five days after her meeting with Pardee, Shanna sat on the fold-out bench in her cabin with her back resting against the wall and reviewed on her compad the latest data from the remote analysis of the alien object.

No change.

Canter had accommodated her request for sensor adjustments, but they yielded nothing useful.

We need a breakthrough!

She stood and began pacing. The constrained hyper-waves produced in that rock tunnel seemed to have no purpose.

It must be a beacon back to the Rhysu universe!

A comm alert ignited a holoscreen in the wall above the fold-out bench.

Shanna turned to face the incoming message. The black screen displayed the header information in large red text, followed by the message:

Comm-Drone E5784
Sender: Clan Erstallius
Origin: Baleiou
Target: Outer District, Section C, Alliance holdings and independent settlements.
Priority: Alert 1
Message begin-
New data indicates the aliens who took Simbic Ur are planning to disrupt our ability to use Compression Drive. We have no data to foretell a precise time when this will occur - see attached files for specific evidence and options.
-Message End

Shanna voiced a skeptical giggle. *This has to be a joke,* she thought. *What are they going to do, destroy all our ships?*

Then she saw signatures as the text scrolled upward:

Madame Benita Gale Waldu-Reyes Erstallius.
Arlud Reynaldo Erstallius, Regent of GSW-183.
Jegen-of-the-Corp, Jamira Melkor, Commander-in-Charge, Division 1.
Vero Singh, Director of Neurosurgery, Regency Medical Center, Mancipa, Baleiou.

Seeing Arlud's name among the other high-ranking signatories forced her to bury her skepticism and investigate the attached data. She focused on the words below the signatures: Ignore or Accept. She touched the word Accept and reviewed the attached data. Three-quarters of the information were facts she had already learned. The remaining data relayed the conversations Arlud had with Bev Colli and the supporting analysis provided by Vero Singh.

Anti-compression waves?

She straddled the bench and spent the next four hours researching Compression Drive on the ship's data-net—the history of development, and the basic principles of how it works. Satisfied she understood enough to make a valid assessment, she fingered the holoscreen controls and displayed the drone's view of the transparent orange-to-green ball of hyper-waves.

Is it really that simple?

She flicked a comm switch to hail the captain via audio only.

"Pardee here."

"Captain, It's not a beacon. It's an emitter."

"Lady Sy. Canter and I have been discussing that for the past hour, along with my Chief Engineer. Impressive you came to the same conclusion."

"What's your analysis?"

"Collapsing the tunnel now looks like a valid option."

"That would only cause the Rhysu to return. We might not survive that—as you said, 'every time these aliens show up, people die.' We should leave the object alone, set drones to monitor its status—"

"So you acknowledge the aliens present a danger? Why the change in attitude?"

"When conditions change, attitudes must change. Stopping our ability to travel between holdings is an action that will cause harm."

"According to Mister Erstallius, Bev Colli insists the Rhysu do not wish to cause harm."

"There are different levels of harm. I believe her about a direct effort to kill humans. Limiting our ability to travel between holdings will still harm many people and indirectly kill many who become stranded in space."

"I'm glad you understand that," Pardee said. "We've planted more sensors in the tunnel. We'll be evacuating the surface once the final relay drones are in place underground. One frigate will remain in orbit to gather the data. All other personnel will either return to Alpha Cephei Four or return with you to Wald-415."

"If anti-compression waves begin, they'll trap the frigate in orbit."

"At first sign of any changes, we'll collapse the tunnel, giving the frigate enough time to flee."

Shanna took a slow breath to calm herself. "That's a potential suicide mission, Captain. The frigate will never escape if the Rhysu return to investigate."

"Why do you say that?"

"The Javelin and the Iron Spear."

Mention of the two Cormed frigates forced Pardee to remember his rescue of the survivors, and the terrible consequences of his actions—his crew under siege by the rebellious Cormeds, and his decision to strand Shanna on GSW-183.

Shanna waited for a reply and after a long minute assumed Pardee missed her reason for mentioning the damaged frigates. "Those ships were attacked," she said. "There was no anti-compression drive detected and yet they could not escape. Leave a frigate in orbit and our guildmen will be in a very dangerous position."

"Arlud told us the attacks were an act of the Shoku," Pardee said. "The Rhysu took the Shoku back to their universe. If the Rhysu return—"

"The Rhysu are hurt by our compression waves," Shanna stressed. "Destroying their means of stopping our engines might spark a more devastating reaction from them. By Arlud's own assessment, they will not tolerate—"

"The aliens must understand we will not allow our way of life to be stolen from us. Should they not expect us to dismantle their effort?"

"Offer a solution without attacking them."

"How?"

"We can try to nullify their anti-compression wave by reducing the impact Compression Drive has in their universe. There's nothing better to end the conflict than the demonstration of a peaceful solution. That would communicate our intentions better than any message."

"And how do we do that?"

"By altering our engines. The Rhysu wave must change the attributes of the sub-quantum wind that's generated by the electro-gravitic gradient of the advancing compression wave. By changing the attributes of the sub-quantum substance, the compression wave will dissolve faster than it can propagate, which will nullify the superluminal acceleration. If we change the amplitude and the polarity of the compression wave, reduce the amount of energy used to induce the wave, and revert to a tri-pole emission system, we may bypass the negative effects of the Rhysu emissions. If our changes work, the hyper-space shock front that disrupts the Rhysu universe will be reduced."

"The effectiveness of any change will be problematic—"

"Not if we revert to a process similar to the old Spatial Warp Generator technology. Instead of seventeen hours from here to Al-phaq, the trip will take seven days. Slower, yes, but still fast enough to be acceptable."

"Forgive me, my lady."

The voice was unfamiliar to Shanna. "Forgive who?"

"Chief Engineer, Krasok, my lady. What you propose won't work."

"Why?"

"Our systems won't support the alterations you suggest. The sub-quantum substance is the foundation for everything in our universe—alter any part of it and our physical universe will cease to exist as we know it. It is more likely the Rhysu emissions affect how our Compression Drive interacts with the sub-quantum realm, rather than changing that realm."

"Both our theories are assumptions," Shanna insisted. "Arlud was sure the Rhysu solution would alter the underlying fabric of space to nullify Compression Drive. How that happens will be determined after the fact. My point is: We can counter the Rhysu effort by not using Compression Drive and revert to the old Spatial Warp system."

"Easier said than done," Pardee remarked. "As the Chief just said, our systems don't support that type of alteration."

"Oh."

"I applaud you, lady Sy," Pardee added. "The effort you've put into this is impressive. I agree with your assessment regarding the frigate. It could be a suicide mission—thank you for reminding me of the past. I've sent a command to leave drones in orbit to monitor the planet and broadcast a warning to stay away. We will all leave orbit in two hours."

"Good choice, Captain. Thank you."

"Come to my ready room. I'll show you the engineering data we've been discussing."

"I will."

Pardee closed the comm link.

Shanna frowned. *I impressed Pardee, but my conclusions were flawed. I was correct with the intent, but wrong with the details, and Krasok is stuck in his own paradigm.*

She remembered Busard Garth-Wallu, her science instructor on Al-phaq. His workbook began with a brief introduction that encouraged the mindset he expected from his students. His statement had a deep impact on Shanna's outlook, and she had memorized every word. She recalled the introduction's main points:

> "Knowledge can propel you toward discovery, but it can also lead you down a path toward oblivion. That's how gravity became geometry and for five-hundred years confined mankind to the boundaries of the Terra Prime system. . . Knowledge is only a beginning. Your goal should be understanding. Understanding is only achieved when we digest knowledge free of opinion. Facts always matter and should be acknowledged without regard for our feelings. . . Reality is the universe of factual data. Facts are the framework for understanding."

We need more facts, she thought. *No one will understand the Rhysu without more data.*

The essential data resided in the Rhysu dimension. That was obvious to Shanna and everyone else involved in the investigation. Arlud revealed that fact when he related his dialog with Bev. Shanna was certain more knowledge would flow if she could establish her own connection with Bev. Arlud and Bev had bonded before she was taken, and that bond kept Bev linked to him. Shanna had no previous association with the young sapi, which made connecting with her a doubtful prospect. *I must try,* she thought. *Perhaps my link to Arlud will be enough?* She fingered the holoscreen controls. The data files from the Erstallius drone message appeared on screen, and she searched for the analysis of Bev's brain waves.

The first brain wave graph displayed five frequencies interlaced along a baseline twenty centimeters in length. The Beta wave was the weakest, with the Theta and Gamma waves most energetic. The Delta and Alpha waves were in the lower frequencies.

This is Bev's scan during her coma.

Shanna searched through more graphs. Each recording in the sequence was different, which revealed the change in Bev's mental activity until she woke. After examining fifty scans, Shanna realized the recordings of Bev's brain function were not consistent enough for a baseline imprint of wakeful consciousness, and worthless for determining a combined frequency for communication. *Besides,* she thought, *Bev is no longer human, so these scans are probably worthless.*

"I'm approaching this from the wrong direction," she muttered and closed the file on Bev. She searched further and opened the analysis of the waves that were flagged, Rhysu Thought Prints.

Thought Prints?

The Rhysu wave patterns were from 2hz to 30hz, with amplitudes that never reached higher than the mid-point of Bev's overlapping waves.

This I can use!

Shanna transferred the Rhysu patterns onto her compad, closed the holoscreen, and rushed out of her cabin.

BEV COLLI: LIARS

Bev twirled in the cyan energy sea. She searched the surrounding plasma streams for any sign of Rhysu.

Where did they go?

She focused on the churning, knotted streams that marked where the rift to Arrilen Po was anchored. The knotted streams bubbled outward, exploded, and flung Rhysu spheres and white-hot plasma into the energy sea.

The shock front hit Bev, pushed her into a turbulent plasma stream that carried her past the shredded rift location.

Rhysu burst out of plasma streams from every direction, a chaotic rush of glowing spheres. Their twisting electric tendrils stabbed outward and linked with each other as they sped toward the explosion site.

Caught in the rush of Rhysu, Bev flowed toward the ruptured knot. "What happened?"

The Rhysu ignored her query.

Bev fought to free herself from the enclosing spheres, but the Rhysu grip was too strong to break. "What happened!?"

Once inside the tattered knot, the Rhysu pressed so close together all Bev could see was their cyan spheres. "Let me go!"

Another shock wave pushed through the cluster of Rhysu, and they splintered into separate spheres.

Bev tumbled free. She moved to isolate herself, ignored the undulating tendrils that tried to reconnect, and dove into a parallel plasma stream that carried her from the main cluster of Rhysu.

White-hot plasma erupted again from the shattered knot.

More Rhysu rushed toward the explosion site.

Bev touched a passing Rhysu and was filled with the knowledge that fueled their activity.

The Shoku!

She grabbed another passing Rhysu and held onto it. "What did the Shoku do?"

The Rhysu paused. "The humans destroyed the emitter. The explosion expanded through the rift and fractured the enclosing streams. The Shoku enfolded through a spatial crack and passed through the rift. We are trying to retrieve them."

Bev released her grip and watched the Rhysu join others who rushed into the fractured streams to repair the knot and anchor the rift. She projected her mind into the rift's whirling vortex, and it threw her consciousness back into the hard place. She ascended through a tunnel behind the Rhysu who rushed after the rebels.

A new path made by the Shoku, Bev noticed. The smooth surface of the rock still radiated intense heat.

Her mind's eye followed the Rhysu to the surface. The terrain had collapsed where station 38 once stood, forming a crater half the diameter of the basin and twice as deep. Above the melted rock, cyan plasma trails left by the Shoku swirled beneath a brilliant white sky.

The white is where they battle, Bev thought. *Like the white that was my prison.*

Thousands of Rhysu spheres poured out of the new tunnel and sped upward, through the gossamer strands of cyan plasma, into the white.

Bev's mind snapped back to her location in the energy sea. She knew the Halva clanmen on the surface were dead, and she could not sense the ships in orbit. "Did you kill all the humans!?"

"The humans brought this destruction on themselves," a Rhysu said.

Bev twirled to see ten Rhysu spheres press upon her, blocking her from the rift. "On themselves?"

"Their violence allowed the Shoku to break free and access the rift."

"You're to blame for not restraining the Shoku. You should have stopped your tests once you discovered the dead humans."

"We did not kill the humans. The Shoku—"

"The Shoku are Rhysu. You are all the same. You are all to blame for this mess!"

Bev's berating forced the Rhysu around her to pause and contemplate their motive. She took advantage of the relaxed state of their spheres, blasted her tendrils to open a path between them, and rushed through their blockade into a plasma current that pushed her away from the explosion site. She looked back—the Rhysu did not follow. She relaxed in the swift current and focused on what she should do next.

What the Rhysu do proves what they say is a lie. They have no genuine concern for human survival.

That reality left Bev with no alternative.

I must escape!

The only other rift Bev knew about was anchored to Alpha Cephei Four.

I must go there.

She focused on the Polinda mine. She no longer had living connections to that place, but her six years there had embedded that hated holding deep in her memory. That was the only link she needed. She saw in her mind the rock hollow where the Rhysu broke into the mine. She saw the melted drill and a spiral tunnel that led to the cavern where the rift opened.

I must learn how to ignite the vortex that opens the rift.

A Rhysu voice boomed in Bev's mind: "You must not pass through the rift!"

Bev turned to see a distant cluster of cyan spheres moving toward her. "Liars! If you wanted to stop the Shoku, you could have done it easily. If they're criminals, why did you use me to save them? You should have let them die. You won't because you're both creatures of the energy sea." She searched for a path and rushed into another plasma stream. *I won't let you catch me,* she thought. She gained more distance from her pursuers by enfolding multiple times into different streams to confuse them. She had learned enough to evade capture, but wondered if she would arrive at the crossing point to Alpha Cephei Four and find a horde of Rhysu waiting to ensnare her.

She buried all thoughts about the Rhysu and focused on Alpha Cephei Four.

The energy streams rushed around her and became a blur—twisting ropes of cyan light that formed an undulating tunnel as her speed increased and her course adjusted.

CLAN ERSTALLIUS: ESCAPE

The day after the fifteen comm-drones were launched, Arlud relaxed on the cushioned bench in the cruiser's darkened port side lounge. He looked through the observation window and watched a salvage ship two kilometers away clean one of the debris fields created during the battle for Balieou. Below the debris, Baleiou was a quarter crescent—white clouds dotted the sunlit side above patches of blue ocean and black, blast-scared land. *We came too close to losing everything,* he thought. *We can't let that happen again.*

He leaned his head back against the wall, closed his eyes, and touched the medpad on his forehead.

Where are you, Bev?

Images of Bev filled Arlud's inner vision.

Answer Me! Where are you? I need to speak to you!

He repeated his plea for contact so many times he lost count.

Jamira Melkor entered the lounge. "Excuse me, sir. You should see this." She flicked a wall switch, and a holoscreen blinked to life inside the window. She fingered the channel controls and Hugo Rusan's square face topped with sun-bleached curls, filled the screen.

". . . and that shall be our focus," Rusan said. "This supposed threat is unrealistic and scientifically impossible. No, my dear Benita, all you and yours have accomplished today is to obscure the real threat to our clan. No matter how powerful the aliens purport to be, they cannot change the fabric—"

Arlud cut-off the holo-transmission, stood, and plucked off the medpad. "I expected that response."

Benita stepped into the lounge. "He's an idiot," she said. She sat on the padded bench. "Mister Tupo just informed me a security team came to the house. The cadre has revoked my privileges. And I have been denied my travel permit. They will prevent this cruiser from leaving orbit."

Arlud faced Melkor. "Did you know about that?"

"No."

"It doesn't matter," Benita said. "If the anti-compression drive thing happens, remaining in orbit will be good. Better than being stranded in the void."

"We have plenty of time," Arlud said. "Bev was certain it would be months before the Rhysu finalized their effort."

Melkor moved to the window. "You're sure about that?"

"I am."

"We're eleven standard-days from GSW-183," Melkor said. "If we can get there before the Rhysu activate their weapon, we can make quick alterations to the Aku transports—they have tri-pole engines. Based on my engine chief's analysis, that will reduce the impact of the Rhysu weapon. We'll have unhindered access to U'galem and Clan Dejoria's shipyards. In a few months, we could have a large fleet of altered ships."

"I was with Winstone Bittle when he examined the Aku engines," Arlud said. "He referred to their output as compression drive."

Melkor smirked. "He was correct technically, but not semantically. It's been so long since the tri-pole method was in general use, I'm not surprised. The Spatial Warp process and the Compression Drive process are similar. Both achieve the same results, just at different intensities and via different methods—they both compress space and pull the ship into hyperspace."

"Oh."

"Bittle's compression drive statement is like the modern use of the word jets when referring to Magnetic Induction Turbines. Our ancestors also had jets, but the method for their propulsion was very different."

"Different methods that achieve the same results," Arlud muttered. "They both compress space, so how can the tri-pole method circumvent the Rhysu weapon?"

"The compression field is formed at lower energies. It's less stable but ignores the alterations we believe will cripple modern compression drive."

Benita huffed at Melkor. "We believe? You mean we don't know."

"We won't know for sure until the Rhysu weapon is activated," Melkor explained. "But it is a workable option based on the math. The quantum phase shift is not as great in a tri-pole field, which may bypass the weapon's effects."

Arlud grabbed the hand railing below the window and stared at Baleiou's bright crescent—it was fatter now, as the cruiser's orbit brought the ship over more of the daylight side of the planet. "It's the only option we have."

"I know the Aku ships are old and in need of retirement," Melkor said, speaking to Benita, "but they may help us achieve victory against the aliens."

"We're not at war with the Rhysu," Arlud insisted.

"Correct," Benita interjected, "we're not at war. In a war, both sides have similar strengths. We are no match for the Rhysu if they choose to obliterate us. That's not war, it's genocide."

Arlud glanced at his mother—her expression echoed the intensity of her words. "We need to avoid escalating the problem," he said, then returned his attention to Melkor. "If we can bypass the Rhysu effort and stop their harmful fluctuations, that will be a victory for both of us. If a tri-pole system will do that, I'm all in."

"Then we should go to GSW-183," Melkor said. "There's no other place we can find enough ships that still use tri-pole field generation."

Benita pointed to the window. "You must convince them first."

Five Class 9 interceptors rushed toward the cruiser and sped past the window.

"I'll take care of it," Melkor said. She turned and hurried out of the lounge.

Benita stood. "If we ignore the High Regent's order, the cadre will brand us as traitors."

"We're not traitors," Arlud insisted.

"Our opinion doesn't matter."

"If we can't resolve the Rhysu threat, upsetting the cadre will be the least of our problems."

Benita recalled what Bev said: "The Rhysu will not stop until they have ended the harmful fluctuations."

Arlud nodded. He understood the consequences and doubt crept into his thoughts at hearing his mother repeat Bev's warning. *Find a solution!*

The cruiser jerked forward, and the deck rumbled.

Benita joined Arlud at the window. She clenched the hand railing. Baleiou drifted to the left, out of view, as the cruiser turned to face a path out of the system.

Two Class 9 interceptors slid into view—they were stationary one-hundred meters from the cruiser.

"They're letting us pass," Benita whispered.

"Melkor handled it," Arlud said. "The cadre won't fire on us—that would cause a civil war, and the clan can't afford more division."

A comm channel buzzed.

Arlud opened the holoscreen in the window. A prompt requested contact with Benita from Hugo Rusan.

"Ignore it," Benita said.

"He won't like that."

"I know."

"You're sure?"

Benita nodded and Arlud changed the holoscreen to view the Task Force Summery. Only one frigate had joined their move to leave the system. "Well," he said, "that's better than none."

"The others are being cautious," Benita said. "They don't fear the cadre. They fear being stranded in space."

"Only the brave will be successful."

"Armand's words," Benita remembered. "I miss his confidence."

"I miss his strength."

Benita saw the worry on Arlud's brow. "You have your own strength. You tolerated ridicule from the cadre with a resolve not common in other men."

"Father's support helped."

"I was wrong to criticize you. Once the cadre knows all the facts, they'll—"

"Do nothing," Arlud insisted. "Their motive has always been more political than practical. I will be an outcast, removed from my position and ignored at the General Assembly, if I'm even allowed to attend after this move."

"Prove them wrong."

"No," Arlud said. He faced his mother. "I'll prove us right."

PETRA SITLYN: INTRUSION

The framing for the new shuttle construction building was completed. The outer walls and convex roof were covered in the first layer of alsteel plates. The extended landing surface was finished—the duranide-infused composite tiles met the building's durroconcrete foundation, and the seam was covered at the wide doorway by a single strip of alsteel.

Petra stooped to inspect the alsteel threshold. The wide metal strip was designed to adapt to potential ground movement and still maintain a smooth transition from tarmac to hanger floor. *Good,* she thought. *Not too tight and not too loose.*

Her compad buzzed.

She stood and brought the device close to her mouth. "Petra," she said.

"This is Bittle. We received a comm-drone message from Baleiou. I'm sending it to you now." Bittle signed off and Petra watched the progress bar for the transferred message.

Why is it so big?

She scanned the header and message:

> **Comm-Drone E5784**
> **Sender:** Clan Erstallius
> **Origin:** Baleiou
> **Target:** Outer District, Section C, Alliance holdings and independent settlements.
> **Priority:** Alert 1
> **Message Begin:**
> New data indicates the aliens who took Simbic Ur are planning to disrupt our ability to use Compression Drive. We have no data to foretell a precise time when this will occur - see attached files for specific evidence and options.
> **Message End.**

"Wow," Petra whispered. She perused the attached files as her crew worked around her, oblivious to the new threat. When she reached the document that detailed how compression drive could be disrupted, Bittle drove onto the new landing surface and stopped his cart a few paces behind her. She spun to face him. "Can this really happen?"

Bittle slumped in the cart seat. "Those who signed the message think so."

"What's Command going to do?"

Bittle motioned for her to sit in the cart next to him. "Let's keep this private."

Petra scanned the Aku workers in the building—all were focused on their assignments. She nodded to Bittle and sat in the cart.

Bittle drove west off the composite tiles onto ground covered with clumps of melting snow. A few hundred meters from the construction site, he turned the cart toward the Mânu and stopped. "Command has ordered us to return to Baleiou."

Petra gestured to the new building. "What about all this? What about the training program?"

"We're done here. I told you this might happen. Jegen-Major Sari believes we can get home before the aliens activate their weapon. We leave in six hours. He's meeting with the Aku elders as we speak."

"They won't like that."

"We either leave or get stranded here. Sari won't strand us if he can prevent it."

"You could get stranded in space—that would be worse."

"The data says that won't happen for months."

"We'll be breaking our promise to the Aku."

"I think they'll understand."

"They'll understand the Erstallius break promises."

"You should give them more credit, Petra. They'll understand."

"Well, I'm staying."

"I assumed you would."

Bittle's compad buzzed. "Another comm-drone message," he said. "From the Guild." He scrolled through the data. "The Guild 3rd fleet arrived at Al-phaq. They discovered an alien object deep under the mine on Alpha Cephei Four."

"What kind of object?"

"They think it's an anti-compression wave emitter. Which means the message from Baleiou is solid data. It's a real threat."

Petra scanned Kuliq'Quad Basin—the rim wall was frosted with what remained of the last snow fall, as were the ancient stone dwellings below Seelay's shrine. The white-washed buildings in the village stood amid muddy roads and narrow streams that helped empty the basin of snow melt. The Mânu, with one grounded transport, and the half-finished shuttle construction building, were the modern buildings the Aku hoped would help them continue to reach orbit. "The Aku survived here on their own for over 160 years," she said. "They'll continue to survive, but once again as planet-bound survivors, if the Aku threat becomes reality."

"Yes, they will," Bittle agreed. "We are not leaving here as enemies. Once we've found a solution to this alien issue, we'll be back."

"Maybe not," Petra said. "Next time the Aku may not let the clan planet-fall. They have no patience for broken promises."

A bulging Erstallius cargo shuttle landed in the yellow landing circle at the center of the new landing surface. The ship was too large to fit through the ten-meter by ten-meter doorway, so the Erstallius ground crew stacked the delivered crates outside, within the safe zone marked by orange striping.

While the cargo was unloaded, Petra spoke to her twenty-man construction crew inside the building. "There it is," she said. "Now you know."

The foreman asked, "Will that impact what we do here?"

"No," Petra assured. "The Erstallius may leave, but we will finish what we started. We'll need to adjust our timeline. Maybe a year, since some assembly components will be manufactured without Erstallius help, but we will get it done."

A worker called out: "An entire year?"

Petra nodded. "That won't matter. If we become isolated because of the aliens, we'll have more time for everything we do. Another year might be a good thing—less need to rush."

Another worker asked: "So you are staying?"

"Yes."

A member of the Erstallius ground crew approach Petra and stopped by her side. "Excuse me."

Petra faced the clanman, and he presented a data pad. She reviewed the cargo manifest—eight two-meter by four-meter crates filled with energy conduits, alsteel pipes, composite plating for the interior walls, and other miscellaneous supplies to finish the building. She signed the signature line and handed the data pad back to the clanman.

The clanman nodded and walked back to his crew, who waited in a six-wheeled ground car next to the cargo shuttle.

Petra watched the ground car roll away toward the Mânu.

The cargo shuttle's engines ignited, lifted her off the ground, and pushed her upward toward the basin's southern rim wall.

Petra clapped her hands and faced her Aku construction crew. "Ok. Let's get those crates unloaded." She moved to the nearest crate and punched in the code to open the doors on the square end as her crew broke into smaller groups to open the other crates. One of the crew joined her as she swung the right-side door open. The crate was filled with bundles of four-centimeter diameter pipe on top of small, rectangular containers.

"I'll get a hand truck," the man said.

Petra nodded. As the man turned to reenter the building, a bright flash diverted her attention to the sky.

High above the southern rim wall, the retreating cargo shuttle, now at least two-kilometers distant, appeared to be on fire and falling.

A warning horn blared across the basin.

The ground crew stopped working and watched the shuttle fall, trailing black smoke.

A double horn blast sounded, and a squadron of ciâfey took flight from the eastern rim above the Mânu.

Along the basin's rim, camouflage covers moved to reveal rail gun installations. The barrels rotated upward and fired.

Petra searched the sky for intruders. Five rapid sonic booms hit her ears, but she could see no aircraft.

Another warning horn blared.

The construction crew ran for the Mânu.

Petra navigated her compad to display the global security update. Twenty cruisers were attacking from three positions around the planet. Ten troop transports had begun to planet-fall.

Five attack drones sped below the clouds above the basin—the source of the sonic booms.

"Damn!"

Two large rail guns emerged from the outer corners of the Mânu and fired into the sky.

Petra watched the attack drones drop in an arc toward the Mânu amid vapor streaks caused by the rail gun projectiles. The intruders returned fire, shooting compact plasma bursts at the grounded transport.

Under the smoke and plasma flak rebounding off the transport, the Mânu rail guns each sited an attack drone and fired explosive projectiles that made contact. Both drones tumbled toward the eastern rim wall and broke apart after hitting the rock face.

The rim wall rail guns targeted the three remaining drones from all sides. They fell out of the sky before clearing the basin. Two tumbled apart and fell into the white-walled village, sending black smoke and flames into the sky. The remaining ship hit the southern cliffs and exploded.

The rail guns went silent.

Petra dropped her gaze to the Mânu—the transport had a large crater in her upper hemisphere rimmed with fire. *She'll be good for spare parts.* She focused on her compad. The Erstallius and Aku defenders were pressing the intruders hard, but more troop transports were entering the atmosphere.

An expanding shock wave from an explosion in high orbit formed a fiery sphere that filled the southeastern sky.

Petra jogged toward the Mânu. *We can't stop this attack! Not enough ships!* She reached the old tarmac and felt a wave of pressure roll over her feet and rise upward—a light press against her body. She stopped. The wave rustled her hair as it left her body, and she noticed a disturbance in the air—a rippling shock-front that agitated the clouds above her as it rushed through them.

Three fireballs streaked through the clouds toward the southwest.

Petra looked at the security update on her compad. The battle appeared to be stalling on both sides. Only the Aku transports moved at attack speed. She fingered the data index to focus on the fireballs. They broke apart and fell out of view—the sensor data showed them to be enemy troop transports.

She gasped. *Clan Tuma!*

A security update showed the orbiting Aku transports were hitting the sluggish Tuma cruisers in strafing runs and ripping them apart.

The Tuma cruisers lost speed. Their troop carriers burned up during planet-fall.

She fingered her compad and changed the sensor input to download data from the Erstallius flagship.

They've lost Compression Drive. We lost Compression Drive!

Petra looked up. The Aku transport was being dowsed by a fire suppression crew. The Mânu's rail guns still pointed skyward. Another squadron of ciâfey flew across the basin toward the northwest. *That's where*

Tuma transports made planet-fall. Our Outpost is in that direction. The Hybrid Farm is in that direction. Ji'dess is that way too.

Another fiery shock wave expanded in the upper atmosphere.

Petra focused on the security update—the explosion came from a Tuma cruiser.

The Rhysu activated their weapon. The anti-compression weapon stalled the attack!

With the immediate danger gone, Petra continued toward the Mânu, her gait slower, her mind focused on the implications of the anti-compression wave.

Looks like the Erstallius won't be leaving after all.

An hour after the battle's abrupt end, Jegen-Major Kurt Sari called a meeting of the remaining Erstallius command officers in the largest conference room in the Mânu. Grénu, the old Aku overseer of the Mânu, joined the meeting with his five lead engineers, along with two local elders and Narèndu, the overseer of the Aku Defense Force. Winstone Bittle stood amid his six lead engineers a few paces inside the doorway.

Petra walked through the narrow hall toward the meeting room. She could hear Sari speaking about the battle before she reached the doorway—his voice was uplifting. She stopped a pace inside the room, behind the Erstallius engineers. No one was seated. Sari was separated from the main group by a holo-display of Ni'apinu—a light-blue graphical sphere map with navigation lines and markers that identified locations.

"The Tuma approached Ni'apinu from the direction of the central sun," Sari said. "Their attack cruisers focused on two main targets—Kuliq'Quad Basin and Dol'anar. Their troop ships targeted both those locations and our outpost in the Sequleg Mountains. They knew exactly where to hit us to keep the Aku from constructing more ships. They were unsuccessful."

"We have the anti-compression wave to thank for that," Narèndu said. "We were grossly outnumbered."

Sari nodded and fingered his control pad. The sphere map dissolved into a view of a 20-kilometer area around the ruined Erstallius outpost. "Tuma successfully landed troops here," Sari said. He used a pointer to mark a spot north of Khemyak Gorge, in the delta region west of the tiny village called Koos on the shore of the northern sea. "We estimate one hundred to one-hundred and fifty clanmen."

"We are surrounding that location," Narèndu said. "We will be done with them by tomorrow."

No prisoners, Petra thought. *The Aku are ferocious when it comes to Clan Tuma.*

Sari changed the holo-display to show the terrain around Dol'anar. "We received word that eight troop carriers landed in this area, about a kilometer from the city." He used the pointer to highlight the specific spot west of the new construction facilities. "We are engaging them now."

A wave of sadness hit Petra. *The Rhysu weapon didn't stop everything.* She retreated into the hall and rested her back against the wall. *Salus is in Dol'anar,* she thought. *He could be dead.* She folded her arms and lowered her head. A tear trickled down her cheek.

Sari changed the holo-display to show Ni'apinu and its two moons, with markers that identified ship locations. "The surviving Tuma cruisers and troop ships are moving away from us," he said. He used the pointer to highlight their present location, two-hundred thousand kilometers beyond the orbit of the outer moon. "Without Compression Drive, they can't leave the system as quickly as they'd like. They're no longer a threat."

"We must remove them," Narèndu said. "We cannot allow them a haven in our system."

"We won't," Sari insisted. "We will remove the Tuma on-planet first—they are the immediate threat. Everyone off-planet is stuck in this system because of the alien weapon. We need to find the source of the anti-compression wave and disable it. We need—"

"Our ships are not disabled," Narèndu interjected.

"Correct," Sari said. "They've experienced only a minor drop in the efficiency of their engines. But you only have ten without damage. They are the only defense we have that can move at attack speed. They are our most precious weapons now. We should use them with caution. If we lose them, we will be exposed everywhere. The Tuma fleet will not attack again. They are limping away to avoid more damage."

"We need to understand why the Aku ships are immune to the alien weapon," Winstone Bittle said.

Sari nodded to the old engineer. "I expect you to lead that investigation."

Petra wiped the tears from her face and shouldered her way through the officers standing in front of the doorway. "Can the Aku ships fire their main weapon in the atmosphere?"

Narèndu shot a puzzled look at Petra—her civilian work clothes hid her status as a retired Erstallius clanman. "And you are?"

"Petra Sitlyn. One of the Erstallius engineers who repaired your ships."

Narèndu flinched at Petra's revelation. He bowed his head as a gesture of respect. "Firing in the atmosphere—we've never tested that. Never saw a need."

"Can you do it?"

"I suppose. In the upper atmosphere. We could stabilize the ship using the plasma thrusters. I would not try it in the lower atmosphere."

"Could we hit the surface with enough force to destroy our enemy?"

Narèndu nodded. "Why?"

"Send two ships to Dol'anar," Petra said, her voice pleading. "Blast the Tuma from the upper atmosphere. They'll never know what hit them and you'll save Aku war-fighters from a ground battle."

Narèndu looked at Sari.

Sari asked: "Will that work?"

"Yes, but we are already engaged."

"Then disengage," Petra said.

"You'll save lives," Sari added.

Narèndu agreed, pinched the metallic ring around his neck and walked out of the room while he spoke in Akün—a quiet command to alter the battle at Dol'anar.

Petra met Sari's gaze. "Thank you, sir."

Sari tipped his head and smiled. "Now," he said, "about that alien weapon. Our Command Center reports the anti-compression wave has affected them." He changed the holo-display to show the station orbiting the system's blue gas giant 720,000,000 kilometers from Ni'apinu. "Our security drones on the same side of the sun as Ni'apinu, near the heliosphere, have also detected a change—their TAC emitters have a slower response time than the drones on the opposite side of the system. That means the emission of the alien wave throughout the system is asymmetrical. Which means the wave is probably being emitted from Ni'apinu or somewhere close—like one of the moons. It's buried somewhere deep. Based on all the reports, the aliens need a strong gravity well to cross over. That's where we'll find their anti-compression emitter."

"It was emitted from Ni'apinu," Petra said.

"How do you know that?"

"I felt it, didn't you?"

"No," Sari admitted. "Did anyone else feel it?"

"It created a mild pressure wave in the atmosphere," one of the Erstallius officers said. "It moved up from the ground."

"Everyone in my ground crew felt it," Bittle said.

"The fire suppression gang said the streams from their hoses fluttered," one of the Aku engineers said. "They thought it was a hose pressure issue."

Sari scanned the room. "Anyone else?"

Petra held firm. "It's being emitted from Ni'apinu. If I were to do something like that, I would want it as close to my enemies as possible to keep them planet-bound, to keep them caged."

"That's a good analogy," Sari said. "We are in a Rhysu cage. How do we break out?"

Petra folded her arms. "That's the most important question we have before us."

The holo-display flashed red, and the image changed to show a TAC prompt.

> **TAC Comm 1**
> **Sender:** Erstallius Cruiser 1108
> **Target:** Erstallius Command, GSW-183
> **Priority:** Alert 1
> **Accept:** Yes - No

Sari fingered the control pad, clicked Yes, and the message text appeared on the screen.

> **Message begin:**
> Jegen-Major Jamira Melkor, Erstallius Cruiser 1108
> We have arrived at the heliosphere of PDN160. Because of an anti-compression wave present in the system, we cannot proceed.
> Light time to GSW-183 is 20.5 hours.
> We can proceed at space normal speed to arrive in 3.5 years.
> We request an Aku transport to off-load the crew.
> Our Chief Engineer has calculated the Aku tri-pole engines can bypass the effects of the compression wave and make the round trip in less than six hours.
> Please respond on TAC frequency 109.
> **Message end.**

Petra looked at Jegen-Major Sari. "I thought the clan was leaving. Why is an Erstallius cruiser arriving?"

"You know as much as I," Sari replied. He faced Grénu. "Ouahi'lef duf'ekly. Ar'ilesu a'hul siedu?"

Grénu exchanged hushed words with his engineers, then faced Sari and nodded.

Sari motioned for his staff officer. "Send this reply: Two Aku transports deployed. Be advised, Clan Tuma has attacked the system and is still present. Sending tactical data. Advise Combat Alert."

"Aye, sir," the staff officer said.

Petra watched the staff officer turn and rush out of the room.

BEV COLLI: RIFT

Bev stopped. Her energy output dropped, but she continued to move, pushed by the current in the plasma stream. She twisted with a brief surge of power and broke free from the energy current. She tumbled into the center of a plasma knot. Twisted cords of cyan energy, entwined and tucked together, blocked her view of the energy sea.

Something is wrong.

A quiet fear pushed all other thoughts to the background of Bev's consciousness, and she heard a distant Rhysu call out, "Have courage!"

Bev twirled to see Rhysu spheres rushing past her through the plasma knot.

She opened her mind to connect with the Rhysu.

They're not chasing me!

Voices called from a thousand Rhysu—a garbled cacophony that screamed disaster.

They activated the weapon. The weapon was a mistake!

Bev dove back into the streams, followed the Rhysu into another void within the knot, and discovered her focus had brought her to the crossing point that led to Alpha Cephei Four.

The rift is open!

A swirling vortex of cyan plasma roared and emitted persistent pressure waves that hit Bev before she saw the opening. She recoiled as the waves flowed over her. *That shouldn't happen*, she thought. *Something is wrong.* She scanned the void but could see nothing that looked like controls to open and close the rift, just black space around the surging vortex.

The gathered Rhysu pressed toward the tornado of energy but balked from entering the rift because of the odd pressure waves.

They're afraid, Bev noticed. She squeezed through the surrounding Rhysu to get a better view of the circular opening. Understanding flowed into her from the Rhysu—the anti-compression emitter was propagating waves through the rift and causing the streams to form knots. *They didn't expect that.* "Shut off the emitter!"

A hundred voices replied: "We can't!"

"Then close the rift!"

A Rhysu brushed against Bev and its tendrils flapped against her energy sphere. "We close it. It may not open again."

"Because of the emitter?"

"Yes. The rift is weakening. The caretakers of the emitter may get stranded in the human universe if the rift collapses."

Bev moved closer to the vortex. The pressure restricted her movement, but she could still move forward. "Tell the caretakers to come back!"

"They can't hear us!"

"It's good you did this test before—"

"Not a test," the Rhysu admitted. "All the emitters are active."

"Idiots!"

Bev pushed away from the Rhysu toward the swirling tunnel of cyan plasma. She saw an opportunity in the surrounding chaos, but now, with the active rift so close to collapse, she hesitated.

What if the knots have changed the sea so a stable rift at this location is no longer possible?

She remembered Cynth Halva's presentation about the colony on Arrilen Po.

The Rhysu were on-planet, surviving there before the humans evacuated. They also proved they could survive in space after they destroyed the mine on Alpha Cephei Four.

She recalled her trip to Ni'apinu and Pigrell. *I survived in space.*

"I've nothing to fear if I can't come back here," she told herself. She pushed against the pressure and inched closer to the whirling vortex.

Behind Bev, the Rhysu erupted with shouts and plasma discharges.

Hundreds of Shoku broke through the wall of Rhysu and rushed toward the vortex.

The Rhysu collapsed upon the advancing Shoku, igniting a plasma spewing, tendril stabbing battle to keep the rebels away from the rift.

Bev turned from the fight and rushed into the vortex. Once inside the maw of the rift, the pressure waves from the emitter moved outward, confined to the swirling walls of energy, leaving the center of the rift free of turbulence. She was pulled through the vortex and thrown into a rock cavern.

Anti-compression waves radiated into the cavern from a small circular tunnel below the vortex. A small section of the waves twisted away from the uniform wavefront and flowed into a funnel shape as they were sucked into the churning walls of energy that formed the rift.

Bev noticed two Rhysu inside the entrance to that small tunnel. *No panic. No sense of failure. They're blind to what's happening on the other side.* She moved toward the surface of the cavern and saw the exit—a circular hole in the glazed rock. "You should close the rift," she yelled to the Rhysu. "Your weapon is destroying your home!"

The Rhysu moved out of the circular tunnel to confront Bev.

Bev turned, faced the exit, and rushed into the rock.

The melted surface of the rock tunnel twisted and turned, but always led Bev upward. She looked back during her assent and did not detect pursuit by the Rhysu. Her energy sphere destroyed five sensor drones as she sped upward—minor obstacles that had no effect on her passage. She stopped when the tunnel made a right-angle turn.

"Eetah!"

The cyan glow from her body revealed the mass of melted metal that had been her mobile drill, and scattered remains of charred environment suits.

"Rest in peace, Josh."

She rose to the tunnel ceiling, to keep the heat from her energy sphere as far from the remains as possible and moved toward the main evacuation shaft. The support frame for the evac lift was warped and melted into the surrounding rock. As she moved up through the shaft, all remnants of the support frame disappeared after level six, and the evac lift was gone.

The Shoku destroyed everything.

Above the shaft, another tunnel began—a four-meter circular hole in the rock ceiling of the assembly area, three levels below the surface. Bev could see a patch of stars through the opening, and with her Rhysu senses a steady stream of radiation from the system's sun. She examined the assembly area—melted scaffolding, glazed rock, and charred piles of shredded environment suits.

If I had gotten on the lift, I'd be scattered with the ashes.

Bev could no longer shed tears, but she felt them anyway.

She moved into the round tunnel. As she neared the surface, she searched with her mind for anyone living, expecting to find Sabballi or Cormed clanmen—the clans Arlud told her were investigating the eruption. She emerged from the tunnel, greeted by deep black shadows that hid most of the surrounding landscape on the airless surface. The sky was awash in the churning solar radiation from horizon to horizon, with brilliant spots of light from ten thousand stars piercing the solar particle streams. She stayed in the shadows—her cyan plasma glow pushed back the blackness and allowed her to find a patch of ground free of rubble. She rested there and projected her mind outward to understand the impact of the anti-compression wave. She sensed fear. Somewhere nearby, humans bemoaned their crippled ships. She pushed her mind farther out and discovered anti-compression waves active within every colonized holding she detected—Roth-513, Boden, Jai'raan, and Wan'tei. She heard Arlud's voice when she examined Ni'apinu but ignored it so she would not mentally jump to his location.

Although the anti-compression waves were expanding, Bev could detect only two major disruptions—the battle at Arrilen Po, where she no longer sensed anyone from Clan Halva, and the reverse pressure issue deep in the rock below her. On the other side of the rift, Shoku fought Rhysu for control, and the outcome of that struggle would impact all humans.

She returned her focus to her physical location. Nothing stirred on the surface, so she looked up to find something in orbit and saw the blinking red light of a comm-drone streak across the southern horizon. With her expanded senses, she followed the path of its TAC transmission through the solar wind.

There they are.

Bev stayed in the shadows and cast her mind toward an armada. The ships were far from Alpha Cephei, moving toward the heliosphere, but at a speed slower than usual because of the anti-compression wave. She deduced they were over four-hundred million kilometers away, closer to the orbit of Alpha Cephei Five.

Guild Ships, she noticed. *What are they doing here?*

Her mind snapped back to her energy sphere, and she moved off the surface into sunlight.

Alpha Cephei's raging solar wind hit Bev as soon as she cleared the rock embankment. The waves of radiation caused the outer surface of her energy sphere to glow brighter and produce a wispy, cyan-colored fog that trailed behind her as she ascended higher. Once high enough to see the entire blazing-white disk of Alpha Cephei, the star's intense radiation increased the production of fog around her energy sphere, and she disappeared inside a thick cloud of cyan-colored particles. She remembered laying on the hill after she escaped the mine and the strange blue cloud that descended toward her. *The Rhysu survived that,* she thought. *I'll survive this.* She examined her body—the reaction was painless, made her tendrils thicker, and her sphere brighter and larger.

The sun is making me stronger! The Rhysu said they could not survive in the human universe. She flexed her tendrils. *I'm surviving just fine!*

She focused again on the fleeing Guild armada and enfolded to hide her presence. To her surprise, the cyan cloud that encased her vanished when she restricted her dimensional presence. *Just like the Rhysu disappeared,* she thought, and she rushed toward the Guild ships.

Captain Erlis Pardee leaned forward in his command couch and watched the rippling distortion on his holoscreen. "You're sure it came from Alpha Cephei Four?"

"Yes," the helmsman said. "It matches the description in the Cormed reports."

Pardee knew that bit of data. *The Rhysu are coming for us!* "Can we move any faster?"

"No, sir," the helmsman replied. "We're still caught in the anti-compression wave."

Pardee flicked a comm switch to broadcast to all ships in the armada. "This is Pardee. Condition Red. Deploy TNMs and evade. Maneuver, Alpha-2 Gamma."

"We'll never out-run it, sir," the helmsman said.

"I know," Pardee replied, "but some of us may get away with no damage." He turned to his weapons officer. "Set Plasma cannons full charge."

"Aye, sir."

Bev watched the Guild armada spew small objects behind them that formed a grid pattern—a curved barrier between her and the ships.

They think I'm coming to attack.

She slowed her advance to better analyze what waited for her and focused her mind on the humans in the dreadnought. *That's the command ship. That's the one I need to approach.*

The Guild armada split into four groups, each heading along a different course out of the system.

Bev stayed focused on the dreadnought and searched within it for a human connection. Her mind roamed through the corridors of the mid-deck, up to the forward lounge below the bridge, where she saw a woman seated at the conference table with four men. A large holoscreen displayed medical diagrams of a human brain, with graphs of brain wave patterns.

Another screen displayed tactical data on a map of the area surrounding the armada. She centered her mind on the woman. *I've seen her before. On Ni'apinu. With Arlud!* She let her mind snap back to her position behind the armada.

The Guild ships had spread out into a hemispherical retreat pattern to target their pursuer from a wider angle, and to enable more ships to escape an attack.

I have only one chance to make contact, Bev thought. Once the battle was over between the Rhysu and the Shoku, either the Shoku would emerge and demolish the Guild ships, or the Rhysu would come and force her back through the rift. She focused on the best course and, using her higher-dimensional attributes, positioned herself in front of the dreadnought, five-hundred meters from the forward deflection field. She matched the ship's speed to keep her distance and unfolded to reveal her three-dimensional appearance. The cyan fog around her body was less intense because of the increased distance from Alpha Cephei, but her energy sphere was still larger and brighter than normal. She focused on the woman in the forward lounge.

Can you hear me?

Shanna Sy stiffened in her chair. The voice in her head yelled at her to listen.

Prompted by a warning message on the tactical display, Leru Cantor changed views to the forward camera. "Look, they're in front of us!"

"They're in my head," Shanna said.

Canter leaned back in his chair. "What?"

Shanna closed her eyes. *I'm listening!*

I'm Bev Colli. Remain calm. I have a lot to tell you.

The transfer of knowledge took less time than Bev expected, and it surprised her to learn her connection reached more people than Shanna Sy. More than half the crew in the dreadnought heard her. Their response complicated the connection at first, but the clamoring faded as the initial shock passed and the crew calmed down and listened.

"The emitter cannot be turned off?"

Bev resolved who asked that question. *Erlis Pardee. The Captain.* She was glad her voice had reached most of the officers. *Yes, Captain,* she responded. *The emitter will block your compression drive and cannot be turned off.*

"You said Clan Halva blew up the emitter on Arrilen Po," Pardee stated. "Can we do that?"

Clan Halva detonated bombs beneath the surface, Bev explained, *but that gave the Shoku an opportunity to break through the Rhysu barriers. They attacked the Halva ships. Sending explosives to destroy the emitter will put everyone here in jeopardy. Do not provoke them!*

"Then what are we supposed to do?"

Your options are limited. As I speak, the Rhysu are fighting the Shoku. The Rhysu want to cage you. The Shoku want to destroy you. If the Shoku defeat the Rhysu, your Armada will be in danger of attack. You should power down your engines and do what you can to shield any power sources you need for life support. If you reduce all traces of energy generation, the Shoku may not notice you. If the Rhysu win, they will come to retrieve me, and you will be stuck here without compression drive.

Shanna Sy had heard enough. "That's not acceptable! There must be a way out of this!"

Whoever wins the battle will defeat you. You have no other options. I cannot stop them.

"Then why," Shanna asked, "do you bother to tell us this?"

I thought you should know the fate that awaits you.

The quiet from the humans was unsettling. Bev broke her connection and wondered if she had made a mistake contacting the Guild ships. She focused on the rift and could no longer sense it.

It's closed!

She rushed back toward Alpha Cephei Four. The increased solar wind thickened the glowing cyan fog around her as she neared the planet. When she entered the rock, her particle cloud stayed on the surface and settled over the terrain like a thick blanket, illuminating the dark ground before fading in the shadows.

Bev rushed through the rock tunnel. She searched ahead with her mind and found no one. She entered the dark cavern, its surface illuminated by the glow of her energy sphere. In the small tunnel at the bottom of the cavern, she saw the emitter, its higher-dimensional structure, turning, twisting, shedding anti-compression waves.

They left me here, she thought. She looked up into the rock tunnel that led to the surface. *The sun gave me strength. If a stable rift is no longer possible here, I will survive, and the Rhysu cannot retrieve me.* The realization she was back in the human universe, free of the Rhysu grip, broke her composure and she let her energy sphere drop to the cavern floor.

I did it!

She focused her mind on the Rhysu. The battle continued. Both Rhysu and Shoku suffered more than in previous battles. The knots in the streams remained, but without an open rift the anti-compression waves could no longer impact the energy sea.

The Rhysu will win. The Rhysu always win.

Bev moved closer to the emitter and examined its design and function. Collapsing the rock around the emitter would not block the waves. *I must destroy it.* She backed away from the emitter toward the exit to the surface. *It's time the humans won.*

She gathered her energy tendrils into a tight ball and fired a burst of plasma at the emitter.

The explosion blasted rock into the larger cavern and a fiery shock front pushed Bev into the exit tunnel. She recovered from the blast and peered into the cavern. Durillium veins in the rock surface glowed pale blue from the infusion of energy. The emitter's original shape had collapsed into itself, and the internal movement stopped.

Bev moved back into the exit tunnel and rushed toward the surface.

THE GUILD: CAGED

Captain Pardee peered into the holoscreen above the course-plotting cubicle and squinted. "Where is she?"

The helmsman shrugged. "Gone, sir. She vanished."

"Engine status," Pardee commanded.

"No go, sir," the Systems Engineer said.

Pardee flicked a comm switch to hail his Engine Chief.

"Chief Krasok here, Captain."

"Mister Krasok, did you hear Bev Colli?"

"Yes, Captain."

"I think it best to follow her advice."

"Aye, sir. I agree."

"Make it happen, Chief. Pardee out."

A few minutes later, the lights in the C.I.C. dimmed because of the reduced power flow. With the main generators turned off, only life support systems and a few external sensors were left at full power.

Pardee moved next to the main sensor station operator and saw the other ships in the armada had followed his lead. "Keep an eye out, Miss Kissel. If the Shoku approach, signal all ships to go black."

"How do I tell if it's the Shoku or the Rhysu?"

"If you spy a distortion of any kind, send the signal."

Pardee returned to his command seat and hailed Leru Canter.

"Canter here, sir."

"Were you able to record any of the voices?"

"No, sir. We were not ready for that."

"Are you ready now?"

"We still need to update the medpad."

"When can you have it done?"

"I can't give you an exact estimate."

Pardee frowned. "Notify me once you have it working. Pardee out." He slumped in his seat and stared at the blank holoscreen. There was nothing more for him to do. *To reach the heliosphere will take almost two years,* he thought. *The anti-compression waves will advance beyond that boundary and continue to restrict Compression Drive. We will die in space.*

No, you will not, Captain.

Pardee mentally recoiled at the sound of Bev's voice. "Where are you?"

I'm in front of you.

Pardee leaned toward the prime sensor station. "Miss Kissel?"

The befuddled operator faced her captain. "She just appeared, sir."

I've been to Alpha Cephei Four, Bev said. *The rift is closed. I destroyed the emitter. The anti-compression waves should stop if they haven't done so already. If you want to leave this system, I suggest you do so now.*

"How is that possible?"

I threw a ball of plasma at the emitter—

"No," Pardee intoned. "How did you get to Alpha Cephei Four and back so quickly?"

Bev thought of an answer and realized she had never considered how her quick movement through space happened. *I don't know. I focus on a destination and I'm there. I'm a higher-dimensional creature now. That must have something to do with it.*

Pardee shook his amazement aside and flicked a comm switch to hail Chief Krasok.

"Krasok here, Captain."

"Power up the Compression Drive, Chief."

"Aye, sir."

Pardee flipped another switch on the plotting pedestal's communication panel. "Attention all ships, this is Pardee. Go for Compression Drive. We have a narrow window, make use of it."

You have time, Bev said. *The Rhysu placed the emitter too close to the rift. They had to close the rift to prevent more damage to their energy sea. They will know the emitter is off once you engage your drive because of the harmful fluctuations. You must flee as fast as you can.*

Miss Kissel faced Pardee. "Captain, if the anti-compression waves propagate at light speed, we won't be free of them for about thirty minutes, and our trip though hyperspace may be a short one—the waves will persist farther out."

Pardee pondered Kissel's warning. *Is she correct, Bev?*

I don't know, Bev answered with genuine regret. *I'm not an engineer.*

Pardee hailed Chief Krasok again. "Krasok, will the anti-compression waves persist even if the emitter is destroyed?"

"Standard energy waves will persist," Krasok replied. "In the sub-quantum realm, wave propagation is not limited to light speed. Sub-quantum effects disperse almost twenty billion times faster than light—think gravity. In theory, once the emitting source is gone, the anti-compression effect will dissipate everywhere it exists in this system. We should be able to jump into hyperspace as soon as the engines are up to full power. It may be rough going at first, like a boat cutting though high swells, but that won't last long."

The helmsman faced Pardee. "Where do we go, sir?"

Pardee looked at Bev's glowing sphere on the holoscreen. "Bev, what holdings are free of emitters?"

Bev analyzed the nearest star systems—five suns and their planets wrapped in the normal energy streams persistent in this universe. *Al-phaq does not have an emitter,* she said. *That may not be for long.*

Pardee sat up straighter on his couch. "Good. We'll swing by the old homestead to gather the rest of our forces, then head to Wald-415. Set a course, helmsman, and broadcast it to the armada."

"Aye, sir."

Pardee focused on Bev. "What about you, Bev? Where will you go?"

Bev focused her thoughts on the image in Pardee's mind. Where is Wald-415?

"Sixteen point twenty parsecs from here. About eleven standard—"

No, Bev interrupted. *Don't tell me how far. Show me in your mind.*

Bev mentally leaped toward the holding in Pardee's memory. The Guild ships stationed throughout the system and around Wald-415 were in sub-light orbits. There were no vessels leaving or arriving. TAC transmissions bounced between Wald-415 and ships in the system's outer regions, but no com-drones. She refocused on her current position. *You'll be safe at Al-phaq,* she said. *Leave. Now!*

"And what of Wald-415?"

They are trapped by an emitter. Do not go there, you won't make it. Leave now! Get to Al-phaq!

BEV COLLI: CELESTIAL

Bev watched the ships in the Guild armada retreat. One by one, they became enveloped in the green wisps of Compression Drive, were pulled into hyperspace, and disappeared, leaving a streak of green particles that dissipated into the space that remained.

The dreadnought was the last ship to activate its engines.

Bev focused on Pardee's flagship and was distracted by a powerful regret from someone on board. She centered her concentration on the sadness and her mind jumped to the rear observation bay to see Shanna Sy gazing out the window. Thoughts of losing Alpha Cephei Four, and how that would disappoint her father, fed Shanna's misery.

It's not your fault, Bev said.

Shanna stepped back from the window. "Get out of my mind!"

The anger shocked Bev. *Why are you mad at me?*

Shanna turned and rushed out of the observation bay.

Bev kept her focus on Shanna. *You should not fear me,* she said. *I'm not your enemy.*

Shanna hurried down the corridor toward the mid-deck personnel lift. "Leave me alone!"

Bev backed away and allowed the young woman her privacy. There was more to Shanna's regret, and it centered on Arlud. Shanna's mental image of the Erstallius Regent hit Bev like a hammer.

She thinks she's lost him.

Shanna's feelings were intense—more than Bev expected. She mentally leaped back to her. *He's not in love with you,* she said. *He never will be.*

"Get out of my head!"

Bev's focus jumped back to her position in space. She glimpsed the gossamer streak left by the dreadnought's Compression Drive moments before it dissolved. The anger in Shanna's response echoed in her mind. *Her feeling for Arlud is a school-girl crush based, not on reality, but on her own inner needs. Everything she's done since she left Ni'apinu has been to bring her closer to Arlud.* Empathy for Shanna's regret stifled her urge to reconnect.

I'd just add fuel to her fire, she thought. *A fire that will burn out once she understands Arlud has no interest in her. She'll get over it.*

Bev refocused on her surroundings. She was alone in space now, but there was no need to panic. She flexed her electric tendrils and puffed up her energy sphere, which pushed a wave through the thin blue fog that surrounded her. The energy emissions from the sun, while less intense than at Alpha Cephei Four, gave her strength and filled her with confidence.

I can survive here.

She spun around to face the Guild minefield. It was a concave mesh of destruction one-thousand meters in diameter. The proximity switches on each mine would detonate once an object came within one-hundred meters. The mines would not kill a Rhysu—the energy would attract them and then distract them.

That'll just piss them off.

She faced Alpha Cephei Four. The Guild armada's jump into hyperspace would attract a Rhysu investigation into the failure of their emitter, but she could sense no Rhysu.

And no rift.

They'll be coming, she thought, *once the Shoku are subdued.*

She rotated to focus on her destination—Arlud. He was near Ni'apinu. So was Gus.

They need help.

Bev constricted her energy sphere and enfolded to reduce her dimensional presence. Her vision narrowed as she focused on Arlud. The stars seemed to twirl around her focal point, then blurred and coalesced into a solid tunnel, bright and warm, a spinning kaleidoscope of blazing colors.

The spatial jump landed Bev inside the trailing edge of PDN160's heliosphere. The brilliant yellow-white glare of the primary star dominated her view, with the minor companion star glowing a less intense orange about forty degrees to her right side. Between the two suns she saw remnant back-scatter halos from failed Compression Drives around two stalled ships—a large cruiser and a smaller frigate.

They're stuck.

Bev projected her mind to pinpoint Arlud and saw him seated in the darkened starboard observation bay inside the cruiser. She stayed enfolded and moved closer to the disabled ship. To avoid speaking to the entire crew, she focused all her attention on Arlud and projected her thoughts at an energy level lower than her previous connections.

Can you hear me?

"Yes!"

You can take off that medpad. You won't need it anymore.

Arlud touched the medpad. "Why?"

I'm no longer in Rhysu space. I'm here, outside your ship.

Arlud ripped off the medpad, jumped up to the window, and pushed the button that opened the shutters. "I can't see you."

I wanted to keep this private and not alarm anyone.

"Are you back for good?"

Bev transferred her memory of the events at Arrilen Po and Alpha Cephei Four, including her last encounter with Shanna Sy.

"Cynth is dead," Arlud said. "No one could have survived that. She deserved a better end."

It is possible they survived.

"It was good of you to help the Guild."

A temporary kindness, Bev replied. *The Rhysu will track them to Al-phaq. If they stay there too long, they will get stuck there, like you're stuck here.*

"Shanna told me she would investigate the aliens at Alpha Cephei Four. She's proved her integrity, even if a bit fanciful with her feelings."

She thinks she's in love with you.

Arlud fell silent as he contemplated everything Bev had told him.

To break the silence, Bev said: *Tri-pole engines. You found a solution. That's great!*

"Yes," Arlud said. *It is great,* he thought. But he also knew it would only lead to a permanent solution if they could get to U'galem and have the Dejoria shipyards produce a prototype powerful enough to showcase to the Rhysu.

The Aku ships will convince them, Bev said.

"Maybe not," Arlud replied in a sullen tone. "The Aku ships may not be powerful enough. The Rhysu crossed over in response to the harmful fluctuations after tri-pole engines were replaced. Their reaction is a direct response to modern Compression Drive engines. We need to demonstrate a tri-pole powerful enough to move modern dreadnoughts through hyperspace. Any other result may not convince the Rhysu that our solution will be maintained. Convincing them will be the only way to stop the Shoku from trying to kill us."

Jamira Melkor entered the observation bay. "Excuse me, sir. The Aku ships are on approach. They will be here in fifteen minutes."

Arlud turned to face the Commander-in-Charge but was distracted by a flash of light outside the window.

Klaxons shrieked a warning and the window shutters closed.

Melkor turned and rushed out of the observation bay.

Arlud opened a holoscreen—the Aku transports were under attack.

The shrieking beat from the klaxons stopped.

Bev moved closer to the cruiser. *What happened?*

"Clan Tuma has crept into range," Arlud said. "Their earlier attack was repelled after the anti-compression wave—"

Oh, I see them, Bev said. *I'll be back.*

"Bev?"

Five squadrons of small Tuma assault ships were running sorties against the two Aku transports from five directions.

The Aku's plasma weapon was too concentrated a blast to be as effective against the fast-moving assault ships as it was against the larger carriers and dreadnoughts, and the rail guns were too slow. Within minutes, one of the spherical Aku ships had diagonal fractures in the hull and began spewing atmosphere and clanmen.

Bev approached the battle enfolded and assessed the tactical situation. *The other Aku ship won't last long.* She glanced back at Arlud's cruiser—too far to save the Aku. The Erstallius frigate was moving toward the battle but would soon be swarmed by the Tuma assault ships and meet the same fate as the Aku. She searched the area for the carrier that brought the speedy Tuma devils to this junction. *Directly below me, a dreadnought and two frigates. More than two-million kilometers distant, hiding in a cometary debris field. They planned this well in advance for the smaller ships to engage here.*

Bev focused on the still active Aku ship—she was throwing everything she had at the enemy.

It's now or never.

Arlud took a step back from the holoscreen as he watched brief bursts of light erase every Tuma assault ship one by one. Within five minutes, all the attackers were gone. "Wow!" He fingered the holoscreen controls to affirm the attackers had been destroyed.

The cruiser's status was upgraded to Yellow Alert and the window shutters opened.

Arlud stepped sideways from the holoscreen and peered out the window. Amid the stars, he saw a small rippling distortion in the direction of the surviving transport. "Is that you, Bev?"

Yes.

Arlud blinked, and Bev revealed herself.

She unfolded fifty meters from the cruiser. Her depleted energy sphere was still strong enough to emit a brilliant cyan glow within the wispy fog created by interaction with the solar wind. *One Aku ship is safe now. The other one is almost dead—survivors are aboard, but they won't last long.*

Arlud gripped the hand railing below the window. "Are you OK? You sound different."

I am speaking to everyone who can hear me inside your ship. The Aku need help. Tuma ships are in that comet cloud south of your position. They are no longer a threat at that distance.

Arlud moved back to the holoscreen. "Rescue shuttles have been sent."

Hundreds of human voices bombarded Bev with questions. The jumbled contact forced her to shift focus back to Arlud. *What did you say?*

"Shuttles are on their way to the Aku."

Bev identified eight small ships racing from the Erstallius cruiser toward the Aku ships. *They're too slow,* she said. *They need to move faster.*

"They're going as fast as they can."

Bev turned and analyzed the status of each Aku ship. *They both have damage to their engines,* she said. *I have an idea. Tell the shuttles to divert to the ship that's still intact.*

"What? Why?"

I'll be back.

Bev enfolded and rushed toward the fractured transport. She sensed live humans inside the cracked hull. *Listen to me,* she said, and transferred her thoughts to the scared clanmen so they would understand her intent.

I am going to save you. Do not panic. You have enough atmosphere in your sealed compartments to keep you alive, but you will die soon if you wait for the Erstallius shuttles. Stay inside your sealed compartments. Keep away from bulkheads that connect to the outer hull. I will need to siphon energy from your core. The interior will get hot. I have never done this before, so you may feel uncomfortable. You must endure it to survive.

The mental response from the clanmen roared into Bev's mind like waters bursting through a dam. She blocked the riotous inquiries and concentrated on the ship. She could reach the core through the main breach, which would reduce the impact on the passengers as they had been secured on the opposite side of the ship. She unfolded, wrapped her electric tendrils around the spherical ship, and pierced the outer hull to establish a firm grip. She shoved a thick plasma tentacle into the breach and tapped into the energy at the core. Her outer sphere expanded while more tendrils grew from her body and encased the crippled ship. *Get ready,* she said. *This won't take long.*

Bev narrowed her vision and concentrated on Ni'apinu. She enfolded and pulled the transport into her higher-dimensional self. The stars swirled around her, a spinning swarm of streaking lights.

The spinning stopped, and Bev saw Ni'apinu—a distant blue and white crescent floating in the black to her left with its small inner moon. The damaged transport was still secure in her grip, and she sensed the humans inside were still alive. She looked to her right—the outer moon was closer—she estimated less than ten-thousand kilometers. She could also see multiple streams of debris that circled Ni'apinu between the moons and two salvage ships at the trailing edge of the clumped ring that was encroaching into Ni'apinu's thin upper atmosphere.

Bev focused on the transport's clanmen. *Everyone OK in there?*

The response was immediate and universal: "Yes!"

This trip isn't over yet.

She pulled information from the Commander-in-Charge inside the transport and focused on the proper destination on Ni'apinu.

Get ready, Commander. This will happen fast.

Salus, ciâfey pilot, Leader of Twenty, and Commander of the Watch, strolled to his parked aircraft to prepare for his early morning flight to the construction site east of Dol'anar. From this outer parking circle, he could see the ancient tarmac at the Mânu across the aqueduct that separated the new landing field from the old. The Mânu was vacant of both ships and ground crews. The naked tarp poles stood rigid against the early morning breeze. The four transport crews who called the Mânu at Dol'anar their Ilju'dalfah—*Home Port*—had been in orbit for two months. All had survived the Tuma attack. Two of the crews had left for the system boundary to rescue the Erstallius clanmen.

Salus pinched his neck ring to respond to a beep in his ear. "Salus here."

A basso voice asked: "Where are you!?"

"At my ciâfey. Flight prep."

"Get back to the command center! Something has—"

A sonic boom broke the morning silence.

Salus turned to face the sound and saw a ball of blazing cyan plasma drop through the clouds over the Mânu. Heat from the object pushed the air away at high speed. The hot wind hit Salus, knocked him off his feet, and pushed his ciâfey to the end of its tie-down line. He rolled to a kneeling position and watched four landing struts extend from the bottom of the fiery cyan ball and touch the tarmac—a perfect landing centered between the tarp poles of landing pad Three.

The plasma ball rose, revealing a damaged Aku transport, then sped toward the clouds and disappeared.

Salus noticed multiple punctures in the ship's composite hull and gaping, diagonal fractures that cut through the ring of rail guns that hugged the ship's equator. He could hear the hull pop and snap as it cooled in the early morning air.

Evacuation hatches opened in the belly of the spherical ship, between the landing struts. Exit ramps deployed, and the crew slid to safety as ground crews rushed to help them.

Salus stood and pinched his neck ring. "I saw a ball of fire like that at Kuliq'Quad."

The voice in his ear was astonished. "What is it?"

"It was smaller the first time I saw it. Arlud said it was Bev Colli."

Bev rose above Ni'apinu's atmosphere and paused to soak up more energy from the sun. She expanded her mind to hear the humans on the surface and in the ships in orbit. Her presence had caused quite a commotion. Many saw her as a threat. *Typical,* she thought, and she remembered Arlud once told her, "The ignorant always fear what they don't understand."

To avoid a confrontation, she paused just long enough for her energy level to rise near its previous state. She enfolded as two Aku ships came within striking distance and jumped back to the stalled Erstallius ships.

Arlud stood at the observation window and watched the shuttles tow the Aku transport toward the cruiser. "Melkor said her Chief Engineer believes we can repair the damage out here."

"He's an optimistic fellow," Eahuda said. He stood a few paces from Arlud at the other end of the window. "The hull looks intact. If it's just the antennae that are damaged, it'll be a quick fix."

Arlud stepped sideways to examine the holo-display that filled the center of the window. "The Tuma ships haven't moved."

"They've nowhere to go," Eahuda said. "They're stuck here just like us. Besides, after watching their fighters destroyed, I would assume fear has them frozen in place."

"Yeah," Arlud whispered. "I'm glad Bev's on our side." Her display of power was a genuine surprise—he had never thought of Bev in that context. He knew the Rhysu had changed her into an energy being, but having the ability to discharge plasma and vaporize durillium plate was beyond everything he had imagined.

"She's back," Eahuda said.

Arlud saw the spatial distortion in the holo-display. It appeared on the right edge of the screen, moved toward the center, and blocked his view of the approaching transport and shuttles. "That was quick."

Yes, it was, Bev said.

"Did they survive?"

Yes. Everyone survived. They're home. She sent an image of the transport resting on the tarmac to everyone in the cruiser. Reactions from the clanmen bombarded her, but she focused on Arlud's question: "How did you do that?"

I'm not sure how, Bev said. Her response was private, sent only to Arlud. *Captain Pardee asked me the same thing.*

"Can you transport all our ships?"

Only the ball-shaped ones. The others are too big. I need to surround the object completely.

Eahuda glanced at Arlud. He'd heard Arlud's question, but not the reply. "Can she do it?"

"No."

"Can she destroy the emitter like she did at Alpha Cephei Four?"

Bev heard Eahuda's question and opened her mind to respond to him. *I could, but I won't.*

"Why?"

That wouldn't solve your problem. It would just attract more Rhysu. They'd repair it and you'd be in the same situation, with more deaths.

"We don't need you to destroy it," Arlud said. "We know a tri-pole engine will work, and we know you can travel faster than any engine we've made."

Me? I'm happy to save these people, but I am not your personal taxi!

Bev's anger was in every word Arlud heard. "I know you're not," he said. "That's not what I meant."

Sure sounded like it.

"What you can do is beyond anything we can do," Arlud explained. "But the fact you jumped across billions of kilometers of space and your human passengers survived, means the process is safe for us. We just need to discover how you do it, and what effect it has on both universes. Can the Rhysu detect when you jump through space?"

They needed my help to find the Shoku. So no, they can't.

"Good," Arlud said. "We'll need you to take the other Aku ship, but this time we'll load it with sensing equipment as well as people. We need to analyze how that process works."

"So we can replicate it," Eahuda said.

"So we can determine if we can replicate it," Arlud corrected. "We may be restricted because of our nature."

"Our nature?"

"Being human."

Bev was sympathetic to the plight Arlud and his people faced. How could she not be? She was human once. Now, as a Rhysu, her choices, while not restricted by human frailty, were still guided by her human personality—everything that influenced the growth of her consciousness while human.

I'm still me, she thought. *I'll never get away from that. I'll always have a connection to this universe, to the people I knew, to the places I've been. But I'm not human. I may survive in this universe, but I am no longer part of it.*

Her struggle to survive in the Rhysu universe had strengthened her resolve. Now that she was back in the human universe, doubt clogged her thinking. With every interaction, the gulf between who she was now and who she had been became wider.

And yet, behind all the inner conflicts, she was still Bev. She was still that poor sapi who escaped a Polinda mine, shot a Polinda retriever, attracted the attention of the High Regent of Clan Dejoria, befriended the Matriarch of Clan Halva, fell in love with the Regent of GSW-183, and formed a mental link with aliens.

I fell in love? Yes, I did. I fell in love. As much as that surprised her, she could not deny it.

Maybe the Rhysu were right. Maybe I should have stayed with them. Now that love will just be an unending regret.

She discounted that thought as soon as it was finished. *Get your head straight, Bev! You got stuff to do!*

Five hours later, the Aku transport was ready. The eighty-five people from the frigate and the forty people from the cruiser had joined the twenty-man Aku crew on board the transport—all jammed together into every available space, made possible by ejecting every bit of non-essential material to create more room. Eighty special sensor packs had been installed on the transport to record the spatial changes that would initiate the jump. If the jump failed and left the transport stranded in space, death would come early for all aboard because of oxygen depletion.

Bev unfolded and moved toward the transport. *What about the other ships? Is anyone staying?*

"The ships are both in hibernation mode," Arlud said. "They'll be fine."

The Tuma are still in that comet cloud. They could take them once you're gone.

"They could," Arlud said. "But they won't."

How can you be so sure?

"They've been watching us. Once we're gone, they'll turn and run."

It's a long way to their home. Your home is closer.

"You think they'll head in toward Ni'apinu?"

That's what I'd do.

"Not to worry," Arlud assured. "Whatever they do, we'll be ready for them."

If you say so.

Bev wrapped her electric tendrils around the spherical transport and found the connection terminal. The engineers had removed one of the rail gun assemblies and replaced it with a direct link to the ship's energy core. Without a breach in the hull, Bev would need to make one to gain enough power to complete the transfer. The large duranide stud made that unnecessary—and the passengers would benefit from an intact inner hull that would help repel the heat from her body.

Her grip needed to be firm and sure, so piercing the outer hull was still necessary—minor damage, the commander-in-charge accepted.

The voices from the passengers hummed in the background of Bev's thoughts. One-hundred and forty-five people rested their hope on her ability to rescue them from the system's outer reaches. She found that reality uplifting. *I was a sapi. I have become a hero to people who wouldn't have given me the time of day in my old life. I've come a long way since Alpha Cephei Four.* She focused on the mission at hand and stabbed her electric tendrils into the outer hull. She pressed her body against the duranide stud. Her energy sphere grew to envelop the transport, and more tendrils wrapped around the ship's hull.

I'm the solution to the Rhysu alternative.

She enfolded and disappeared with the Aku transport firmly in her grip.

A sonic boom preceded Bev's energy sphere as she rushed into the atmosphere above the Mânu at Dol'anar.

Get ready, Commander!

The Aku commander's response to Bev's warning was the mental image of his tight grip on the landing strut lever on the helmsman's console; no words were necessary.

Bev reduced speed as the landing field came into sharp focus five-hundred meters below her. She aimed for landing pad One. It was diagonal to pad Three, where she had placed the other transport.

Now, Commander!

The landing struts dropped into place, and the transport touched the tarmac.

Bev released her grip and rose back into the blue sky.

Everyone OK in there?

The response was a vocal cacophony of positive remarks.

Bev sorted through the clamor and focused on Arlud. *Did the hull block the heat?*

"Wasn't too bad," Arlud said. "No one was injured."

Good.

As she left the streams and eddies of the upper atmosphere, Bev was overwhelmed by how much the radiation that enveloped the planet resembled the energy streams in the Rhysu universe. The particles flowed along the magnetic field lines generated by Ni'apinu's rotating core. She looked beyond the local environment and peered in all directions at the connected streams that filled the space between the primary sun, its brood of orbiting planets, and the smaller companion sun and its own siblings. Then, farther out, she examined connections between the neighboring star systems. Her extended vision confirmed an understanding always present, but never acknowledged: *Everything is connected.*

Bev floated in orbit and opened her senses to everything. She saw ripples from the Rhysu emitters, the stalled ships throughout the district, and the Rhysu emerging once again from Alpha Cephei Four.

They're looking for me.

She sensed searing pain, and a distant scream she recognized as the voice of Cynth Halva, but this time Cynth was not dying in a cave. She saw charred Halva cruisers and a white prison encasing Arrilen Po.

"Bev, what are you doing!?"

Arlud's exasperated query broke Bev's concentration, and she shifted her focus to her immediate surroundings. Her energy sphere had grown to immense size, roughly equal to the diameter of the second moon. The increase did not affect the gravity well of Ni'apinu like another moon would have so close to the surface. Her enlargement was only an expansion of her relaxed energy sphere. The energy she soaked up from the sun was stored in her higher-dimensional body—her three-dimensional mass had only a slight gain. Her enlargement shocked those on board the ships in orbit and caused the nearest Aku transports to move away to avoid a collision.

Sorry, Bev replied. *I didn't realize.*

Arlud heard the surprise in Bev's voice and wondered how much she still had to learn about being a Rhysu. "Is that normal?"

Must be, Bev said. *Don't worry. I'll be fine.* She compressed her energy sphere and shrunk her three-dimensional size to a more manageable proportion, then focused again on Arrilen Po.

I must leave, she said. *I'll be back.*

CLAN ERSTALLIUS: GROUNDED

Arlud watched Bev enfold and disappear on a holoscreen inside the Aku transport.

Eahuda stepped next to Arlud. "Where did she go?"

The old Degen-of-the-Corp's question caused Arlud to face him. "She didn't tell me." He and Eahuda waited on the evac-deck walkway for the rest of the passengers to debark—the few remaining were being prompted by a security officer to drop into one of two evacuation shoots.

The Aku commander-in-charge descended the ladder from the bridge and gestured for Arlud and Eahuda to evacuate.

Arlud nodded to the commander and stood at the threshold of the port shoot while Eahuda walked to the starboard shoot. At the security officer's signal, they dropped into the oval tubes to exit the transport.

The twelve rescued Erstallius officers gathered with Arlud and Eahuda inside the main hangar at the Dol'anar Mânu to learn what had happened when Clan Tuma attacked, and the battles that followed to remove them from the terrain east of the village.

"We hit the Tuma drop-troops near the construction site," Salus said. "Here." He pointed to a map that hung on the wall outside the engineering workshop. "They knew where to hit us. They had the precise data they needed to destroy our ship-building industry."

"Remote surveillance." Eahuda muttered, but he kept silent about what that knowledge implied. *We failed. If we had a full division here, Tuma would not have been able to gather their surveillance. Our internal disagreements cost us in more ways than one.* He glanced at Arlud, who belied his own understanding with a regretful look Eahuda had seen too often in recent days. He faced Salus. "It's good you were able to stop their efforts."

Salus nodded to Eahuda. "We used our plasma weapons against them. Fired from high altitude, they never knew what hit them. Scorched a bit of forest, but the result was worth the cost."

Jamira Melkor wondered: "You got them all?"

"Jegen-Major Sari ordered a survey of the entire planet," Salus explained. "If any are left, your ships will find them."

"The rest are headed this way," Eahuda said. He raised his compad and showed everyone the data screen. "They've left their hiding place in the comet cloud."

The Erstallius officers accessed their own compads to read the updated security report for themselves.

"Without compression drive, they won't reach us for two years," Melkor said. "Plenty of time to deal with them."

Salus looked at the data on Arlud's compad. "Can they survive that long?"

"Maybe, maybe not," Arlud said. "If they can't, they can still program their ships to hit us at a speed high enough to cause major damage. We must intercept them before too long, no matter what they have planned."

"If I were stranded without a working compression drive," Eahuda said, "and I saw my enemy exit the field via unknown technology, I'd do everything I could to understand that new tech."

"Yeah," Arlud agreed. "They witnessed two transports leave with Bev's help. They're coming to uncover that new tech."

"We'll stop them," Melkor said.

Arlud nodded. "Yes, we will."

PETRA SITLYN: OPTIONS

Petra strolled out of the main hanger at the Mânu in Kuliq'Quad basin and stood at the northern edge of the tarmac, near empty landing pad Two. The crippled, spherical transport sat on pad One, surrounded by a clean-up crew, and engineers preparing to dismantle the port hull to repair the damage caused by the Tuma attack. She focused on the construction site—it was void of activity. Supply crates still littered the landing pad in front of the open doorway.

All my workers returned to the village, she thought, and she knew they would not be coming back anytime soon.

The Rhysu emitter changed everything.

There was no need to build modern shuttles that incorporated Compression Drive. The focus now would be on tri-pole engines, and they had no equipment or supplies to build that kind of engine. After the fleet regrouped, they would design and plan the manufacture of tri-pole components, but she could not foresee a return to construction for at least two months.

It's back to the hybrid farm for me.

Winstone Bittle paused a few meters behind Petra. "You OK?"

Petra turned and shot a confused look at the old engineer. "What do you want?"

"I'll be leaving for Dol'anar in about an hour. Would you like to go?"

"I can't. Why are you going?"

"What do you mean, you can't?"

"I agreed to the Bi'au's demand to keep my distance from Salus for one year. That contract has not ended. If I void the agreement, we will not be allowed to marry."

Bittle frowned and turned to leave.

"Why are you going?"

"Our regent has returned," Bittle said. "I'll be traveling with him to U'galem to help oversee tri-pole engine construction."

"Arlud's back? How did he get through the emitter field so quickly?"

"Bev Colli."

"Bev?"

"Two Aku transports were sent to retrieve crew and passengers from our stalled ships—a cruiser and frigate. They were attacked by Tuma raiders. Bev brought them back. Only took a few minutes. She initiated a dimensional jump somehow. We're analyzing the data."

"On her own?"

"Yeah. You sure you want to stay here?"

"Not staying here. I'm going back to the hybrid farm."

Bittle nodded and headed to the row of mag-jet-enabled shuttles parked along the southern edge of the tarmac.

Grénu, the overseer of the Mânu, peered from behind the hangar door at Petra, then glanced over at Bittle as the old engineer advanced toward his waiting shuttle.

Bittle caught sight of Grénu and flicked a subtle farewell.

Grénu returned a brief salute. Bittle had done his bidding—he had offered to take Petra to Dol'anar. Her refusal made her promise firm and sure. She would not lose her status as betrothed to Salus. Grénu smiled and retreated to his office inside the hanger, where he would compose a message for the Bi'au about Petra's honor and determination.

Petra faced the abandoned construction site, saw her cart parked inside the open doorway, and began walking in that direction. Her thoughts shifted to Salus, and the news he had survived the battle near Dol'anar. Jegen-Major Sari's push for the Aku to use their energy weapons had eliminated the Tuma ground troops and saved countless Aku and Erstallius fighters. She had received no acknowledgment from the command staff for her suggestion to use the weapons, but she was beyond the need for accolades. That Salus was still alive was all that mattered.

He's alive and time moves forward. One day closer to being united.

She smiled to herself and sat in her cart. The trip to the hybrid farm would take about thirty minutes, once she boarded a ciâfey at the landing site beyond the security checkpoint at the entrance to the basin. The cart's power level was low, so she drove to the charging station outside the main hanger at the Mânu, then returned to her quarters to bundle up her belongings and a small cache of food and water.

An hour later, she drove through the security checkpoint and parked her cart next to a bungalow at the ciâfey landing field. She waved to a waiting pilot, who gestured for her to board. Ten minutes later, she was seated behind the pilot as they flew north toward the western end of the Wassûa Caphâga, and the hybrid farm.

CLAN ERSTALLIUS: CONCERNS

Winstone Bittle led Engine Chief Maximilian Sands to the narrow, ring-shaped engineering deck below the central Kottrel Sphere. The outer bulkhead was lined with display screens, control knobs, and insulated conduits. The inner side of the deck, below the sphere, was dominated by four pillars that supported the sphere, and the conduits and pipes that led from the sphere to the main engine couplings below the deck plates.

"Much more cramped than I imagined it would be," Sands said.

"Yes," Bittle agreed. "The original Mayfair-Courkos design was more open. The Aku made major modifications." He moved to the primary engineering display on the port side. "This will show you the initial power flow and how the antennae are charged before the tri-pole bubble is formed."

"The initial power flow?"

"Yes," Bittle said. He knew Sands was a talented engineer, but he had never seen an Aku engine, so he expected him to discover a few surprises. "The flow changes after the bubble is formed to ensure the primary weapon is always available. The Aku were fleeing from slavery. They were not about to let Clan Tuma capture them."

"Then the charge is self-sustaining—"

Footsteps rebounded off the metal deck and Bittle turned to see Arlud approach from the starboard stairwell.

"Pardon the interruption," Arlud said. "I just wanted to see how you two are getting along."

"Chief Sands has never seen these Aku modifications," Bittle said. "I thought it best to get him up to speed before we lift-off."

Arlud smiled at Bittle and stepped sideways to face Sands. "Well, Chief, what do you think so far?"

"Very impressive modifications," Sands said. "I'll spend most of our trip analyzing what they did and how we can incorporate some of the changes into our new design. They made improvements beyond what I thought possible for that time."

"Seelay was a genius," Arlud said. "Without him, the Aku would not have survived. Without you and Segen Bittle, we may not survive."

The Aku transport made orbit and twenty minutes later left Ni'apinu behind on a course for U'galem.

The interior of the ship was cramped, even with a minimal crew of five—the small crew would extend resources in case their journey was prolonged. It was a ship designed for efficiency and power, not comfort. The interior corridors were narrow and the sleeping bays for the crew not much wider. The only private cabin was for Ruñal, the Commander-in-Charge, and it was also used as a briefing room.

Arlud sat on the narrow bench against the convex bulkhead next to the hatchway and listened to the navigator explain their necessary course corrections. The young officer stood a step inside the hatchway and faced Ruñal, who sat on the only chair in the room.

"We'll avoid the gravity well at PDN172," the navigator said, "and swing back toward PDN163 five hyper-hours after we pass. That detour will have us reach U'galem in four hyper-days."

"Twelve standard-days," Arlud said. "That's not too bad."

"Yes," Ruñal agreed. "Thank you, Jarol."

The navigator nodded and left the room.

Ruñal asked: "The reduction in power, is it necessary?"

Arlud sat up straighter. "I know the normal trip time was around thirty-one hyper-hours—that was how long it took us last time—but with the Rhysu on the prowl against compression drive, I think it best to travel with less chance of disrupting their universe."

"I thought you said tri-pole engines were invisible to them?"

"I did. Speculation based on the fact they ignored us until the upgrade to compression engines, but that doesn't mean tri-pole fields don't impact their space. By reducing power, we reduce the chance they can track us. We do not want to confront them in space."

"Where's Bev?"

"I don't know."

"Why not?"

Arlud shrugged.

"Is that like her, to not tell you?"

Arlud frowned and shook his head. "She was distracted by something. It must have been important because she lost touch with me and her immediate surroundings shortly before she left. Her focus was somewhere else."

"Any possibilities?"

"No. Her senses have expanded to a degree I can't fathom. Could have been anywhere."

"Even in the Rhysu universe?"

"Anywhere."

Ruñal leaned back in his chair. "I'm not comfortable knowing she's a loose cannon—that she's beyond our understanding and out of our control."

"She's not a threat."

"Not yet."

"Excuse me?"

"I heard she denounced being your personal taxi. Rather combative, if you ask me."

"She can be stubborn, always has been. Very strong-willed. That's how she survived the mine. Once she understood what I meant, she relaxed. She does not hold grudges for minor misunderstandings."

"Not yet."

Arlud folded his arms and held his voice. He disliked where the commander was leading this conversation.

Ruñal leaned forward and whispered, as if to hide his thoughts from Bev: "She's more powerful than this ship. She destroyed all those Tuma attack ships in five minutes! If she rebels against our wishes, we won't be able to stop her!"

Arlud relaxed his posture and leaned forward to meet the commander's gaze. "I understand your concern, Commander. Bev was human once. She has affection for me and others who helped her. While she may no longer have a human body, she's still human at heart. She is not a threat. Reverting to tri-pole engines will demonstrate our interest in stopping the Rhysu's harmful fluctuations, but Bev is our mediator, and her contact with the Rhysu is the bridge we need to reach a compromise. She may be the only hope we have to deter the Rhysu and stop the Shoku from wanting to annihilate us."

SHANNA SY: TRAPPED

Shanna stood at the west window in her father's old library and watched the sky shift to orange above the domes and spires of the sprawling keep. The sunset's fiery glow was a beautiful sight—an attraction that lived in her memory and now was a reality once again.

I haven't seen the last of these sunsets.

How many Al-phaqi sunsets were in her future were uncertain, but she expected more than she cared to count, now that the Guild fleet was trapped here.

The flight from Alpha Cephei Four had been unhindered. Forty minutes after arriving at Al-phaq, the fleet's Compression Drive engines failed.

"The Rhysu must've repaired the emitter on Alpha Cephei four," Pardee had said.

The engineers had agreed, and Shanna fell into an instant depression, compounded by having to leave the investigation, and the troubling assertions made by Bev that Arlud had no interest in her.

She's just jealous, Shanna thought. *She's no longer human, so she hates the idea that I can form a physical bond with him. She wants me to doubt. She wants me to reject him.*

Shanna shrugged off her thoughts about Bev's motives and focused on the fact that separation from Arlud was a physical reality that may never be overcome. That was more infuriating than everything Bev had told her.

I'll probably die here!

She bowed her head and felt tears trickle from her closed eyes.

"Excuse me, lady."

Shanna turned away from Ross Cordova's voice to hide her tear-stained face. "What?"

"Pardee would like you to meet him in the debarkation center."

Shanna wiped her face and turned toward Cordova. "Are we leaving?"

"No," Cordova said, with a hint of regret. "He's in the briefing room with the senior captains, and he would like you to attend. I am to escort you."

Shanna stepped into the debarkation briefing room and assessed the mood.

Grim.

The nine senior captains had moved seats to the center of the room and were sitting in a circle. Pardee was the focus of attention as he droned on about ship supplies and shuttle readiness.

Shanna hovered in the doorway while Pardee spoke.

"Lady," Cordova whispered.

Shanna glanced behind her and saw Cordova's hand gesture to advance into the room. She took a few steps forward and grabbed the back of an empty chair.

The conversation stopped between Pardee and the senior captains. They stood and faced Shanna.

"Lady Sy," Pardee said. "Please take a seat."

As Shanna sat, Pardee followed, but the senior captains left the room, and she noticed Cordova now stood a step inside the doorway, his posture relaxed but ever ready. She faced Pardee. "What would you like to discuss, Captain?"

"We are stranded here," Pardee said. "My fellow captains and I just reviewed our status. We may be stuck here forever, but our future may be short-lived. I thought you should be aware."

"I understand the circumstances, Captain. I expect to die here. Why do you expect a premature demise?"

"The supplies we need to make this planet livable will not last forever, and we do not expect to reestablish trade routes."

"I was born here," Shanna said. "My parents lived here for 23 years. Can we not fare the same?"

"No."

"Please explain."

"Living here was a struggle. A struggle, not with the Alliance, with the planet. Why do you think the clans avoided this place? The Guild was founded here because it was remote, and a place no one wanted. The atmosphere and climate are deadly to us. That helped keep the clans from dropping an invading force to the surface, but it also demanded constant vigilance on our part to maintain the systems that keep us alive. Those systems break down over time because of the extreme cold. We can produce oxygen to breathe, the power generators will continue to supply heat, and maintenance will prolong the life of the mechanical systems, but food is limited. The farming stations froze after we left and getting them reactivated is proving more difficult than we expected—complex systems always fail when abandoned, especially when the environment has an average temperature of minus one-hundred degrees Celsius."

"How did the first settlers survive? There were no farm domes here when they arrived."

"We survived because we had constant access to off-planet supplies, like seeds and fertilizer. We don't stock seeds on our ships."

"So we will starve."

"Eventually. The combined stores from our ships can support us for a year if we ration. During that time, we may be able to resurrect some of the frozen plants, but that's being overly optimistic."

I was a fool, Shanna thought. *I have returned to my grave.*

"Unfortunately," Pardee added, "food is not our only problem." He flicked a switch on the console behind him and a holoscreen appeared above the circle of chairs.

Shanna examined the holo-image of a star field. "Where's that?"

"Above us," Pardee said. "That bright star near the center is Alpha Cephei. The view angle encompasses one hundred and twenty degrees, as seen from my ship."

Because the view centered on Alpha Cephei, it did not display the position of GSW-183, the only Alliance holding Shanna knew how to find while on Al-phaq. "Have we been able to contact someone off-planet?"

"No." Pardee said in a flat tone. "But we have detected this." He moved a slider on the holoscreen control panel that magnified the center of the starfield, and revealed three rippling distortions. One near the display's top left, one a few degrees right of Alpha Cephei, and a third near the bottom right edge.

Shanna gasped. "The Rhysu!"

"Yes, the Rhysu."

"How long have they been there?"

"We noticed them about an hour ago."

"How many?"

"Multiple at every direction we look. We are surrounded."

Shanna stood but kept her gaze on the holoscreen. "What do we do?"

Pardee leaned back in his chair. "We've powered down our ships in orbit and seventy-five percent of our crews have made planet-fall with about sixty percent of the cargo. We should have all the ships in hibernation mode within the hour and all crew and cargo on-planet."

Shanna lowered her head and dropped back into the chair. "Transmit Bev's brainwave patterns."

"Why would we do that?"

"It might prompt them to contact us. They need to know our intentions."

"They have stayed at a safe distance. Contacting them may change that."

"They don't need to move to communicate with us."

Pardee sat up straight. "Every time these things show up, people die. We need to avoid them, not attract them. Besides, they're probably looking for Bev and have no interest in us."

"You don't surround a planet if you have no interest," Shanna insisted, and she noticed Pardee's expression relax, his posture slump, and the focus of his eyes shifted to something distant. "Captain?"

The Rhysu vision hit Shanna as it had Pardee. She was overwhelmed by images of Bev—Bev as a human; Bev in an environment suit in the mine on Alpha Cephei Four; Bev in blue overalls on U'galem; Bev in the tactical environment suit of Clan Halva on the surface of Arrilen Po; Bev in the flight suit aboard the Erstallius cargo shuttle, and Bev as a ball of cyan colored plasma that rushed up to Shanna and dissolved, leaving only blackness around her. Then the visions of Bev repeated, again and again.

Shanna could hear a distant drone and sputters of electric discharge behind the images of Bev, but no voices. She tried to speak, but heard no sound, only her inner voice, full of a hesitant panic, confused and rimmed with fear, that shouted, "Stop it! We do not know where she went!"

The Rhysu visions persisted and overwhelmed Shanna's consciousness—a mental rape that left her exhausted when the Rhysu retreated.

Shanna's sight returned to her immediate surroundings, and she discovered she was on the floor, lying on her side. She pushed her torso up and turned to see Pardee still slumped in his chair. "Captain!"

Shanna watched Pardee stir from the Rhysu visions as footfalls approached from behind her and a hand touched her shoulder. She spun her head to see Cordova's concerned face. "I'm OK," she said, and she allowed the old soldier to help her to her feet.

Pardee stood and rested his hands on his hips. "Wow. That's what that's like. A lot different from Bev's mental conversation."

"Yes," Shanna said. "An intrusion more than a conversation." She looked at Cordova. "Did you —"

"Yes," Cordova said. "I saw Bev."

"They're searching," Pardee said. "They're angry. They would've attacked our ships if we weren't evacuating them."

"Yes," Cordova said. "They think we destroyed the emitter on Alpha Cephei Four."

"Bev did that," Shanna said.

"But we were there. We were the reason."

Shanna looked up at the holoscreen that still displayed the magnified view of the Rhysu distortions. "No more compression drive."

"We will never get off this planet," Pardee said. "They will confine all humans, wherever we are, or we will die."

BEV COLLI: RESCUE

Stars swirled, a spinning tunnel of streaking lights.

Bev sensed Rhysu ahead, and humans.

Clan Halva.

Detecting only a handful of human voices caused Bev to halt her advance toward Arrilen Po. She dropped out of the higher-dimensional pathway and scanned the charred Halva cruisers and the white prison encasing Arrilen Po.

She estimated PDN1527, Arrilen Po's dwarf yellow sun a few degrees to her left, was a few hundred million kilometers away based on its apparent size and brightness—but close enough to recharge her energy level, and obscure her presence from the Rhysu in its energetic solar wind. She projected her mind's vision and saw multiple energy spheres roaming along the limb of the white prison, bobbing in and out of the opaque cage which she estimated was more than twice the diameter of the planet it covered. The Rhysu voices were many—a jumble of emotive complaints aimed at the Shoku.

The Rhysu are restraining the Shoku.

She could still detect the mass of Arrilen Po and wondered: *Will it be taken like Simbic Ur?*

Then she heard the humans again. Faint murmurings—angry, full of sorrow and fear. None of the voices were familiar. She focused her mind's eye on the disabled cruisers. They had left Arrilen Po and their momentum had carried them toward the edge of the system, just inside the outer asteroid belt.

Satisfied the Rhysu had not detected her arrival, Bev moved toward the cruisers. Her focus on the human voices brought her alongside the charred hull plates of the vessel with the least amount of damage. The other ships had large breaches in their engine pods and central hulls—lifeless hulks devoid of energy.

Bev maneuvered herself to the port side to put the disabled cruiser between her and Arrilen Po, out of sight of the Rhysu. She let her mind enter the ship, pulled by the voices of survivors. In the mind of one of those still living, she saw a flicker of a memory of Cynth Halva. She used that memory as a homing beacon and rushed through the unlit corridors until she reached the cabin where the vision of Cynth originated. The cabin hatch was sealed, but she peered with her mind to see a woman floating in the narrow room, inside a hard-shelled, red environment suit, tethered to the utility wall's oxygen spigot via a thick gray hose that connected to the suit's coupling under the right arm.

Bev's hope to find Cynth inside the cabin faded as she realized this woman was someone she had never met.

Can you hear me?

The woman jerked as if woken by Bev's voice. "What? Who's there?"

I'm outside your ship. Do you know where Cynth Halva is located?

"Who are you?"

I'm a friend of Cynth's. I am here to help you.

Bev waited for the woman's response. She could sense her fear. *I am here to help you.*

"How am I hearing you? My comm hasn't been able to pick up transmissions since the attack. All I get is static."

Telepathy.

"What? Who—Are you the Rhysu!?"

I am Bev Colli. Do not be afraid.

"That's impossible!"

Why?

"Bev Colli is no longer human. She's in the Rhysu universe."

Yeah, my human body is gone, but I am outside your ship.

Bev dove into the woman's mind to collect the data she needed and ran into a scattered quagmire of thoughts and emotions. *Please calm down. I am here to help you.*

After a long silence, the woman asked: "How can you help me?"

What's your name?

"Tara Quin."

Well, Tara Quin, I intend to get you and the other survivors out of this wreck and take you home. But I can't do that without your help.

"Well, Bev Colli, I can't get out of this cabin without your help. The heat from the attack warped the door seals. It won't open."

Bev pulled her mind's vision back into the corridor and examined the hatch frame. She sighted along the row of hatches and saw the ripples in the bulkhead. *I see the problem,* she said. *I can't cut you out without doing more damage that might harm you. I'll find the others still alive, and they can use a torch to breach the seals. If not, I'll try to get you out, but you might get injured.*

"I understand," Quin said, her voice a distant whisper.

How long have you been stuck in there?

"Four days."

Wow. How much time do you have left?

"Enough water for seven days, longer if the main supply is still intact. Enough air for two more days from the cabin supply. My suit tanks are full—they last about eight hours."

And food?

"None. Haven't eaten since the attack. Which is probably best since my waste output has been less. I can't smell outside this suit, but it must really stink in the cabin—I emptied my suit's waste tanks, but the evac tube in the lavatory doesn't work."

You have air inside the cabin?

"Yes, according to the gauge on my suit. Not sure if it's breathable."

Where is Cynth Halva?

"We were in the forward lounge. She pushed me out when the Rhysu were coming. She told me to get into this suit."

That wasn't the Rhysu. Is Cynth still in the lounge?

"I don't know. What do you mean it wasn't the Rhysu?"

The Shoku attacked you, not the Rhysu.

"Who are the Shoku?"

The bad guys.

"Are you really Bev Colli?"

I am. I'm going now to find Cynth, but I'll be back.

The cruiser's forward lounge was above the rear bulkhead of the froward engine pod. That position was perfect for the one-hundred-and-eighty-degree panoramic window, but proved to be a disastrous engineering choice once the engine pod was decimated. The panoramic duraplex window, along with its protective duranide shielding, had collapsed into the space used for the lounge, creating a narrow rip in the hull.

Bev floated outside the cruiser's damaged bow. She dove into the constricted interior with her mind and found a charred body pinned beneath one of the ceiling support girders that had been warped inward and pushed into the deck plates. When she saw the crushed metal legs, she knew the blackened torso was Cynth. Shock pulled her mind back to the exterior of the cruiser. She last spoke to Cynth on this same cruiser while in orbit of Arrilen Po. Their separation had no impact on her then, because she had always expected to see the old matriarch again.

I was never able to thank her, she thought.

When they first met, Bev was nervous Cynth would dismiss her as an unwelcome sapi, but Cynth proved to be accommodating and willing to listen to Bev's unrefined rambling about aliens and her fear of Polinda retrievers. They connected in a way Bev had never thought possible. They related to each other where it mattered—via truth hidden in the past and revealed in dreams.

She cared about me, because I cared about what happened to her.

Bev returned her mind's vision to the crushed forward lounge, and after examining Cynth's blackened torso, she surmised Cynth had died when the air in her lungs was blown out into space after the hull was ripped open. That gave her some comfort, knowing Cynth did not suffer. Death would have been quick—a warm fall into unconsciousness before the searing heat burned her body.

Captain Pardee's words echoed in Bev's mind: "Every time these aliens show up, people die."

Anger flared inside Bev.

The Shoku killed Cynth, Bev reminded herself, forcing a separation in her mind between the Rhysu and the Shoku. *They're the same creatures, but with a murderous difference in their purpose regarding humans.* Up to this point, the battle between the Rhysu and the Shoku had been a distracting conflict that she sought to use to her advantage. She had always understood the danger to humans, but Cynth's death now made that conflict personal.

I can't allow this to happen again!

Bev subdued her anger, turned from Cynth's corpse, and focused on the survivors. There were seven. Three on the med-deck, three in the main engineering core, and Tara Quin in her cabin. She pulled her mind's eye from the forward lounge and headed along the outer hull toward the closed shuttle bay doors.

The crew had been briefed—they came to Arrilen Po knowing who Bev was and what had happened to her. When her voice sounded in their heads, they were surprised but not overwhelmed.

Do you all have access to environment suits?

The senior engineer responded: "Yes, that's not a problem. Freeing Tara Quin will take time, but it's doable, as long as we have access to her cabin."

I'll guide you there, Bev said. *I suggest only those necessary to free her go to her cabin.*

"Agreed," the senior engineer said. "We can meet-up with everyone else outside the shuttle bay. Is access to the bay clear?"

Yes, an intact route to the bay from both the med-deck and the engineering core.

Bev found an open path to Quin's cabin through the crippled ship, and forty-five minutes later, the stuck hatch was open. With the GPGs not working, the passage to the shuttle bay was a micro gravity swim through dark corridors. Bev guided them through the difficult areas where the corridors had been warped and the bulkhead collapsed inward. The two engineers arrived with Quin at the entrance to the shuttle bay to find the other four survivors huddled in front of the closed doorway.

This next part is important, Bev said. *You all need to do as I say, or you could die.*

Bev waited for a reaction, but no one flinched.

Good, Bev said. *Once this hatch is open, I'll need you to attach an energy node on the exterior of the largest shuttle, with a direct connection to the main power source. It will need to be as close as possible to the generator to help shield it from the crew cabin.*

"Why?" the senior engineer asked.

I'll need power to make this rescue happen. That node will allow me to feed off your generator.

"We can do that," the senior engineer said, "but that'll take time."

How long?

"About an hour."

Good. Until that's done, everyone else not needed for that work must enter the shuttle, strap in, stay quiet, and no unnecessary fiddling with equipment.

"Why?" Quinn asked.

Bev focused on each survivor one by one and planted a vision of the white prison around Arrilen Po and the Rhysu roaming around the limb. *If they detect us, they will come quick. You do not want that to happen.*

Bev sensed a rise in anxiety among the survivors.

Once the node is in place, I will cut through the hull and release the outer hatch—it's warped and will not open on its own. Once that's done, you will activate the shuttle systems and use the docking release to push you out of the bay. I will catch you and take you to safety. Do not engage the main engines.

The senior engineer was confused by Bev's intent. "You'll catch us?"

Yes. I've done this before. You must stay away from the hull, and you'll need to withstand a fair amount of heat for a while. Once we are out of this system and away from the Rhysu, we can make adjustments that may make you more comfortable, but I will still need to envelop the shuttle.

"How much heat?"

Bev focused on Quin. *Enough to be uncomfortable, but survivable.* My trip here took four days. The trip to your home will take a similar amount of time.

Quin frowned. "Will we need to stay in these suits?"

Yes. For your safety.

The senior engineer flicked a glance at each of his comrades. "If that's what it takes, that's what it takes."

"We're ready," the senior engineer said.

Bev saw in her mind all the survivors seated in the shuttle. They attached the energy node atop the fuselage, above the generator compartment, a meter aft of the crew cabin. *That should be far enough,* she thought. She positioned herself alongside the jammed bay doors and focused on the charred hull plates surrounding the entry. Her first analysis told her to focus a continuous plasma burst like a cutting torch, but she realized that would take too long, attract too much attention, and most likely deplete her energy reserves before she made contact with the shuttle's energy node. This situation demanded a novel approach. *It will test me to my limit,* she thought, *but has less chance of damaging the shuttle and killing the survivors.* She knew it might slow her reaction time if the Rhysu came to investigate, but that was a risk she had to take.

She unfolded and inflated her energy sphere to equal the size of the bay doors. She was still hidden from the Rhysu by the cruiser, so did not hesitate. Six energy tendrils grew from her center, rippling strands of plasma she punched into the charred bay doors. Once locked on, she expanded the tendrils and twisted the streams to bore deeper through the duranide. Six more tendrils grew out of her energy sphere and punched into the blackened hull around the edge of the entry threshold. She pivoted the tendrils attached to the doors and yanked. The doors ripped free from their damaged sockets. She tossed the doors aside and watch them tumble away from the cruiser.

Bev's expenditure of energy caught the attention of the Rhysu. She sensed them coming. She heard their voices. She focused on the survivors in the shuttle.

Power up. Let's go!

The docking clamp moved the shuttle toward the exit and released.

The shuttle's momentum carried it toward Bev in the micro-gravity. Once the vessel emerged from the cruiser, Bev enveloped it and pressed against the energy node. Her tendrils increased in size and her energy sphere grew thicker and more brilliant.

The Rhysu reached the stern of the cruiser and attempted to flank Bev from four different angles.

Bev enfolded as the Rhysu advanced and their energy spheres bumped against her hyper-dimensional form, but she escaped the tendrils that tried to grab her, and her jump propelled her and the shuttle beyond the system's heliosphere.

Bev held an advantage over the Rhysu—she was familiar with Alliance holdings. She knew holding locations within a small margin of error and had human connections she could use as real-time navigation points, and memories of landscape, cities, atmospheres, and population distributions at each location that would act as their own beacons. This made evading pursuit easier, along hyper-dimensional pathways the Rhysu could not anticipate. This ability also enabled her to recognize areas to avoid when she detected Rhysu incursions that blocked her path.

We cannot continue to Cestratha.

Quin was roused from a light sleep by Bev's voice. She opened her eyes to the darkened crew cabin and adjusted her reclined couch to its upright position. Her environment suit was cumbersome but necessary—the cabin had not been pressurized to reduce convective heat transfer from the hull. "What did you say?"

I need to change course. We cannot continue to Cestratha.

"Why?"

The Rhysu are there.

"Oh. Have they attacked?"

I can't sense that. But they are in our way. We'll plow into them if we stay on this course.

Quin glanced at the other survivors. They were asleep. "Should I wake them?"

No need for that. Let them sleep.

"Why would the Rhysu go to Cestratha?"

They know Clan Halva sent your team to Arrilen Po, Bev explained in a harsh tone, revealing her frustration. *They know Clan Halva is from Cestratha. They expect you to return there.*

"How do they know that?"

Because I was on Cestratha, and they were linked to me. I was human then. They used me to understand humans. They used me to help capture the Shoku. And I knew Cynth. I went to Arrilen Po with her. They know you will return to Cestratha.

"Why do they care where we go?"

They want to capture me.

"Oh."

Bev analyzed her energy level and shifted her focus to a new destination. The change in course would add another day to the journey, but they would survive the inconvenience. The hull of the shuttle was holding up against the constant pounding from Bev's radiated energy and the dimensional warping of space around it. The power streaming into her from the shuttle's generator was steady and could last for weeks. *We'll make it,* she thought. *Another day won't matter.*

"Where are we going?"

Ni'apinu.

"Where's that?"

GSW-183, the Aku homeworld. Clan Erstallius has an outpost there.

Bev's ball of cyan-colored plasma punched through the clouds above the surface of Ni'apinu as it descended toward the Mânu at Dol'anar. Aku Transports stood under repair scaffolding on pads One and Three, so Bev guided her descent to pad Two.

Extend your landing pads, Bev said.

The senior engineer, now the shuttle pilot, reached down and pulled the landing pad lever. "Got it."

Bev held the shuttle within her energy sphere, then pulled away as the landing pads touched the tarmac.

Nice landing.

The senior engineer killed the power flow to the descent thrusters, which were not used, and opened the valves to pressurize the cabin equal to the local atmosphere. "Thank you, Bev."

You're welcome!

"Yes," Tara Quin said. "Thank you, Bev!"

Bev ignored the gratitude from the other survivors and rose through the clouds, continued her ascent out of the atmosphere, and settled into an orbit beyond Ni'apinu's magnetosphere to bathe in the full impact of PDN160's solar wind. The Aku defense force had recognized her as she approached the planet and gave her a wide berth to land and exit. She could sense they were apprehensive about her presence, even though she had proven she was not a threat. News had spread fast about her actions against the Tuma raiders. *They fear me,* she thought, *as do the Erstallius clanmen.* She relaxed and let her energy sphere expand into the streams of charged particles. If she was still human, she would have closed her eyes to focus on her internal feelings, but being alien, she had to force her focus inward and allow the material space around her to dim and fade.

The trip from Arrilen Po had taken five days. The power node had kept her energized enough the journey had not fatigued her. Sleep was foreign to Rhysu, but relaxation was a welcome condition, because it gave her time to focus on what she had discovered and mourn those who had died.

Rest in peace, Cynth. I will miss you.

Memories of Cynth flowed into memories of Arlud, and Bev called to him.

Can you hear me?

She heightened her awareness and focused on Ni'apinu.

Where are you?

She had been gone only nine days. She expected Arlud to still be on-planet. With no response from him, she searched the minds of the Erstallius clanmen at Dol'anar and Kuliq'Quad.

He left!

Bev detected the anti-compression wave everywhere she looked.

Al-phaq is caged. Roth-513 is caged. Jai'raan is caged. Wan'tei is caged. Every holding is isolated!

And then she saw him.

U'galem! He's on U'galem!

U'galem was also caged.

Bev pulled her sphere inward to compress her body, then enfolded and jumped toward U'galem.

CLAN DEJORIA: ENGINES

Clan Dejoria's shipyards were in the high desert, five-hundred kilometers from the coastal city, Kythria, where the High-Regent, Jhared Dejoria, stayed while on U'galem. Today the High-Regent approached his shipyards aboard a Zephyr-class shuttle at the request of Arlud Erstallius, who had arrived in orbit a few hours ago, claiming his clan had the solution to the anti-compression wave that stymied travel off-planet. Arlud's best proof of a solution was the fact he had arrived from GSW-183 after twelve standard days, despite the Rhysu emissions.

Jhared sat in his plush passenger couch as the shuttle sped through the stratosphere. He reviewed data displayed on a holoscreen floating above his lap. The ships in the Dejoria Security Fleet were being reassigned to orbits closer to stations that could help sustain their crews for longer periods. The data indicated the outer-most deployments would take four years to return to U'galem without compression drive. Those ships would divert to one of five support hubs placed between the orbits of the two outer-most planets, with a maximum rendezvous time of three months. The ships closer to the orbit of U'galem had more stations to support them, so their hubs were on average less than two months away from their current locations.

This will work, Jhared thought. The safety of his clanmen was his priority. *Even if Arlud has a solution, we can't rely on things that only exist elsewhere.*

He rubbed his hairless head and leaned back in his couch.

"Regent?"

Jhared glanced up at his pilot. "Yes?"

"Arlud Erstallius is on-planet and waiting at the shipyard landing field."

"Good."

Heat waves rose off the tarmac in the mid-day sun and shimmered off the black hull plates of the spherical Aku transport that had landed in parking circle Nine, thirty meters from the nearest hanger. Ground crews had rolled two cranes next to the Aku ship to drape white tarps over it to reflect the sunlight and help cool the hull.

Jhared noticed the cranes and tarps at the Aku transport from inside his private hangar as he bounded down the steps of his shuttle's boarding ramp. He wore his typical ankle-length tunic over his plump frame, and open-toed sandals covered his bare feet, which was unusual as he preferred no shoes. He noticed Arlud as he took his last step off the ramp. "Black hull plates?"

Arlud flicked a glance at the Aku transport. "Yes. Stealth plating. We are at war. Clan Tuma invaded our system. Their remnants are still there."

Jhared stopped a few steps from Arlud and surveyed the young regent's two-man entourage. "Where's Salus?"

"He did not join us on this trip."

"Oh. I liked him. And of course, Bev is not here. She was a beautiful girl. Perhaps she should have stayed here."

"Perhaps," Arlud agreed. "She is now something very different."

Jhared noticed the sadness in Arlud's response. "But she is still Bev. She always will be. A wonderful girl."

Arlud nodded to that kindness and introduced Jhared to Bittle and Sands.

Three hours later, the proposed engineering changes and the proof-of-concept had been reviewed in a nearby conference room. Most of the objections from Jhared had been resolved by Bittle and Sands, but he was stuck on the timeline to a workable tooling change for tri-pole engine production and installation.

"Realistically," Jhared said, sitting at the conference table next to his Director of Assembly, "eighteen months before we are at full capacity with these changes."

"We've got to do better than that," Arlud replied from across the table. "Eighteen months is beyond the tipping point when people stranded in space and on hostile holdings start dying by the thousands."

"Hundreds may die long before that," Bittle said.

Jhared pushed away from the table but remained seated. "I will not accept the blame for that. Do you want these modifications or not?"

Arlud leaned back. "We're not blaming you. We need to consider the ramifications of a lengthy delay. There must be a solution to speed-up the process. Comm-drone communication has stopped. As we speak, every holding is isolated. Every ship stuck in deep space has begun to die."

Chief Sands stood. "We've been focused on altering production to customize current assembly-line models with tri-pole engines. Those designs were built around modern compression drive engines. The two drive systems are not compatible, so don't change them. Build smaller ships with a known, proven design. Like the Mayfair-Courkos Transport. Like the one standing on your tarmac."

Arlud and his engineers focused on Jhared and waited for his answer.

Jhared looked at his Director of Assembly. "How long?"

The old man shrugged. "Based on that old design, three months, maybe six if we hit any problems. That design is relatively simple compared with modern designs. But it's small with limited storage, so not sure how effective it will be."

Bittle cleared his throat. "It'll get off-planet and bypass those damn Rhysu waves. That's all we need."

"Three to six months is acceptable to me," Arlud said.

Jhared faced his director with a stern look. "Do the estimates, set a definite date for the first completed ship, and get the data to me by tomorrow morning."

The next morning, Arlud, Bittle, and Sands entered Assembly Building Two, to see the construction process in person. Assembly Building Two was one of ten massive structures, each 100 meters wide, 400 meters long, and 50 meters high, that housed assembly lines dedicated to different parts of spacecraft construction. The workers in building Two focused on conduit installation inside the skeletal air-frames for energy transfer and life support systems. Once completed, each air-frame would go to the next line for interior bulkhead finishing.

They passed the first assembly area, which housed three cargo shuttle air-frames. The second area held two medium-sized frigate air-frames. The last area supported midsections for two light cruisers and another cruiser midsection was being prepped for placement into the last air-frame cradle.

Arlud asked: "What's the average build time for these?"

Bittle shrugged.

"Their efficiencies are very high," Sands said. "I asked the Assembly Director, and he showed me stats. They vary from model to model and were faster than I expected. One month average for shuttle assembly. Two for the frigates. Three for the cruisers. The tooling is already in place and the parts are always available. That helps keep things moving, especially when assembly is nonstop with four work shifts."

"That's encouraging," Arlud said. "Twenty-six hundred hours to assemble a light cruiser! Amazing."

"That's only the construction phase," Sands explained. "Another four months for systems testing and adjustments."

"Still, very impressive," Arlud said.

"Mister Erstallius!"

Arlud turned to see Jhared's assistant standing in the aisle between the workstations about ten meters away—the small, red-haired woman he had met during his last visit.

"The High-Regent is ready for you," the woman called. She gestured for Arlud and his engineers to follow her toward the front of the building.

Once they were seated back in the conference room, Jhared prompted his Director of Assembly to report his recommendations.

"We understand the urgency of this project," the director said, "so I have laid out two paths for us. Path One will continue the original plan to modify our existing ships. This is necessary for the long-term victory against the Rhysu wave. Path Two will be our immediate focus—to build smaller vessels based on the old Mayfair-Courkos design. Path Two will get us off-planet faster—because of the simpler design, we can build them faster. I estimate fifty transports completed in two years, with a two-month start-up time for assembly-line refits and tooling."

The director activated a holoscreen that floated above the table. The two assembly paths were displayed from the beginning to the end, with animated graphics that highlighted every dated goal.

"Well done, Director," Arlud said. "When do you start?"

"Path Two was set in motion before dawn," Jhared said. "We have already begun to retool the line in Building One. We need your input about the internal engineering changes you mentioned. We have access to the original Mayfair-Courkos designs, but I understand the Aku made modifications you'd like to keep."

"Yes, we would," Bittle said. "I can download the changes to your design team from the ship. And they may benefit by coming aboard to see the changes for themselves."

"They may see something," Sands added, "that can do what the Aku intended, but in a better way. There have been inconsistencies with the Aku modifications."

The director stood. "Then let's get to it," he said, and gestured for the Erstallius engineers to follow him out of the room.

Arlud stayed behind with Jhared. "Thank you, Jhared."

Jhared pushed away from the table and stood. "No, thank you, dear friend. Without your insight, we'd be stuck on this rock for much longer. Come, I'll treat you to a wonderful U'galem brunch." He gestured for Arlud to join him. "We can discuss the construction details later."

PETRA SITLYN: WARRIOR

Petra stood at a work counter in the food pantry next to the entry to the sipá boarding stalls. She stuffed into a basket two clumps of pristal berries, a small bundle of large tègo roots, four apples, three grapefruits, and two hand-sized sweet melons.

"You're here early," a male voice said.

Petra turned to see Tryol standing in the doorway. "Yes," she replied. "I want to get this basket to Aluk before I begin my session with Serra. Is Aluk outside the gate yet?"

"I didn't see him. He's usually there not too long after sunrise. Give him another thirty minutes. If he's not there when you get there, once he gets your scent, he'll come running."

Petra nodded to that truth. The old sipá still had his keen sense of smell and would detect her from kilometers away, if the wind was right.

Tryol smiled and stepped away from the doorway as more trainers began entering the pantry.

Ten minutes later, Petra was at the main gate. Aluk was nowhere to be seen. She opened the gate and headed for the chest-high grass in the field south of the farm that sloped down to the river. A light wind blew toward the tree line about two-hundred and fifty meters distant.

If Aluk is there, he'll smell me.

She stopped amid the chest-high green grass, leaned down to set the basket on the ground, and froze. Less than a meter away she saw half-hidden by the grass a clanman squatting low, wearing a helmet, goggles, and mouth filter, holding a short barrel magar rifle pointed at her head.

"Get down," the clanman said in Englo'ni.

Petra knelt in the grass and noticed a Clan Tuma patch on the clanman's green uniform. *He didn't kill me,* she thought. *That means he's either hesitant about harming a woman, or he doesn't want to reveal his location by shooting me. If he's alone, that'll make this easier. If he's with others, there is trouble ahead.*

The clanman duck-walked through the grass toward Petra and gestured for her to lie on the ground.

Petra dropped to her hands and knees, but kept her eyes focused on the clanman.

A swish of movement sounded in the grass behind the clanman and ended with a heavy thud.

The clanman glanced behind him.

The crack of a magar rifle discharge caused Petra to flinch.

Another swish and thud.

The clanman pivoted and aimed his rifle toward the commotion behind him.

Petra lunged. She placed a rear choke hold on the warrior and squeezed the sides of his neck to restrict blood flow to his brain, and he flopped unconscious. She disarmed the clanman, and with the long cord he had stuffed into a utility pocket, she bound his wrists behind his back, then tied the remaining length of cord around his ankles. She hefted the magar rifle and stood to see Aluk nearby, swatting at something in the tall grass. Blood stained the grey fur on the old sipá's shoulder but didn't restrict his swiping motion.

Two dead Tuma clanmen were stripped of weapons and clothing and left in the grass.

"Whatever the carrion birds and insects leave during the day," Tryol said, "the klâwpa will finish during the night."

The surviving clanman was carted to a sipá stall and left there as Petra had bound him, under the watchful eyes of two armed men ordered to guard him.

Petra waited inside the medical facility as Aluk's wound was being repaired by the vet. She faced Tryol, who stood next to her. "There may be more Tuma out there."

"We understand that," Tryol said. He turned from Petra and peered through the doorway into the operating room. Aluk was on a padded pallet that had been wheeled into the room. He was unconscious as the vet worked on his shoulder injury.

"We've notified the authorities," Tryol said, still focused on Aluk. "The Erstallius are sending ground troops and attack shuttles. The orbital surveys have been increased. If more Tuma are on-planet we'll find them."

Petra hugged herself. "Will Aluk be OK?"

"The projectile grazed him," Tryol said. "He'll be sore for a few days." He faced Petra. "I'd like you to interrogate our prisoner."

"Me? Why?"

"You know about off-world things. That man is an off-world warrior. You were an off-world warrior. You have a similar background."

"Yeah, but Erstallius Security should—"

"No," Tryol insisted. "We will handle this ourselves."

Petra paused a moment to consider Tryol's reasoning. *This is vendetta,* she thought. *This is Tryol's way of allowing me to settle my dispute with the man who threatened me.* "OK," she said, "but I wasn't trained as an interrogator."

"That doesn't matter."

Petra squatted next to the bound Tuma clanman. He was young, with brown eyes and a shaved head. His complexion was light olive-tan and his eyelids had a slight epicanthic fold—typical of the Priam people from Keikos-40, a Tuma holding.

"You're new to this uniform," Petra said. "I can tell from the way you reacted in the grass."

The clanman ignored Petra's words.

"I could have killed you today instead of restraining you. You really need more training."

The clanman was silent.

"I know you won't tell me where the rest of your troops are to be found. It's obvious you don't know. You and your comrades were separated during one of the earlier battles and found your way to our farm, thinking it was a good target to hit—a way to gain success from an obvious failure."

The clanman closed his eyes.

"Do you know the history between Clan Tuma and the Aku people?"

Petra waited longer for a response, and when there was none she added: "I don't mean the propaganda used to indoctrinate you. I mean the real history. The history of abuse. The history of neglect. The history of slavery and genocide against the Aku people on Kainogae that led to their rebellion and eventual escape. Do you know about that history?"

Still no response.

"Well," Petra said, "that history was real. I know you had nothing to do with that. You're too young to have been part of it. But here you are, a warrior for the Aku's historic enemy. What do you think that means for you?"

"Death," the clanman said.

Petra nodded. "But not if you help us. You are a pawn in a game that is hundreds of years old. What benefit is in it for you?"

"The honor of serving my clan."

"Honor is worth nothing when you're dead."

"My honor brings worth to those who come after me. To my family, to my descendants, to my clan."

"Honor is a mental outlook, a point of view based on our myth-making imagination. It's not tangible. It's of no material value."

"Honor is a value we hold in our minds, and our values unite the clan."

"Values also destroy, like the way Clan Tuma seeks to destroy the Aku. Is that honorable?"

"Honorable for all who serve Clan Tuma."

Petra stood. She sympathized with this young war fighter—the Aku had killed many of his ancestors and annihilated every Tuma fleet that pursued them to Ni'apinu. *Inherited hatred is a persistent evil for both sides,* she thought. *And because of that, this young man will die today.* She turned and exited the stall. On her way out of the stall-way, she approached Tryol. "Waste of time," she whispered as she strode past the old overseer. She stepped into sunlight and heard the crack of a magar rifle echo inside the building.

Three hours after his shoulder repair, Aluk woke in one of the outdoor recovery pens next to the medical building.

Petra stood outside the pen with a med-tech, waiting for the old sipá to regain consciousness. "He's awake."

The med-tech entered the pen and knelt a few paces away from the groggy old sipá. "L'dyém, Aluk," he said.

Petra stepped into the pen and stood behind the med-tech.

Aluk huffed and pushed up to a sitting position.

"Ahákiah si'ou, Aluk," the tech said. He stood and gestured for Petra to exit the pen with him. "Give him some space."

A few minutes later, Aluk was up on his feet. His injured shoulder was shaved of fur around the wound site—a rectangular patch of bare skin covered with a thick bandage. He did not hesitate to leave the pen. He trudged forward, stopped next to Petra, sat on his haunches, and dropped his head to sniff her face.

Petra reached up and rubbed Aluk's chin. "U'aliou, yáhir guáfi," she said and led Aluk to the main gate, stopping once at a water trough, and then again to give him a clump of pristal berries.

The med-tech followed to make sure Aluk was fully recovered before setting him free.

Upon reaching the main gate, Aluk stood on his hind legs, sniffed the air and roared.

"He must smell the dead," the med-tech said.

"I'll try to steer him away from that place," Petra said. "I'll head down the main road until we've passed that area."

Aluk roared again.

Sipá in the paddocks roared.

Petra looked over at the training paddocks and noticed four sipá standing on their hind legs like Aluk. Their roars continued, like some strange sipá song only they understood.

Petra looked at the med-tech. "What's happening?"

"I don't know."

The sipá in the boarding stalls roared.

Aluk dropped from his hind-leg stance but continued to roar.

Petra scanned the farm. More trainers were now outside and looked as dumbfounded as the med-tech. "What's happening?" She shifted her gaze from the farm to the surrounding terrain, and then to the sky.

The distortion was difficult to see at first, then a spectral shift happened that caused the clouds in the southwest to shimmer with subtle, rainbow-like halos.

"Up there," Petra said.

The med-tech focused where Petra pointed. The spectral colors twirled and spun the clouds into different shapes and ripped them apart. "What is that?"

The colorful distortions moved out of the southwest, across the horizon, eastward toward the Dekeg Mountains, creating more turbulence that punched holes in the cloud layer.

"The Rhysu," Petra said. "That has to be the Rhysu.

Multiple energy spheres plunged into the upper atmosphere above the farm—their shimmering, multi-colored halos filtered the sunlight.

Petra examined the sky. "They're everywhere."

From horizon to horizon, Rhysu filled the sky above and below the clouds. Pressure waves traveled through the atmosphere and hit the terrain hard, causing trees to sway. The people and animals at the farm cowered from the hot wind.

Petra saw Bev Colli in her mind. The sudden rush of visions and the influx of Rhysu emotion blocked her surroundings from her senses. She was pulled into a kaleidoscopic review of Bev's last days as a human, and her current life as something different.

And then the visions stopped.

The hot wind receded.

Petra regained her composure and looked at the sky.

The Rhysu were gone.

The trainers and other farm workers gathered outside the main office to discuss what had happened.

Tryol pushed through the perplexed crowd and clapped his hands above his head to hush everyone. Once the conversation stopped, he said: "The sipá are quiet and there has been no damage. We know the Rhysu are looking for Bev Colli. Their visions made that clear. She is not here, so they left. I know it was a shocking experience, but now we must return to our duties. Our lives continue. Our purpose has not changed. Get back to work."

The stunned workers dispersed, but Petra stayed to speak to Tryol. "You know the Rhysu are a threat. Didn't you sense their anger?"

"Yes, I know, and I did."

"They've stranded everyone on-planet. They intend to keep us caged."

"They are angry at Bev Colli, but they care nothing for us. They only wish to end human space travel. The Aku have been on Ni'apinu a long time, and we'll continue to be far into the future. Our lives changed more because your people came here than because of what the Rhysu have done."

"You resent Clan Erstallius?"

"No. I resent Clan Tuma for forcing us to come here, but that turned into a blessing. Our isolation allowed us to prosper without the negative influence of your Alliance. Based on what I've learned, the clans cause much of the violence among off-worlders."

"Yes," Petra admitted. "The Rhysu are still a threat."

"Those with great power are always a threat to the weak. We accepted the Erstallius presence because we recognized our weakness. Your presence here attracted your enemies, but that was the price we paid to survive. We had to partner with your clan to protect Ni'apinu. If you had not been here, the Tuma invaders would have destroyed us all. If your reports are true, the Rhysu are everywhere. We would have met them eventually, even without you being here. Because you are here, we understand the Rhysu's motives, and our lives will continue as always. You may come to appreciate isolation can be a good thing, as we have learned."

"I chose to stay on Ni'apinu. I chose a planet-bound life. But I still worry for those off-planet. The Rhysu threat is very real."

"There are always threats," Tryol said. "Sipá can be a threat, as the Tuma war fighters discovered. How we manage our threats determines our future. The Rhysu threat is not on-planet. It could have been, but they left."

Petra considered Tryol's pragmatic outlook and wondered if the Aku mindset had developed from their years of slavery, or if isolation here on Ni'apinu was the reason for their lack of concern for threats to humanity off-planet. "If the future of humanity is fractured into isolated holdings, our civilization will dwindle and fade away. We must be united with access to all holdings if we hope to build a future in this galaxy that will persist and thrive for everyone."

"Change can be good. Your Alliance needs change. It hasn't created a peaceful civilization for everyone. If it had, we would not have had to flee Clan Tuma."

Petra could not disagree.

"Our future is on Ni'apinu," Tryol insisted. "What happens elsewhere in the galaxy is not our concern."

CLAN ERSTALLIUS: TRANSPORT

Arlud watched the glow of sunlight rise above the jagged peaks along the horizon—white rays that diminished the orange and red bands of color in the cloudless sky above the tarmac at the Dejoria shipyards. PDN163 was a main sequence star with an average surface temperature of 5837°K, cooler than PDN160, Ni'apinu's primary sun, but produced more heat on U'galem because of the planet's orbital parameters.

Today will be a hot one.

Behind Arlud, the doors to Building One were open half-way, and he could hear the rattles and bangs from the tooling changes underway inside the building. He spent the night at the shipyard as a courtesy to Jhared, but would leave with him for Kythria after breakfast. "We should head over to the cafeteria."

"Right, lad," Eahuda said. He stood behind Arlud, more interested in the cargo shuttles on the adjacent field that were delivering supplies for the tooling changes. The bulky aircraft were planet-bound transports not designed to leave the atmosphere.

"Let's go," Arlud said.

Eahuda focused on Arlud's back and followed him as they walked toward the cafeteria south of Building One.

Can you hear me?

Bev's desperate voice bellowed in Arlud's mind. He stopped walking. "Yes!"

"I can hear her too, lad."

Arlud spun to face Eahuda, but focused on Bev's voice.

I found you, Bev said.

"Where are you?"

I'm above you, in orbit of U'galem.

"Where did you go?"

Bev narrowed her focus to Arlud and dumped her experiences since leaving Ni'apinu into his mind.

Arlud dropped to his knees and lowered his head under the mental weight of Bev's memories.

Eahuda stooped and placed a hand on Arlud's shoulder. "You OK?"

"I hate when she does that."

Nothing faster than a mental dump, Bev said. *Sorry if it makes you uncomfortable, but we don't have time for casual conversation!*

"I know," Arlud said. He stood with Eahuda's help. After a moment to realign his thinking, he straightened his posture and looked into Eahuda's eyes. "Where's Jhared?"

"Probably waiting in the cafeteria."

"Get to the transport and tell Ruñal we're leaving after we make adjustments to his ship."

"Why?"

"I'll fill you in once I get there."

"Where are you going?"

"To tell Jhared."

I'll tell him, Bev said. *That'll save time. You go with Gus!*

Jhared Dejoria stood at the open entry to his private hangar, just inside the shaded interior to keep the scorching sun off his tender feet. He watched a maintenance crew working on the outside of the Aku transport, at one of the magar-cannon installations along the equatorial weapons ring. "What are they doing?"

"Removing the cannon," Arlud said.

Jhared turned to face the young Erstallius. "Why?"

"Bev didn't tell you?"

"I must have missed that. She told me so much."

"They're installing an energy node, so she can feed off the power supply."

"Feed?"

"She'll need the energy. Normal trip time from here to Arrilen Po with this transport would be twenty-two standard days. With the adjustments to reduce our impact in hyper-space, the time increases to one-hundred and seventy-four standard days. We don't have that much time. Even twenty-two days is too long. Bev can get us there in five days."

"Oh. How does she do that?"

"She wraps herself around the ship and holds it."

"She wraps around it?"

"Yes. After that crew installs the energy node, they'll attach U-shaped hand-holds to the hull so Bev can grab them. When she rescued us in the Aku transports, she had to pierce the hull to hold on."

"How does she do that?"

"She has a Rhysu body with multiple limbs."

"Like tentacles?"

"No. Limbs of energy. Think strands of plasma lined with lightning bolts."

"Oh. How does she propel the ship through space?"

"A dimensional jump."

"Dimensional? How does she do that?"

Arlud shrugged. "We're investigating, but we may never know for sure."

"I would like to discover that."

"I'm sure you would. If we uncover how she does it, I'll let you know."

"Why is time so precious? Isn't everyone there dead?"

"The sooner we can dialog with the Rhysu, and prove to them our sincerity about reducing our impact in hyperspace, the sooner people will stop dying."

Jhared pursed his lips. "I've met no one from Clan Halva. They were ostracized by the General Assembly, so were recluse on Cestratha. I understand Gustus came to the annual meetings, but I was never introduced. So sad about what happened to Cynth."

"When she met Bev, her outlook changed," Arlud said. "I think she found solace knowing someone else had experience with the Rhysu. Bev proved she wasn't to blame for Ludi Prell's death. She needed that validation. She helped Bev deal with the Rhysu intrusion and other things. They cared for each other. She'll be missed."

"Can't ask for anything more than that," Jhared said. "How do you rate your success at Arrilen Po?"

"A larger ship might be more convincing, but we'll use what we have. The result will depend on the Rhysu."

BEV COLLI: REVELATION

The hull resonated with a rattling noise from the interaction with Bev's energy sphere. The noise had become an irritant to Arlud. This was the second day on the journey to Arrilen Po. This was the second day his sleep cycle was disrupted.

You worry too much, Bev said. *I can feel it. You'll never sleep if you don't let it go.*

"Some things are tough to ignore," Arlud whispered. He turned on his side. His bunk was a narrow pallet inside one of the bottom-level alcoves in crew sleeping bay Two, and comfortable enough for a refreshing sleep. His only real distraction was his concern about the future, and his insomnia was the byproduct.

Stop worrying. Whatever happens, you'll be glad we tried.

"The odds are not good," Arlud muttered. "You have your own doubts."

Yes, I do, Bev admitted. *Doubts are good, they keep us on our toes.*

"You don't have toes."

You know what I mean!

Bev's doubts concerned the white prison, and that bothered Arlud more than anything else. If the prison was still there, then the Shoku were still there. A peaceful encounter might not be possible under those circumstances.

The Rhysu will accept the proof of what they observe, Bev said. *The Shoku will see the same results. That should cause them to stop their effort to eliminate all humans.*

"It should," Arlud agreed. "It's the other possibilities that bother me. There is no time for compromise when you are trying to survive."

The Rhysu will restrain the Shoku, and we will adapt to what we find. Quit worrying! Go to sleep!

Three standard-days later, Bev ended the journey to Arrilen Po six million kilometers from the planet. She sensed the white prison was still active, so released the Aku Transport far enough away to reduce detection.

Hold this position, Bev told Ruñal. *I'll see what's happening.*

Bev heard Rhysu voices, but they were less vocal than she remembered. She projected her mind's eye and saw the white prison was smaller—half the diameter of its original size, but still large enough to encase the planet.

There is movement through the rift.

Surprised the prison had lasted this long, but confident the situation was stable, Bev moved inside the orbit of the second moon and announced her presence to the Rhysu.

The lack of response surprised her, so she transmitted graphic images of the human plan to replace Compression Drive engines with tri-pole engines. "You will see a demonstration," she said, and projected her mind back to Ruñal. *You can begin, Commander.*

A dozen energy spheres unfolded around Bev.

Bev broke her link with Ruñal and focused on the energy spheres pressing toward her. "Stay back!"

The Aku transport's tri-pole engine activated and pulled the ship on a course at sub-light speed that would orbit Arrilen Po and her moons. Faster speeds were planned along the route so the Rhysu could witness the reduced impact in their universe no matter the power level.

The energy spheres were distracted by the transport and stopped advancing toward Bev.

"Notice the lack of harmful fluctuations," Bev said. "This solution will work. Witness how little an impact this new design has on the energy sea."

A dozen more energy spheres unfolded near Bev and formed a wall between her and the transport. "We are here for you."

Bev scanned the new arrivals and realized they were the ones who had been searching for her since she destroyed the emitter on Alpha Cephei Four.

The twenty-four energy spheres joined their energy tendrils and rushed toward Bev.

More energy spheres emerged from the white prison and swarmed around the Aku transport.

Ruñal, seeing no way to break through the tightening cluster of energy spheres, powered off the tri-pole engine to avoid a collision. As soon as the hyper-bubble around the ship vanished, the crew was bombarded with mental intrusions that incapacitated everyone aboard.

Bev sensed the attack on the crew. She projected her mind to contact Arlud, but could not create a link. She expanded her energy sphere to five times normal size and blasted the approaching spheres with a massive release of energy.

The spheres tumbled away from Bev. The blast had ripped them open and their brightness dimmed as they bled plasma.

Bev turned her focus to the spheres surrounding the transport and enfolded.

The spheres at the transport formed a tight wedge to confront Bev, but it was an effort too late. Bev unfolded behind them and, in less than a heartbeat, pierced the spheres with a crippling discharge of energy that split their bodies apart.

Once the threats were gone, Bev reduced her size. Her attack against the Tuma fighters had been quick, but this brawl surpassed her expectations. She scanned her surroundings. *I never thought I could beat so many Rhysu at once.* A new understanding grew out of that realization. *I'm different. I am not Rhysu. I can do things they can't do.* And within that thought, she sensed her purpose. *They made me to help them defeat the Shoku!*

Hundreds of energy spheres emerged out of the white prison and hugged the surface.

The injured spheres lost illumination visible to humans, and even with her expanded sight, Bev could no longer see half of them. *Did I kill them?* She had never heard of a Rhysu dying, but knew they needed repair when injured. She noticed the spheres at the white prison made no attempt to help the injured. *They fear me,* she thought. *They've faced nothing like me.*

Bev sensed the humans on the transport were alive and recovering from the mind rape. She focused on the white prison and positioned herself nearer the transport. She broadcast a message to the new arrivals at the white prison: "Stay where you are and witness the reduced impact of the tri-pole engine."

New energy spheres continued to populate the surface of the white prison, but none ventured beyond it.

Bev connected to Ruñal. *Are you OK, Commander?*

"Yes."

And your crew?

"We're all fine."

Fire up the engine!

The tri-pole demonstration continued.

Bev sensed anger from the energy spheres at the white prison. "Restrain yourselves! Witness the solution!"

Hundreds of energy spheres advanced toward Bev. She connected to Ruñal. *Power off the engine!* She retreated toward the transport and once the hyper-bubble faded, she backed into the plasma node and sucked up more energy.

"The humans attacked," a voice told Bev. "Their bomb destroyed our emitter. Our streams were damaged. We cannot trust the humans. They must be removed!"

"You are not Rhysu," Bev said. "You are Shoku!" She pulled away from the energy node and focused on Ruñal. *Leave, now!*

The tri-pole engine ignited and the Aku transport lunged forward at hyper-velocity on a course out of the system.

Hundreds of energy spheres surged toward Bev.

Bev swelled to her largest size yet, twenty times normal, with five times the energy tendrils. She met the approaching energy spheres head on. As she made contact, she pierced them and sucked their power into herself. Her size grew with each Shoku she disabled.

Energy depleted, the wounded Shoku tumbled back toward the white prison, pushed by the shock front of Bev's massive energy sphere.

The Shoku will not win today!

Arlud watched Bev push the energy spheres toward the white glowing mass that had been Arrilen Po. "I was afraid this would happen."

"She's doing well against those odds," Eahuda said. "Did you know she could do that?"

Arlud flicked a glance at his old friend, who stood with Ruñal on the other side of the plotting pedestal, looking at the image of Bev displayed above it on a holoscreen. "No. Never imagined she could do that."

"Did she know she could do that?"

Arlud focused on the holoscreen. "I don't know."

The exterior cameras followed Bev's progress as she forced the Shoku toward the white prison. With each contact, her energy sphere grew larger and more Shoku lost energy and were pushed back. A few Shoku enfolded and rushed Bev from behind, above, and below, but each contact ended with her massive tendrils flinging them toward the prison, energy depleted and tumbling.

"She's stronger than she was before," Ruñal said, looking at Arlud.

"She's no threat to us."

Eahuda gripped Ruñal's shoulder. "Look!"

Bev had reached the white prison, and her energy sphere was half its size. Once the Shoku had been forced to retreat within the white glow, Bev grew larger. Her tendrils extended outward, wrapped around the white, and compressed it.

Eahuda leaned toward the holoscreen. "What's she doing?"

The white prison collapsed under the pressure of Bev's tendrils until it equaled the size of the planet within it.

"Oh, no," Arlud whispered to himself.

The holoscreen flared white.

Stunned, the Aku crew stood motionless as the brilliant white glare on the holoscreen faded.

The Shoku were gone.

Bev was gone.

Arrilen Po was gone.

Arlud was the only person in the sleeping bay, so Eahuda sat on the edge of the bunk across from him. "The anti-compression field is still gone."

"Clan Halva destroyed the emitter and the Rhysu never replaced it," Arlud said. He rose to a sitting position, swung his feet to the deck, and sat on the edge of the bunk. "We'll hit the anti-compression field again as we get closer to the more populated section of the outer district. Is Ruñal still following the low power guidelines?"

"Yes. Fifty-seven hyper-days to reach Ni'apinu. One-hundred and seventy-one standard. You think the Rhysu will believe we're sincere?"

Arlud shrugged. "That depends on what happened to Bev once she crossed back into Rhysu space."

"Taking all those Shoku with her must account for something with the Rhysu. She may not always be agreeable, but she has always been truthful. They must see that."

"We'll know we were successful when the anti-compression waves stop."

"With the tri-pole engines, the waves won't need to stop."

"Yeah, but it would be the most obvious way for the Rhysu to let us know they believe us."

Eahuda could see in Arlud's eyes his worry for Bev. "She'll be fine," he said. "Bev's strong. Look what she just did. They'll think twice before—"

"She's gone, Gus. She was back and now she's gone. They tried to retrieve her. They didn't want her here. By forcing the Shoku back, she did what the Rhysu always wanted—she returned to their universe. What she did was a massive display of power, but don't think for a minute the Rhysu are weaker than her. They made her. They will control her. They were probably controlling her the entire time."

"You really believe that?"

"She's gone, isn't she?"

NI'APINU: MOTIVES

Petra sat at the desk in her quarters and opened her journal on her compad. Through the window above the desk she noticed red dawn light had filled the sky along the horizon, framed by the rocky foothills of the Dekeg Mountains to the south and the rugged hills of the tree-covered Umelk Range to the north.

Beautiful morning.

She returned her gaze to her journal. After the shuttle crash, when Salus found her with Arlud and Eahuda, she began recording what she learned about the Aku, and the change in their attitude toward the Erstallius off-worlders. Her recordings soon drifted into other areas, both technical and personal—a robust daily diary of everything she experienced.

She opened a fresh page and spoke:

"Today marks the end of seven months since Arlud Erstallius left with Gustav Eahuda, Winstone Bittle, and Maximilian Sands, aboard Aku Transport Eighteen commanded by Ruñal. We have heard nothing of their journey because the comdrone network is still down. The anti-compression waves persist.

"Grénu and Narèndu have refused to send another transport to check on Arlud's status. Their focus is on Ni'apinu now. All other matters are outside their concern. I have scheduled an interview with Narèndu and Jegen-Major Sari later this afternoon to record the current policy regarding planet defense and the Tuma ships still approaching from the system's outer rim. Why the Tuma ships haven't been neutralized yet troubles me and has become a regular complaint from Tryol and the other trainers."

She leaned back in her chair.

"My year-long training is now past the three-quarter mark, so only a few months left before Salus and I can unite.

"I composed a letter this morning to send to Naña. She's in Squa Paln with her parents. The letter should arrive by the end of the week. I hope she can come visit.

"I will go to Kuliq'Quad after breakfast. The first tri-pole shuttle has been completed. Grénu wants me there early to witness the launch."

She closed her compad and stared out the window. The sipá were awake—she could hear their faint rumblings through the glass.

Thirty minutes later Petra squatted in the ankle-high grass outside the main gate. The air was cool and the morning sun's rays caused the dew to glisten around her. She chewed on a carrot as she watched Aluk devour the fruit and vegetable assortment she had brought him. She noticed his fur had grown enough around his shoulder wound to hide it. "U'aliou, Aluk."

"It's great how you interact with those animals."

Petra stood as she spun around to see who spoke, but only saw Aluk. She checked her compad—it was off.

Aluk stopped eating, sat on his haunches, and looked up into the sky.

Petra followed the old sipá's gaze and saw a rippling distortion in the clouds above her. "You're in my head. Is that you, Bev?"

Yes. My voice is in your head. I'm far above you. Do not be afraid.

"I'm not afraid."

A compact ball of cyan-colored plasma dropped through the clouds and descended toward Petra. The hot wind that preceded the ball of energy hit Petra and Aluk, and they flinched away from the pressure wave.

Aluk lumbered toward Petra and stood in front of her to shield her from the oppressive down-draft.

Petra stepped away from Aluk's furry blockade and faced the energy sphere once it stopped about twenty meters above her. The hot wind evaporated the dew and pressed the grass to the earth. "What do you want?"

The energy sphere backed away and morphed into a human shape—a female shape.

The sweltering wind subsided.

Sorry, Bev said. *I must remember to keep my distance.*

"What do you want?"

Thank you for helping to save Arlud. I never got the chance to thank you while I was human.

Petra was flooded with visions of Arlud's rescue from the crashed shuttle and her attention to his head wound. She saw everything from Arlud's perspective, and she understood she was seeing his memories. "How can you do that?"

I have seen his memories. I learned from him you were here. Thank you for your kindness.

"Where is he?"

At Dol'anar. He returned last night.

That revelation caused multiple questions to arise in Petra's mind, but Bev ignored them.

It's great how you interact with those animals. Rhysu interaction with humans is similar.

"How?"

The communication is limited between you and the sipá, but you understand each other enough to be successful together. The Rhysu will learn a lot by observing how you interact with the sipá.

"They're observing us?"

Yes. Do not be afraid. Where a lack of trust exists, everyone must be monitored to ensure they fulfill their promises. The Rhysu will monitor your progress with tri-pole engines, and while doing that, they will come to understand more about everything you do. I will monitor the Rhysu agreement to stop the Shoku from annihilating you.

"Annihilating us?"

Do not be afraid. I will stop the Shoku if the Rhysu fail. I was created for that purpose. Thanks again. I must go now.

Bev's appearance changed back into an energy sphere. A pressure wave hit Petra and Aluk again, then faded as Bev rose into the clouds and disappeared.

"Wow."

Aluk faced Petra and huffed.

Petra kept her conversation with Bev to herself. No one else reported contact with Bev, so unlike the previous mental intrusion by the Rhysu, Bev's contact was not for everyone.

A private conversation.

That understanding impressed Petra, not because she felt privileged, but because Bev had taken the time to thank her for helping Arlud. *Such a little thing,* Petra thought. *I did what anyone in my position would have done, and I wasn't alone. Eahuda was there, and he helped too.*

Out of that humble reflection, Petra realized Bev's experience in the Polinda mine stifled all actions based on good motive—everyone confined to that slavery had been focused on themselves. And she remembered Arlud told her Bev once said, "I'm a selfish survivor. Everyone in the mine did what they did to save their own butts. Which is probably why so many died."

Arlud would have died if injured in that mine, Petra thought. *Bev would have let him die, but she's grown since then.* Bev's "thank you" was heartfelt—a sign her motive was good.

She's a genuine help if she can keep the Shoku at bay. How long has she known that's why the Rhysu changed her?

Petra pondered that question while Aluk leaned against her and buried her face in his thick neck fur. She stepped back and placed a hand on Aluk's chin to keep him at bay, and focused on the southern sky.

The ciâfey that would fly her to Kuliq'Quad had not arrived yet, so she gave Aluk a farewell rub under his chin and headed to the training paddocks to see Serra. She found the cub in a paddock, loping behind his new trainer, who jogged in front of him.

Exercise first, then command training.

Serra now stood almost one and a half meters at the shoulder when standing on all four feet. He could out-run the trainer, but kept pace because that was what the trainer expected.

We've taught him well, Petra thought. As she watched Serra jaunt around the paddock, she saw him with a fresh perspective. Bev had forced her to think in broader terms regarding inter-species relationships. *Serra is a sipá, but he is more than the physical creature. He is a conscious living being with his own likes and dislikes, with his own needs, his own self-worth, his own ability to make friends and enemies. Serra is as much an alien to humans as the Rhysu because of the limitations in the way we communicate. Sipá and humans share similar biology, but the conscious part, the unseen element that guides what that biology does, is as far from being human as the consciousness that guided the Rhysu. Both have needs. Both have a self-preservation motive behind their actions. Both have the ability to understand the actions of other species.*

Knowing the sipá-to-human bond was real and lasting, Petra knew in time the Rhysu-to-human bond would also succeed.

Hopefully, with no more casualties.

She turned at the sight of an approaching ciâfey and headed to the landing zone.

-End-

APPENDIXES

The following information is supplied to enhance the reader's understanding of various terms and phrases contained in the chronicles.

EXCERPTS FROM CATALOG OF HOLDINGS

ALPHA CEPHEI FOUR: Fourth planet of PDN203 (Alpha Cephei). Abundant metals attracted Clan Polinda to this barren world where they established a successful mining operation. A source of pure durillium.

AL-PHAQ: Fifth planet of PDN198 (Eta Cephei). A fortress of the Guild of Free Traders. Colonized by Wolfram Sy in 3502.

ANDERS PRIME: Second planet of PDN220 (Epsilon Eridani). Homeworld of Clan Bree.

ARRILEN PO: Fourth planet of PDN1527 (Trigelle's Star). An attempt at colonization by Clan Halva failed and the world was abandoned in 3478.

BALEIOU: Fourth planet of PDN306 (Pi-3 Orionis). Adopted homeworld of Clan Erstallius. Old World designation: Pi-3 Alpha.

BODEN: Fourth planet of PDN133 (Eta Cassiopae A). A holding-complete of Clan Sabballi.

CESTRATHA: Third planet of PDN169 (Lambda Serpentis). Homeworld of Clan Halva.

COLLIRI-3: Third Planet of PDN201 (61 Cygni A). A Joint Holding of Clan Tuma and Clan Emlito.

GLASEL-221: Fifth planet of PDN607. A Joint Holding of Clan Tuma and Clan Emlito.

GSW-34: Fourth planet of PDN145 (Tau Ceti). Homeworld of Clan Brandi. Old World designation from Guide to Surveyed Worlds, first edition, published in 3278.

GSW-183: Second planet of PDN160A (26 Draconis A). Independent Holding of the Aku people. Old World designation from Guide to Surveyed Worlds, first edition, published in 3278.

JAI'RAAN: Second moon of Wald-181 (The third planet of PDN150B [Zeta Herculis B]). A holding withdrawn from Clan Halva in 3478. Noted for its exotic mineral deposits and hot springs.

KAINOGAE: Fifth planet of PDN158 (Zeta Tucanae). Adopted homeworld of Clan Tuma. An agricultural holding. The Kainogae School is the major school of agronomy in the Alliance. Where K. H. Epstein developed his Gamma-2 strain of Pennisetum glaucum (millet). Old World designation: ZT5.

KEAEH: Third planet of PDN136 (Nu-2 Lupi). Adopted homeworld of Clan Cormed.

MAKENZIE: Second planet of PDN209 (Epsilon Indi). A holding-complete of Clan Vestlok. The location of the annual Conference of Great Clans. The original homeworld of Clan Sy, which was forfeited after the First Rebellion when the Clan was removed from partnership in the Alliance of Great Clans.

OIKÍA: Third planet of PDN165 (70 Ophiuchi A). Homeworld of Clan Sabballi.

PIGRELL: Fourth planet of PDN103 (Surphra). Homeworld of Clan Polinda.

ROTH-513: Third planet of PDN193. A holding-complete of Clan Cormed. A micro-bionics research and development center.

SIMBIC UR: Third planet of PDN185 (Sigma Draconis). A holding-complete of Clan Dejoria. Mined for water.

TERRA PRIME: Third planet of PDN100 (Helios). Considered the homeworld of all mankind. Old World designation: Earth.

THRUM DAU: Second planet of PDN438 (Alpha Mensae). A holding-complete of Clan Erstallius. Thought to be the original homeworld of both Clan Erstallius and Clan Tuma. Old World designation: Mensae 2

U'GALEM: Fourth planet of PDN163 (Chi Herculis). A holding-complete of Clan Dejoria.

WALD-415: Fourth planet of PDN1592. Unclaimed world. Surveys are scheduled to begin in 3530. No sanctioned settlement.

WAN'TEI: Second planet of PDN185 (Sigma Draconis). Homeworld of Clan Dejoria. Old World designation: Sigma Prime.

AKÜN VOCABULARY

AHKHÉ: A shrub native to GSW-183. A sour spice used to flavor food. Used as a natural barrier against insects.

AKÜN: The original language of the Aku people, and the predecessor of various dialects persistent on Kainogae and Jai'raan, that stems from an undetermined root whose origin among the Old Worlds is not certain.

BI'AU: The mediator. A central figure of Aku government.

CIÂFEY: A two-man, winged aircraft. Developed by the Aku after their arrival on GSW-183.

GÁSAH KAHÁFA: Name given to an astronomical event seen in the skies of Ni'apinu in 138 A. E.

IPÀG: A large avian native to GSW-183. Wingspan averages 2 meters for adult females and 1.5 meters for adult males.

JI'DESS: Largest settlement on GSW-183, located on the north-eastern coast of the Wardu Sea. Population: 1,200.

KLÂWPA: a small, carnivorous scavenger of GSW-183. It is characterized by its muscular build, black fur, pungent odor, keen sense of smell, and ferocity when feeding. Average length 90 centimeters from nose to tip of tail.

EDSUA'FAYAK: Knife of Unpleasantness. Any deliberate act of repugnance directed with a specific purpose at a specific person or persons.

KULIQ'QUAD: Place of Safety. A derivative of an old Akün expression, and the name of the first settlement established GSW-183.

L'DYÉM: A formal greeting, most often used when meeting strangers.

MÂNU: 1. A noun meaning a covered, or enclosed space. 2. A verb meaning to cover, to conceal, or to collect.

NELA'OGU: First People. The Aku who settled GSW-183.

NI'APINU: Secure Abode. Name given to GSW-183 by the first settlers.

NI'DESIAH: Leader of Twenty, Commander of the Watch.

OMÈU: A broad-trunk Pinaceae with green or yellow-green needles. Native to GSW-183. Needle length can reach 500 centimeters on the largest specimens, which have been measured up to 150 meters high.

PAUK: A legume native to GSW-183. Its green and white leaves fan out to seven points that each support needles five centimeters long. A source of gum used for tanning leather.

PRISTAL: Shrub-like plant native to GSW-183. The leaves are large, and the six-centimeter-wide lavender flowers produce a berry fruit averaging fifteen centimeters long. Height: 70 to 120 centimeters.

SIPÁ: Omnivorous mammal with gray and brown fur of the family Ursidae, bred on GSW-183 from stock originally from Wan'tei. The largest cataloged specimen was four meters in length.

SÌJ YÊBU: Akün term for the Common Language of the Alliance. A hybrid form of Englo'ni, whose origin has been traced to various language groups persistent among the Old Worlds.

SQUA PALN: Small settlement in the foothills of the Umelk Mountains. Population: 160.

UAH'EKI: 1. A pervasive, controlling force that blinds the mind to reality. 2. The imagining of the conscious mind that subverts logical thought.

U'ALIOU: Informal greeting between friends.

WASSÚA CAPHÁGA: Valley of Streams. The rift valley between the Umelk and Dekeg Mountains that runs from the coastal plain east of Squa Paln, to the foothills south of Quel Pass and north of Kuliq'Quad basin.

MAPS

The following are maps of holdings mentioned in the chronicles, and were taken from The Planetary Database. Complied in the 116th year of the Merchant Alliance of Great Clans.

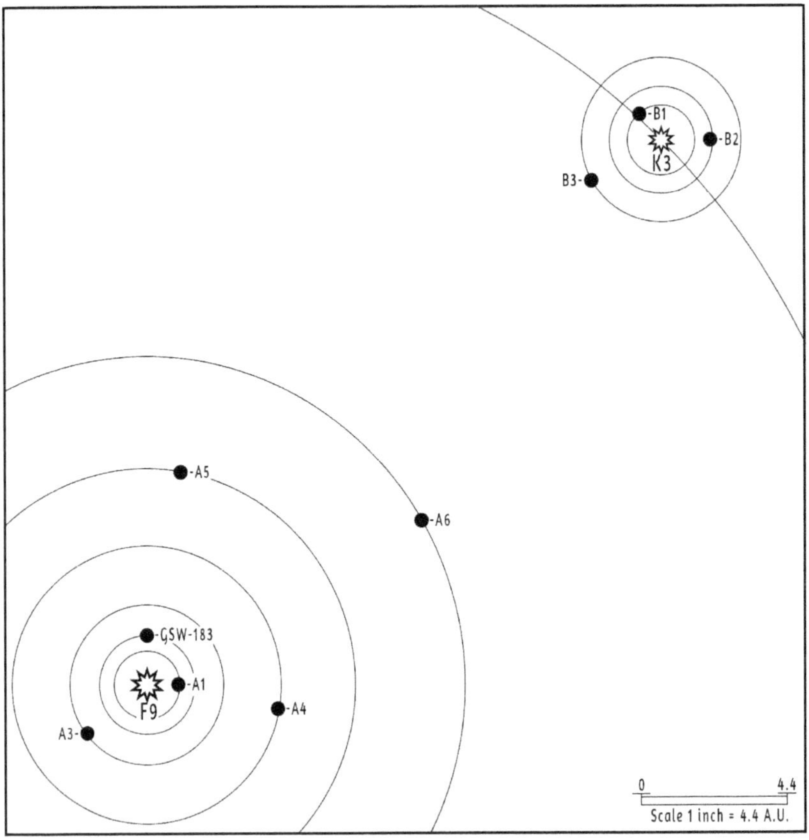

PDN160

F and K Type Dwarf Multiple Star System

Old World Primary Name: 26 Draconis AB

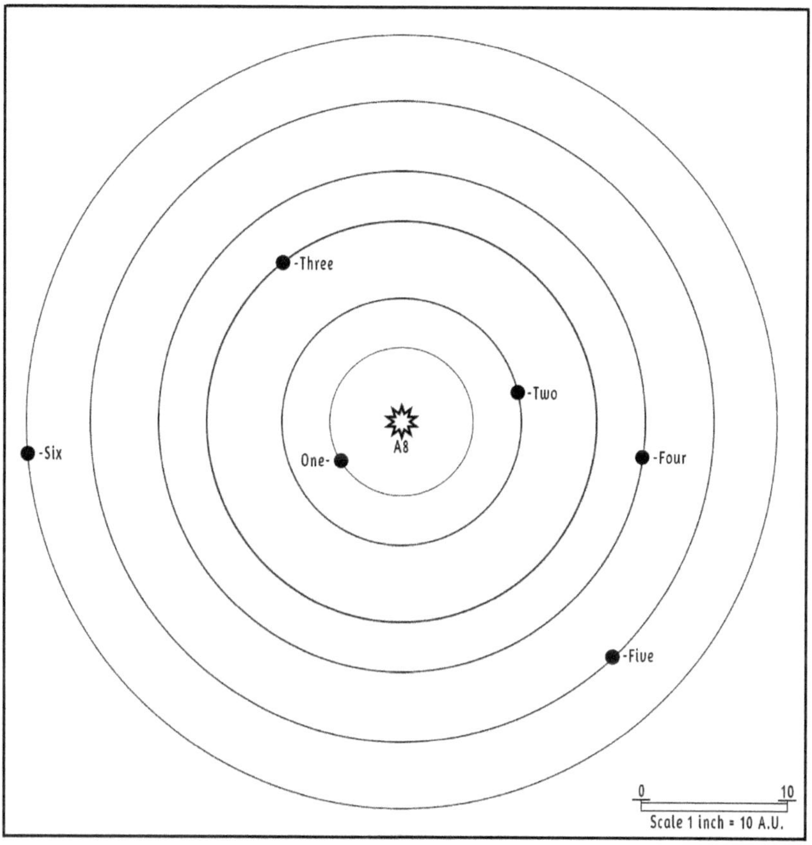

-Three
-Two
A8
-Six
One-
-Four
-Five
0 10
Scale 1 inch = 10 A.U.

PDN203

A Type Subgiant Primary

Old World Primary Name: Alpha Cephei

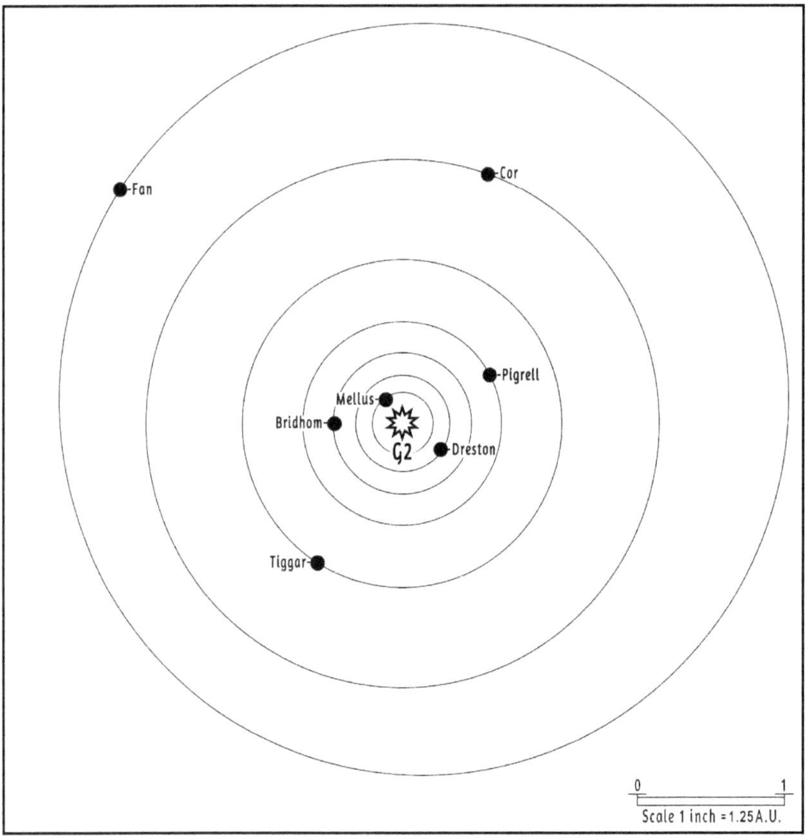

Fan
Cor
Pigrell
Mellus
Bridhom
G2
Dreston
Tiggar
0
1
Scale 1 inch = 1.25A.U.

PDN103

G2 Type Dwarf Primary

Old World Primary Name: Surphra

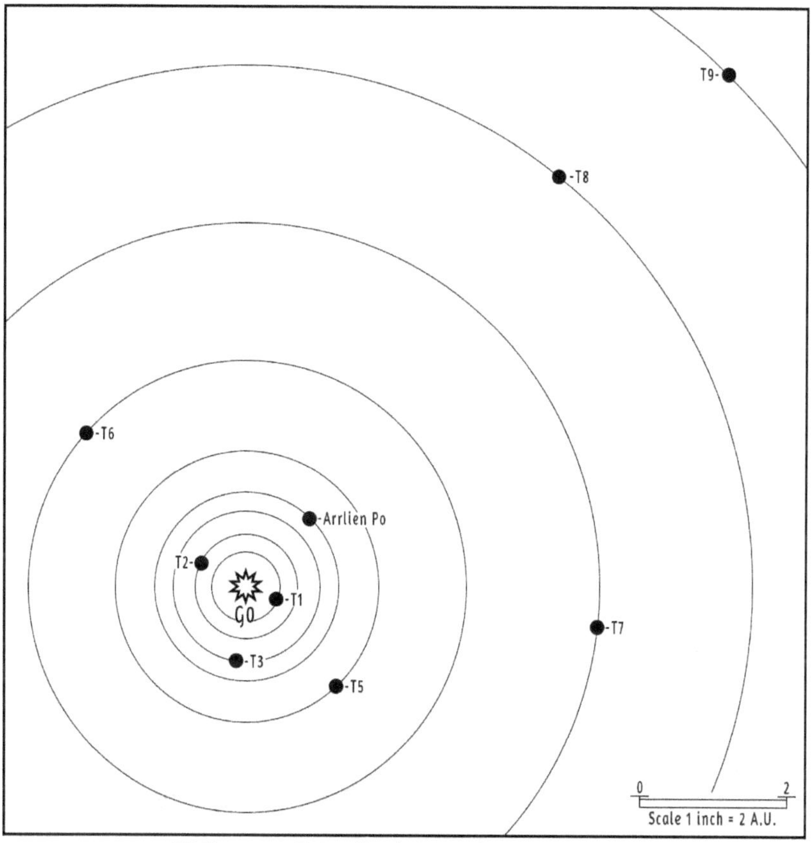

T9-
-T8
-T6
-Arrlien Po
T2-
G0
-T1
-T7
-T3
-T5
0 2
Scale 1 inch = 2 A.U.

PDN1527 - Trigelles' Star (inner system)

G Type Dwarf Primary

Old World Primary Name: HIP 82636

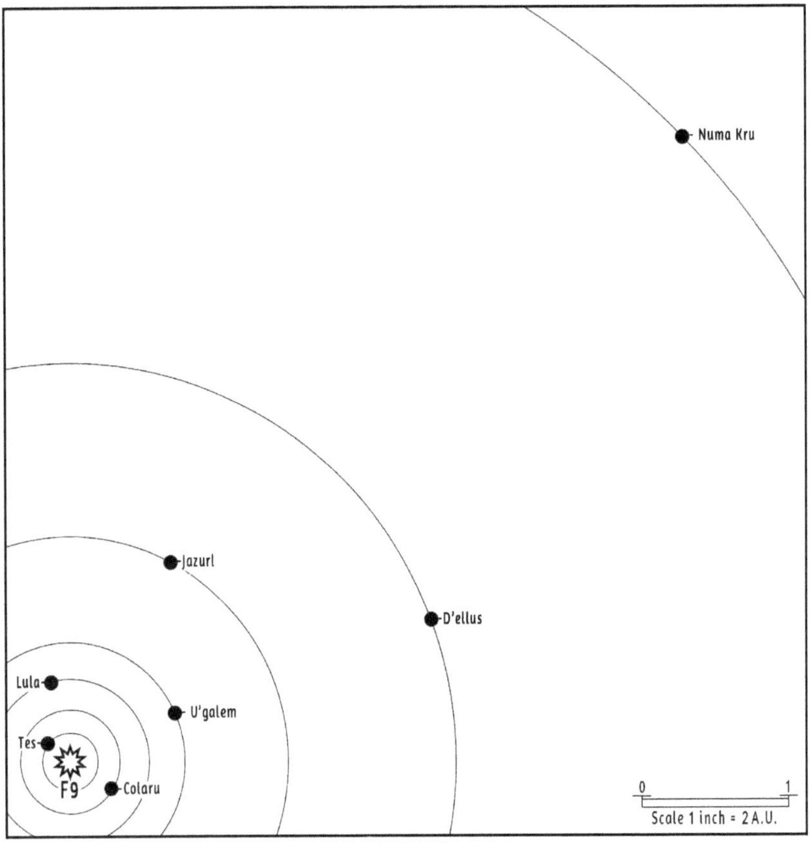

Numa Kru

Jazurl

D'ellus

Lula

U'galem

Tes

F9

Colaru

0 1

Scale 1 inch = 2 A.U.

PDN163

F9 Type Dwarf Primary

Old World Primary Name: Chi Herculis

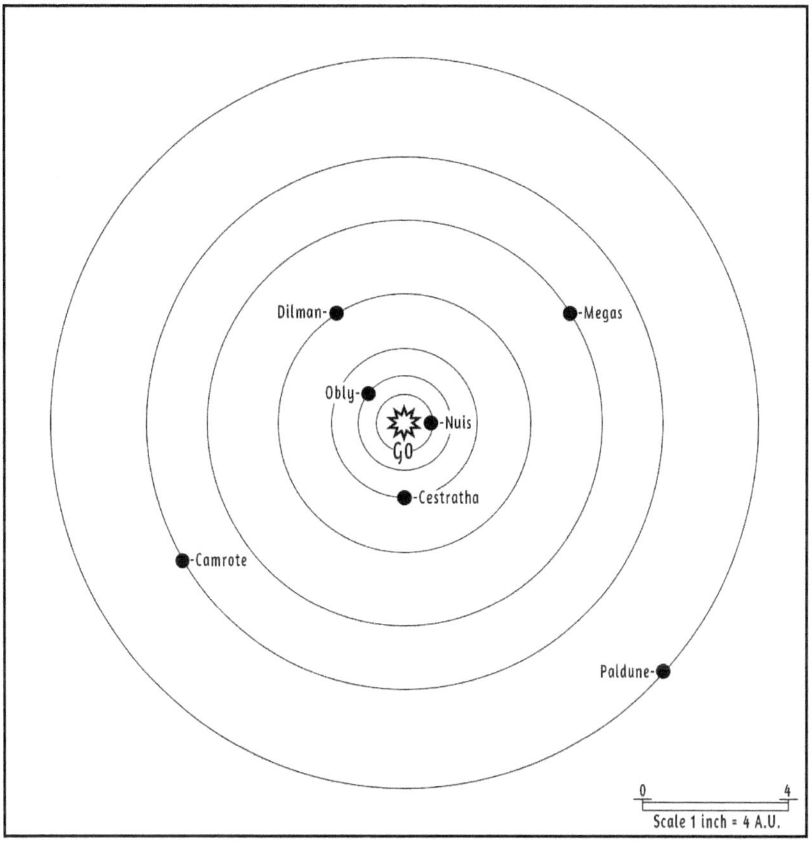
Dilman-
-Megas
Obly-
-Nuis
GO
-Cestratha
-Camrote
Paldune-
0
4
Scale 1 inch = 4 A.U.

PDN169

G Type Dwarf Primary

Old World Primary Name: Lambda Serpentis

HALVA
THE NEW ALLIANCE OF GREAT CLANS

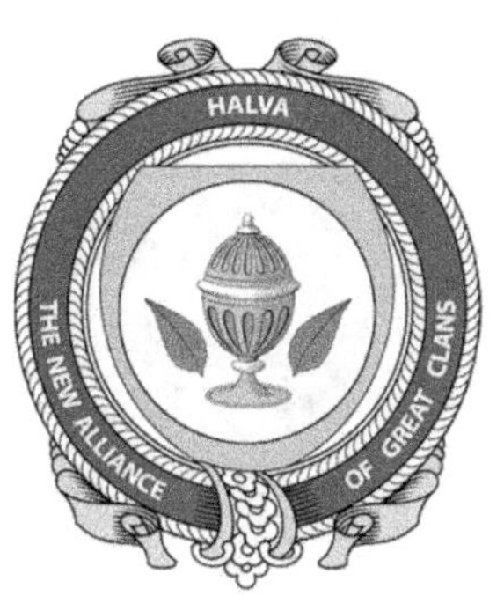

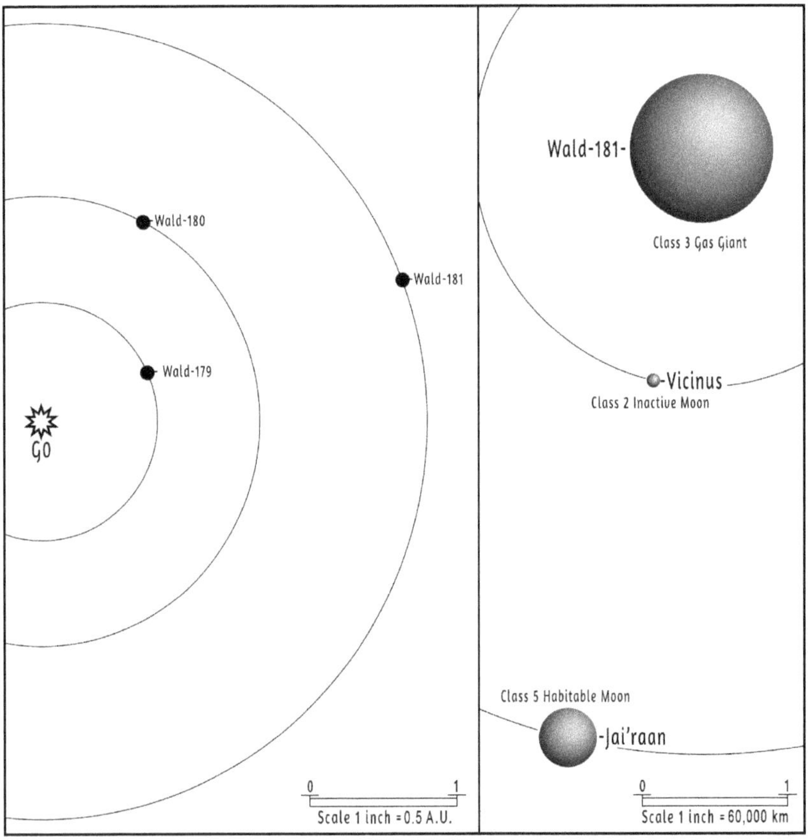

Wald-180
Wald-181
Wald-179
G0
Scale 1 inch = 0.5 A.U.

Wald-181-
Class 3 Gas Giant
-Vicinus
Class 2 Inactive Moon
Class 5 Habitable Moon
-Jai'raan
Scale 1 inch = 60,000 km

PDN150B

G0 Type Dwarf Primary

Old World Primary Name: Zeta Herculis B

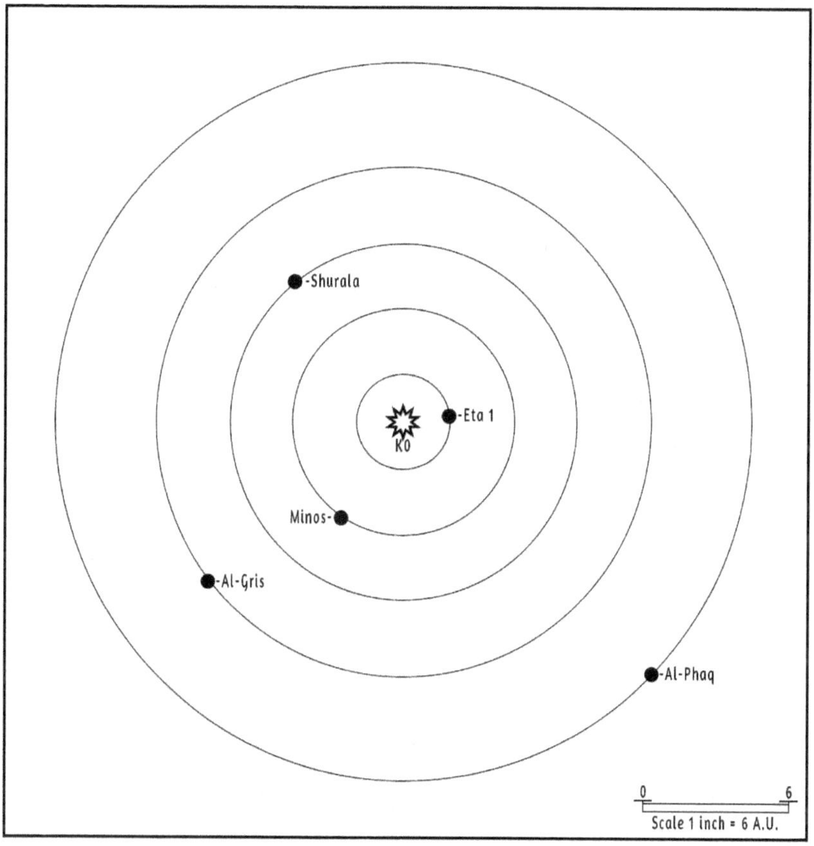

-Shurala
K0
-Eta 1
Minos-
-Al-Gris
-Al-Phaq
0 6
Scale 1 inch = 6 A.U.

PDN198

K Type Subgiant Primary

Old World Primary Name: Eta Cephei

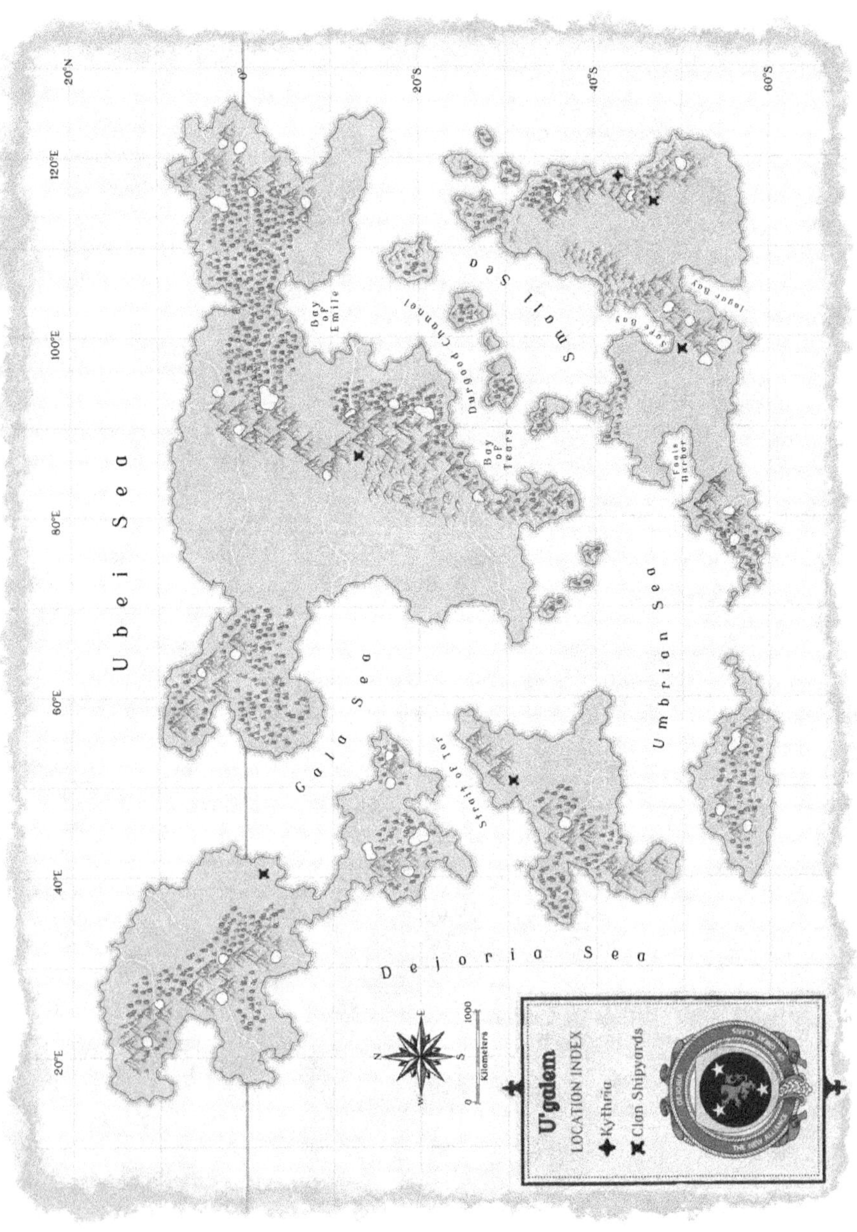
Ubei Sea
Gala Sea
Dejoria Sea
Umbrian Sea
Small Sea
Bay of Emile
Durgood Channel
Bay of Tears
U'galem
LOCATION INDEX
Kythria
Clan Shipyards
Kilometers
20°E
40°E
60°E
80°E
100°E
120°E
20°N
0°
20°S
40°S
60°S

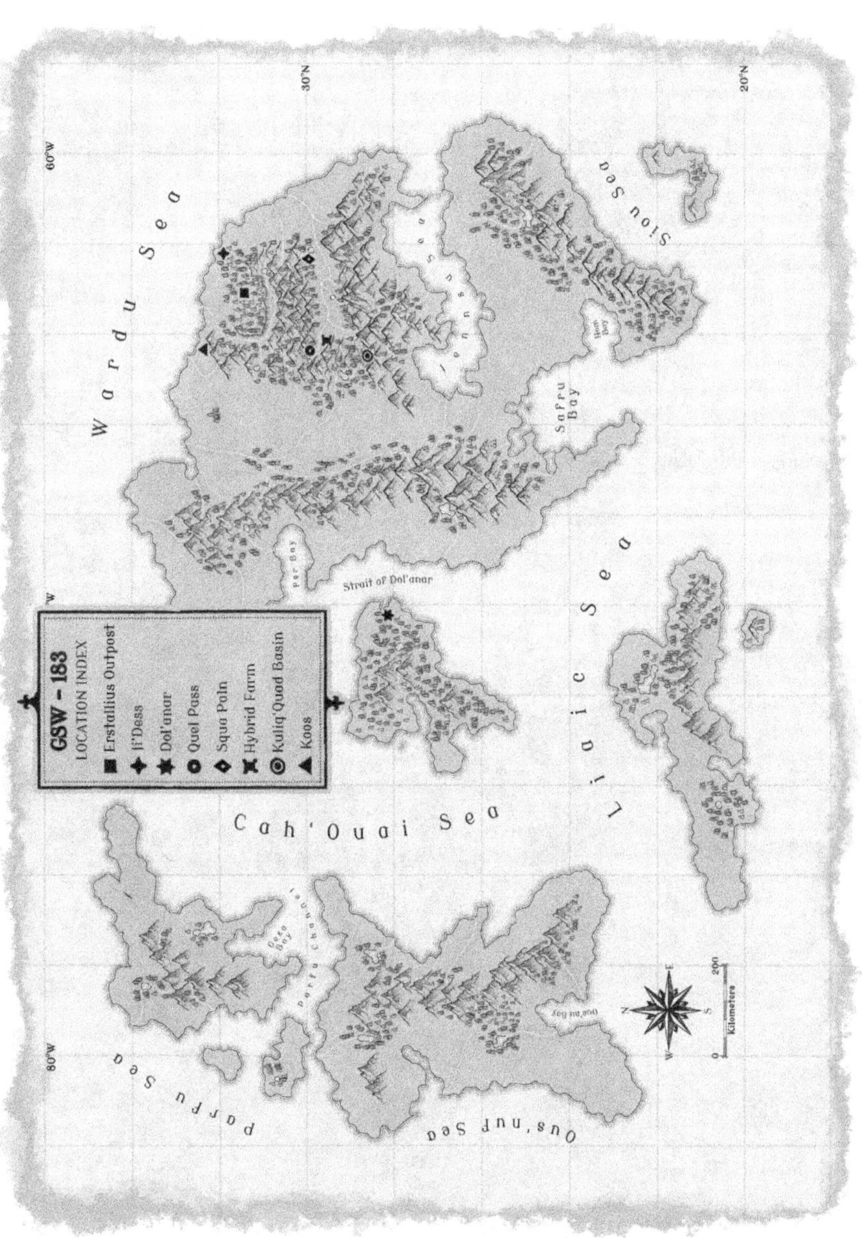
GSW - 183
LOCATION INDEX
Erstallius Outpost
Ji'Dess
Dol'anar
Quel Pass
Squa Paln
Hybrid Farm
Kuliq'Quad Basin
Koos
Wardu Sea
Siou Sea
Saffru Bay
Per Bay
Strait of Dol'anar
Liaic Sea
Cah'Ouai Sea
Parfu Sea
Ous'nuf Sea
60°W
80°W
30°N
20°N
0
200
Kilometers

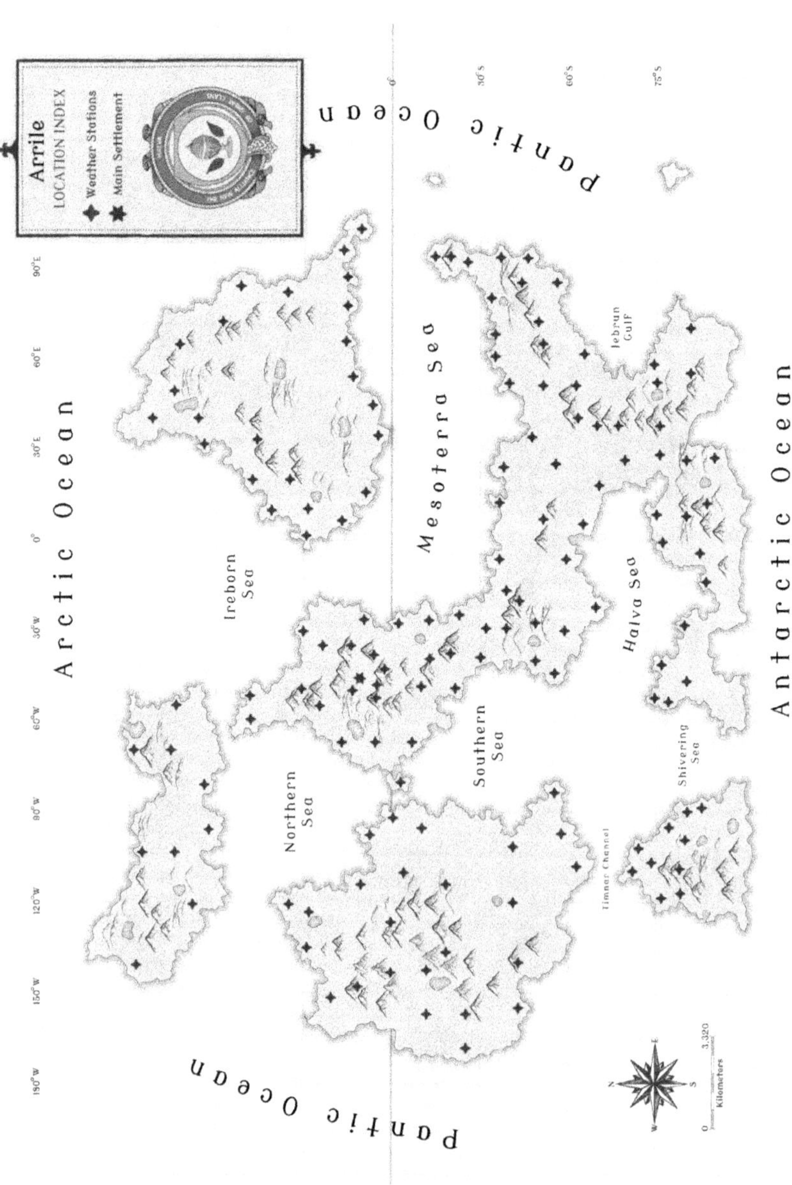
Arrile
LOCATION INDEX
Weather Stations
Main Settlement
Arctic Ocean
Pantic Ocean
Mesoterra Sea
Antarctic Ocean
Ireborn Sea
Northern Sea
Southern Sea
Halva Sea
Shivering Sea
Pantic Ocean
Kilometers

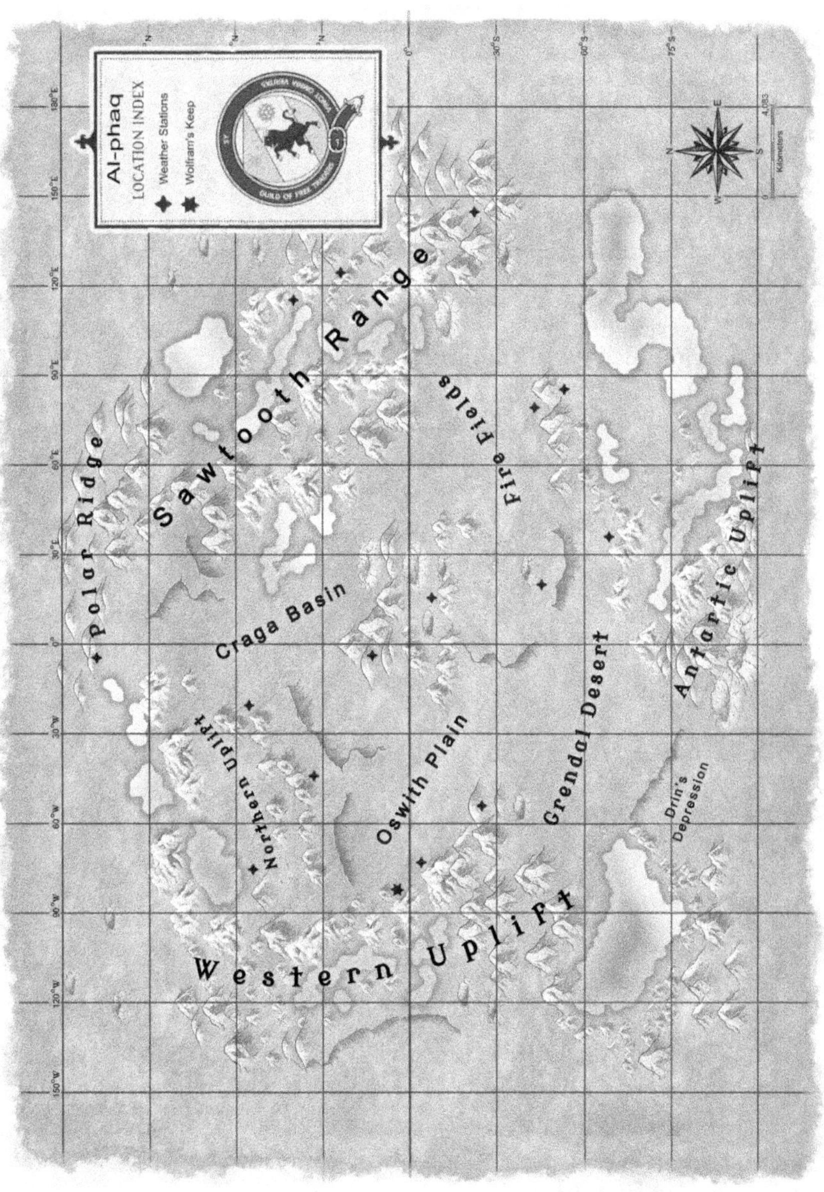
Al-phaq
LOCATION INDEX
Weather Stations
Wolfram's Keep
GUILD OF FREE TRADERS
Polar Ridge
Sawtooth Range
Fire Fields
Craga Basin
Northern Uplift
Oswith Plain
Grendal Desert
Antartic Uplift
Drin's Depression
Western Uplift
Kilometers

GLOSSARY OF CHARACTERS

The Aku

Aluk - Old Sipa
Lyda - Na'alief, Teacher of Children
Mérol - Overseer of the Depüfah'ahuah
Naréndu: Commander-in-Charge of the first Aku transport to leave GSW-183.
Naña - The Depüfah from Squa Paln.
Ruñal - Commander of Aku Transport 18
Serra - Sipa cub
Tryol - Overseer of the Quel Pass Hybrid Farm

Clan Brandi

Levion Cellius: Envoy sent to the Merchant Symposium on Jai'rran

Clan Cormed

Milos Fore: Envoy and Regional Director of Clan Affairs.

Clan Dejoria

Jhared Dejoria: Patriarch of his Clan.

Clan Erstallius

Arlud Reynaldo Erstallius: Regent of GSW-183 and son of Armand.
Armand Reynaldo Erstallius: High Regent and Patriarch of his Clan.
Avery Barick Erstallius: Second cousin of Armand Erstallius.
Benita Gale Waldu-Reyes Erstallius: Wife of Armand Erstallius.
Hugo Rusan Erstallius: Son of Patrus Rusan Erstallius.
Patrus Rusan Erstallius: Armand's older brother.
Gustav Eahuda: Degen-of-the-Corp, and Commander of Erstallius Security on GSW-183.

Jamira Melkor: Commander-in-Charge of cruiser 1108.
Jens Orr: Nared, and Senior Shuttle Pilot.
Kurt Sari: Jegen-Major and Outpost Commander on GSW-183
Lester Isard: Envoy to Clan Halva
Lon Pavan: Jegen-Major, and Commander-in Charge of the Erstallius Fleet at GSW-183.
Maxillian Sands: Engine Chief assigned to cruiser 1108.
Mister Dal: Nared and Reconnaissance Officer aboard the Erstallius Dreadnought sent to Anders Prime.
Mister Tupo: House Manager for Clan Erstallius
Newt Vellion: Segen and Science Officer assigned to cruiser 1108.
Omba Khan: Nared and Recovery Team Leader
Petra Sityln: Segen and Lead Construction Engineer on GSW-183.
Rena Vellion: Nared-Major and Security Officer on Baleiou
Winstone Bittle: Segen and Lead Aircraft Engineer on GSW-183.
Vero Singh: Director of Neurosurgery, Regency Medical Center, Mancipa, Baleiou.

The Guild of Free Traders

Cala: Attendant to Shanna Sy
Donté Cegla: Marine assigned to Shanna Sy's Personal Guard
Eber Kurnes: Security Minister for the Guild.
Erlis Pardee: Captain of freighter 107.
Gretel: Attendant to Shanna Sy
Leru Canter: Commander-in-Charge of the survey on Alpha Cephei Four.
Minister Len: Envoy to Clan Halva
Mister Egin: First Officer aboard Erlis Pardee's battleship.
Mister Han: Lead Engineer on Al-Phaq
Ross Cordova: Marine, and Head of Shanna Sy's Security Group.
Shanna Sy: Daughter of Wolfram and Wellen Sy.
Wellen Talillia Sy: Wife of Wolfram Sy.
Wolfram Sy: Patriarch of the Guild of Free Traders who led the First Rebellion.

Clan Halva

Cynth Halva: Matriarch of Clan Halva, sister of Gustus.
Gustus Halva: High Regent and Patriarch of the Clan.
Tara Quinn: Servant to Cynth Halva.
Stephan Russo: Jegen-Major and Commander-in-Charge of the Halva Fleet sent to Arrilen Po.

Clan Sorrell

Ronon Venau: Envoy to Clan Halva

Clan Rastee

Jera Pellion: Envoy to Clan Halva

Clan Tuma

Fiorello Darmanti: Envoy sent to the Merchant Symposium on Jai'raan
Jacob Vindel: Envoy sent to the Merchant Symposium on Jai'raan

Clan Polinda

Bev Colli: Sapi, and Mad Japer assigned to the mine on Alpha Cephei Four.

ABOUT THE AUTHOR

P.D. Blackwell is a lifelong student who began studying theology, religion, and physics in 1980. He practices the guitar and piano everyday, and enjoys a good game of chess.

www.pdblackwell.com

PRAISE FOR CHAOS RISING

"A compelling, complex, and cinematic work of science fiction with plenty of chilling psychological undertones and all-out action scenes."
— K.C. Finn, *Reader's Favorite.*

"If you enjoy complex, well-developed science fiction novels, you'll want
to check out Blackwell's book. I loved how this adventure takes the reader to many new destinations full of diverse cultures, vivid landscapes, and honored pasts."
— Erin Dydek, *Online Book Club. Org.*

"Blackwell excels at characterization and vivid portrayals of each scene. Chaos Rising is edgy, clever, and layered. It kept me glued to its pages."
— Lit Amiri, *Reader's Favorite.*

PRAISE FOR THE RHYSU ALTERNATIVE

"I already had high expectations before starting The Rhysu Alternative. I was expecting the same level of intricate plot, smart characters, and impressive narrative. I was completely surprised when P.D. Blackwell exceeded all of my expectations and gave me a lot more."
— Rabia Tanveer, *Reader's Favorite.*

"Author P. D. Blackwell presents a worthy sequel after the excellent worldbuilding and complex emotional dynamics of the first foray into this incredible universe. After what Bev went through in the opening novel, I thought it would be hard to top, but her journey of empowerment in her new situation was really inspiring."
— K.C. Finn, *Reader's Favorite.*

"Blackwell creates conflict at multiple levels without taking away from the story the balance it deserves. The crisp prose is enriched by the engaging dialogues, but the strength of the narrative lies in the author's expert handling of plot points and the conflict which escalates to an explosive climax."
— Romuald Dzemo, *Reader's Favorite*

PRAISE FOR LAWLESS TRADITION

"Lawless Tradition is a tour de force with an engaging literary style that educates the reader along the journey."

— Kimberly Vargas, *Award Wining Author*

"Lawless Tradition is a book of divine wisdom, understanding, and discovery. A guide to help true Christians better understand God."

— Anthionette Ejimofor, *Goodreads.com*

"The amount of study and preparation put into this work is evident and instills in the reader a fair amount of confidence in the authenticity of this book. Nothing is pulled out of thin air; everything is backed up with evidence."

— Nzube Chizoba Okeke, *Online Book Club .Org*

This is a solid book with so much scriptural backing and commentary from theologians to support its interpretations that it cannot be reasonably ignored. Very highly recommended.

— Asher Syed, *Reader's Favorite*

P. D. Blackwell takes a deep dive into word meanings and cultural context . . . Explaining in easy-to-understand terms how to develop a first century understanding, Blackwell leads to a logical conclusion.

— Philip Van Heusen, *Reader's Favorite*

www.ingramcontent.com/pod-product-compliance
Lightning Source LLC
LaVergne TN
LVHW020527100826
845148LV00010B/1365